Praise for Melissa Caruso

Praise for *The Last Hour Between Worlds*

"A charming fantasy mystery that kept me guessing until the very last page—I completely adored this book and would read a dozen more of Kembral's adventures."
—Shannon Chakraborty, *New York Times* bestselling author of *The Adventures of Amina al-Sirafi*

"This book has everything you've been craving: sword fights, time loops, complicated feelings about parenthood, and banter with your sworn enemy. What an absolute delight!"
—Alix E. Harrow, *New York Times* bestselling author of *Starling House*

"A brilliant, breathlessly twisty fantasy adventure that I utterly adored. Melissa Caruso is a powerhouse."
—Tasha Suri, World Fantasy Award–winning author of *The Jasmine Throne*

"A masterpiece filled with excitement, romance, and characters you would protect with your life. The wobbly time effects in this book reach past its pages, making hours of reading blink by in a moment. Unmissable!"   —Andrea Stewart, author of the Drowning Empire series

"To say *The Last Hour Between Worlds* hits the ground running would be an understatement: This book starts at a sprint and never slows down. It's funny, and scary, and weird in the very best way. Melissa Caruso's writing is razor-sharp and this book is one heck of a page-turner!"
—Nicholas Eames, author of *Kings of the Wyld*

"Equal parts sheer adventurous fun and creepy, dimension-bending tension, featuring a relatable and instantly engaging protagonist. This is totally unlike anything I've read before; Caruso has pulled off a wonderfully creative premise with skill and panache."
—Freya Marske, author of *A Marvellous Light*

Praise for Rooks and Ruin

"A classic, breathtaking adventure brimful of dangerous magic and clever politics. This is a book that will thrill and delight any fantasy fan."
—Tasha Suri, World Fantasy Award–winning author of *The Jasmine Throne*, on *The Obsidian Tower*

"*The Obsidian Tower* deftly balances two of my favorite things: razor-sharp politics and characters investigating weird, dark magic. A must-read for all fantasy fans."
—Emily A. Duncan, *New York Times* bestselling author of *Wicked Saints*

"Block out time to binge this can't-stop story filled with danger and unexpected disaster. From the fresh take on time-honored tropes to a crunchy, intrigue-filled story, *The Obsidian Tower* is a must-read."
—C. L. Polk, author of *The Midnight Bargain*

"Full of tension and immediately engaging....Caruso builds a vivid universe...filling the pages with personality and depth."
—*BookPage* (starred review) on *The Obsidian Tower*

"With *The Obsidian Tower* [Melissa Caruso has] hit another level in terms of prose and tension. This is a truly excellent fantasy, and an epic beginning for a new trilogy."
—*Locus*

"Full of magical and political intrigue, Caruso's latest novel will surprise and delight fans and new readers alike. With rich worldbuilding, nuanced characters, and ratcheting tension, *The Obsidian Tower* is a fulfilling read from start to finish."

—Tara Sim, author of *The City of Dusk*

Praise for Swords and Fire

"Charming, intelligent, fast-moving, beautifully atmospheric, with a heroine and other characters whom I really liked as people. (I overstayed my lunch break in order to finish it.) I would love to read more set in this world."

—Genevieve Cogman, author of *The Invisible Library*, on *The Tethered Mage*

"Brilliant and complex."   —*Library Journal* on *The Unbound Empire*

"Caruso's heroine is a strong, intelligent young woman in a beguiling, beautifully evoked Renaissance world of high politics, courtly intrigue, love and loyalty—and fire warlocks."

—Anna Smith Spark, author of *The Court of Broken Knives*, on *The Tethered Mage*

"*The Tethered Mage* is a riveting read, with delicious intrigue, captivating characters, and a brilliant magic system. I loved it from start to finish!"   —Sarah Beth Durst, author of *The Queen of Blood*

"Breathtaking. . . . Worth every moment and every page, and it should make anyone paying attention excited about what Caruso will write next."   —*BookPage* on *The Tethered Mage*

By Melissa Caruso

THE ECHO ARCHIVES
The Last Hour Between Worlds

The Last Soul Among Wolves

ROOKS AND RUIN
The Obsidian Tower

The Quicksilver Court

The Ivory Tomb

SWORDS AND FIRE
The Tethered Mage

The Defiant Heir

The Unbound Empire

THE LAST SOUL AMONG WOLVES

THE ECHO ARCHIVES: BOOK TWO

MELISSA CARUSO

orbitbooks.net

This book is a work of fiction. Names, characters, places, and incidents are the product of the author's imagination or are used fictitiously. Any resemblance to actual events, locales, or persons, living or dead, is coincidental.

Copyright © 2025 by Melissa Caruso
Excerpt from *The Last Vigilant* copyright © 2025 by Mark A. Latham
Excerpt from *How to Become the Dark Lord and Die Trying* copyright © 2024 by Django Wexler

Cover design by Lisa Marie Pompilio
Cover images by Shutterstock
Cover copyright © 2025 by Hachette Book Group, Inc.
Maps by Tim Paul
Author photograph by Erin Re Anderson

Hachette Book Group supports the right to free expression and the value of copyright. The purpose of copyright is to encourage writers and artists to produce the creative works that enrich our culture.

The scanning, uploading, and distribution of this book without permission is a theft of the author's intellectual property. If you would like permission to use material from the book (other than for review purposes), please contact permissions@hbgusa.com. Thank you for your support of the author's rights.

Orbit
Hachette Book Group
1290 Avenue of the Americas
New York, NY 10104
orbitbooks.net

First Edition: August 2025
Simultaneously published in Great Britain by Orbit

Orbit is an imprint of Hachette Book Group.
The Orbit name and logo are registered trademarks of Little, Brown Book Group Limited.

The publisher is not responsible for websites (or their content) that are not owned by the publisher.

The Hachette Speakers Bureau provides a wide range of authors for speaking events. To find out more, go to hachettespeakersbureau.com or email HachetteSpeakers@hbgusa.com.

Orbit books may be purchased in bulk for business, educational, or promotional use. For information, please contact your local bookseller or the Hachette Book Group Special Markets Department at special.markets@hbgusa.com.

Library of Congress Cataloging-in-Publication Data
Names: Caruso, Melissa, author.
Title: The last soul among wolves / Melissa Caruso.
Description: First edition. | New York, NY : Orbit, 2025. | Series: The echo archives ; book two
Identifiers: LCCN 2024047375 | ISBN 9780316303941 (trade paperback) | ISBN 9780316304047 (ebook)
Subjects: LCGFT: Fantasy fiction. | Thrillers (Fiction) | Novels.
Classification: LCC PS3603.A7927 L377 2025 | DDC 813/.6—dc23/eng/20241029
LC record available at https://lccn.loc.gov/2024047375

ISBNs: 9780316303941 (trade paperback), 9780316304047 (ebook)

Printed in the United States of America

LSC-C

Printing 1, 2025

*To Kyra,
my magical forest creature.
Being your mom
is the best adventure.*

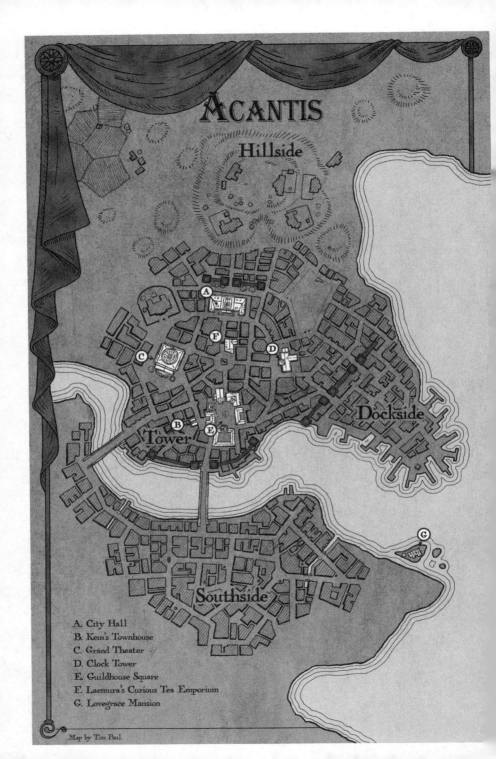

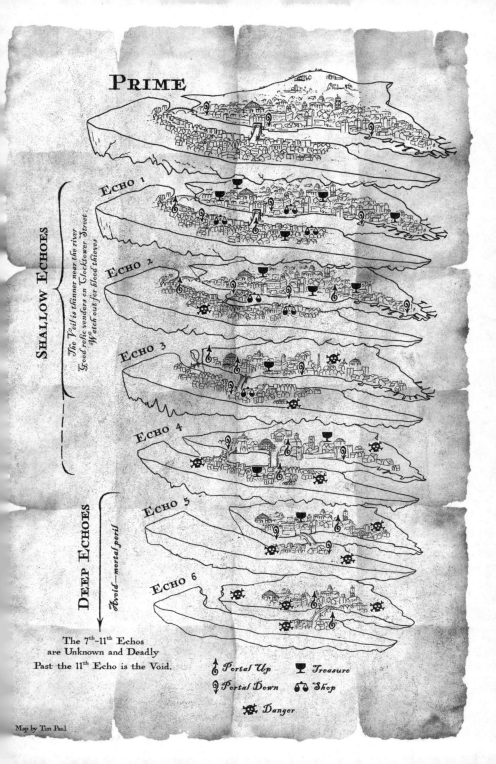

GET YOUR CREW TOGETHER

Like so many things, it was Jaycel's fault.

It'd be an exaggeration to say it was *always* Jaycel Morningray who got me involved in trouble, but not by much. We had a long history with an established pattern: She got us into scrapes, and I got us out. It was a natural rhythm, like breathing.

So when she asked me to come with her to our old Southside neighborhood for a moderately urgent personal matter, I brought my sword. I considered bringing *two* swords, but that seemed alarmist.

It was weird, strolling with Jaycel through streets we'd haunted as kids. I hadn't been back much since my parents moved away, and the heart-achingly familiar mixed everywhere with the new and therefore jarringly *wrong*.

The cobbled plazas and soot-stained brick storefronts snapped into their waiting places in my memory with a deep, satisfying *click*, down to the gritty shine on the stones from the light misting rain. Scents wafting from street carts awakened a deep nostalgic hunger: fried cheese rolls and sweet sticky buns, some hawked by the same old Viger immigrants. But for every detail that unpacked perfectly from my memories, something else had changed: shops come and gone, houses painted the wrong color, a broken water pump replaced with a planter full of flowers.

I'd changed, too, an adult and a mother and a guild member. I felt like an outsider in my new red coat and my Damn Good Boots, with a sword on my hip and the keys to a Tower townhouse in my pocket. My old neighborhood and I were two puzzle pieces that didn't fit together anymore.

We passed a certain right turn to an achingly familiar little plaza with a dried-up mermaid fountain, and I averted my eyes. The narrow building across the far side would no longer bear a sign that read THORNE'S MINIATURES, and the window of the smallest bedroom above the shop wouldn't have purple curtains lovingly hand-painted with a spangling of crude golden stars. I didn't need to see that; I had enough feelings to grapple with these days, with Emmi *still* not sleeping, and my memories raw from the blood-soaked year-turning party ten weeks ago—not to mention Rika and I navigating the complicated new territory of our relationship.

Besides, this place hadn't really been my home in... Holy shit. *Seventeen years?* My math must be wrong.

I eyed Jaycel, who bounced along bright-eyed at my side. She didn't look seventeen years older. Did she?

I pulled up my collar for a little more protection against the chill of the miserable late winter drizzle and tried not to think about it.

"Are you going to explain what's so important that I needed to hire a babysitter and come all the way out here with you?" I asked.

Jaycel waved an airy hand. "It'll all be clear in time."

"You only say that when you know I won't like the answer."

"Which is exactly why I need your help, darling. If you'd *like* this situation, I could manage it on my own."

I instinctively glanced northward, but too many buildings lay between me and the great clock in the Tower district to read the time. "This had better not be one of your more involved and dangerous bad ideas. Achyrion is expecting me back in five hours."

"Ah, your mysterious babysitter! I'd like to point out that *Achyrion* is a very odd sort of name."

"That's his business. He takes great care of Emmi."

Jaycel gave me a smug sort of grin. "Well, if you can be secretive about your babysitter, I can be secretive about where we're going."

Her gaze slipped sideways, a guilty glance that my own eyes followed with an alarmed leap.

She'd taken us to the far edge of our old neighborhood, within a couple blocks of the river. There was nothing in that direction but a final row of buildings and then a stony jumble sloping down to where the mouth of the river met the sea. It was too rocky on this bank for ships and piers, though locals tied up small boats in places, and at low tide a bit of mucky beach emerged. That beach was a great place to find crabs, mussels, and the occasional oyster. A sometimes-submerged permanent rip to the first Echo made it an even better place to mudlark—and far too dangerous an area for kids to mess around. So of course we'd spent countless hours there.

"We're not heading to the Echo portal, are we? Because if we are—"

"Oh, no, of course not!" Jaycel waved a reassuring hand, but she wouldn't meet my eyes.

There was nothing else over that way, except a few houses, a fried fish shop, and—oh.

At the lowest tide, for about an hour, that bit of mucky beach turned into a sandbar reaching out partway into the mouth of the river, dividing it from the sea. At the far end of that sandbar sat a little island, just a pile of rocks and jumbled trees, crowned by a crumbling old mansion every child in Southside swore was haunted. Some of the bravest and most reckless claimed to have run across the sandbar to touch its bramble-clad walls before racing the tide back to safety. I was never sure whether I believed them, but I absolutely believed the stories about the kid who'd failed to make it before the sandbar vanished beneath the hungry waves. Or the ones about the drunken youth who'd gone into the water too near the rip in the Veil trying to impress a girl and gotten eaten by sea horrors. The place was plenty dangerous without ghosts, though of course that didn't stop us from making up countless ghastly stories—and never mind that Ravens still debated whether ghosts were even real, or just Echoes of deceased people passing through the Veil to Prime.

"Don't tell me we're going to the old Lovegrace house," I said.

"You will note that I am already going to commendable lengths to avoid telling you this very thing."

I stopped in the damp street. "Come on. You can't just leave it at that. Why are we going to the Lovegrace place?"

She waggled her fingers. "It's a mystery."

"Jaycel."

"Oh, fine. It's a bequeathal. All official and everything. I do hope I'm dressed for it."

I blinked. "Wait, old lady Lovegrace was still alive? And she died? And she *bequeathed* you something?"

"Apparently." Jaycel suddenly wouldn't meet my eyes. "You know how sometimes when you're a kid, things happen, and later you convince yourself they weren't real, and that's usually the end of it? Emphasis in this case on *usually.*"

"You're not making me feel better about this."

"Oh, I'm sure it'll be fine, with you there." She flashed me a bright smile. "You always did keep us out of trouble. But then you went off to join the Hounds, and trouble stayed behind with the rest of us. And now here we are!"

"Here we are." I stared suspiciously between the buildings, toward the water. It was possible, of course, that Jaycel just wanted company during boring legal proceedings. But I doubted she'd describe that as urgent.

"Come on, darling. It'll be easier to explain inside, where it's dry, and the others can help."

"Others?"

"I would never want to spoil the surprise!"

I muttered some uncharitable things under my breath. "Five hours, you hear me?"

"Five hours at most," she agreed. "You know you're too curious to back out now."

The worst part was that she was right. Sure, I wouldn't back out regardless—even setting aside that Jaycel was my friend, I owed her too much after the year-turning—but I wanted to know what in the Void was going on.

I huddled deeper into my coat and followed her, ignoring the fluttering of old candlelight story ghosts in my stomach. I wasn't a kid anymore; I was a grown Hound who'd faced far worse things in the Deep Echoes than could possibly be waiting in some run-down old house on a rock.

I should have known better than to even *think* that.

It was low tide, and the lumpy ridge of the sandbar had emerged from the restless dark water, scattered with driftwood and seaweed on the wave-sculpted oceanward side and calm on the sheltered riverward one. Gulls stalked the sand, busily searching for crabs and snails left stranded during this brief hour before the sea reclaimed its scuttling secrets.

Near the place where the curve of the sandbar merged with the wide stretch of mucky beach, a blur like a heat shimmer hung above the water, a glimmering subtle smear in the air with its bottom edge beneath the lapping waves. The rip in the Veil our parents had endlessly warned us about as kids—the one Jaycel had thrown rocks through on a dare. It stood in dangerous wading distance of the shore at the lowest tide. I'd done a few retrievals through there, bringing back kids who'd been less cautious than our crew. Once I'd helped dispatch a dangerous Echo that had wandered through, a thing like a pony-sized, ten-legged crab with a dozen fanged mouths gaping from its shell. When we were little, I'd seen the gap between worlds disgorge a slick of oily tentacles into the water once, thin as glass noodles, which had tentatively caressed the surface of the waves and then retracted back through the portal.

"We should never have played around near that thing," I muttered, thinking of Emmi. "They should fence it off, or something."

"Oh, come on, you know a fence would just be an invitation." Jaycel gave me an amused sidelong look. "You sound like our parents."

"Yeah, well, maybe they knew what they were talking about. Just keep an eye out, all right? Nasty Echoes live in the water, and something could come through."

"Yes, mom."

Damn right I was a mom. It meant I listened to common sense now. But it spoke in a language Jaycel had never learned, so I grunted to acknowledge the hit and started out onto the sandbar.

The Lovegrace mansion hadn't changed. The intervening years that had seen other derelict buildings in the neighborhood fixed up or torn down had passed this house by without touching it. I expected to find it stripped of the looming spooky significance of childhood, looking a bit run-down and lonely on its island but otherwise pretty normal, the exaggerating fog of years dispelled. But no—it still looked absolutely, aggressively haunted.

The island itself was one of a scattering at the southern lip of the river; ships steered wide of them as they came into Dockside at the north edge. Jagged rocks girdled the little mound of land like broken teeth. Beyond a few patches of trees, its bramble-choked slopes rose up to an overgrown garden behind a spiked black iron fence; dark scraggly bushes half obscured the soot-blackened brick of the mansion's walls. Sharp-crowned turrets reared against the grey clouds, surrounding a lonely widow's walk, and empty windows gaped below, several with cracked panes. Gulls wheeled overhead, letting out mournful cries.

The only thing that had changed was the gate, which stood open. It had always, always been chained shut, the thick links visible even across the water, a message to local kids not to even think about it. That open gate felt like a dangerous aberration, as if it could let hungry Echoes through from the deep and nasty cellars of reality. I couldn't help pausing as we reached the end of the sandbar, reluctant to cross that forbidden boundary even with the grey waves creeping closer and the rainy wind stinging my face.

Jaycel's sharp elbow nudged my ribs. "Scared?"

"You went out to the island once, right? And no hungry ghosts ate you."

"Ha! I'm too tough for ghosts to eat. They'd spit me out."

There was an unusual edge to her tone. Was she *nervous*? Jaycel Morningray, who feared neither shame nor pain nor death? All right, now I was progressing from suspicious to *concerned*.

THE LAST SOUL AMONG WOLVES

"What did you get into? What are you getting *me* into?"

She bit her lip. "Come on in, and I'll tell you. The day isn't getting any longer."

She was right about that; sunset ruddied the westward clouds. The wet sand dragged at my Damn Good Boots as we took the final strides from the sandbar to the island. A flight of barnacled stone steps led up to the gates, the black iron weeping rust. We passed between their teeth and climbed the hill.

The salt-weathered front doors swung open as we reached them. I half expected the old lady's shrouded corpse to glare at us from the gloomy entryway, hissing *Trespassers* at us with vengeful sibilance.

Instead, it framed a woman with a thick chestnut-brown braid whose pointed chin and wide brown eyes I'd know anywhere, even in a face far more sun-weathered than I remembered it. She still wore the blue that had always been her favorite color, but instead of a faded dress with the skirts tied up for better scrambling, it was a sharp royal-blue coat with knee-length swishy skirts.

Linna Vycross. The youngest member of our little gang of friends, a fiercely determined tagalong we'd all embraced and protected after initial attempts to shoo her away with the cruelty of youth had failed. (I *still* felt bad about that.) It was difficult to reconcile the wide-eyed kid I remembered with the sharp-edged face before me now, an old scar slashing a cheek that used to be baby soft. I hadn't seen her in ages. I'd always meant to get together with the old gang more often, but the Hounds had kept me so busy that years slipped by—and then suddenly Vy had jumped on a ship chasing adventure and sailed away from Acantis. Stars, it must have been *ten years.*

She blinked at us as if we were a tremendous surprise, then broke into a shy smile.

"Morningray! You're here! And Moon bless me, is that Kem?"

"Vy! Look at you!" I pulled her into a quick, fierce hug, feeling weirdly displaced in time. "Little Vy! You're half a foot taller than me. I used to have to give you a boost to climb up on that statue of a horse in Pennyworth Market."

She laughed. "Now I'd have to give *you* a boost. Did you get smaller?"

8   MELISSA CARUSO

"Come on, I'm not *that* short." I grinned. "What are you doing here?"

"Oh, you know." Her smile went suddenly sheepish. "Same thing as all of us."

Jaycel shook her head. "She wasn't with us, Vy. It was after she moved to the guildhouse dorms. Remember?"

"Oh! That's right." She raised a hand to her lips. "I've got the memory now. You made me swear not to tell her."

"I'm having an increasingly bad feeling about this," I said.

"Oh, just you wait!" Jaycel clapped my shoulder. "Can we finish the reunion indoors? I want to get out of the rain."

"You don't like the rain? I love it. But of course, come in." Vy stepped aside, letting us into an expansive foyer with a grand ceiling lost in shadows and cobwebs, the marble tiles of its floor chipped and stained with worn-in grime despite someone's brave attempt at sweeping. "Petras, look who's here!"

A slim gentleman in a charcoal-grey tailcoat turned from an open doorway with the casual ease of power in his movements and a glass of red wine in his hand. His cravat and the silk shirt beneath it showed a daring deep red that matched his drink; rubies glinted in his ears. A sleek dark ponytail fell halfway down his back, and a neat line of beard edged his jaw.

An incredulous grin stretched my face. "Petras! Looking good as always."

"Kem." His low, velvety tenor still surprised me, even though I'd seen him a few times over the years since I'd left Southside; his voice had gotten so much deeper when he finished his gender transition. "And Jaycel, of course. Always a pleasure."

I liked adult Petras just as much as I'd liked the nimble-fingered, quick-witted boy who'd always beaten me at tiles—a skill he'd apparently capitalized on, since he now ran a string of questionably legal gambling houses and Moon only knew what else. It was always strange but satisfying to see the nervous kid I remembered now radiating so much confidence and strength.

I hadn't done quite as rotten a job keeping in touch with Petras as I had with the others; he'd hired me once to recover his bartender's kid who'd slipped into an Echo, and had helped me navigate the underworld for jobs a couple of times. Still, there was a certain distance between us now, the closeness of our youth worn away by the erosion of years. I envied Jaycel's seemingly effortless and eternal friendship, which by the grinning arm clasp they exchanged was as warm as ever.

"So what *is* this?" I looked between the three of them, half expecting some prank to drop like a belated punch line. "Did you lease the place for a reunion of the old crowd? If so, I have to say it's a weird choice of venue."

"Don't I wish." Petras raised one dark brow. "Jaycel, didn't you tell her?"

"Not exactly," Jaycel said evasively. "I just mentioned it was a bequeathing."

The three of them exchanged a long glance. It was the same *What are we going to tell Kem* look I remembered from when they tried to explain how they'd lost my kite, or why they needed to hide in the back of my father's shop from an angry grocer.

Vy gave me her big brown eyes. "You won't be mad, will you?"

"Just tell me what happened already. You're killing me."

Petras had mercy on me. "Not long after you left the neighborhood, Jaycel got the idea that we should sneak into the Lovegrace mansion."

"I remember. She invited me." I shifted, a bit uncomfortably. "The Hounds had a curfew for the youngest apprentices, and I couldn't go."

Petras shook his head. "Only you would actually consider a curfew binding and not try to sneak out."

"So you broke into the mansion. And what? Found some horrible head in a jar and got cursed?"

"Basically," Jaycel agreed. "Only it wasn't a head. It was a book. And I'm still not sure we're cursed."

"Oh, we are," Petras muttered.

"Are we? It was just a lark." Vy's brows pinched. "I don't *feel* cursed."

Petras lifted an eyebrow. "You touched the book with your scraped palm and your name appeared written in blood."

I pressed a hand to my temple. "Tell me you didn't do that, Vy."

"Okay," Vy said cheerfully. "I didn't do it."

There was a pause while everyone stared at her.

"Well...not on *purpose*."

Times like this I wished I could drink. "What about the rest of you?"

Jaycel drew herself up. "I couldn't let her be cursed *alone*. She was so upset."

"She was crying," Petras clarified.

Vy flushed. "I don't remember crying."

"You did," Jaycel declared. "You were sobbing. So I told you whatever happened, we'd face it together, and I cut my hand and put it on the book, and my name appeared in it, too."

That sounded like something Jaycel would do. "Two cursed people is *not* better than one cursed person."

"That's what Petras said you'd say. But you weren't there, so we all ignored you."

I turned to Petras in despair. "You too? You actually had sense sometimes."

He shrugged. "Well, after Jaycel did it, and Mareth did it—"

"Mareth! He should have *known* better!" Mareth had always been obsessed with Echo stuff, a lanky kid who flitted around like a moth and wore a lot of black. It was no surprise that he'd wound up a Raven. He'd lectured us enough about not touching anything that might be Echo flotsam when we went mudlarking; he had no excuse.

"I'll bet he just didn't want to be left out if anything magical happened," Jaycel said.

"All right, I can see that. So wait, all four of you bled on some Echo relic book? Out of *solidarity*?"

"Nothing came of it, though," Vy said, a bit defensively. "I think."

"Until now," Petras amended.

"Until now," Jaycel agreed, "when a Wasp guild advocate sent us messages asking us to come to a special bequeathing of certain possessions of the late Auberyn Lovegrace. And I thought to myself, you know who I wish we'd had with us back when we got into this mess? Kembral. And you know who I want with us when we have to face the presumed consequences some seventeen years later? Also Kembral."

Lovely. I'd left my childhood friends alone for a few days and they'd immediately found an Echo relic to bleed on and probably gotten themselves cursed, and I was only finding out about it now, when Jaycel wanted help cleaning it up. I couldn't even be mad, given that I'd done basically the same thing at the year-turning. Stars, if it had happened a few months earlier, before I got whisked off to live with the Hounds, I'd have been right there with them—though I liked to think I'd have stopped things from getting out of hand.

Which made it somewhat my responsibility if they *were* cursed, in a backdoor sort of way.

I rubbed my forehead. "You don't need a Hound. You need a Raven."

Vy brightened. "Well, as it happens, there's one in the drawing room!"

"Let me guess. Is it Mareth?"

"You win the prize," Petras said.

"What's the prize? Do I get a curse, too? I'd better not get a fucking curse."

"Just don't bleed on the book."

The drawing room was in somewhat better shape than the foyer. Old lady Lovegrace's impeccable eye for dread-inducing decor seemed tempered here by the need for actual usable living space; the exceedingly dark wood paneling of the walls and the heavy brocade curtains could arguably *not* harbor ghosts, and in the massive marble fireplace crackled a fire that could almost be considered cheerful. Someone (probably the Wasp) had brought in some lamps to make the place a bit less dismal, and had set up a couple rows of chairs and a podium as well.

Mareth had a streak of silver in his hair now, and it was totally weird seeing grown-up man shoulders on someone who should be a gangly twelve-year-old. The silver earrings and studs climbing his ears were new, and his face had deep adult creases instead of the soft roundness of boyhood. But I'd still have recognized him anywhere. His angular slouch was the same, and the long robe-like black coat he wore with full split skirts and silver trim was totally something that young Mareth would have aspired to. About half a dozen different amulets hung around his neck, an assortment of runic rings decorated his fingers, and the only way his appearance could have screamed *I am a Raven* louder would be if he rolled up his sleeve to show his tattoo.

I couldn't help a little twinge of guilt that he'd been right across Guildhouse Square from me for years and I'd never gone over to say hello. Come to think of it, it was a bit strange that I hadn't seen him around town before now. I ran into most of the field Ravens now and then while I was on Hound business. Maybe he was the type that never left the library.

He was chatting with a tiny wisp of a woman with spectacles and a silver bun, wearing a crisp sage-green dress with a cream scarf. She clasped a well-worn leather portfolio full of papers against her side. The Wasp, then. They both looked worried, which couldn't be good.

They weren't the only ones in the room. A man and a woman sat in the double line of chairs, as far from everyone else as possible, their seats drawn tight together. The woman wore the kind of expensive bleeding-edge-of-fashion clothes you saw on Tower district merchants trying to impress each other; the man sported a large diamond brooch, a number of ostentatiously large rings, and a tailcoat of opulent burgundy velvet. Their hair was so carefully styled with the latest creams to perfect, glossy waves that you could have bounced a penny off them. They whispered to each other, heads close, casting dubious or downright hostile glances at the rest of us.

I couldn't decide if they were Hillside aristocrats trying to look as fashionable as Tower merchants, or Tower merchants trying to look as patrician as Hillside aristocrats. They both had the dark hair, deep-set eyes, and warm brown skin of the old Acantis ancestry prevalent among the Hillside crowd, but that didn't mean anything—so did Petras and Vy. The sprawling archipelago of the League Cities

THE LAST SOUL AMONG WOLVES

had lain at the intersection of all the major trade routes for ages; like her sister city-states, Acantis had welcomed immigrants from all over the world for centuries. Anyone might trace their Acantis citizenship back far enough to be a scion of one of the old ruling families—including people with pale, hawkish Viger features like me, or deep brown, sharp-cheek-boned Cathardian ones like Almarah and Marjorie, or the omnipresent hard-to-pin-down mix, like Jaycel, Mareth, and Rika.

"Maybe we shouldn't bother Mareth, if he's talking to someone. I think that might be rude?" Vy worried her lip with her teeth. That was new—both the gesture and the uncertainty.

"Bah. Nobody likes talking to Wasps. It's all legally binding contracts and musty old archives and enough figures to make your eyes fall out." Jaycel started toward them.

I hooked the back of her jacket. "Wait."

The Wasp's stern voice wasn't hard to overhear in the dusty, quiet drawing room. "I'm sorry, but I can't let you see them. The instructions are clear. No one is to enter the sealed room until after I read the statement."

"But if there's a risk to the safety of the people here..." Mareth suggested.

"Then I expect you will be well suited to deal with it, as the Raven present. I am the Wasp presiding, and my duty is to follow the instructions of the deceased as laid out in the documents entrusted to the care of my guild."

Jaycel's eyes lit up, and she turned a grin on us that meant trouble. "A sealed room! Could you get us in, Petras?"

"I'm hurt that you feel the need to ask."

"Hey," I protested. "This is exactly what got you into this situation in the first place. It's probably even the same room."

Petras gave Jaycel a narrow look. "You had to bring her."

I cleared my throat. "So, what have you all been up to?"

Petras rubbed his knuckles modestly on the lapel of his jacket. "Let's just say business has been good."

Vy straightened. "I've been on a ship!"

"Just like you always wanted!" Jaycel slapped her back, and Vy jumped a little. "You used to play at being Captain Vycross, remember? I was your dashing first mate, but I kept getting mutinous."

Vy gave a surprised little laugh. "That's right, you did! I didn't mind, though."

"Ha! You hit me and ran off crying once." Jaycel shook her head. "I deserved it, naturally. What kind of ship? Are you a pirate?"

"No, no. That would be a grand adventure, though." Vy looked dreamy at the thought. "It's a courier ship, running the express route between Acantis and Cathardia."

"The express route!" Petras gave her a keen, assessing look, and I wondered whether he might be involved in a little smuggling on the side. "So you've got a Dolphin guild tide skimmer?"

"Of course!" Vy bounced on her toes. "A tide skimmer can really get you places."

"Isn't dipping down an Echo on the open ocean like that risky, though?" I asked dubiously. Almarah had always told me never to touch the Veil at sea.

Vy's grin didn't fade. "Oh, yes. Terribly dangerous."

I shuddered. "Yeah, no thanks. I'll travel the long way." The ocean was full enough of strange horrors in Prime; it got exponentially worse as you descended through layers of reality. Plus the Veil was always thinner near water, so even though tide skimmers only took their ships down one Echo, things could wash up from much deeper.

The fashionable couple in the back corner seemed to conclude a whispered argument. The woman straightened, radiating disdainful impatience, and called out to the Wasp.

"It's two minutes past the hour. Are you ever going to get started?"

The look the Wasp leveled at her was unimpressed. "Not everyone is here yet. We'll wait a little longer."

"I see no reason we should have to suffer for their lateness."

"If you experience suffering when sitting still for a few minutes, I recommend you speak to a physicker. In the meantime, we will wait. If we're still missing anyone at a quarter past, I'll start without them."

THE LAST SOUL AMONG WOLVES   15

Vy shrank a bit in her chair, eyes wide on the Wasp. "Maybe we should follow the rules here."

"Maybe we shouldn't get caught breaking them," Petras countered. "Speaking of which..."

He gave me a guarded look, and I had the feeling he was weighing whether to mention something I wouldn't like.

"Oh, spit it out," I grumbled. "I can already see things are going to keep getting worse, so no sense trying to spare me."

Petras glanced to Jaycel. "I had the same thought you did, about inviting a guest in case things turned out dodgy."

"Oh, did you bring a bodyguard? Maybe that one with the incredible shoulders you had with you at the club last time?" Jaycel glanced around eagerly.

"No. I hired a different kind of professional." Lips twitching, he nodded toward the door.

I turned, curious, and froze as if I'd been turned to stone.

Standing in the doorway—looking for one brief instant as surprised as I felt—was Rika Nonesuch.

NEVER ARGUE WITH A WASP

It wasn't that seeing Rika was a shock. I'd seen her that morning. She'd come by my place almost every day while I was recovering from my wounds after the year-turning, and the habit had stuck in the two months since. She showed up at my door with the unpredictable frequency of a well-fed stray, sometimes stopping by for a few minutes between jobs, sometimes staying half the day. She played with Emmi, cuddled up and read to me while I nursed, and made sure I ate. She insisted I get out of the house, dragging me to cafés and parks and even the Grand Theater once, when we could get someone to watch Emmi. We'd inched our way into an intimacy that was hesitant at first—Rika was elusive by nature, and I was still a bit burned from Beryl unceremoniously ditching me—but growing alarmingly comfortable.

No, it was her appearance *here* and *now* that felt like a rumble of thunder. If she was on a job, this was serious. There was no way Petras had paid Rika's steep fee to have one of the best Cats in Acantis come to a bequeathing with him as moral support.

"What are *you* doing here?" The second it left my mouth I realized what a stupid question it was—if she was on business, she couldn't answer. My only consolation was that Jaycel clearly wondered the same thing, given the sharp rise of her eyebrows.

THE LAST SOUL AMONG WOLVES   17

Petras offered her an elegant bow. "Signa Nonesuch. Thank you so much for coming."

Fine, Petras. Show me up, why don't you.

Rika had recovered her composure; she gave him a warm smile, her eyes barely sliding sideways in my direction.

"Always a pleasure working with you." She turned to me. "I could ask you the same thing. Who's watching Emmi? Achyrion?"

Petras blinked at me. "*Achyrion?* What kind of name is Achyrion?"

"A babysitter kind of name," I said. "And yes, he's with her."

I suspected I was the only one who noticed Rika's shoulders relax a little. It gave me a warm tickling feeling to know she cared enough about Emmi to worry if she was safe. Given the enemies I'd made, it was a valid concern—but between the time shield the Clockmaker had given her and Achyrion's substantial capabilities, Emmi was probably the safest person in Acantis right now (a fact I had to keep reminding myself whenever we were apart).

None of this explained why Rika was here. Probably she and Petras were plotting to steal something—and fine, that was none of my business. They could strip the place bare for all I cared, especially if the snooty rich couple so studiously ignoring us were an example of the relatives who would otherwise inherit whatever old lady Lovegrace had squirreled away. But you didn't need a Cat of Rika's caliber to loot an old ruin like this.

If I couldn't ask her about her job, I wished I could at least wrap an arm around her waist and banter comfortably about the creepy house and my impulsive friends. But she was working. Despite years of what in retrospect had probably been flirting on the job, I had no idea whatsoever how to be her girlfriend while she was being a Cat. This was new territory, and it was all definitely too complicated for my rusty social skills.

Jaycel, undaunted by any such concerns, grinned a welcome to Rika. "This is shaping up to be an exciting day! A Cat, a Hound, a Raven, and a Wasp walk into a haunted house..."

Rika's brows lifted. "Haunted? Petras, you didn't mention it was haunted."

"Well, look at it!" Jaycel gestured around expansively.

"Haunted is an imprecise term," Petras murmured. "Jaycel is applying it loosely."

Rika did a Cat thing where she edged forward and changed the angle of her shoulders and suddenly she was part of our conversational group, smooth as if she'd always been there. She flicked her eyes toward the sour-faced rich couple, dropping her voice to a near whisper. "Speaking of who's walked into the house, do any of you know who *they* are? They're not part of your old neighborhood crew, surely."

I knew she was redirecting our curiosity away from herself, but I wanted to know the answer, so I kept my mouth shut.

Jaycel smothered a laugh. "Ah, Willa Lovegrace. Old lady Lovegrace's niece. Cheap vinegar in an expensive bottle."

Vy snickered. Then she confessed, "I have no idea what that means."

"She used to live not so far from us in Southside, though you'd never know it—she puts on a fake Tower accent and everything."

Petras grunted. "I don't know who she thinks she's fooling."

Jaycel's eyes gleamed wickedly. "Her husband, darling. Regius Moreland, a classic boring Hillside twat. Not the sort of man you'd marry for anything but his money."

A clammy draft swirled in as the outside door opened and closed. Hard on its heels, an absolutely stunning woman sailed into the room with the grace of a swan. Delicate gold embroidery climbed from the hem of her brilliant fire-orange gown. Gold and amber ornaments graced the dark fall of her hair, and a shimmer of gold makeup highlighted her lovely eyes, standing out against her warm brown skin. She took her seat at once without speaking to anyone, with the aloof grace of someone used to having every eye on her.

Petras froze, staring at her with the lost, desperate hunger of a starving man at a bakery window. I'd seen him react less to getting punched in the gut.

"Ah, good," the Wasp said, with a pragmatism that seemed almost blasphemous as the rest of us caught our collective breath. "Signa Glory."

"Signa Silena Glory!" Jaycel's eyes kindled with the spark of good gossip. "My, my. Fancy seeing her here."

Even I had heard of Silena Glory, the famous alto, jewel of the Butterfly guild and the Acantis opera, whose shows at the Grand Theater sold out weeks in advance. I couldn't for the life of me imagine what she could possibly have to do with old lady Lovegrace, or why the sight of her should make Petras look like he was dying.

"You know her?" I whispered to him.

He gave a mute, agonized nod, without taking his eyes off the singer. Her gaze landed on him, widened, and then immediately flicked away. *Well.*

"Everyone's here, then," the Wasp declared. "Why don't you all sit down while I get things in order." It was clearly more of a command than a question.

The five of us took up an entire row of chairs by ourselves; I sat between Jaycel and Rika. I had no idea how much space to leave between us in a professional context anymore and awkwardly scooted my chair an inch away from hers, then back toward it. Rika seemed content to let our hips just barely touch. She kept giving me little shuttered, searching glances, probably wondering if we were going to be at odds on this job of hers. Stars, I hoped not.

Mareth settled behind Jaycel with a grave nod to all of us. "I'd say good to see you all, but given the circumstances, I'm not sure that's appropriate."

Vy gave him big calf eyes. "It's good to see you anyway, even if we're in a spot of trouble."

"If it's only a spot, I'll be pleased enough," Mareth said darkly. But his cheeks reddened.

"Do you know anything about these Echo relics, then?" Petras asked, hooking his arm over the back of his chair and turning to face Mareth.

"Echo relics?" I asked sharply. "You didn't mention relics, plural. Just the book."

"There was a suspicious-looking mirror, too." Petras gave one of his liquid shrugs. "I may be jumping to conclusions."

20 MELISSA CARUSO

Sure he was. By the unruffled look on Rika's face, this wasn't news to her, either.

Mareth laced his fingers studiously on his knee. "As it happens, I was just discussing the matter with the Wasp, as the Raven present, and—"

The Wasp in question tapped her papers authoritatively on the podium. The room went silent.

"Let's begin," she said crisply.

"Finally." A sour edge sharpened Regius's Hillside drawl.

"I'm Beatrix Clement, an advocate with the Wasp guild. I have called you all here according to the posthumous instructions of Auberyn Lovegrace, duly registered with my guild, for a special bequeathing. This is separate from the disposition of her funds, goods, and investments, all of which she has donated to various charitable causes in her will."

Willa Lovegrace's mouth pinched as if she'd sucked on a lemon. "That bitch," she muttered.

"I have been instructed to gather you here and read a sealed document, the contents of which are unfamiliar to me. As a senior Wasp, I am prepared to interpret the law accordingly should the document prove irregular or imprecise."

She settled her golden spectacles firmly on her nose with the air of someone just *daring* that document to step out of line, then drew a large envelope from her leather folder and tore it open with practiced ease. I leaned forward, ready to learn what accursed foolishness my friends had gotten themselves involved in.

The Wasp slid out a thin sheaf of papers, skimming them quickly. She made a small tutting noise, sharp as a slap against the tense silence. We all exchanged alarmed glances.

"Well." Signa Clement cleared her throat. "I'm going to read this now, but please bear in mind that these are the words of the deceased, not mine."

"That's a bit ominous," Mareth muttered.

"If you are reading this," the Wasp read, "then I have passed beyond this life and left behind my most terrible burden. It grieves

THE LAST SOUL AMONG WOLVES

me that I must now bequeath it to another. But remember: I did not put this upon you. You chose it. Despite all my efforts to prevent this very thing from coming to pass, you elected to circumvent my precautions and claim this fate for your own. And now you reap the consequences."

Jaycel gave me a look and spread her hands, mouthing *Oops?*

"Several of you were rash children, trespassing foolishly in places you would have done well to leave alone. One of you is my own flesh and blood, who should have known better."

Willa sniffed disdainfully, clasping her husband's arm.

"One of you took advantage of my goodwill to seize your own undoing."

Glory bowed her head, elegant hands folded in her lap.

"Not one of you is blameless. All of you are now linked irrevocably to the relics that cruel fate has placed in my care. As some of you know, they have the power to grant health, wealth, and—most powerfully of all—a wish."

A murmur of excitement rustled through the room. I didn't try to hide how my stomach sank—wishes were always bad, bad Echo business. By the Wasp's disapproving expression, she knew it, too.

"The next weeks will determine which of you will inherit these relics, as I did many years ago. The manner of that determination is unfortunately rather simple." The Wasp paused, the slightest hesitation, her gaze fixed on the document in her hands. She continued with great reluctance, as if only the stern, invisible hand of duty could compel the rest of the words from her lips.

"Only one of you will survive."

WISHES ARE ALWAYS BAD NEWS

Silence fell, brittle and jagged as the cold tracery of windowpane frost. Nobody breathed. My brain was still stuck in *I couldn't possibly have heard that right* while my gut plunged with the dread certainty that yes, I did.

Vy let out a startled little laugh, as if it might be a joke, choked off at the end as she realized it wasn't. She pressed trembling fingers to her mouth, too late to recapture the sound.

That was all it took to set the whole room off. Half the audience leaped to their feet; Willa and Regius started shouting. My skin came alive with the familiar electricity of danger, mind sharpening into the acute wakefulness that comes when you know something has gone horribly, deadly wrong.

The Wasp's voice cut through the chaos like a whipcrack. "If you would please sit down."

Everyone sat at once except Willa Lovegrace, who stood with her fists at her sides, eyes smoldering with fury. The Wasp met her gaze, unflinching. After an agonizing handful of seconds, Willa sank stiffly back into her seat.

"That's the end of the first document. My instructions are to now open the second one." The Wasp's tone suggested we were all a

THE LAST SOUL AMONG WOLVES   23

bunch of unruly children. "I trust you can control yourselves enough to give me a moment to read it, as I can assure you I have as many questions about this rather irregular situation as you do."

Irregular situation was a uniquely Wasp way to describe an ominous statement of impending doom. I wasn't ready for more deadly Echo nonsense, damn it, not so soon after the year-turning. I exchanged a glance with Rika; her grey eyes reflected the same trouble that roiled in my mind.

A tense silence fell. After a moment, Signa Clement looked up from her papers and cleared her throat.

"The second document pertains to the set of Echo relics housed in a certain room in this house, which the deceased refers to as the 'lantern room.'"

Petras lifted his head like she'd called his name. *Interesting.*

"To summarize, the relics in question are a book, a lantern, and a mirror. The document claims that some unspecified demise will fall upon each person whose name appears in the book in turn, until only one remains. That person shall inherit all three relics and the benefits they confer." She frowned disapprovingly at the page before her. "Allegedly this inheritance is magically binding, and the deceased could not bequeath them otherwise if she tried."

"But she didn't try very hard, did she," Willa muttered bitterly.

The Wasp ignored her. She tapped her papers straight against the podium and tucked them away in her leather folder. "This is clearly a situation where the potential danger posed overrides certain usual protocols. Fortunately, we have a Raven present." She turned to Mareth. "If you would be so kind as to accompany me to examine the relics, Signa Overfell?"

Mareth rose at once, all looming importance, brushing imaginary dust from his robes. "Of course, Signa Clement."

"Wait," Jaycel objected. "You can't say a mysterious doom will overcome us one after another without telling us *when*. It's simply not done. You have to say that one of us will die at midnight, or on the third day, or something dramatic like that."

"The document does not specify." The Wasp's mouth pursed in

dissatisfaction. "It does say that the interval will be halved each time, but fails to state when we should expect this process to begin. It *is* a rather glaring omission."

Great. Because what we all needed was an *exponentially accelerating* death curse. I could immediately tell by the range of reactions to this statement which people in the room understood the alarming math behind that little tidbit.

"Hopefully Signa Overfell can determine the answer," said Clement (who certainly did understand the math, but probably didn't want to go into it with a roomful of people already given to dramatics). "You are free to go if you wish. If you wait peacefully here, however, we may have more information in a moment."

She and Mareth left the room together, a solemn professional purpose in their stride.

"Oh dear," Vy murmured from behind her fingers. "This isn't how I thought it would be at all."

Jaycel patted her shoulder sympathetically. "If you'd thought it'd be like this, I would have some serious questions for you, Vy."

Regius whirled on his wife the moment Signa Clement was gone.

"You didn't say anything about people *dying.*" His voice had the throttled quality of someone who probably thought he was being quiet. "Stars, Willa, you said all we had to do was bleed on that book and we'd be sure to get the relics, since none of the others were family. You didn't mention the little detail that only *one* of us would be alive to inherit them!"

"I didn't know!" Willa snapped. "All I knew was that she got heaps of money from putting her name in that book. She never said anything about people dying, either!"

"You expect me to believe that? You're trying to kill me, aren't you! You manipulative little bitch."

Glory edged her chair away from them with an expression of acute discomfort.

"So," Jaycel said brightly, "impending doom! Very exciting. What do we do now?"

She looked at me. Behind her daring smile, worry strained her face.

THE LAST SOUL AMONG WOLVES

The trust in her eyes—the certainty that I would have an answer—twisted a knife in my heart.

I wanted so much to assure her that I would fix this somehow. But I knew too well from the year-turning that there was no guarantee I could protect the people I cared about. I didn't know what to tell her—what to tell any of them, as all eyes fixed on me, waiting for my answer as a seasoned expert in dealing with weird, dangerous stuff.

Those relics could be mere cosmic rubbish a Raven like Mareth could disenchant in an afternoon. They could be designed and wielded with purpose by some asshole human in an attempt to win the wish. Or they could be the mechanism of an Echo game, with powerful beings lurking behind the scenes, betting on their favorite mortal to win. That last option was my personal nightmare. But until we knew which it was, there wasn't much sense worrying everyone with dire possibilities. They all looked anxious enough.

"We wait for Mareth to take a look at those relics." I tried to sound calm and professional. "He's a Raven. This is Raven stuff. Hopefully he comes back and tells us he knows how to break the curse."

Vy looked a little wistful. "I wouldn't mind a wish, though."

Petras let out a disbelieving huff. "At the expense of all our lives?"

"Oh, well, maybe there's a way to get the wish without people dying?"

"There isn't," Petras said flatly.

"The Echoes will always claim their price," I agreed, eyeing him. First he'd hired Rika, and now this certainty. "You sounded pretty sure there, Petras. Do you know something about this?"

He bit his lip, a brief flash of the uncertain boy he'd once been. "Maybe. Just vague stories about a curse and a lantern, you understand—I'd much rather have Mareth's professional opinion."

I glanced toward Rika to catch her reaction—but she was gone. Probably spying on the Wasp and Mareth, getting a peek into the sealed room.

Regius's voice rose up painfully loud. "Why did you have an aunt living in some moldy old house in Southside, anyway? I always *hated* coming here—you *know* I only did it because you said if we were nice to the old bat we could get the wish and the money, and now look what's happened!"

The noise drew Petras's attention to the side of the room where Glory sat, edging farther away from the quarreling couple. That haunted look came over his face again, and he rose suddenly.

"Excuse me. I'll be right back."

He crossed to stand just out of touching range of Glory, murmuring something too low to hear. She glanced away from him at first, but then her gaze pulled back, and she rose with all the grace of a sunrise. The two of them withdrew to a corner and began an intense, whispered conversation.

Jaycel shook her head. "Poor bastard. He should know better, after what she did to him."

Before I could ask what *that* meant, Vy blurted out, "Do you think he's mad? Is that why he left?"

"Petras?" I blinked. "No. Why would he be mad?"

"Because...because I'm the one who got him into this, touching that awful book." Her hands twisted in her lap. "Or because I said the wrong thing. Oh, I'm off to a bad start already! I've been at sea so long, and I forget how to talk to people."

I knew how that felt, being home with Emmi so much. The new hesitancy I'd seen in her suddenly made sense.

"You're fine, Vy. He's not mad. You haven't said anything wrong, and no one blames you for touching the book."

"Not in the least." Jaycel flung an arm around Vy's shoulders. "Old lady Lovegrace shouldn't have left that book out in the open like that in a locked room in the middle of her house if it was so dangerous."

"So you're not mad, either?"

"Never at you, darling. Only at whoever is playing games with us." For a flicker of a moment, a haunted look shadowed Jaycel's eyes—she'd been caught up in the Echo game at the year-turning, too. Then she sprang up and started pacing, rapier hilt winking in the dim light. "We'll see what this doom is. If it can bleed, I'll cut it."

"And if it can't bleed?" Vy asked anxiously.

Jaycel flashed a grin. "I'll find a way to make it."

THE LAST SOUL AMONG WOLVES   27

It was unlikely to be that simple, of course. But far be it from me to interfere with Jaycel's glorious coping mechanisms.

Vy laughed. "If anyone can, you can, Morningray."

Jaycel gave her arm an affectionate, gentle punch. The look that lit Vy's face was everything I remembered, all bright with wonder at being taken along with the big kids, eager to earn our approval. My throat thickened perilously.

My salvation from unwanted feelings came in the unexpected form of Willa Lovegrace, whose voice cut across my thoughts in a hiss she seemed to think was far quieter than it really was.

"If you didn't want your name in the book, you shouldn't have bled on it!"

"You *know* I need this wish." Regius leaned close and took her arm. "You *know* the state of our coffers. Stars, Willa, if this doesn't break our way, you can forget having a new wardrobe for the spring season."

Jaycel caught my eye. *Poor babies*, she mouthed.

Willa shook his hand off. "Well, it hardly matters, because one of us will be *dead*! This is serious, Regius—you need to pull it together!"

Regius leaped to his feet. "Pull it together? Hardly. I've had enough. This whole affair is an insult. We're leaving."

Willa stayed in her chair, crossing her arms. "You heard what she said—they're going to have more information for us in a minute. If we're going to be cursed, I'd like to know how."

"Come now, Willa, we can't stay in this moldy pit." His lip curled. "Unless it feels like *home* to you. I notice your Tower accent is slipping, *dear.*"

Willa reached out to him, alarmed. "Regius—"

He turned away from her. "Stay here if you like. *I'm* going home."

Regius Moreland stormed out, the outer door admitting a swirl of chilly wind before banging shut behind him. Willa's cheeks blushed a furious red.

We all exchanged grimaces—even Petras and Glory, from across the room. Jaycel mimed tossing something out a window, and I wasn't sure whether she meant Willa should dump her husband, that

Regius had just dumped Willa, or that we should defenestrate the both of them.

"Well! That was awkward," Vy declared cheerfully, without dropping her voice at all. Willa scowled at her.

Under cover of the distraction, Glory gave Petras's arm a quick, gentle touch—far too intimate a gesture for a stranger—and turned away, brow furrowed. Petras stared after her, hands curling at his sides, before heading slowly back toward our seats.

Maybe not the best possible time to talk to him, but probably the best I was going to get. I rose and met him halfway.

"Hey," I murmured. "You okay?"

"Yeah. I just...used to know Silena, before she joined the Butterflies and got famous. I already knew she's changed, so I don't know why I keep being surprised." He squared his shoulders and smoothed out his cravat, carefully arranging the unsettled pieces of himself. "Not to mention that we just heard, rather dramatically, that we're all going to die. Why would anything be wrong?"

"Yeah, that was a fun surprise." I chose my next words carefully, stepping around the question I wanted to ask. "Though you must have suspected *something* was up, if you hired Rika."

"I didn't expect *that*." He gave me a narrow look. "You're not going to leave me alone until I tell you why I hired her, are you?"

"Look, I'm a Hound. We're not known for letting things go."

"And that's exactly why I can't tell you."

"Petras—"

"I like you, Kem, I do. But when you left us to join your guild, you made it pretty clear where your loyalties lie."

It wasn't an accusation—his tone was almost gentle. But it stung.

"Hey, I didn't ask to leave so abruptly. It was because of that whole kidnapping thing. By the time I woke up in the guild infirmary, my parents and Almarah had decided I'd be safer with the Hounds, and they'd already moved my things into the apprentice dormitory."

"But you weren't exactly upset about it, were you?"

"I— No." I'd been thrilled. Disoriented, maybe, but it had been a dream come true.

"You'd already made your choice long before you left Southside." Petras's voice softened, but he continued, relentless. "The point is, you're a Hound through and through. You investigate things, all right? Some people don't like being investigated." He shrugged, an angry tension in his shoulders that I didn't think was directed at me. "I got a tip from someone that the lantern might relate to a personal matter. I had to promise discretion. I hired Signa Nonesuch because I've worked with her before and I know she's the best. End of story."

"What personal matter?"

"I don't want to talk about it."

We used to tell each other everything, in our little crew—all our hopes and fears and secrets, sharing all our treasures. But fine. He was a grown man now, and we hadn't talked much in years. It was normal and natural for him to have personal things he could talk about in a professional capacity with my girlfriend and not with me.

I gave a stiff nod. "All right. I won't push you. But think about what you can safely share, will you? I want to help."

"Sure."

Rika swept up to us. "Excuse me, Kembral, are you bullying my client?"

I forced a grin. "No. I'm bullying my friend."

"No one *bullies* me." Petras chuckled, breaking the tension. "Except you, Kem. You were always a bossy little bitch."

A reasonable approximation of the warmth of our old friendship washed over me in sweet relief. "*Somebody* had to take you bunch of scoundrels in hand."

"I'd say that's a load of horseshit, but the evidence seems to support your case." He slid a sideways glance at Rika. "Did you..."

She gave her head a tiny shake. "We should talk."

"All right." Petras gave me a gracious half bow. "Sorry, Kem. The job, you know."

They stepped out into the foyer. What they talked about was none of my business, of course. Petras didn't want to confide in me, and Rika was a Cat doing her job. Except she was also my girlfriend now, and having secrets from each other felt weird in a way it never had before.

No, that wasn't it. Rika always had secrets. She was made of secrets. What bothered me was that two people I thought should trust me were keeping secrets from me *with each other*. Which was a pretty childish thing to be upset about, and probably had everything to do with my emotions still being a mess from new motherhood and how isolated I'd felt for the past four months.

Still, this was important, damn it. They could at least give me some better hints.

They'd left me standing an awkward intermediate distance from Signa Glory, who leaned against the wall alone, head tipped back, eyes closed. I prepared to withdraw and give her space, but she opened eyes that were weary and knowing, as if some great irony weighed down on her.

"Signa Thorne," she greeted me, my name honey on her lips. "It's a pleasure to meet you."

Her voice was so beautiful my knees went to water. I'd forgotten— she was one of a handful of Butterflies in the city who could use resonance, one of her guild's secret Echo skills, like blink stepping was for Hounds. A Raven had tried to describe the theory behind it to me once—something about pitching your voice through the Veil so that it reverberated with power and emotion from more than one world. The difficulty was that unlike a blink step, the more you used resonance, the more difficult it was to turn it off. A little crept through even into casual conversation.

No *wonder* she'd been so quiet. It must get old having your off-hand comments evoke overly emotional responses and having people imprint on you like little baby ducks.

"Likewise." My own voice sounded flat and awkward in my ears.

Her gold-lidded eyes searched my face. "Forgive me for not introducing myself a moment ago, but I didn't want to intrude in case you were talking about something private."

In that instant I had no doubt it showed in my face that we'd been talking about her.

"No, no," I assured her hastily. "We were just discussing the unexpectedly dark turn this bequeathing has taken. I'm sorry you were drawn into this."

She shook her head. "It was my own fault. I was young and foolish and desperate, and I made a mistake. Auberyn would have no pity for my remorse now."

That got my attention. "You knew her?"

"You could say that. She was my first patron." A touch of wistful affection warmed that gorgeous voice; my heart ached with the echoes of it. "When I was a little girl, she heard me singing in the street, and she paid for my voice lessons. I'd never be what I am today if it weren't for her. I suppose I paid her back poorly for her kindness."

"Oh?"

"She never wanted anyone to be hurt the way she was. She warned me to stay away from that book."

Everything she said sounded like a rehearsed line, reverberating with significance and feeling. As if she weren't a mere human being, but a carefully crafted stage character.

"Did she talk about how it happened? How she wound up surviving, or—"

"No." Glory sighed. "I should have asked her. I should have listened. But instead I did the one thing she didn't want me to do, above all others."

"Well, we all do foolish things when we're young, and a wish is hard to resist."

"Yes. Yes, it is. Especially when you're desperate for an escape. But I found another way out." Her dark eyes went knowing and sad. "Do you have any regrets, Signa Thorne?"

"I suppose we all have a few." I couldn't help thinking of what a shitty job I'd done keeping in touch with everyone except Jaycel. Or how it probably wouldn't have been so hard after all to sneak out of the guild dorms and go with them to the Lovegrace house on that fateful night.

"I've tried to live my life without regrets. I thought it would be easier as I got older and wiser, but I'm finding it's only becoming more difficult." Glory shook her head. "It's no matter. I do hope we can finish here soon. There's ... someone I need to talk to about all of this. I was hoping to get his help earlier, but well—he can be elusive."

"A Raven?"

"Something like that."

Before I could try to unpack that—or really anything about the conversation—Signa Clement poked her head through the doorway.

"Excuse me. Signa Thorne, would you mind joining us?"

I turned to her without hesitation, eager to do *something* with all this nervous energy. To take this problem in my teeth and shake it.

"Of course."

Everyone's eyes burned into my back as I left the room, following the Wasp down a dusty, wood-paneled hall. Time to get a look at these relics that threatened to destroy my friends.

LEAVE THE RELICS TO THE RAVENS

Candles in sconces lit the small, dim room, the lower half of its walls done in yet more dark paneling and the upper half in poisonous green and age-splotched silver. No windows let in moonlight; it was located right at the heart of the house, as if the mansion had been built around it. The room contained no furniture besides a sleekly polished wooden table set before a tarnished oval mirror. On it a small, age-yellowed book lay open.

Mareth stood over the book, scrutinizing it through a silver hand lens ringed in arcane symbols.

"Ah, there you are, Kembral." He glanced up, all business. "Come take a look at this. I want your professional opinion."

I stood beside him and eyeballed the book. Sure enough, there was a list of names in it, all written in some crumbly, dark, reddish ink—oh, I wasn't fooling myself. It was long-dried blood. *Fantastic.*

The first four names were in various childish handwriting that I recognized, and the rest were more adult and refined, as if the book had copied their penmanship as well as taking their names.

"My professional opinion is that I can't believe you all fucking touched that thing."

The Wasp made a tutting sound that could have been disapproval or agreement.

"Not the book," Mareth said. "That's simple enough; it binds each of us into the enchantment. I meant the lantern."

I blinked. "There is no lantern."

"Exactly."

My first thought was *Did Rika steal it already?* But Mareth didn't have the look of someone who was outraged and distressed at a criminal act; he had the eager expression of someone waiting for me to catch up to the point he'd reached in unraveling a mystery.

I sharpened my attention and *really* looked around the room.

I felt it as soon as I focused my senses. A faint prickle along my nerves, a hum of possibility in the air—the closeness of a thin spot in the Veil.

The shining silver oval of the mirror in its ornate frame wasn't tarnished after all. It was clouded, blurry, the image it reflected obscure.

I reached out and hesitantly touched the smooth, cool glass. It gave slightly under my finger, a small softening. I had no doubt that if the circumstances were right, I could push through.

Heart quickening, I took my fingertip back.

"It's an Echo portal."

"Yes." Mareth let out an uneven breath, as if he'd been worried I wouldn't confirm it. "It's closed at the moment, but it could open at any time. So you can see why I wanted your expertise."

"My expertise with Echoes is mostly about traveling into them."

"But you also know something about what might come *out*."

Ah. Yes. There was that. I puffed a dubious breath between my lips. "Any sense of how deep it is?"

"Hmm." Mareth turned the ring of the hand lens, lining the symbols up differently; mist began to swirl in the glass. "I'm seeing a refractive depth beyond the shallow layers. The portal probably goes at least four or five Echoes down."

"Well, shit. It could be anything, that deep."

The Wasp had been watching each of us in turn, her eyes bright. She cleared her throat. "Perhaps you'd like to share your theory about the relics with Signa Thorne?"

Mareth sighed; he'd been enjoying the diversion. "Yes, I was

THE LAST SOUL AMONG WOLVES   35

getting to that. My guess is that the lantern is *in* the mirror. Or else something that unlocks the lantern comes out of it."

"I am somehow not reassured."

"I think each relic has its own role." Mareth gestured to the book. "Those who mark the book with their blood effectively enter into a pact with the relics."

"Makes sense."

The little book seemed to be open somewhere shy of the middle. I tried to turn the pages back, to see if there were other names, a traceable history—but though it felt like paper, I might as well have been trying to open a block of solid wood. If there were previous lists of earlier unfortunates who'd suffered the curse, the book wasn't going to divulge them to me.

I glanced over the one visible list of blood-scrawled names, just in case there were any clues buried in there...and froze.

There was an extra name in the list.

I read it twice to be sure:

Linna Vycross
Jaycel Morningray
Mareth Overfell
Petras Herun
Silena Glory
Willa Lovegrace
Regius Moreland
Tylar Amistead

"Who the fuck is Tylar Amistead?"

The Wasp all but shouldered Mareth aside to peer at the book, adjusting her spectacles.

"How vexing. Someone must have been added after the will was written." She straightened, frowning. "I do think the intent of the deceased is clear, given the documents we have and the nature of the relics as we understand them. We'll have to contact this eighth person."

I'd heard that name before, or at least the surname. The Amisteads were a wealthy Hillside family, old and moneyed, known for their occasional fits of philanthropy. There was an Amistead Park and an Amistead Library, and an Amistead Hall at the Acantis College of the Arts. They'd sponsored an annual children's festival in Southside that had been a highlight of my summers.

"Poor bastard's day is going to be ruined. All right, so that's the book. How about the mirror? What's its purpose?"

"Well, it's closely linked to the book. You can't even move them more than about ten feet apart—the magic won't allow it." Mareth peered at the silvery glass. "I think the mirror admits whatever essence or entity comprises this doom of which Signa Clement's document speaks. And the lantern..." He hesitated.

"Yes?"

"I'm guessing it either unleashes the doom or grants the wish. Or both."

An uncomfortable silence fell between us, shaped like a truth we both knew.

"You're sure it's a wish," I said at last. "Like, an actual *wish*, not some Echo-fueled power that could be used to get a lot of things you might wish for?"

"Let's hope it's not," he said grimly. "But given what little I can tell about these relics without proper equipment, I have to entertain the possibility that it is."

Only the most powerful Echoes could grant true, open-ended wishes. The last thing I needed was to draw that kind of attention, after the year-naming business.

I studied the book. Its pages were brittle and slightly yellowed, the cover mottled with apparent age. "That book looks old. And it's open to almost halfway through. This could have happened before—possibly many times." I turned to Signa Clement. "Wasps might have been called in to handle the earlier bequeathings, right? Your guild could have records."

She pressed her lips together. "If our guild doesn't, no one does. I'll seek authorization to open sealed files and gain any answers I can."

"The Ravens might have been called in to examine them before, too," Mareth offered. "If we were, my guild will have records of it."

The Wasp gave a sharp nod. "I propose that the three of us cooperate on this matter as representatives of our guilds. I am sufficiently senior that I feel confident in promising you both appropriate compensation for the job."

"Of course," Mareth said, without hesitation. "My life is on the line; I'm going to put all my effort into getting to the bottom of this regardless. Making it a formal investigation will only get me more access to guild resources."

They looked at me, expectant. A strange, bitter tangle knotted my throat. I'd only just recovered from the last Echo game I'd been drawn into. I had Emmi waiting for me at home; I already missed her, with a deep yearning ache. Sure, I'd been planning to go back to work in a couple months, but I'd figured I'd start small: easy retrievals to the first Echo, consulting, low-stakes stuff so I could ease back in without risking myself—and therefore Emmi's future.

This did not feel like it was going to be easy or low stakes.

"Well," I began slowly, "I've been...I'm officially on leave."

It sounded pathetic to my ears, the flopping of a grounded fish. They waited, clearly confident that my next word would be *but*.

And how could it not be? My friends were going to die if we didn't fix this somehow, and while it wasn't *because* I hadn't gone with them all those years ago, well...it might not be happening if I had. I could hardly walk away and shrug it off and let some horrible Echo doom fall upon them.

Pearson was going to be *ecstatic*.

I sighed. "So I can't put in long hours. I have a baby at home. I'll take the job, of course, but..."

The Wasp waved a hand. "Of course. We all have other duties. We're not going to be here around the clock."

That all sounded good, but with my friends facing potential imminent death, I'd work as late as I had to. Provided I could get someone to watch Emmi, since there was no way I was taking her to work near a bunch of cursed relics and an Echo portal.

"I'll see to putting through the paperwork," Signa Clement said. "Now, we'd best inform everyone of this situation and send them home. There's not much point in people milling around here waiting to die."

Wow. Wasps could be brutally practical.

With an authoritative stride, she started back toward the drawing room. We followed, though Mareth shot a last longing glance back over his shoulder. Puttering around with mysterious Echo relics was much more to his liking than public speaking.

We made it down the hall, around the corner, and almost to the rectangle of light that was the open drawing room door before everything went straight to the Void.

The air turned cold and heavy, like the deepest and slowest eddies of the river in winter. A shiver rippled through me as a familiar, awful feeling prickled my skin.

Mareth flinched. "Was that—"

I whipped around to face the way we'd come, ripped my sword from its sheath, and stepped in front of him and the Wasp.

"Get back! That's the portal opening. Something's coming through!"

IF YOU SEE THEIR EYES, IT'S TOO LATE

Signa Clement scrambled backward like a startled cat and then fled to the drawing room, papers clutched protectively to her chest. That was good—one less person I needed to guard. Mareth let out a low moan, which was not what I needed him to be doing.

"You're an Echo worker! Put up a barrier or something!"

"Right," he gasped, but no barrier manifested.

The hallway stretched dark and cobwebby in front of us, its green-and-black wallpaper peeling. The far end was lost in shadows. The dim, flickering light of a lamp shone from the intersecting hallway that led toward the relic room.

All at once, the lamp guttered and went out. A soft, bluish-white phosphorescence took its place, slowly brightening.

"*Mareth*," I barked.

"Working on it," he said through his teeth.

I risked a glance at him; his hands were lifted before him, fingers angled and flexing as they sought to part the Veil and draw power forth from the Echoes, but no glow haloed his fingertips or split the air. His eyes were scrunched shut, his lips a flat line. He must be too panicked, too grounded in the moment in Prime, to reach the Echoes. This was all up to me.

The whole house shuddered. Paintings knocked on the walls; startled exclamations came from the drawing room behind us. Bluish-white fog hazed my vision.

Whatever was coming through the mirror, it was already here.

A terrible, chilling howl rose up above and around and within the house.

It resonated in my bones and my mind alike, awakening an ancient, visceral fear of being hunted. My sharp puff of breath frosted in the suddenly icy air.

And then it passed. My vision cleared, the cold lost its biting edge, and everything went still.

I whirled. Mareth stared at his hands, miserable.

"I'm sorry, Kembral, I just—"

"Shh! Where did it go?" I strained to listen, sword still bare in my hand, not remotely foolish enough to believe this was over.

The awful howl sounded again, mournful and hungry, great and empty as the wind itself. But this time it was no longer right on top of us; walls and distance muffled its power. Mareth let out a small sigh of relief.

The fear gripping my gut didn't lessen. I knew that sound. I'd heard it in the Deep Echoes. I prayed I was wrong, but...if I was right, that thing getting loose in the city would be *bad*.

I burst into the drawing room, scanning frightened faces. Everyone was still here except Regius. Why it would bypass everyone in the house to pursue him, I couldn't guess, but knowing its target would make this simpler.

"I'm going after it! You all stay here, where it's safe." It probably wasn't actually safe, but I wanted to know where they were.

Jaycel was already on her feet, sword in hand, ready for action. "I'll help you."

"No, it could be hunting you! Stay here." I sheathed my blade— because charging around in the dark with a sword out for no reason was asking to have an embarrassing and painful accident—and started for the door.

THE LAST SOUL AMONG WOLVES   41

"I've got her back, Jaycel," Rika said, her voice firm as steel.

There was no time to argue. I might not know what she'd been hired to do, but one thing I knew without a shadow of a doubt: I could trust Rika with my life.

"Fine. Just be ready to run if things get bad."

Another howl sounded outside, muffled by the wind, raising gooseflesh all along my arms. And something else—a scream.

Like a pair of fools, we chased after it, out the door and into the falling night.

—∞—

The air bit our skin, raw and cold, as we sprinted through the dim sloping tangle of the garden. My nerves sizzled with the jagged energy of fear.

The sea stretched black and restless in the grey remains of dusk. Waves lapped up against the rocks girdling the island, and a dark rush of water flowed freely across the middle of the sandbar, cutting us off from the kindling twinkle of lights on the shore. But I couldn't picture Regius and Willa tromping through the sand to get here—they must have taken a boat. Regius would have headed for the docks on the northern, navigable side of the island. With all the creature's other targets inside the house, I had no doubt which way it had gone.

Rika must have come to the same conclusion. She swerved onto the weedy pathway that led down through a windbreak stand of pines toward the docks at the same time I did. Another cry of pure, wordless terror came from that direction—not Regius, but an older voice, maybe his boatman.

"Kembral," Rika panted as she ran beside me, "that sounded like one of those things that chased us in the seventh Echo at the year-turning. The ones you said we shouldn't look at, or they'd kill us."

"Yes. Deepwolves. I'm *really* hoping it's something else."

"And why exactly are we running after it? I distinctly recall you said that we couldn't fight them."

"Because if it doesn't go back through the mirror after it gets what it came for, someone needs to warn the city."

"Ah," she said faintly. And then, with vehemence, "You know, all my other jobs since the year-turning have been positively routine. These things *only* happen when I'm with you."

"Me? I live a quiet, domestic life."

"I'm not going to dignify that with a response."

I couldn't muster a retort; fear for my city closed my throat. A Deepwolf could walk on water, loping easily across to the mainland. It could leave a trail of death across Acantis, killing hundreds. It'd take a whole band of Ravens to drive it off. Emmi was safe with Achyrion, thank the Moon, but everyone else I knew was in danger.

We burst through the pines onto a broad stretch of sloping lawn adorned with dramatic, crumbling statuary. At the far end, a couple of small boats bobbed in the water, moored at a weathered dock that had seen better days. An old man cowered in one, frantically casting loose. That wasn't what commanded my attention, though.

A massive shadow hulked above the boats, nearly two stories high.

It had a lupine shape, bristling with hackles of darkness; its tail flowed into the twilight like boiling black mist. The scattering of lights in the city across the water shone dim and flickering through its dark, spectral form. Twin pits of whirling blue fire burned where its eyes should be.

From its jaws hung a lantern, golden lights quivering in it like fireflies. A dark, unmoving heap lay beneath one of its massive paws.

I froze, my heart spasming with pure terror in my chest. It had seen me, and I had seen it. The only protection I knew against a Deepwolf was that they seemed reluctant or perhaps unable to finish quarry who had not yet beheld them. Now that fragile shield was gone.

Rika went still at my side, her breath ragged from running. "*That's* where the lantern is?!"

The twin blue flames of its eyes dropped as the Deepwolf lowered its shadowy head. The lantern swung gently with the motion, dipping toward the still, silent shape on the ground. As the lantern's light fell over it, I could no longer tell myself it was anything but a body.

A tiny spark of golden light lifted from the still, huddled form

The Last Soul Among Wolves

with liquid reluctance. It drifted up into the lantern, joining the others that danced there.

"What the Void is that?" I whispered.

Rika shook her head, eyes wide and dark with horror.

The Deepwolf lifted its muzzle to the cloud-smothered sky and let loose a howl that set the earth beneath my feet to trembling. Rika's fingers clawed through my coat sleeve, seizing my arm as if she could stop me from doing something rash. But I had no interest in trying to fight that monster. We were far too near it already.

I stayed motionless, pulse racing—running would only draw its attention. If it decided to kill me, I would die.

Those baleful glowing eyes turned toward the Lovegrace house on the crown of the island above us. The lantern swayed from its jaws. I held my breath.

The Deepwolf let out a gravelly huff of a growl. It loped past us, uphill toward the mansion, with the unhurried pace of a predator returning home from a successful hunt. It slipped into the stand of pines; its great shadowy back appeared in glimpses between the treetops, and then it was gone.

I exhaled sharply. My hands were trembling.

Rika's gaze fixed on the dark lump lying by the docks. "Is that..."

"I'm sure it is. But we should check."

The old boatman was rowing vigorously away, swearing; no one tended the other small craft tied up at the dock. Only the one sprawled body remained, the sea wind picking at its clothes but unable to stir the slick glossy sculpture of its hair.

I'd seen more than my share of corpses, but I still didn't like looking at them. Something about the absence of life where it should be, the sad dull emptiness of them, the transformation from *person* to *thing*—it struck a deep wrongness in the pit of my stomach. So I didn't look over Regius for longer than I had to. Just enough to confirm everything I already knew.

An expression of pure terror remained frozen on his features. There was no mark on him, his expensive clothes unbloodied.

He was most thoroughly and entirely dead.

THE LIVING COME BEFORE THE DEAD

I burst into the cobwebby foyer of the Lovegrace house on a damp curl of wind, Rika at my heels, heart pounding with dread at what I might find. But nothing dire waited for me in the gloomy drawing room—only a bunch of frightened faces, my news already reflected in their eyes. Jaycel stood in front of the others, ready to defend them from all the horrors the Deep Echoes could muster.

"The monster passed back through here, whatever it was," she reported. "That same unnatural fog and awful chill. I despise an opponent without a heart to stab or ears to burn with shame—it's simply unsporting."

Vy stared off deeper into the house, eyes wide and dark with fear, as if she could see through the walls. "It went back into the mirror," she breathed. "It's gone."

The tension twisting my muscles eased up a bit. My friends were safe. The Deepwolf had departed, its purpose complete.

Which meant that whatever created those relics had the power to bind a Deepwolf to a task. I didn't want to think about that.

"What happened?" Petras asked. "For Void's sake, tell us."

THE LAST SOUL AMONG WOLVES   45

"I'm sorry." My words came out rough and uneven. "Regius is dead."

Willa's hands clenched in her skirts. "What killed him? Did you see?"

"It looked as if it was quick. He...It was a Deepwolf." That didn't mean anything to anyone but Mareth, who sucked in a sharp breath. "A very powerful and dangerous Echo."

Glory rose to her feet, bright and sudden. She stood there like a living flame in her brilliant gown, her face haunted, eyes dark.

"I need some air." She hesitated, then turned to Willa. "I'm sorry about your husband."

The look Willa gave her was a little glazed. She uttered a short, harsh laugh. "Thank you, but I'm far sorrier about what's going to happen to *us*."

Glory didn't seem to have anything to say to that. She nodded and swept out of the room. In a moment, a draft of cold night air announced her departure. Petras made an abrupt movement as if to get up and follow, then checked himself and leaned back in his chair, lacing his fingers broodily in front of his lips.

"Why did it go after Regius?" I asked Mareth, desperate to sort this nightmare into some kind of sense. "It went right past the rest of you to get him."

He shook his head, face pale with shock. "I don't know."

"And how soon will it be back? The interval is halved each time, but when are we counting from?"

That got him thinking. He bit his lip. "The death of the previous owner, I'd say. It's the only thing that makes sense."

I turned to Signa Clement. "How long ago did Auberyn Lovegrace die?"

She didn't even need to check her paperwork. "Four days ago. Nearly to the hour."

Willa stood with her hands on her hips, gaze flicking back and forth between me and Mareth. "So two days? Is that all we have, then?"

Vy covered her mouth. "Two days! That's barely time for a nap and dinner."

Jaycel gave her a brave grin. "It's all right, Vy. We've got the old crew back together again! Think of everything we used to get up to in a day. That's plenty of time, for us."

The gaze Vy turned on her was all but worshipful. It was the same look she'd worn when struggling to copy Jaycel's movements as she invented flashy pretend sword moves with a stick. I wished to the Moon I had that kind of confidence we were up to this.

Signa Clement gathered her papers. "Two days is a rather tight schedule. We'd best get moving. Signas Thorne and Overfell, I'll leave you with a full set of keys to the house so you can continue your investigations; just lock up when you leave. I recommend the rest of you go home and take the opportunity to rest. You've had quite a shock. I'll make sure you're informed immediately if there are any new developments."

She handed Mareth and me the keys, then sailed out with her papers clasped under one arm, striding briskly with the air of a woman who has other appointments. She had barely left when Willa broke out in disbelieving laughter.

"That's it? She just leaves us here with doom hanging over our heads? That thing *killed* Regius!"

Vy winced, extending a sympathetic hand. "Are you all right? Do you need—"

Willa ignored her, whirling on Mareth. "Is this how it's going to be? In two days another of us dies? We just wait for our turn to be slaughtered by some horrible Echo beast?" Her voice rose and rose, panic pushing it higher.

"No." I tried to project a calm I didn't feel. "You have a Raven and a Hound on the case. We're not going to sit on our hands and let that happen."

Mind you, I didn't *want* to be in charge of fixing this. I was out of practice. I had a baby at home who deserved (and demanded) my full attention. I was tired, and having all these lives depend on me was terrifying. But these were my friends, no matter how much time and circumstance had come between us. I'd abandoned them once when I joined the Hounds; I wouldn't let them down again.

"Knew I could count on you." Jaycel clapped my shoulder. "And when you get to the part where you need my sword, I'll be there before you can snap your fingers. Until then, I'm afraid research gives me a headache, so I'll leave you Signas to it while I perform my own investigation in the local pubs. I welcome anyone who feels the need for a drink after tonight's excitement to join me."

"That doesn't sound like a bad idea, actually," Petras murmured.

"Oh, yes!" Vy agreed. "It'll be like old times! Only I suppose with more alcohol."

They all headed off toward the docks, Jaycel linking arms with Petras and Vy, Willa maintaining an awkward aloof distance. Only Mareth, Rika, and I remained. I could feel all our collective forced bravery draining out with the others gone, and we exchanged the grim looks of professionals knowing we'd been set an impossible task.

"I should head to my guildhouse," Mareth said, "but a word first, Kem. That portal in the mirror—it stayed open after the Deepwolf went back through it. I checked."

That was a bit alarming. "Any sense of how long it'll stay open?"

"It's slowly reverting to its closed state. It should seal completely within a few hours. Nothing else seems to be coming through from the Echo, but it's permeable from this side."

"I suppose I could look through," I offered, with immense reluctance. "See where it goes."

"Oh, no." He held up a hand, alarmed. "It cuts straight to the fifth Echo. That's too deep."

"I've been down that far before."

"Then you're lucky to be alive. Seriously, I know you're good at this, but you've got to know how dangerous it is to go that far down."

"I do, and I'll admit I'm not keen on it. Shall I poke a stick through, then?"

Mareth gave me a mildly scandalized look. "A *stick*."

"Or a fork, or something. It's what I do before going down an Echo on missions. If it comes back on fire, corroded, or covered in slime—well, I've learned something."

"I can see that, but still, it lacks..." He gestured vaguely, like he was trying to pluck something from the air. "Gravitas. Ceremony. Crossing between worlds should be a serious and significant action."

I shrugged. "It's a job."

Mareth shook his head. *"Hounds."*

"Right?!" Rika agreed, with an insulting amount of feeling.

I decided to ignore that. "Can you think of any way to stop the Deepwolf from coming through again?"

Mareth's face fell. "I...Maybe. Sealing it would take a major Echo working woven from scratch, which, ah..."

"So not something you can just whip up," I cut him off, to avoid a descent into mind-numbing technical details.

He gave me a grateful, tired smile. "Right."

I hesitated, then put a hand on his shoulder. "Mareth. How are you doing?"

Unexpectedly, he laughed. There was an odd edge to it, but it sounded real enough.

"How am I...? Moon above, I don't know." His fingers curled around one of the many amulets hanging from his neck. "It's funny. When it happened—when we bled on that book, all those years ago—I was so excited. I'd been waiting all my life for something magical to happen to me, you see, and I was sure this was finally it."

"You were excited about a curse?" Rika asked incredulously.

"Oh, yes." Mareth gave me an amused glance. "Kem knows what I was like back then. I was so full of the stories I'd heard about my ancestors. My grandfather Hiram Overfell, who defeated the Scourge of Callisport. My great-grandmother Alyana Overfell, who devised a new means of scrying and saved Acantis from invasion by the Sigil Empire. My—"

"I remember," I said.

"I was so sure my turn would come. That I would be called to do great and magical things, and my portrait would hang in the Raven guildhouse someday as an inspiration to new generations. A mysterious Echo relic curse seemed like the perfect opportunity—but nothing happened." He shook his head. "And now here we are, seventeen

THE LAST SOUL AMONG WOLVES

years later, and my adventure is finally beginning. But I'm afraid it's too late for me to rise to meet it."

I stared at him. "Mareth, you're only thirty."

"Twenty-nine," he corrected, reddening.

"Whatever. It's hardly too late. Ravens keep doing spectacular things until they're ancient. You could have sixty more years of adventure ahead of you."

The little smile he gave me was an adult's expression, tinged with aching irony and all too painfully honest, nothing like the mirror-practiced haughty looks he'd tried on us when we were young.

"Provided I survive the week."

"We'll make sure you do."

"We'll try our best, anyway." He straightened, his tone becoming brisk, pushing away any further false assurances. "I've got to get to my guildhouse, and I don't want to miss that boat. Are you coming, Signa Nonesuch?"

Rika shook her head. "I'll stay and help Kembral search the house."

Ha. Stay and help herself to whatever she needed for her job, more like it. But I'd be glad of the company.

Mareth stalked off after the others like an overly tall and ruffled crow, and Rika and I were left behind alone. The lamps of the foyer sent subtle shadows racing across her face in the draft from the closing door.

"Well." She sighed. "This job has gotten unexpectedly complicated, hasn't it?"

"You could say that."

A silence fell between us, heavy with unspoken worry, and I knew we were both thinking about the year-turning.

"Rika..." I hesitated, reluctant to cross a line. But no, I had to ask—things had gotten too serious to hoard information. "What did Petras tell you? What do you know about the relics?"

"I can't tell you anything without asking my client first." She spread her hands, helpless and commiserating. "You know how it goes."

"Yeah. I know it doesn't go like *this*, with giant spectral wolves coming through mirrors to murder people."

Her lips twisted. "Except for us, lately."

"Except for us." My shoulders fell in a sudden, exhausted slump. "Last time we only survived because we worked together. I hate having secrets between us again. I'd much rather know I could trust you on this job."

She glanced away. "Can you ever really trust me?"

"Of course. And I do. But now you're working, and it's your job to be devious." I stared at the familiar curve of her cheekbone, the stark black edge of her lashes. My hand moved toward her face in a distinctly unprofessional fashion. I stuffed it into my pocket instead.

"Rika...do we have a conflict of interest? Tell me that much, at least."

Her brow furrowed. Shit, she had to think about it. There was a time when it would have been natural for us to be pitted against each other—when I might have relished the challenge—but after what we'd been through on the year-turning, and how Rika had become a part of my life since, the idea of being in direct opposition made me queasy.

"I don't think so," she said at last. "Petras is as invested in not dying as anyone, so given that your job is to stop that from happening, I think we can safely work together. At least for now."

"Will you tell me if that stops being the case?"

"Of course."

"It had better not," I grumbled, kicking at the broken floor tiles. "I don't want anything to mess this up."

She gave me a quizzical look. "This?"

I waved my free arm around at the foyer, as if the cobwebby chandelier and dusty windows were responsible for the messy knot of feelings unwinding in my chest.

"You here, at my side, in my life. Us." The word felt strange on my tongue.

"Us," she whispered. "Moon help me. What am I doing?"

"You're, uh, avoiding answering my questions?"

"Naturally. That's not...I mean..." Her breath hitched, and something vulnerable fluttered across her face in the uneven moody light. "I haven't really had much occasion for there to be an *us* in my life before."

I opened my mouth to say something inane like *surely not*, then closed it again.

"I was looking at you with your friends today and thinking about how that could have been me. We lived in the same plaza, played together—I could have been one of you." A trace of wistful bitterness edged her voice. "But I had to move out of your neighborhood because someone saw...Well, I hadn't figured out all the nuances of illusion yet, and some creepy people started following me. I had to move around a lot, back then."

I swallowed a sudden roughness in my throat. "I wish you could have stayed."

Rika brushed it off, a tired gesture. "It's the past. Suffice to say that when you spend your whole life making sure no one ever sees you sleep, your opportunities for an *us* are rather limited. So forgive me if I make rookie mistakes."

"Making sure no one sees you sleep? Why, are you...Do your illusions lapse or something, so people can tell you're—"

"Don't say it." Her voice had gone knife-sharp. "Don't bring that up, even in private. I can't even *think* about it."

It was like that any time I so much as hinted at her Empyrean heritage. She shut it down hard and fast, as if the topic were poison to her. Fine. I wouldn't press, no matter how desperately curious I was about how much of her human appearance was reality, illusion, or some strange transformative mix of the two.

Either way, the sheer loneliness of never having had an *us* made my heart ache.

"Anyway, don't worry about rookie mistakes. You're doing fine," I said gruffly.

A stray tendril of hair hung in her face, still damp from the misty rain. I couldn't stand not to do anything about it, so I reached out and tucked it back. It felt far too clammy to be an illusion.

"I don't know what I'm doing, either," I murmured. "I just don't want this job to come between us, that's all. I like being on the same side."

The lines of her face softened. "We do make a good team, don't we?"

"Besides, you'd run circles around me right now. It wouldn't even be a challenge for you. I'm so damned tired all the time, Rika."

She slipped her arms around my waist. So much for maintaining a professional distance. "You see, this is why you need me to help you. To keep you from making exhausted mistakes."

"Hmph. To take advantage of my exhausted mistakes, more like it." I planted a quick kiss between her brows, where the trace of a worry line lingered. "Come on. Let's shake this house and see what secrets fall out."

***

It turned out the house harbored more dust and spiders than secrets. I didn't know what I'd expected—a diary chronicling a dark past, a box full of the skulls of trespassing children, the old lady's desiccated corpse. Instead, we found room after room neatly made up and abandoned to time, in such an orderly state that I doubted they'd ever seen much use.

The spare furnishings in the parlors and salons sat at perfect right angles, fabrics pristine but blanketed in dust. The ballroom stood completely empty, its floor unscuffed by dancing. Curtains shrouded most of the windows, leaving the rooms dim and stuffy, with a few exceptions where a bare break of moonlight looked out to the restless sea. The place felt blank as a tomb without a corpse.

Rika shivered. "I enjoy privacy myself, but this level of isolation seems excessive."

Her gaze lingered on anything valuable, in the same automatic way mine noted entrances and hiding places, but she seemed reluctant to touch anything.

"I think she knew what she had, and she was trying to protect everyone from it," I said.

"Why didn't she just give the whole horrid set to the Ravens, then? They could have put it in their vaults with all the other cursed relics."

"Maybe she didn't trust them enough. A wish is a powerful temptation."

THE LAST SOUL AMONG WOLVES   53

Aside from the drawing room where we'd gathered, a mere handful of rooms looked lived in. The kitchen, whose multiple brick hearths and sprawling iron stoves could have served up a feast for hundreds, showed signs that a solitary woman had been cooking simply here for herself and eating directly from a worktable. Cloths covered most of the instruments and furniture in the music room, but the pianoforte didn't have a speck of dust on it, and much-riffled sheets of music stood propped open and ready above use-polished keys. Similarly, a single chair by the window in the library had cushions asymmetrically squashed and dented by years of someone sitting with her legs tucked up. The shelves with scholarly books remained dusty, but the cheap dime novels looked heavily thumbed.

This giant mansion was meant as an aristocrat's showpiece, a dramatic location for hosting social events, and Auberyn Lovegrace had lived in its corners like a mouse. But it had been her own choice, and she had books and music and a fantastic view, so maybe she'd been living out her dream life.

In the master bedroom, I found a box of papers—not official paperwork, as she'd clearly left that to the Wasps, but personal stuff. Letters, notes, an age-yellowed academic commendation from Hopeworth Day School. *Huh.* Hopeworth was a charity school for poor kids in Southside. Apparently old lady Lovegrace was no pedigreed scion. I tucked the box under my arm to take home and go through at my leisure (such as it was).

"Kembral, look at this."

Rika had opened the door to one of the guest bedrooms that lined the upstairs hall. At first glance, it looked just like the others—but the heavy brocade curtains had been thrown open to reveal the glimmer of lights across the river, and someone had given the dust at least a cursory wipe-down. The bed was made, but it didn't have the impeccable neatness we'd seen elsewhere—someone had pulled up the covers and called it good enough. A cup left on the bedside table still had a bit of water in the bottom.

Someone had been here, and by the look of it, quite recently. But old lady Lovegrace had died four days ago.

"This has to be from the past couple of days." I stared at the bed and the empty glass, frowning. "Do you think someone might have broken in?"

Rika peered over my shoulder, standing close enough that I could feel the warmth of her body. "What, without stealing any of those silver plates in the dining room?"

"It could have been a kid, doing it on a dare." I thought it over, and my skin prickled with unease. "Or it could have been someone trying to mess with the relics. There *is* a wish at stake."

Rika shook her head. "It doesn't make any sense. Why sleep here?"

"Maybe they came on the sandbar and missed the tide. Or maybe..."

"Yes?"

"Maybe they're still here."

Rika stared at me. "Congratulations, Kembral. Somehow, you found a way to make this place even creepier."

We swept the Lovegrace house from cellar to widow's walk, checking its outbuildings and gardens. The only sign we found of the mysterious squatter was in the solarium, where a cracked pane of glass in the door to the garden and fresh mud tracked across the floor suggested they'd entered that way.

If the trespasser was still hiding on the island, however, they were too good to be so easily found.

"I think we've gotten everything we can out of this place," I muttered, acutely aware of the passage of time. Emmi adored Achyrion, but part of my brain kept whispering *What if she misses you? What if she's crying right now?*

Rika, reading me like an open book, lifted an eyebrow. "Heading home?"

"No. I took this job, and I'm going to do it the right way." I scrubbed my face, pushing away weariness. "I still have some time left. Let's go to Guildhouse Square."

THE GUILD PROVIDES

Stepping into my guildhouse was like coming home.

Guildhouse Square was a hub of power in Acantis, sure as the city hall and its grand plaza were. The stately, embellished facades of the guildhouses reflected their importance, with sculptural details, gilding, and Gothic flourishes. They stood cheek by jowl around the perimeter of the square, with the sprawling Raven guildhouse anchoring one end, its palatial soot-darkened spires reaching to the sky.

That grandeur was calculated. The balance between the guilds and the governments of the League Cities was complex and delicate, enshrined in charters and upheld by oath and tradition. It was vital that everyone respected the guilds' neutrality, and part of winning respect was displaying power. So every city-state in the League had a square like this, with guildhouses grand to the edge of ostentation, to make a point.

It had certainly worked on me. I'd been terribly impressed whenever I visited the square as a child, looking up at these storied buildings in awe of the near-legendary people doing exciting things inside them. I'd gazed especially long at the golden stylized hound over the doors of the second guildhouse on the left, dreaming of what it would look like tattooed on my arm.

Now I flung open those doors with the casual ease of seventeen years of belonging, striding in beneath that same golden hound. (Rika had gone across the square to the Cat guildhouse.) Never mind that it was only an hour or two shy of midnight—in the guildhouses, someone was always on duty.

Warm light and gleaming wood paneling surrounded me in the soaring two-story reception hall; another golden hound ran in a circle inlaid on a floor of caramel marble. Curving stairs and an assortment of archways led to offices and archives and armories. A fire crackled merrily in a grand hearth on one end, and a long desk backed by shelves of folios and racks of keys anchored the other. An assortment of comfortable leather chairs scattered around the room, and a light tea and coffee service lay waiting on a table by the fire. All in all, the place felt like a cross between a cozy tavern and a grand library. I breathed it in, the scent of leather and old wood and coffee, and something deep inside me unknotted.

A couple of my colleagues stood together by the fireplace, one leaning against the mantel with a mug in his hand, the other holding what appeared to be some kind of skull and gesturing as if explaining something. An apprentice scurried through the hall from the infirmary toward the practice rooms, trailing a flying streamer of bandages and grimacing.

Lydra was on desk duty, Moon bless her, petite and competent behind a stack of papers. She leaped to her feet and braced both hands on the reception desk when she saw me.

"Signa Thorne! You're back!"

"Yeah, I am."

The Hounds by the fireplace looked up; the apprentice with the bandages slowed and gawked over her shoulder. A door slammed open upstairs, and pattering footsteps approached the long second-floor balcony that ran between two sweeping staircases. *Uh-oh.*

"Is that—" I began, glancing upward with some trepidation.

Pearson skidded onto the balcony as if summoned, grinning widely. "Kem! Hey, Kem! You're back!"

Of *course* Pearson was working late tonight. "I do seem to be."

THE LAST SOUL AMONG WOLVES 57

"Great! Could totally use you on the—"

Lydra cut him off. "I just got a contract for you, Signa Thorne, sent over from the Wasp guild."

Pearson looked at her, then me, his thick dark brows rising. "You have a contract with the *Wasps*?"

Lydra pulled a stack of papers from her pile and slapped them on the table. "She does, and we have to send it back to them right away or they'll be breathing down my neck. So if you could sign here?"

I headed for the desk, feeling the familiar excitement of a new job closing around me like a trap. "Sure."

Pearson leaned over the rail so far I worried he might fall. "Well, when you're not working on the Wasp job, maybe you could consult on this Echo incident investigation at the courier berths in Dockside. It's a weird one."

Lydra handed me a pen. I dipped it in the inkwell and signed where she pointed without reading it. Lydra would've let me know if the Wasps tried to slip in anything fancy.

"This job is top urgency," I told Pearson. "Lives at stake, time limit, the whole deal. So I won't have time to consult until after."

"Should have said that first." He straightened, eyes shining. "Top urgency. Right. I'm ready. What do you need?"

A wave of gratitude washed over me at those words. Blood on the Moon, it was nice to hear them, after months of constantly taking care of someone else's needs and never my own.

"I want any records we've got about Deepwolves coming through to Prime in and around the city over the past two hundred years, and any deaths related to those appearances. Plus anything you can find about a matched set of relics including a mirror, a book, and a lantern."

"You got it!" The bastard was practically quivering with excitement at getting me back to work. "Anything else?"

"Do you know anything about the death of Auberyn Lovegrace?"

Pearson's brows flew up. "Funny you should ask. Why Auberyn Lovegrace?"

Well, now. Sounded like I might have already hit on something.

"The job centers around a bequeathing. Part of her estate. Let me guess—was she murdered?"

"The city investigators called it an accident." He grimaced. "Not my place to second-guess them."

"But you do."

"Carriage accidents happen, sure. Fatal carriage accidents, tragic, but those, too. Fatal carriage accidents where a swarm of Echoes drive the horses wild, then disappear all at once as soon as one old lady gets run down? Not so often."

My skin prickled. "Not a lot of people have the power to set Echoes on their enemies."

"Probably would take a Raven. Your guess is better than mine. Not my specialty."

"Right." I rubbed my neck, unsettled. If there was direct Echo involvement, that changed everything, and not for the better. "If you find anything else out about that, definitely let me know. You can send it all along to my house."

"You're going? It shouldn't take long to pull that stuff for you."

"I've got to get back to Emmi."

He looked blank for a moment; then his eyes lit up. "Right. The baby."

Lydra tapped the last page of the contract meaningfully. I signed it, and she took it with a warm smile. "Welcome back, Signa Thorne."

A few more familiar faces peeped out of doorways or over the balcony now: desk Hounds, apprentices, a couple of my field colleagues. They were all grinning like loons. A scattering of waves and greetings echoed her:

"Hey, yeah, welcome back, Kem!"

"Welcome home!"

"Yeah," I grumbled, my cheeks feeling unaccountably warm. "It's good to be back, I guess."

—⁓—

I'd barely stepped out into Guildhouse Square when Rika manifested beside me, slipping up out of nowhere as usual. One moment there was no sign of her, and the next she was at my side, walking along as if she'd been there the whole time. Rain misted her black hair, giving it a silvery sheen beneath the streetlamps.

"I'll walk you home," she offered, without preamble.

"It's got to be past midnight. Is my place even on your way?" I still had no idea where Rika lived. She guarded every little piece of information about herself as if she were being paid to keep it secret.

She gave me an *I see what you're doing* look. "It's not even eleven o'clock."

"That early? Bloody Moon. Today has been ten thousand years long." I rubbed my face.

"You're right about that part."

A chill wind swept through the nighttime streets, setting the lanterns to guttering, their reflections dancing on the wet cobbles. The few people we passed huddled into warm coats, hats pulled down against the insistent drizzle. My mind buzzed, full of names written in blood and Deepwolf eyes burning through the dark and a flock of Echoes that had driven a woman to her death. It was all forming a shape I couldn't quite see yet, the shadow of a great ship slipping through midnight waters.

We turned onto my street, tree-lined and cobbled with a strip of green in the middle. Narrow townhouses flanked it, built a couple hundred years ago; at least half of them had been bought up by the guilds over time and converted to housing for guild members. One of the benefits of being a senior Hound with a rare and irreplaceable skill was that I got the smallest townhouse all to myself.

It was never a *busy* street, but at the moment it was utterly quiet. My neck prickled. This wasn't an early-to-bed neighborhood; guild members stayed up late, and things usually remained lively until after midnight—but there was *nothing*. Not the loud voice of old Murvey, whose hearing was going, chattering away to his husband as they got ready for bed. Not the clatter of pots and pans from the apartment of the Wolf who was always cooking dinner at this hour. Not the young apprentice Butterfly singing to herself as she took her evening bath.

A faint whiff of damp smoke clung to the air.

Just a rainy evening. No signs that anything terrible had happened here. But the feral animal in the back of my mind that loved to imagine threats to Emmi woke up, and irrational fear surged along my nerves.

I all but ran to the familiar weathered brick townhouse with the red door, Rika eyeing me strangely as I leaped up the steps and jammed the key in the lock.

"Achyrion? Is everything—"

The door opened before I could turn the key. Achyrion stood there in the lamplight, his glorious copper mane of hair tumbling loose over his shimmery bronze waistcoat and rolled-up shirtsleeves, a finger pressed to his lips. His yellow-green, slit-pupiled eyes took me in knowingly.

"Shhh. She's sleeping."

DON'T LET THEM FOLLOW YOU HOME

Relief poured through me like an ocean tide. My shoulders slumped as Rika caught up to me, nodding a greeting to Achyrion over my shoulder.

"Come on in out of the rain." Achyrion moved aside for us. "Everything's fine. Emmi was delightful, as always."

I stepped in with a sigh of relief, sweeping off my sodden scarlet coat to hang it on the peg by the door. "Thank you. I'm sorry I'm a bit late. Things got... interesting."

Rika chuckled darkly as she slipped out of her own coat. "That's one way to put it."

Achyrion waved a languid, long-fingered hand, his nails pointed like claws. "It's quite all right. I enjoy your hatchling's company very much." A pause, during which he seemed to consider something. "You may, ah, hear something from the neighbors. I don't want you to be distressed. Everything went well."

I stopped in the act of removing my sword belt. "What happened? Is Emmi—"

"I told you, she's absolutely fine. She slept through the whole thing."

That was a relief, but also somewhat ominous. I exchanged a worried glance with Rika. "Did you—"

"There was no mess," he said quickly. "No humans were hurt. There was very little property damage, and I made it right with them."

"Achyrion. For love of the Moon, just tell me."

He sighed. "If you must know, a few Echoes tried to get into your home. I'm sure someone sent them. Horrid things, too many spikes, from about five Echoes down."

My stomach turned to ice. "Were they after Emmi?"

"No," Rika muttered, her eyes narrowing. "They were after *you*."

"I have no idea what they wanted, but I couldn't take chances, could I?" Achyrion gave me a sideways sort of look, catlike eyes gleaming, as if judging whether he was going to get away with this line of explanation. "Emmi was napping, and I didn't want them to wake her up. So I, ah, slipped outside and dealt with them."

I parsed that a few ways in my head, meeting Achyrion's steady, innocent gaze. That could mean...several things.

His tongue flicked out to lick his lips, quick and satisfied, and all right, it could mean one thing. I put a hand over half my face.

"You ate them."

"It seemed tidiest."

"And the neighbors saw?"

"They were quite understanding. I explained that it was important not to wake up Emmi when she's napping, and everyone stopped screaming at once."

Rika made a little noise in her throat that could have been a hastily swallowed laugh, but I'd do her the credit of assuming it was a groan of despairing sympathy for me.

"And this was in your—"

"My true form, yes." Achyrion studied my face, a little anxiously. "I remembered what you said last time."

"About how if my neighbors complain, the guild could kick me out of this house."

"And we can't have that happen to dear little Emmi. So I made sure they wouldn't complain."

"Holy Void, Achyrion, please tell me you didn't—"

"No!" His eyes widened. "Blood on the Moon, of course not. Your neighbors are lovely. I mean I was nice to them."

Which had probably left them even more terrified than if he'd eaten a few as an example to the others, but I let it go. "Thanks for letting me know. And thanks for taking care of the Echoes. I hope they didn't taste too bad."

"They were all right, once one crunched through all the spikes." He tipped his head. "Nice soft center, with a bit of a nutty aftertaste, like—"

"Thank you, Achyrion," I said firmly. And then, because it was true, I added, "I'm really glad you're here to take care of Emmi and keep her safe. I'd worry about her all the time if it weren't for you."

He grinned at that, pleased, displaying his sharp white fangs. "It's my pleasure. Emmi is a fine creature. All my own young grew up centuries ago, so it's a treat to look after her. I'm so glad little Almarah told me about you."

My eye twitched a bit at *little Almarah*. My old mentor was a couple inches shy of six feet in reality, but more like eight feet tall in my mind. She'd referred me to Achyrion, saying he'd practically raised her—which was a story I *really* needed to weasel out of her someday— and that he was wonderful with children and the only person she'd trust to keep Emmi safe from my rather alarming enemies.

She had failed to mention that he was a fucking *dragon*. Small details. I had no doubt she'd laughed for an hour after sending me off straight-faced to meet him.

"Me too," I said. "Here, let me pay you."

I rolled up my sleeve. Rika winced as I pricked the back of my arm with the tip of my dagger; a single drop of red blood welled up. Achyrion watched it with the intense interest of a cat eyeing a wind-blown feather.

I offered my arm to him, and he scooped the ruby bead up with the curved tip of one claw and popped it delicately into his mouth. I couldn't help but be aware of Rika's eyes on the exchange, making something that had become a routine piece of business feel weird.

"Do you need a second drop? I know I was late."

"No, no. One is plenty." He hesitated, then added a bit grudgingly, "I don't think you quite realize how valuable that is."

Rika gave me a searching glance, then turned to Achyrion. "Maybe *I* should know."

"She named a crux year," Achyrion explained. "The Year of Hope. In the Echoes, her blood binds hope into things and shapes reality." He turned his glance back to me. "One drop might be enough to increase the chances of my hopes coming to fruition for a week. Given the frequency with which I watch Emmi for you...let's say all my beloved hatchlings and fosters will probably be doing quite well for a long while." A deeply satisfied smile curved his lips; something about it didn't look remotely human.

"Well, if that includes Almarah or Emmi, I might as well be paying myself."

"It does. I think little Almarah's arthritis has been doing a bit better lately, in fact."

Little. My eye twitched again. "That's good."

I asked him if it wouldn't be too much trouble to be on call at odd hours for the next few days, since I had an urgent job; he agreed cheerfully before saying his goodbyes and heading out the door. I had no idea where he went when he wasn't babysitting. Whatever Deep Echo he came from, maybe. Though he occasionally referenced his knitting club, and I couldn't tell whether it was a joke.

The second the door closed I turned to go have a quick peek in at Emmi, to make *sure* she was really all right—but Rika gripped my arm.

"Why are Echoes targeting you?"

"We *know* why." I didn't much like it, but there it was. "You heard Achyrion. My blood makes me like a walking diamond mine to them."

"No, we *don't* know that's why." She tapped my sternum. "You're supposed to be the analytical one here. Do you have any reason to believe that word has gotten out about you in the Echoes generally?"

"No. But what other reason could they possibly—oh." I sighed. "I suppose Rai could be sending them. For vengeance."

"Or certain other Empyreans." Rika avoided putting her mother's name in her mouth as if it were poison. "They all but promised they'd come after us again. I thought we'd have longer than this."

"Look, we don't know it was them, and if it was, we can't do anything about it."

"You seem awfully calm." She gave me a suspicious look. "Wait. Has this happened before?"

Oops. Caught. "Uh, maybe once or twice, since the year-turning."

"Void's sake, Kembral, *tell* me about these things!"

"You don't tell me about most of the stuff *you* do," I pointed out.

"That's because most of the *stuff I do* is protected by guild contract confidentiality clauses!" She visibly wrestled herself under control. "When I ask you if anything interesting happened in your day, if monsters from another world tried to kill you, don't say 'Oh, nothing much' next time. It's just rude."

It occurred to me belatedly that she was the one being normal here. That maybe most people didn't get attacked by Echoes and shrug it off as a hazard of the job and move on. Though even for me, an attack in Prime was far from normal. It was just maybe possible that I'd been avoiding the issue because the idea that Empyreans might be pursuing vengeance upon me was sufficiently terrifying that once I started thinking about it, it'd be hard to think about anything else.

I lifted my hands. "All right. Point taken. If it happens again, I'll let you know."

She gave me a long, searching look, and seemed to be about to say something. Then a shiver passed through her, and she closed her eyes.

"It had better not be *her*," she whispered. "Anything but that."

I could almost see the dread settling over her like a cloak. Which made no sense; so far as I could tell, we had no reason to think her mother was involved—Rai was a far more likely culprit, since he was the one with a grudge against me.

Unless she knew something I didn't. Suddenly, I was sure she was holding something back. A truth she'd almost told me just now, some secret she still held close to her heart like a stolen jewel. A reason to fear we might be in more danger than I'd guessed.

I had the instinctive urge to push her like I would an informant, to chase down what exactly was upsetting her. What the tension in her rigid spine was about, what burden her shoulders were tightening to hide. I opened my mouth to say some stupid, sharp thing, prodding for details.

It occurred to me at the last second that maybe treating your girlfriend like a reluctant source on a high-stakes case the moment she displayed vulnerability wasn't the best thing for your relationship.

So instead I smoothed her hair back from the tension in her brow, then slid my hand down to cradle the delicate angles of her cheek. Her whole body seemed to relax at once, and she leaned into my palm, eyes still closed.

"Hey," I said softly. "We're all right. Achyrion took care of the Echoes. And this relic business is intense, but it's just a job. We've faced worse."

She sighed, her dark lashes lifting the gate on the stormy depths of her eyes. "I hope you're right."

"It's the Year of Hope, remember?" I smiled, though thinking about that still made me uneasy. "My year. That means no matter what happens, we can handle it."

A dry touch of humor stirred her lips. "There's hope, and then there's excessive optimism." All her vulnerability smoothed suddenly away, her usual competent confidence sliding back on like a well-tailored jacket. "But very well, we *are* on a deadline. Let's get to work."

—⟋⟋⟍—

I *meant* to dive right into the papers Pearson had sent over, but of course I was a fool and couldn't resist looking in on Emmi first to make sure she was all right, and of *course* she woke up. Achyrion had the right idea, literally eating anyone who threatened to disturb her sleep—but no, I just had to peek, and she preternaturally sensed my presence like she always did.

Emmi's round little face broke into a wide, toothless smile of pure joy at seeing me. It melted my heart every time. I scooped her up and kissed the top of her head, breathing in the scent of her peach-fuzz hair, letting it do strange and wonderful things to my brain. She was so small, like my mother said I'd been, with my sea-colored eyes. There were little bits of Beryl in her here and there too, I supposed; her skin was a shade or two darker than mine, and her mischievous face held faint anticipatory traces of her father's roguish smile. But it was easy to think of those as just parts of Emmi, not leftover bits of the lout who'd dumped me. She was herself, and the most precious thing in existence.

Blood on the Moon, I'd missed her, and I'd only been gone five hours. Going back to work was going to be *hard*.

It might be nice to be the sort of person who could let her be my whole world—who could throw my entire self into being her mother and slough away all the rest of this messy, alarming existence. Forget every woe that wasn't hers, and be hers alone. But that wasn't who I was. Or who I wanted to be.

"Hey, gorgeous," I greeted her. "I bet you want to help me read some papers!"

Emmi made an enthusiastic noise. Showed what *she* knew.

Rika laughed. "You read. I'll make dinner. I know we're in a hurry, but you can't skip meals on a job like this."

I would never have guessed Rika could cook—she didn't seem like a creature who would deign to learn the simple arts of living, even before I knew she was a half-divine being with starlight for blood. But her hands were skilled and sure as she cracked cloves of garlic out of their papery skin and diced them fine and even, her wrists just as fluid and confident as when she picked a lock or purloined a letter. I stole glances at her while I settled a squirming Emmi, who finally relaxed enough to wrap my hair around her fist and stuff it in her mouth, her storm-blue eyes serious, like soaking my hair with drool was a vital matter of important baby policy. I settled in my most comfortable chair in the parlor to paw one-handed through the stack of papers from the guild archives while I nursed her.

Most reports of Deepwolf sightings in the city had been dismissed as drunken flights of fancy. But there were a few clusters of possible incidents over the past century, some linked to deaths. One disturbing pattern emerged: All the deaths had been in Dockside or Southside. And the latest round, about twenty-five years ago, had been mostly children.

A Hound had investigated the kids' deaths, as a charity case (about half of guild jobs were, to make sure the guilds didn't become simply tools of the rich and powerful). He'd connected them to the Deepwolf but was unable to trace the monster back to its origin. The witnesses he interviewed seemed to agree, however, that it came from the direction of Hillside.

I held Emmi's drowsing warmth close against me and struggled with the dark, violent thoughts of what I'd do if I found out some rich bastard had been setting this curse on poor kids on purpose. This stank of someone manipulating the process, using the relics to their benefit. Which didn't fit with the theory that it was an Echo game, but *did* make me want to strangle someone with my bare hands.

A knock sounded at the door.

Rika answered it for me, soft as a shadow to avoid waking the baby (see, *she* got it). She was back in a moment, frowning.

"That was a courier from Mareth."

"Oh?"

"He says everyone needs to come back to the Lovegrace mansion right away. He's found something, and it could be a matter of life and death."

I tensed. In my arms, Emmi stirred and made a noise of sleepy protest. "Well, shit."

"If it's an emergency, they're more likely to need your skills than mine. You go. I'll take Emmi until Achyrion can get here."

I didn't want to go so soon. It seemed unbearable to leave Emmi when I'd hardly had time to be sure she was all right, to warm the part of me that was cold when I wasn't holding her. But Rika was right. Emmi would be fine; my friends needed me more, and I had a job to do.

"All right," I said, and rose.

"Kembral…" Rika bit her lip. I could see that secret in her eyes again, clouded with some hidden anguish.

The Last Soul Among Wolves

"Yes?" If I didn't push her, if I stayed calm and still like I would with a wild animal, maybe she'd tell me.

Rika shook her head. "Just be careful."

"I'll bring a second sword."

This had definitely escalated to a two-swords situation.

SOME JOBS JUST KEEP GETTING WORSE

Wasp historians claimed that the third month was called the Blood Moon because it was the time of year when the snows melted in the northern continent, and the petty kings who had ruled there before the rise of the Viger Republic could resume their incessant wars. Ravens said it was because under that Moon the auspices aligned for violence and sacrifice, conflict and victory. In the Tower district, it meant all the shops were full of everything fashionably red. But pragmatically speaking, in Acantis, it meant a whole lot of rain.

By the time I arrived at the Lovegrace house, I was dripping wet. I shook myself off in the foyer and peered into the dismal drawing room.

Signa Clement was there, along with an older man I'd never seen before. His champagne frock coat looked expensive, but like it had been tailored for comfort over style, and its elbows showed wear from years of use. Gold gleamed from his cuff links and a lapel pin in the shape of a sickle—probably his birth Moon. Everything from his clothes to the lack of styling oil in his slightly scruffy white hair and beard suggested he was the kind of old-money Hillside

THE LAST SOUL AMONG WOLVES

71

type who felt secure enough in his fortune and place in society that he didn't give a damn about the latest Tower fashions or trying to impress anyone.

"Ah, Signa Thorne," the Wasp greeted me. "Signa Overfell should be here soon; he's on his way from his guildhouse. In the meantime, meet Dona Amistead, our surprise extra guest."

Dona Amistead. So he was a member of the Council of Elders—or a former one more like it, given that I didn't remember an Amistead among our current city leaders.

"Good to meet you," I said. "Sorry about the circumstances."

"Delighted, Signa Thorne!" Dona Amistead eyed me with a sharp, assessing intelligence. "I've heard wonderful things about you from Marjorie. I'm glad to have you on our side in this dreadful situation."

"Dona Marjorie is too kind." I returned his gaze with frank curiosity. "So how'd *you* get pulled into this mess?"

"I was just discussing that with Signa Clement." He spread his hands. "I'm afraid I have no idea. I've never seen this book she was telling me about. My best guess would be that one of my enemies wrote my name in it, in an attempt to do me in." He said this last with good humor, as if the idea were exciting but a little scandalous.

I raised an eyebrow. "They would have needed your blood. Do you leave a lot of that lying around?"

"My dear, when you're my age, the physickers want to stick you with pins for a bit of your blood every other Tuesday. I imagine some of it wound up on the black market. It happens when you're in politics, you know—I lost a colleague to a curse that way."

"I suppose you can buy anything in this city, if you can pay enough for it," I said dubiously.

"Isn't that the truth."

"Any idea which enemy would be likely to use such a convoluted method to try to take you out?"

He tipped his head, considering. "Hard to say. I've been out of politics for ages. Although I suppose it could be one of my dear Hillside neighbors getting worked up about my plans to turn my brother's old estate into a charity hospital. Some of them have been ranting to me about how it's an insult to his memory to let the unwashed poor of Dockside wander his halls, and insist he wouldn't have wanted it."

"Would he have?"

"Oh, stars, no. He was an arrogant prick. We argued a lot, and this is my way of getting in the last word." He chuckled.

"You seem to be in remarkably fine spirits for a man who's just learned he's fallen under a deadly curse," I observed.

"Well, over the years I've seen some things." Amistead waved a hand. "My goodness, when I was on the council, people tried to kill me every other year. And I got used to some occasional peril back in my navy days."

Behind me in the foyer, the outer door opened and closed, letting in an icy swirl of damp air. I spun with a jolt of irrational alarm, but it was just Mareth, come in from the rain. I went to meet him; he removed a dripping black greatcoat with a dramatic swirl that spattered droplets in my face.

"Oh, sorry, Kembral."

"I was wet already. I'm glad you're here. How are you?"

"A bit on edge, to be honest."

He looked it. He'd always cultivated a certain broody appearance, but now he held himself as if a sudden move in the wrong direction could cause all his bones to fall apart in a clattering heap.

"I take it you learned something fun and exciting from your research?"

"Well, my first discovery actually *is* exciting. That's what I called everyone here to tell them. The second..." He glanced into the drawing room, where Amistead was talking to Signa Clement. He slid the door closed, then turned to me again, his voice soft and his face pale. "I don't know how to put this. It's...it's bad, Kembral."

A miserable fear dripped from him, sure as the rain from the tips of his hair. His dark eyes had gone big and haunted, like they had when we were looking for Echo relics in the river mud as children and he'd found a severed human finger instead.

"Hey," I said. "We'll get out of this. We always do. Tell me whatever horrible truth you've unearthed. I can work with it."

The Last Soul Among Wolves

73

"I'm not so sure. But all right." He took a shaky breath. "When you found Regius, did he...Did the wolf take something from him?"

An awful feeling unfolded in my stomach like a flower. "A little light. The lantern was full of them."

Mareth looked downright queasy. "I was afraid of that."

"What is it?"

"While I was at the Raven guildhouse, I checked whether we'd been called in to examine the relics when Auberyn Lovegrace inherited them, some twenty-five years ago." He began fiddling with the silver amulets tiered on his chest, carefully arranging them so their chains didn't cross. "We were, and I managed to talk to the Raven who did the analysis; she'd had access to the lantern as well, and it was her conclusion that it acted as a sort of storage receptacle."

"Storage for what?"

"This is where it gets a bit macabre. Another of my colleagues examined the body of Regius Moreland this evening and determined that his...that something was missing."

"His heart?" I guessed, apprehensive.

"No. It was his soul."

A chill went through me like the ice-laden wind of winter. "His *soul*?"

"Yes." Mareth's throat bobbed. "My colleague's conclusion was that the collected souls are what gives the lantern the power to grant a wish."

This was bad. This was *so* bad that I didn't have any context from my long years as a Hound to tell me just how bad it was. I stared at Mareth, feeling lost.

Souls weren't something people talked about in practical terms. Ravens and philosophers argued over what exactly they were, or where they went after death; my Viger ancestors believed the souls of the dead ascended to rejoin the Moon, while in the League Cities many believed in reincarnation. One thing everyone agreed on, though: The composition of souls was mostly an academic point, since not much could interfere with them.

But now something had.

"What...what does that mean? If he doesn't have a soul, is he..."

"I don't know." Mareth's fingers twisted in the amulet chains, disarranging them after all his careful work. "Our best understanding is that the soul is the spark of consciousness. So Regius—and everyone else who's been killed by this curse over however many lifetimes those relics have existed—they're all still *in* there. Trapped and suffering."

"Blood on the Moon," I breathed.

Mareth gave me a desperate, despairing sort of nod. "Exactly."

The drawing room door slid open, and Signa Clement stuck her head into the foyer. "Signa Overfell? A word, if you please."

Mareth straightened, pulling together the tattered shreds of his Raven mystique. "Of course."

I stared after him as he followed the Wasp into the drawing room. How did this keep getting worse? There had to be some point at which we'd reach maximum terribleness, surely. I wished I could stop the sinking feeling that that might still be a ways off.

The outside door banged wide, a spitting gust of rain blowing in with it. A loud, drunken jumble of my friends burst through.

Jaycel had the loose, dangerous grace she acquired after moderate drinking, her already dubious judgment decreased but her martial skills still largely intact; Vy's cheeks shone red and merry, and a soft fondness brimmed in Petras's eyes that I couldn't imagine seeing when he was fully sober.

My stomach sank and kept sinking, through the floorboards and down into the black bones of the earth. These were my friends, ridiculous and precious to me for knowing the secret lore of our shared youth. They belonged to the sunny inviolate realm of my childhood, foundation stones in the edifice of my heart. The idea that they might all be dead soon—not just dead, but with their *souls* ripped out—was intolerable.

And it was my job to protect them. My hands curled into fists. I couldn't fuck this up.

Jaycel waved cheerfully and shucked off her wet jacket without missing so much as a beat on the story she was telling.

THE LAST SOUL AMONG WOLVES 75

"—And *that* is why you should never invite an Echo to a party on a first date."

Vy frowned anxiously. "But what if it's a very *nice* Echo?"

Jaycel waved an airy hand. "Oh, you can still absolutely date them. Just don't get other people involved. Lesson learned."

Petras lifted an eyebrow. "You? Learn a lesson? Did we slip into an Echo?"

"You're one to talk, darling! Speaking of poor romantic decisions, I've seen you making eyes at Signa Glory. She had her chance with you, frankly, and she can go straight to the Void."

A certain ruddiness crept into Petras's warm brown face. "I'm not quite fool enough to open that wound again."

"That's good to hear, but be careful. She looks about ready to cut it wider for you."

I shifted uncomfortably, unsure whether it was all right to ask, or if it'd be worse not to. I settled for muttering, "Um," which was probably the worst possible solution.

Jaycel glanced at me, eyes bright. "Oh, right! You left before that whole debacle."

"Jaycel," Petras said, sounding pained. "Please."

I lifted my hands. "I respect your privacy. Just let me know if I should start graffitiing her show posters or anything."

"No, nothing like that. Jaycel makes it sound worse than it was." He sighed. "She moved into the neighborhood about three years after you left. She was...in a bad way."

"She looked like a starving waif," Jaycel contributed. "Petras started out just helping her, but then he fell hard. Gave her his whole heart on a platter."

Petras shot her a withering look, which Jaycel ignored. "Look, it was my first serious relationship, all right? I thought...Well, I thought it would be forever. But when she got into the Butterflies, she dumped me. Said she was going to be famous and couldn't be involved with someone with *seedy Dockside connections.*"

Vy's hands flew to her mouth. "Oh, that's awful!"

Petras shrugged. "It happened a long time ago. I'm over it."

It was the most obvious lie I'd ever heard him tell.

"Seedy Dockside connections, huh? I hope she steps on a tack," I grumbled.

Jaycel gave an emphatic nod. "A whole box of them."

Petras looked conflicted, like he might defend her but didn't really want to. Before he could say anything, Signa Clement peeked into the foyer.

"Thank you for your patience. If you'll take your seats now, we have some announcements to make."

We all filed into the drawing room, settling into the same rows of chairs facing the podium. Amistead was there already, so of course everyone had to stare at the newcomer.

"Well, now," Jaycel murmured. "Dona Tylar Amistead."

Petras startled. "Amistead! He sponsored a fund for widowed parents in Southside. My mother lived off it when I was small. What's *he* doing here?"

I didn't get a chance to reply; as we settled into our seats, a damp draft rushed over us one more time. The outer door admitted a somewhat aggrieved-looking Signa Glory in a spectacular but sodden coral dress. Willa Lovegrace trailed half a step behind her, complaining loudly about the weather as she stripped off a stylish powder-blue jacket and matching gloves. The moment she spotted Amistead, she detached from Glory at once, taking a seat at his side and greeting him with almost fawning familiarity.

Glory breezed past us and sat a little apart from everyone, looking studiously out the window. Petras couldn't take his eyes off her. If he was trying not to reopen old wounds, he was doing a lousy job of it.

Mareth stood at the podium, a lanky bundle of nerves, swaying slightly. He cleared his throat.

"Ah. Now that we're all here . . . I'm sorry for the abruptness with which I called you back, but I do have some vital new information."

"Life or death, you said," Willa snapped.

"And I meant it." His voice warmed with excitement, despite everything. "As I was studying the enchantments on the mirror, I noticed that in addition to the obvious portal, there's a subtle

THE LAST SOUL AMONG WOLVES 77

disruptive ward layered in. And strangely enough, it's keyed to the transverse anchor Echo, if you can believe it!"

He gave an eager pause, presumably for our startled exclamations.

"Smaller words, Mareth darling," called Jaycel.

"Right, right." Mareth flashed a smile, undaunted. "It has a ward that repels Echoes. But *specifically* those from the fifth Echo, which is the one on the far side of the portal. It would make it rather uncomfortable for the Deepwolf—or any Echo from that layer—to remain near the mirror in Prime. As if it were emitting a painfully loud noise only they could hear."

"Excuse me, I know I'm just a fool with a sword and an occasional stinging retort, but that doesn't make any sense," Jaycel objected. "Why would anyone make a relic that summons a creature to Prime and then immediately repels it?"

"Because then the mirror's owner is safe from the Deepwolf." I said it even as the pieces fit together in my mind. "So they can call it through with impunity. Set it on others with no risk to themselves."

Like those Southside and Dockside kids from Pearson's reports. A tide of rage began to slowly rise in me. Somebody had done this on purpose. Someone had set this curse in motion to farm the souls of the poor and reap themselves a wish.

"You're likely right," Mareth agreed. "Importantly for us, it also means that this house might be safe—or at least, safer than anywhere else. You'll notice when the Deepwolf came through, it passed by all of us to go after Regius, the only one who was outside. It will be repelled from this place; whether that's enough to keep it from its task, I don't know."

Vy looked around, eyes wide. "Oh! Maybe we should all stay here, then. It's spooky, but if it's safe..."

The Wasp gave a sharp nod. "If you wish to remain here as a protective measure until this issue is resolved, my guild will allow it while we hold the house in trust awaiting the resolution of the deceased's will."

"You can't possibly mean to go through with this unholy business," Willa objected.

"The *unholy business* will no doubt attend to itself. It is my sacred duty as the Wasp entrusted with executing Auberyn Lovegrace's estate to follow the dictates of her will, which indicates that the house and relics will pass to whoever is the last alive from the names in that book."

Petras stroked his beard. "Wait. So if everyone else dies from, say, accidents or natural causes, the last one alive still inherits?"

The Wasp frowned. "Yes, though the deceased did include a contingency clause if the curse was actually broken."

"Foolishness," Willa sniffed, but said no more under the Wasp's level stare.

"Well." Signa Clement gathered up her papers. "I must file the appropriate paperwork. I'll send over a boat crew to assist with any messages you wish to send or possessions you wish to retrieve. Signa Thorne, Signa Overfell, I leave it to you to come up with a plan to deal with the curse situation."

I blinked at her, astonished once again at the sheer speed and assurance with which she dropped this mess in our laps and made her exit. I couldn't help a bit of wistful envy as I watched her go.

Willa shook her head in disgust. "Ugh, this is intolerable. How am I supposed to entrust fetching my things to some unwashed boat crew? And who will cook and clean for us while we're here?"

Jaycel leaned forward as if she were about to impart a great secret. "Some of us," she whispered dramatically, "can cook and clean for *ourselves*."

"Oh, shut up, you horrible little—"

Glory's beautiful voice slid smoothly across Willa's before she could say something that would get her challenged to a duel. "I'd like to understand the limits of this enchantment to which we're entrusting our lives. Do you know how far its protection extends, Signa Overfell?"

Mareth stared at her with a somewhat dazzled expression. "It should at least cover the house itself, and probably the immediate garden. Mind you, if we *all* stay here, we'll be pitting the strength of the compulsion on the Deepwolf against the deterrent of the ward, and I can't say which will win. But you really don't want to be the only one outside of its range."

Vy crossed her arms. "Well, I like being alive, and I like my friends alive, so I think we should all stay here until this blows over. We can make it a jolly party."

Willa's face twisted with revulsion at the phrase *jolly party*.

"That would probably be safest," I agreed.

Glory's brows drew together. "But surely we can't stay here the entire time. I have... people I need to meet with. It's urgent."

"Ask them to come here," I suggested. "I'm sure they'll understand, given the circumstances."

She didn't look quite satisfied with that, but Amistead broke in before she could respond.

"If we're all staying here, I'd like to claim the ground floor bedroom, if no one minds. I fear my joints aren't what they used to be, and I do hate stairs."

Willa rose to her feet, jaw working. "It's intolerable that you're all just inviting yourselves to my aunt's house. This is *my* family's home, a place I've visited time and again from childhood. You have no right to sleep in beds that belong to my family and befoul our home with your... with your..."

Jaycel leaned back in her chair, eyes glittering. "With our what? Go on."

Even Willa couldn't ignore the eager menace in her voice. She made an exasperated noise, turned on her heel, and stalked off. A moment later, stomping footsteps ascended a flight of creaky stairs deeper in the house.

"A shame." Jaycel sighed. "I'll miss her sparkling conversation."

"Well, she *did* just lose her husband," Amistead pointed out reasonably. "And she's in fear for her life. I assure you, I've talked to her at parties, and she's usually a bit less..." He trailed off, seeming to seek a word that wasn't rude.

I didn't get to hear whether he found one. Mareth had slipped out from behind the podium the moment the focus shifted away from him and now bent beside me.

80 MELISSA CARUSO

"Kembral." He glanced toward the others, voice low. "Can I have a word?"

It occurred to me that he hadn't told anyone else about what was in the lantern. Just thinking about those golden dancing lights made the room feel colder and darker. I wasn't sure I *wanted* to know what else Mareth needed privacy to tell me.

But it was my job to face all the horrible things no one else could overcome, so I nodded. My evening was already ruined; might as well make it worse.

We stepped out into the long, dim corridor leading to the relic room. Mareth stopped me once we were around the corner and out of earshot. The lamps washed his face in jumping shadows.

"Kembral. I . . . wanted to apologize." He must have seen me blinking in confusion, because he added, "For earlier."

It took me a moment, but finally I realized he must mean for freezing up in this same hallway when the Deepwolf came through.

"Ah. Don't worry about it. Hard to relax your brain enough to reach the Veil when you might be about to die."

"Yes!" He looked relieved. "I should've known you'd understand."

"Took me five years of training every day to get from the point where I could blink step reliably to the point where I could blink step *while fighting*. Everyone freezes up now and then."

He fiddled with one sigil-embroidered cuff. "That's the thing, though. It's not just now and then. I'm afraid I'm . . . Well, you see . . ." His voice dropped to a whisper. "I'm no good."

I blinked. "What? But you've been studying Echo working since you were a kid! You used to drag these tomes around, and practice the hand gestures. And your family line—you must have told us a thousand times that the Overfells—"

"I'm aware that I've let down my family legacy." He said it with an edge, then let out a tremendous sigh, his shoulders slumping. "Frankly, I'm a terrible Echo worker. Completely unworthy of the Overfell name."

"That can't be right." I frowned. "What's holding you back? I know you, Mareth, and I know it can't be because you don't grasp the

THE LAST SOUL AMONG WOLVES

81

arcane mysteries or anything. You always grasped the arcane mysteries so tight they could barely breathe."

"Ha. That's exactly the problem." He gave me a defeated little half smile. "What do you have to do to reach beyond the Veil?"

Almarah's voice sounded in my ears, chastising me as a child when I had been concentrating so hard my face scrunched up. "You have to let go."

"Right. Suffice to say I struggle with that. I'm too focused. To be a good Echo worker, you need to be able to let your mind wander— wander so far, in fact, that it reaches another world." He gave a rueful shrug. "I'm working on it, and I'm making progress. But it's slow."

"Oh, I can imagine. It took me fifteen years to learn to blink step properly, after all."

"It doesn't help that I'm absolutely *humiliated*." Mareth made a face. "I joined the Ravens at eighteen thinking I would be some legendary prodigy, and here I am eleven years later, unable to pierce the Veil half the time. When I *can* do it, I assure you I can work Echoes with some skill, but...Let's just say you should under no circumstances count on me. Especially in a crisis."

"Well, I appreciate the warning. And as for the current situation, what we really need is to keep it from coming to a crisis again in the first place." He looked lost; I needed to give him a path forward. "Can we destroy the relics? Would that do it?"

"I...Maybe. I don't know if we *can* destroy them." He took a shaky breath. "I should try."

I gestured toward the lantern room. "Shall we? I'd love to find out whether we can conveniently solve this problem with a hammer. I need to send a note to Achyrion soon to let him know if I'm staying here overnight."

Mareth's eyes widened. "*Achyrion?* Like the Elder Dragon?"

"No, like my babysitter."

He shook his head, bemused. "I don't dare ask. Come on, let's see whether this complicated problem has a delightfully simple solution."

The lantern room was as we'd left it. The mirror's cloudy silver sheen seemed sinister in the flickering lamplight. The age-yellowed book lay open, its pages stained in blood. When I approached the relics, I noticed one difference: A stark red line had appeared through Regius's name, as if someone had sliced the page and it bled from the slash.

Mareth shuddered when he saw it. "How morbid. All right, let's try to destroy that one first."

It appeared, however, that this wasn't one of those cases where brute force was the answer.

Fire wouldn't burn the book. Water wouldn't wash the pages clean. No amount of pounding would smash the mirror. Mareth tried Raven stuff, too, drawing sigils and weaving wisps of power from the Echoes—which seemed to work just fine when he wasn't in a panic—but nothing put so much as a smudge or a dent on either of the relics.

"Whoever or whatever made these was very powerful," Mareth said, sweat beading on his temples. "*And* very skilled."

"Can't say I'm surprised. If it were that easy, someone would have gotten rid of them already."

He gave me a sideways look. "Dragons have incredible destructive power. If that name you dropped wasn't a joke or a coincidence and you're somehow friends with *the* Achyrion, maybe he could..."

"No. He made it *really* clear that part of the babysitting deal was that I can't bring my non-childcare-related problems to him." I grimaced. "Sorry. I think he gets asked for favors a lot and he's tired of it."

Mareth sighed. "Fair enough. To be honest, I doubt it'd work anyway. I've never seen relics this resilient against any kind of physical or magical force."

"Are you out of things to try?"

"Not quite, but..." He gave me a sympathetic glance that made me realize I'd maybe not succeeded as well as I thought at hiding my impatience. "Nothing I need your help with. If you have things to do, by all means, go."

THE LAST SOUL AMONG WOLVES   83

"Thanks." I started toward the door, then hesitated and turned to face him. "And, Mareth...I'm sorry I didn't stay in touch. All those years, you were just across Guildhouse Square. I kept hoping I'd run into you, but I shouldn't have left it to chance. I should have—"

He let out a strange noise. I stopped, staring. His face turned pink, and for a moment I wondered if he were somehow choking.

At last, he drew in a gasp and managed, "I'm the one who's sorry, Kembral. I didn't...Oh dear. This is going to sound awful, but I was avoiding you."

I felt as if I'd walked face-first into a wall. "Oh."

"No, no, no." He waved his hands, getting redder and redder. "Not because of you. Because I...Well, my skills aren't reliable enough to qualify as a field Raven. And I knew you'd probably ask, or assume, or say *something* about how I was doing, and I would just...sink into a hole and die." He slumped against a wall. "Like I want to do now."

"Mareth, that's ridiculous. You know I wouldn't think any less of you for—"

"I told you, it was never about you." He brushed a hand through his dark waves of hair with a mortified grimace. "You're just... everything I wanted to be. Senior in your guild, renowned for an exceptional and rare skill, looked up to by all, nearly a legend..."

Now *my* face was getting hot. "It's not like that. I'm just a Hound."

"Pah. You're just a Hound the way my grandfather was just a Raven. Which is, of course, exactly the problem." He shook his head. "I kept telling myself I'd give it one more month, until I had some kind of exciting accomplishment to report, and then I'd meet up with you for lunch. But there were never any accomplishments. I kept hearing about amazing things *you'd* done, though. So whenever I saw you across the square, or if you came to visit the Raven guildhouse for some reason and I spotted you in the hall, I'd duck behind something like I was a criminal avoiding the watch."

"Stars, Mareth." I felt about ready to melt into the floor, myself. "I had no idea."

"I know. It's silly." He let out a miserable little laugh. "A terrible reason not to stay in touch with an old friend."

"I'm no better. I should have hunted you down instead of waiting to run into you by chance." I drew in a breath. "Listen. Let's fix this. When I'm working at the guildhouse, I get lunch at the little noodle shop next to the Wolf guild."

"I know." He ducked his head. "It's, ah, why I never went in there. Sorry, I'm a fool."

"You've been missing out. Their noodle bowls are delicious, especially the seafood one." I clasped his shoulder. "Let's meet up there once a week. Forget about accomplishments. Tell me what you're reading, or about guildhouse drama. Why not make something good out of all this mess? Maybe we can get the whole gang back together."

"I'd like that." He smiled, and it was genuine at last. "I'd like that a lot."

—⋙—

The young oarswoman who showed up to take our messages back to shore had the keen energy of an athletic twenty-year-old who knows something is going on and is dreadfully curious about what. Signa Clement must have impressed on her not to pry, though, because she didn't ask any questions, despite accepting notes addressed to everything from Hillside mansions to underworld lieutenants, with a smattering of guildhouses to boot.

I was the last person to hand over my messages to the oarswoman before she cast off under the cloud-muffled moonlight. I sent one note to Rika updating her on new developments, and one to Achyrion apologizing for needing to spend the night away at such short notice. Not that I thought he'd mind, given how much he seemed to genuinely dote on Emmi—but still, it felt strange and wrong to be away from her overnight. I had tried six different ways to convince myself I didn't need to stay at the mansion, but there was no way around it—we had so little time, and lives were at stake. The only way I was going home tonight was if I solved this thing first.

As I turned toward the house, a flicker of silvery light caught my attention. Just a glimpse, through the trees that crowded the sloping shore beyond the docks, but bright and clear—and then it was gone.

THE LAST SOUL AMONG WOLVES 85

It didn't look anything like lamplight, or lightning, either. I could only think of one thing it might be.

An Echo.

Well now. It could be something that slipped through the offshore gap in the Veil at random—or it could be tied into whatever hidden force moved the pieces in this terrible game. A flock of Echoes had killed Auberyn Lovegrace and set the whole thing off, after all. Either way, it might be dangerous.

I'd promised Rika I'd be careful. But I didn't have to get close— just close enough for a better look, to know what we were up against.

I traced the familiar use-worn grip of a sword hilt for reassurance and headed after the light.

EVERYONE HAS SECRETS

I wished Rika were here. Her absence at my side in this potentially dangerous moment felt as if I'd forgotten my sword.

All senses alert, I crept toward the tree line. The silvery light had disappeared without a trace, and only paler patches of water and sky showed in streaks between the trunks and tangled boughs. The rain had tapered off to a light mist, but a thick blanket of clouds still smothered the Moon; everything was shades of black and deepest indigo, save for the lights across the river and the diminishing gleam of the oarswoman's lantern.

On a jumble of rocks that jutted into the water beyond the last tenacious tree, a silhouetted figure crouched, facing out toward the ocean.

I stopped, hand resting on my sword, trying to pull more details out of the darkness. It wasn't quite the right spot to have been the source of the light, but that didn't mean it wasn't an Echo—or a human with unknown intent, for that matter. I couldn't help thinking about that slept-in bed Rika had found.

The figure shifted, and I made out the edge of a coat, the bumpy line of a braid: Vy.

Relieved, I made my way over to her, minding my step on the slippery rocks in the darkness and the slap of the waves near my Damn

Good Boots. She gazed out toward the open ocean, crouched on the tips of her toes with her fingertips trailing in the lapping edge of the water. She didn't look back, but she angled her head in a way that let me know she'd heard my approach.

"Oh, hi, Kem. Want to see something neat?"

I blinked. "Uh, sure."

Vy scooped up a double handful of dark salty ocean, lifting it dripping for my inspection. "See?"

Lights danced in the cupped water. Tiny fish, about the size of a sunflower seed, blue and ghostly.

"Are those Echoes?" I asked, peering closer. This couldn't have been what made that light—but if there was this much Echo activity right at the shore, I could see why Almarah had warned me about blink stepping on the ocean.

"They're so small now," Vy said, a little wistfully. "They grow to be bigger than you are, and sometimes they prey on humans. But at this size, they're so cute."

"Very pretty," I said, since I wasn't sure *cute* was quite the word I'd personally use.

"Yeah." She slipped her hands back into the water, freeing the fish, and then stood, staring out at the waves again. She didn't seem to mind that her hands were still dripping.

I wondered for a fleeting instant whether whatever Echo emitted the silvery light might have somehow dazed her, because this all felt a little weird—but no, Vy had been acting weird since she'd opened the door for me. This was just who she was now, after a decade on a ship with a tide skimmer. I probably seemed strange to her, too— Moon knew I'd changed enough.

"So, uh, did you see anything just now?" I asked. "A light, over that way?"

"Oh, that! Yes. Just a glimpse, moving off." She shrugged. "I wouldn't worry about it. Probably something that came through the portal."

"It's kind of my job to worry about things that come through Echo portals."

Vy laughed. "I suppose so! Okay, you should worry, then. But not too much. It looked like it was leaving."

"That's...provisionally reassuring." I tried to follow her gaze. "What are you looking at out there? Please tell me there aren't *more* Echoes surrounding us."

"No, no. Well, there undoubtedly are, but I wasn't looking at them. I was just looking at the sea." She gave a shy sort of smile. "It's so beautiful at night."

"Ah. That it is." For a moment, standing there on the rocks with the waves lapping at our feet, a comfortable silence eroded the gap time had made between us. "Do you miss it?"

"Yes, terribly." Her eyes gleamed in the diffuse moonlight. "When I'm on land, I miss the sea, and when I'm at sea, I miss the land. Isn't that foolish?"

"I think it's just human nature."

"Is it?" She seemed surprised at that.

"To want whatever we don't have at the moment? Yeah."

"I must be very human, then." A wistful smile crossed her face. "You make it look so easy—you and Petras and Mareth and Jaycel. Joking and talking and touching one another. I want so badly to feel a part of that— for things to be like I remember between us—but I'm not that person anymore." She gazed out at the ocean again. "It's different at sea, Kem."

"Oh? How?"

"There's only one question that matters, out there," she said quietly. "It's the one the ocean asks, and it has no answer."

I blinked. "That's poetic."

"Oh, maybe it is!" She seemed to like that notion. "I wasn't trying to be. I really do feel like I've forgotten how to live ashore. I hope I'm not annoying everyone with my lack of proper land manners."

"Not at all. It's good to have you back."

I wanted to say more, to reach out to her and rekindle the light of our old friendship. There was some wound in Vy I couldn't understand. Some sadness I could hear in her voice, beneath her clear love for the sailor's life she'd always wanted. I didn't know how to ask about it, and I wasn't sure that I had the right anymore.

But the look she turned on me was warm and delighted. "Oh, excellent! It's wonderful to be here. Even with all these terrible things going on—it's so nice to have such good company."

"We should get together whenever you're in port from now on," I suggested. "No sense letting it go another ten years. We can get a drink or something—all of us, together."

"That would be lovely, wouldn't it?" She gave me a wistful smile. "Yes. Yes, let's do it."

We watched the sea together a few minutes more. I finally excused myself to search the trees for any sign of that silvery light—but whatever it had been, it was gone.

—⚍—

After a fruitless search through the small patch of woods and along the rocky shore, I returned to find the drawing room full of warmth and sound. It wasn't quite the jolly party Vy had hoped for, but it was closer than I'd expected.

Someone had stoked up the fire and kindled all the lamps, and a thorough raid had clearly been conducted on old lady Lovegrace's liquor cabinet. Everyone but Willa was there—I could imagine her upstairs, trying to sleep with gritted teeth and wishing extra curses on everyone. They'd pushed aside the simple chairs used for the bequeathing and lounged on the room's proper furniture, well into an ongoing conversation.

I hesitated in the doorway. I needed to go look through the Lovegrace papers, but I longed to drink in the warmth and company for a moment before heading off to some dusty corner of the mansion to work by myself.

"How about you?" Jaycel, one leg hooked over her chair arm, gestured grandly with her glass in the direction of Dona Amistead. "If you had the lantern right now, and nobody had to die for it, what would *you* wish for?"

"Ah, well." Amistead took a sip of his brandy. "You get to my age, and you start thinking about your legacy. My family has a long history, and it's starkly clear that some of us left behind a better world

90   MELISSA CARUSO

while others, I regret to say, made it worse. But I must confess that it's one small piece of that world that concerns me most."

"Which piece?" Vy asked.

Amistead caught my eye across the room and raised his glass to me. "I'd lay odds that Signa Thorne knows. You're a mother, aren't you?"

"Yes."

"Then you understand." He nodded, his eyes crinkling. "Of *course* I'd use it for my children and my grandchildren. For their happiness, health, and prosperity. How could I do anything else?"

"You've got me there."

I wanted to say that I would never dream of using an Echo wish on Emmi, because they had a tendency to twist around and bite you in the ass. But given that I'd accepted help from multiple Echoes in making sure she was safe from my enemies—well, I didn't have much of a leg to stand on. They were *reliable* Echoes, though, who came with very good references, damn it.

Amistead regarded the drink in his hand, his face softening as he watched the play of firelight through golden brandy. "I know it must seem silly to the rest of you. They were born into wealth, and I've given them everything they could need. But last year Allione— my youngest grandchild—caught the red fever, and we nearly lost her." His face fell into deeper creases, ones carved by worry and pain. "The physicker says she'll have lasting complications. There are some things money can't protect you from, it seems. So yes, even a lucky old fool like me with far too many advantages has use for a wish."

Our gazes locked, and an understanding passed between us. For a moment, the room was silent save for the crackling of the fire.

Jaycel shook her head, breaking the spell. "Moon above, so serious! How about you, Vy?" She grinned. "You got your wish to go to sea, so what would you wish for now?"

Vy's cheeks flushed. "Well, that's the funny thing. I think...Oh, you'll laugh at me."

"No, no, we won't laugh," Jaycel promised, already laughing.

"Oh, all right." Vy lifted her hands to her face, peeping over them. "This is going to sound silly, but...I think I might like to have friends like you again. For things to be more like in my memories, when we were all so close, and had adventures together."

Mareth's gaze fixed wistfully on her face. "I think that's a beautiful wish."

Jaycel pressed her hand to her heart. "An excellent wish, and one we have it in our power to grant! Brace yourself, Vy. I'm taking you along on my next adventure."

Vy let out a delighted whoop, her eyes bright as stars.

"And you, Signa Glory?" Mareth asked politely. "What would *you* wish for?"

Glory's sculpted brows lifted. "I suppose one is expected to wish for something noble and selfless, like to end hunger for the orphans or find a cure for the wasting pox."

"No, no, that's boring," Jaycel chided her.

"I think Echo wishes usually have to be for yourself, anyway," Mareth said.

"True." Glory tilted her head, seeming to think it over. "I'm not sure. Perhaps to sing in the amphitheater at Rainnes, in the heart of the League Cities—they say it can seat thousands, and the king of Rainnes is a great patron of the arts." No longing stirred the warm, cloying resonance that imbued her words; I wondered if she had any idea how obvious her power made it that she was lying.

Mareth's brow rumpled in a frown. "Wouldn't you want to get there on your own merits, though? It'd feel like cheating to use a wish."

"At the level at which I perform, the competition is so fierce one must take every advantage one can get."

Petras scowled and took a long swallow of wine. That must cut awfully close to the bone, given her reason for dumping him.

"Maybe you shouldn't take *every* advantage." His gaze burned into her. "Maybe some things aren't worth sacrificing."

Glory's eyes flicked away from him, dismissive. "On the contrary. Every sacrifice I've made has been worth it. To get where I am today, I had to cast aside anything and everything holding me back."

"Holding you *back*?" Petras's head jerked as if she'd slapped him. "I'm the one who got you your first singing job, for Void's sake."

Some sharp note entered Glory's voice—contempt, perhaps. "Yes, in a Dockside gambling hall. To be the greatest star of the Acantis opera, however—"

"But you're not that anymore, are you?" Jaycel hadn't changed her lounging posture, but suddenly she oozed menace.

Glory stiffened. "Excuse me?"

"You didn't get cast in the leading role in the Grand Theater's main show this season, did you? It was that new, younger alto with resonance, the really brilliant one. What was her name? Ah yes— Irida Velar."

For an instant, naked hatred flashed across Glory's face. But her expression smoothed out immediately, and when she spoke, her voice dripped resonance to the point that my head felt fuzzy.

"I'm pleased that Signa Velar is being given a chance for her talent to shine, but I assure you, that does not in any way diminish my own standing." She rose. "Now, if you'll excuse me, it's quite late, and I should be getting to bed."

Glory swept from the room; I had to step aside to let her pass.

Amistead looked around with his brows raised. "Apparently one doesn't need to attend the Grand Theater to see Signa Glory in a drama."

Petras smoothed out his cravat. "On the stage of the world, only a fool goes up against Jaycel Morningray. Or, it appears, those lucky enough to be her friends."

Jaycel laughed and raised her cup to him. Then she sloshed it in my direction for good measure. "Kembral darling! Speaking of friends, come join us! We're making good use of old lady Lovegrace's finest legacy."

"I'd love to, but I've got to get to work. Saving your lives, and all that."

I ducked out of the room before my friends could draw me further in. It would be nice to sit down with them and drive the specter of death away with laughter. But I had less than two days to find a more permanent solution for said specter, and I was feeling the press of time. Not least because that silver light made yet another sign of Echo interference, which I didn't like at all.

I started for the library, where I'd stashed my box of papers. I'd hardly made it half a dozen steps when a voice startled me, a breathless desperate whisper floating down the hall.

"*No.* No, he won't do it. I won't let him."

It was Glory. She'd paused a few steps up the staircase, leaning on the banister, head bowed. There was no one else around—she must be talking to herself. I hesitated, embarrassed to come across her in such a private moment.

She caught sight of me and straightened, going from vulnerable to regal in an instant.

"Signa Thorne. I suppose you're here to chastise me for being callous to your friend."

"Actually, I was just heading to the library."

"Ah." She eyed me like she wasn't sure she believed it. "What did Petras tell you? About... about *us*?"

Oh, this was *so* awkward. "That you had a relationship. Not much. He's a private person."

"Yes. We were very young, and I was in a bad situation. Petras helped me escape it. He saw worth in me at a dark time when few others did, and made me see I could be more."

There was such genuine regret in her voice, her resonance pushing it through me in an aching wave. It didn't match with how she'd just treated him. "But you..."

"I broke his heart." She sighed. "I'm not proud of what I did to him. He didn't deserve it. But it was made clear to me that to reach the heights to which I aspired, I could allow no weakness or distraction. I don't regret claiming the place I have now, and I mean to keep it—even if the price I pay is a life alone."

The husky catch in her voice tugged at my sympathy, but her words didn't line up with what I'd heard from my friends in her guild. "I thought Butterflies tended to form close bonds with each other. And I've never heard of them avoiding romantic relationships."

"Maybe it's like that for some people. Once you learn resonance, though, it sets you apart." A bittersweet half smile pulled at her lips. "Don't you find it the same, with your blink step?"

An ache of understanding swelled up in my chest, and I opened my mouth to say yes, of course I did. But no, wait—that wasn't true at all. I had plenty of friends, and being able to blink step only got in the way for the sort of competitive jackasses I wouldn't want to be friends with anyway. She was using her resonance to pluck my emotions like a harp string.

Anger sparked a fire on my tongue, and I was ready to snap at her—but for all I knew she might be doing it instinctively, without any intent to manipulate. I gave her the benefit of the doubt and swallowed my indignation.

"Not really. But you must have had to train very hard, to learn how to do that."

Glory gave a fluid shrug, glancing away. "It came to me more easily than most. I've been lucky."

"Lucky enough to have help," I pointed out.

For an instant, a wild flash of emotion transformed her face. I couldn't tell if it was surprise, anger, or fear—but it was gone in an instant, her shoulders relaxing in apparent relief.

"Auberyn and Petras, you mean. Yes, they were invaluable to my career, and I'm well aware I showed them poor gratitude for it. I want to make amends."

Her dark eyes read my face hungrily. I wasn't sure what to think, or what that fleeting expression had meant. Maybe it was all true; maybe Auberyn Lovegrace's death had filled her with the urge to make things right with Petras while she still could, and she was just bad at it. Or maybe she was trying to manipulate me.

She might not even know which. Glory struck me as someone who played her own life as a role, lost from the truth of herself in the lights of the stage.

"I'm not the one you need to talk to about making amends," I said at last.

"I suppose not." Her gaze dropped from mine. "Good evening, Signa Thorne."

She started up the stairs toward the guest rooms, moving as if her body were made of lead.

She was hiding something. I had no doubt of that—and given how quickly she'd turned the conversation to Petras when she realized I'd overheard her, it probably didn't have anything to do with him. It was also none of my business. Still, given the mounting evidence that these relics might be part of some larger plot, I filed that away in my brain as I continued toward the library.

A change in the pressure of the air and a faint whiff of honey clove perfume informed me of Rika's presence. I turned to find her at my side, her face carefully smooth and clear of any smugness at having once again snuck up on me.

"Thank the Moon you're here," I said, before I could think better of it.

Rika's focus sharpened to a knife edge. "Did something happen?"

"No, no. I just...You're competent, and I like having you around."

A little smile crooked her mouth. "Why, Kembral. How romantic."

"How's Emmi?"

"She woke up when Achyrion arrived and cried at first, but when I left he was swooping her around like she was flying, and she was squealing and having the time of her life. Don't you worry."

Something in me unclenched a little, with a pang of irrational jealousy as a chaser. I would have loved to see that, damn it.

"He's so good with her. How long can he stay?"

"He said to do whatever you need to do. He's good for at least two days. I told him how to contact your sister if something came up."

I tried to imagine my practical, bossy sister meeting Achyrion. She'd be trimming his claws and scolding him about his nail care before he knew what hit him.

"I really hope this won't take two days." The thought of being away from Emmi that long made my chest ache. "I was heading to the library to finish going through old lady Lovegrace's papers, just in case there's some kind of handy note that lays out all the secrets of the relics. A long shot, I know, but it's the lead I have."

"That's more than *I* have." She gave a sort of frustrated shrug. "This job is awful. It's a matter for the Ravens, not for Cats or Hounds."

"Yeah. Or part of it is, anyway." I groped to express the thoughts that had been nagging at me. "The relics, the Deepwolf, the Echo swarm that killed Lovegrace—those all point to an Echo game. But someone breaking into the house to put Amistead's name in that book, and the curse targeting people in Southside and Dockside specifically... *That* sounds all too human. I'm starting to think it's a case of Echo and human working together."

Rika went still. "Like an Empyrean and their anchor?"

"I hope not," I said. "That's even worse than an Echo game with human pawns. But maybe."

We were standing close together in the dusky hallway; the lamps cast her face into a harsh play of shadows and slips of light. She looked honed, intent—frightened.

If Rika Nonesuch was frightened, I was concerned.

"What is it?" I took her hand, gently, and felt the tension in it. "Something's bothering you. Tell me."

Her voice dropped, so low I could barely hear her. "I have a bad feeling."

"What sort of bad feeling?"

"The same kind I had at the year-turning. It's probably nothing." The edge in her subdued voice suggested that it was absolutely something.

I suddenly felt small and wild and helpless in the dark, a mouse hearing the call of an owl. I strained my senses, alert for the prickling feeling of a thin spot in the Veil, or of the portal opening. But her statement had raised goose bumps on my arms, and it was hard to tell.

"I'm begging you to be more specific. Do you have some extra sense that detects Echo meddling, or are you having a premonition, or is this just a regular human sort of—"

"I don't know, all right?" she snapped. Then her voice smoothed out all at once—too smooth, light and false. "A Hound should understand that sometimes, your hackles go up."

"Yeah. Mine too. But, Rika..." I hesitated, unsure whether I was about to step onto solid ground or fragile ice. "You know you can trust me, right? You can talk to me about stuff. You don't have to pretend everything is all right."

She let out a soft, hopeless little laugh. "Kembral, I trust you like I trust the ground I stand on. But I've been pretending every moment of my entire life. I don't know how to stop."

"Look, this isn't going to be like last time." I squeezed her hand. "We're not trapped here, we're not part of the game, and we're not targets. We can do the job, save the day, and go home."

"It *can't* be like last time. I know that. But if there's any chance..." She trailed off, unable or unwilling to give the shape of words to whatever fear haunted her.

I brushed a loose tendril of hair back from her face. "We'd better be careful. Just in case."

Some of her tension evaporated under my fingers, as if my touch steadied her. "Much as I loathe the idea of shadowing you while you do tedious Hound things, we should stick together."

I snorted. "Are you sure? I'm going through a box of old letters. You might die of boredom."

"Ugh." She shook her head, equilibrium restored—or at least, mask back in place. "Take it as a sign of how much I like you that I'm willing to touch *paperwork* to keep you safe."

That struck me as an odd choice of words—to keep *me* safe? I wasn't the one with a Deepwolf coming to rip out my soul. But I was still working on the whole not-treating-every-conversation-like-an-interrogation thing, so I didn't press her.

She slid her arm through mine, pulling me maybe a bit closer than was technically necessary, and we headed for the library.

Going through a dead woman's letters with imminent doom hanging over our heads shouldn't have been this cozy. Sure, there was a certain background aura of dread; I missed Emmi desperately, and I had to pause to use my horrid glass pump to deal with my milk at one point. But damned if it wasn't nice to sit in a quiet place with Rika and be able to have a continuous train of thought from beginning to end without being interrupted by the baby. I wished we were doing this for any other reason, and maybe reading some of the tenpenny novels on the shelves rather than dry old correspondence.

Most of it *was* dry. Messages of gratitude from various charities, fawning letters from obnoxious fortune-seeking relatives like Willa, household business. There was one real ongoing correspondence with some childhood friend who'd moved to Cathardia and clearly had no idea what turns Auberyn's life had taken since they were kids together in Southside. That one sent a pang through my heart; even a recluse like old lady Lovegrace had done a better job keeping in touch with her friends than I had.

After a while I gave a stack of more recent stuff to Rika to sift through, while I flipped to the oldest papers. If there was going to be anything talking about how she'd come into these relics or what they did, surely it would be there.

At last, I found something. An irregular stack of strange, half-finished, unsent letters.

There were dozens of them. Draft after draft of basically the same letter, with changes in wording, addressed to the same handful of names. None of them got very far before breaking off, some with a distressed blot of ink.

Dear Geraline Clay, I write with the most heartfelt condolences on the death of your son. I understand that nothing can possibly assuage your grief, but I feel that while I am not responsible for his death, as the one who survived I owe you some explanation of the

Dear Vedhra and Bastor Pellin, I am sorry beyond my ability to express for your recent loss. I want to offer you what small solace I can, for it could as easily have been me who

Dear Everton family, My heart breaks for your loss. If I knew someone so young had been drawn into this, I would have

Dear Mina Herun, I have tried to write this letter seven times, and I am hoping this time I may finally have the courage to complete it. You deserve to know the truth about what happened to your husband, and since the perpetrators will doubtless remain silent, I am the only one who can tell you. Yet despite being their victim myself, I find this task impossibly hard—for in surviving, I have unwillingly profited from the deaths of the innocent, and I don't know how to

I stared at that last one. The ink grew thicker and darker as she wrote, the lines harsher and pressed more deeply into the paper, as if she'd been forcing herself to continue against a terrible and increasing weight; it ended with a splash and a tear where she'd clearly broken her nib. The confirmation that Auberyn Lovegrace, at least, felt there were *perpetrators* using the relics deliberately against her was important. But that wasn't what held my attention.

Mina Herun. I knew that name.

"Holy fuck," I said. "That's Petras's mother."

It was time to have a nice little talk with my old friend.

THE PAST SHAPES THE PRESENT

Rika chose the music room to have our conversation, because it was rather long and we could sit by the pianoforte at the far end to put as much space as possible between us and any potential eavesdroppers (which we all understood to mean Jaycel). After giving Petras a moment to read the unfinished letter and process it, we settled down in a half circle with Rika in the middle, like she was some kind of Wasp mediator.

I crossed my arms. "All right, Petras. You're clearly in this up to your eyeballs, and things have gotten too serious for secrets. Are you finally ready to spill?"

Petras straightened his wine-red cravat with an air of weary inevitability. "Much as I might prefer to maintain an aura of mystery, it seems I have no choice."

"It's about time."

"I know, believe me, but this is hard." His jaw worked a moment, as if he chewed through some obstacle to speech. "I'm a private person, Kem, and you're a Hound. This might be easier if I could be sure you were looking at me as a friend, and not some reluctant witness who's been holding back key information."

I winced and uncrossed my arms. "Sorry. I... You have a point. I'll try to do better."

"Good. Now, I know we don't exactly have time for you to practice your social skills, so I'll trust you to do that and skip to the important part." He drew in a breath. "You probably already know I'm in this for the lantern."

"I thought you were in it because you bled on a cursed book with the rest of our dimwit friends when you were a kid."

He shook his head. "This is what I get for asking you to treat me like a friend. Fine, I suppose it's more accurate to say that I brought Signa Nonesuch into this for the lantern."

"Because your family has some connection to it?"

"You could say that." An edge came into his smooth tenor, undermining its perfect control. "My father's in there."

"Well, shit." I rubbed my face, feeling exhausted by the sheer awfulness that kept accumulating around these relics. "I'm sorry."

"My mother always told me he died of a fever. And I believed her, until a couple of days ago."

I gave him a sharp look. "What happened to change that?"

"Someone gave me a tip." He raised a hand. "Before you ask, I promised not to say who. Someone I've worked with before, when I've needed to deal with Echo matters."

Probably a relic smuggler, then, or maybe even an Echo. "Are you sure this information is accurate?"

"Setting aside the question of why someone would make up something like that...I confronted my mother, and she admitted the truth and told me her end of it." His hands curled tight in his lap. "Look, do you want to hear what I know, or not?"

"Sorry. Go ahead."

"My mother said it happened at a festival. Prick your finger and touch the magic book, and if your name appears, you win a prize." Petras's voice took on a harsh edge. "Apparently, they tried to get me to do it, and I wanted the prize very badly, but I was afraid to prick my finger. So my father did it for me."

"Void below, Petras," I whispered. "Did you...Do you remember..."

"I don't remember any of it—I was too small. And my mother

wasn't there. But I remember the prize: a huge stuffed rabbit. I was so proud of that damned thing." Petras shook his head, his voice roughening. "Losing my father plunged my mother into a deep, black depression. She pushed on through it for me, and the physickers gave her medicine that helps, but... Whoever did this to my family stole the light from her life and left her to struggle in darkness. She never really recovered."

I remembered Petras's mother as quiet and kind. In the typical obliviousness of children, I'd had no idea what she was going through.

"There's no words, Petras. I'm so sorry."

"I don't understand what a soul is," he said, with quiet intensity. "That's Raven stuff. But whatever piece of my father remains in that lantern, I'm going to set him free. I'm going to get my mother closure at last. And I'm going to find out who did this to my family, and if that person is still alive, I'm going to make them wish they weren't. I'm not a nice person, Kem. I'm good to the people I care about. But I'm not nice." He drew in a breath, and his usual calm settled back over him like a cloak. "And that's why I hired Signa Nonesuch."

"To get the lantern, I hope," I said, my mouth a little dry. "Not for the vengeance part."

Petras shaped a mirthless slit of a smile. "I can do that on my own."

"This source of yours." I considered carefully how to phrase this, how much to say, given the weight of everything he'd just shared. "The timing seems a little... convenient. After all these years, someone thinks to tip you off that your father's soul is in there, right around the same time Echoes cause Auberyn Lovegrace to have a fatal carriage accident. And within a day or two of *that*, someone breaks into this house and writes Tylar Amistead's name in that book."

Petras looked startled at the extra details. "Someone's orchestrating this, then." His brows swept down in a scowl. "Someone's *using* me."

"Looks like it," I agreed. "Any idea who would benefit if you stole the lantern? Did your source ask for anything in return?"

He hesitated, then shook his head. "Only that I protect his identity and not ask where the information came from. This is someone I've known and worked with for years, though. I suppose he could be passing on tidbits someone fed him, but I'd be surprised if he was knowingly involved."

An idea struck me. One I didn't like at all. "It seems a little weird that you got pulled into this curse after your father did. Is there any chance someone could be deliberately targeting your family?"

"Damn. I never thought of that." Petras sank back in his chair like I'd stunned him. "I can't think of any reason they would. Sure, I have enemies now, but back then we were nobodies."

"Whose idea was it to break into the Lovegrace house in the first place? Did someone suggest it to you?"

Petras stared at me like he'd seen a ghost. "Jaycel. Someone dared Jaycel. Said she'd be too afraid."

Neither of us needed to say anything; our eyes passed the message between us. There could be no surer way to ensure that Jaycel did a thing, and Jaycel always brought her friends along.

"Any chance I can meet this delightful source of yours?" Rika asked, an edge in her casual tone. "I might have some questions."

"Oh, believe me, I do, too," Petras agreed heavily. "But I'll ask him myself. No offense, but I promised discretion, and I need to keep his goodwill—my father's soul is at stake."

Everything in me yearned to follow this trail. I could always look into the matter on my own, using my Hound sources to figure out who Petras dealt with for Echo business—but he'd made it clear he didn't want that, and no lead was worth sacrificing my friend's trust.

"Tell me what he says," I said instead. "And if you do decide you want me to use my skills as a Hound to look into this, they're at your service."

He raised an eyebrow. "For free? My budget is already at its limit paying Signa Nonesuch."

"No need to work for free." I couldn't quite keep the satisfaction out of my voice. "This is all related to the relics. I can bill the Wasps."

—◦◦◦—

We talked and theorized and spun ideas so dubious I couldn't even call them plans, but it all came down to the simple fact that the portal

104 MELISSA CARUSO

was closed and the lantern was on the far side of it. I was on board with helping retrieve it, of course—from everything Mareth had said, I suspected we'd need it to break the curse anyway, and I certainly didn't want to let anyone's souls languish in there—but without any idea where in the fifth Echo the Deepwolf had taken it, we had no way to track it down.

Finally, I started back to the library to finish looking through the last of the Lovegrace papers. Rika said she'd make tea for us and catch up, which I suspected was as much a way to postpone more paperwork as anything.

Just past the stairs I came across Amistead, standing in the hallway in his nightgown, holding a cup and staring pensively out a window at the dark and the sea. The lines of his face had fallen from their usual merry animation to something exhausted, private, and much older.

"Dona Amistead?" I greeted him, uncertain.

"Ah, Signa Thorne!" His face lit up at once. "Pardon my current state. I was already in bed when I realized I hadn't gotten a cup of water—I do get a dry mouth when I sleep. And then I ran into young Petras Herun. I hadn't realized..." He trailed off, his brow creasing.

"Yes?"

Amistead shook his head. "He thanked me. For a fund I'd set up for his mother—one of my charitable programs, you know, to benefit poor widows. And it's damned awkward. I didn't know what to say."

I raised an eyebrow. "I think the phrase 'You're welcome' pretty much exists to get us through circumstances like that."

"Ha! I suppose it does. But, Signa Thorne... why do you think a man like me, from a family like mine, gives a large portion of his money to good causes?"

"A sense of civic responsibility?"

"Ah, but responsibility for what?" His gaze drifted out the window again. "I assure you, every old Hillside family has at some point in its history done reprehensible things. And we, as their heirs, have profited from them. I'd love to tell you that I'm acting out of pure kindness of heart, or in service to some grand vision to make the city a better place. But the truth is, most of us philanthropists are motivated by guilt."

"I suppose it beats sitting on your pile of money and never thinking of how it got to be under your ass."

"Perhaps." He sighed. "Forgive me; I'm rambling. I've had to do a lot of hard reckoning lately, Signa Thorne, and it weighs on my mind. But the hour is late, and I'm getting maudlin. I should get to bed, and let you go about your business."

"Good night then, Dona Amistead."

My gaze lingered on him as he turned away. I couldn't help wondering what exactly his family had done, and whether it might be vengeance for those actions that inspired someone to put his name in the book.

I returned to the library and delved back into the pile of documents, but it was hard to focus when so much new information was buzzing around in my head. Rika brought the tea and joined me, and I hardly noticed.

I could almost see the shape of things, now. I was on the brink of putting the pieces together, making the last connection that would draw back the curtain and show me the shadowy presence hidden behind everything that was happening, the hand moving the pieces in this deadly game. But the answer kept eluding me, like a forgotten word on the tip of my tongue.

I was too tired to think; that was the problem. I hadn't gotten a good night's sleep in so long, and this chair was so comfortable, and there was no baby here demanding my attention. My chin nodded onto my chest, and my eyes closed. I felt the papers slide from my grasp and hit the floor.

Something warm folded around me. Rika's hands smoothed a soft knitted throw into place, tucking me in as if I were a child. I made a mumbled incoherent noise, half protest, half thanks. It was nice, but I needed to get up and get back to work. Lives were at stake.

"Shh." Rika's warm lips touched my hairline.

My thoughts swirled in a jumble of silvery Echo light and

ink-stained apologies. Then they blew out the window into the dark and waiting sea.

I couldn't have slept long. Not more than a few hours. But it was enough.

I woke to Rika whispering my name.

Other information filtered through the clinging barrier of sleep: I wasn't in my bed at home. There were raised voices in the distance, sounding upset. My neck was stiff from sleeping in a chair, but not because I'd fallen asleep nursing again—Emmi wasn't here, an absence that sent prickles of alarm up arms that expected to be holding her. But it was Rika's tone that riveted my attention and shredded any remnants of sleep—the quiet urgency in it, deadly serious.

I sat bolt upright, heart slamming against my ribs, pulling my knife from my belt because my swords were in too much of a sitting-down tangle. Rika drew back, the grey-gold light of a cloudy dawn falling full across her face. I stared at her in muzzy confusion.

"Rika? What's happening? Who's yelling?"

"Get up, Kembral. There's bad news."

That woke me up. I was standing in an instant, blanket and papers forgotten on the floor, knife still in my hand because she hadn't told me to put it away.

"What is it?"

"I'm sorry. I don't know how to tell you this." Her voice went hesitantly, terrifyingly gentle. "Signa Overfell is dead."

"Mareth? *Fuck.*" I sank back onto the edge of the chair, stunned. "But we were supposed to have until tomorrow night before the Deepwolf came back! It wasn't supposed to—"

She laid a hand on my shoulder. It felt like a warning.

"The Deepwolf didn't kill him. He was murdered."

SET YOUR FEELINGS ASIDE

Dawn hung pale and miserable over the Lovegrace mansion. I hated the dingy light that filtered in through the shrouded windows, hated the peeling wallpaper in the halls I stomped through toward the drawing room, hated everything about the moldering old house that had eaten my friend.

I didn't want to be a Hound right now. The last thing I needed was to investigate my friend's murder. I wanted to kick things and scream and tear this house down and throw the scraps into the sea. But feeling things about Mareth's death was a terrifying prospect; it was easier and safer to slip into professional emergency mode and cram it all down into the same little bottle I'd packed full of excitingly awful happenings during the year-turning.

I'd spent the last two months slowly emptying that bottle and working through the pent-up tangle of raw, terrible emotions, but apparently I'd just been making room for more trauma. *Fantastic.*

My mood was a black cloud around me as I stepped into that same awful drawing room with its gloomy wood paneling and that despicable podium (now shoved into a corner) and only ashes in the hearth. I was ready to hate everyone and everything, because some jackass had decided to make this bad situation infinitely worse with a bit of selfish, senseless murder and had taken my friend from me.

Everyone was there already; I was the last one up. Never mind that I usually woke every time Emmi's breathing changed—I was apparently exhausted enough to sleep through an actual murder. And, it became immediately apparent, the ensuing drama.

There in the center of the room stood Jaycel Morningray, tears streaming down her face, sword out, its gleaming tip pointing accusatorily from one terrified face to another. *Of course.* Ready to help the situation with more fucking murder.

"Which of you did this?" she demanded. "If you'll kill a man in his sleep, I invite you to try me wide-awake, or have the whole world know you for a coward!"

"Easy, Morningray," Amistead began, like he was calming a riled-up horse.

"It's too late for *easy*," she retorted. "Some bloody-handed villain decided to make this hard. And by the Moon, if we're making this hard, I'm ready to call it steel and put an edge on it."

"Jaycel, stand down," I barked.

She whirled to face me, sword tip dropping, eyes wild with anguish. "Kembral! Did you hear what they did? Did you hear what these bastards..."

She sucked in a choked breath, unable to continue.

"I heard," I growled. "I'm here. We'll find out who did this. Sheathe your sword, Jaycel. You don't even know who to fight yet."

"When I do," she promised, "the Void itself will tremble at my vengeance."

She slid her gleaming blade back into its sheath, its tip unsteady enough she almost missed the opening. Vy jumped up at once and threw her arms around her; I half expected Jaycel to push her away, but she held Vy tight, head bowed over her shoulder. I had to look away. I needed to be a Hound, clear-headed and professional; I couldn't burst into tears right now, no matter how much my chest hurt.

"Signa Thorne!" Amistead rose from his chair with evident relief. "Thank the Moon, a Hound is here to get this situation under control."

THE LAST SOUL AMONG WOLVES

"Have you sent for the watch?" I asked no one in particular.

Vy's head lifted, and she stepped back from Jaycel. Tears streaked her cheeks, but her eyes were clear. "They're coming. Petras sent me to get them right away. The tide was almost out, so I ran across the sandbar. I didn't want to wait for an investigator, so I ran back ahead of them—but they should be here soon."

I noticed that *almost*. Pretty brash to cross the sandbar while the tide was still flowing across it, especially when it might be full of dangerous Echo flotsam—but I supposed Vy knew these waters, and she'd always been brave. The investigator would likely be more cautious, so I had to assume this murder was my responsibility until the watch arrived.

Which meant I couldn't look at Vy and Petras and Jaycel as my grieving friends. Everyone in this room had to be a suspect. Void below, I hated this.

"Who found him? Has anyone messed with the scene?"

"I found him," Vy said, her voice shaking. "I woke up when I felt the wolf come through the portal, and—"

"Wait." My heart froze. "The wolf?"

"I was going to tell you," Rika said, subdued. "Apparently after he died, the wolf came for his soul, even though it wasn't time yet."

"Blood on the Moon."

I should have figured that death would be no escape from this sadistic Echo game. Apparently if someone managed to die before the deadline, the curse would still take its due.

Which in this case was Mareth's soul.

"It was awful," Vy whispered.

I took a sharp, ragged breath and let it out slowly, trying to release the feelings threatening to overwhelm me, as if I were venting poison.

"The wolf," Glory whispered huskily, clutching a delicate lace shawl around her shoulders. She clearly hadn't had time to perform her morning toilette and had the look of a magnificent but slightly wilted flower. "If it came ahead of schedule...do we know when it will come again?"

Silence fell. A hollowness filled the moment when Mareth should have answered. I could almost hear the abacus beads clicking. Would it still come two days after Regius's death, so we'd have a day and a half left? Or did this reset the clock? If the time was halved again, the Deepwolf would return tomorrow morning instead of evening. We might have lost half a day.

"That's a good question. We'll contact the Raven guild and find out." I tried to sound calm, assured, like it was just an interesting math problem. "So...Vy found him. Then what?"

There was a heavy pause. At last, Petras volunteered, "A few of us were awake at that point. I sent Vy to get the watch, then closed off the room. No one's been in there since."

The Hound part of my brain clinically noted that Vy had had time alone with the scene, and Petras might have as well. I was going to have to include that in my report to the city investigator, much as I didn't want to. This was why Hounds weren't supposed to work on cases involving people close to us. Until the watch got here, however, I had to do my best.

"Did anyone hear anything last night? Or notice anything unusual?"

Willa lifted her chin. "Oh, I heard *plenty*."

Every head swiveled to stare at her.

"I heard a bunch of rowdy trespassers stealing *my* aunt's liquor, tromping about *my* family's house, and tarnishing *my* cherished childhood memories with their brash drunken presence."

"*I* heard a whiny, entitled bitch complaining about trivialities while my friend was dead," Petras snapped.

I held up a hand before they could escalate to shouting, or Jaycel could reach for her sword again.

"This isn't the time," I barked. "Focus. *After* that. Once everyone went to bed. Did you hear anything coming from Mareth's—from Signa Overfell's room?"

Willa twisted her hands together. "I did wake up, in the middle of the night. I might have heard a thump. And then the stairs—they always did creak awfully. I assumed it was those hooligans staggering around—they were up until *all* hours of the night, a complete disgrace."

Jaycel blew her a kiss. Willa recoiled, looking about ready to double today's number of murders.

Vy straightened in her chair. "I heard that, too! The steps creaked late at night, really loud. I had almost finally drifted off—it's hard to sleep on land—and it kept me awake." She frowned thoughtfully. "They creaked a couple of times, in fact. I'm not sure how far apart. You know how time gets funny when you're almost asleep."

"Interesting. Did anyone else hear anything?"

Amistead shook his head. "Not a thing. But then, my hearing isn't what it used to be, and I was on the ground floor."

Glory tilted her head pensively. "I didn't hear anything, but I *felt* something." Her answer washed over me in a warm wave; I had to concentrate to focus on the words instead of basking in her voice. "My room was at the top of the stairs, and I felt that horrible icy draft that always comes in when someone opens the outside door." She shivered, perhaps with a touch of additional drama. "It took me a while to get back to sleep after that."

"*Very* interesting." So either whoever had taken the stairs had gone outside—to dispose of something?—or we'd had an intruder. "Thank you, Signa Glory. Did anyone else notice anything unusual or out of place?"

Willa gave a disdainful huff. "One of the decorative axes was missing from the hall. And they've completely disarranged the drawing room. Not to mention the matter of my aunt's liquor cabinet."

Amistead chuckled at that, earning a glare from Willa.

"Good to know about the axe. Anyone else?"

Petras frowned. "I don't know if this is relevant, but...My window looks out toward that rift in the Veil. It seemed really active last night—lots of flickering and glowing." He winced. "I had a headache, and it made it hard to fall asleep."

Rika gave me a significant look. She'd had that bad feeling last night. I wasn't sure whether the thought that it might have been due to high Echo activity in the area was alarming or a relief.

"Maybe an Echo killed Signa Overfell," Amistead suggested, his usually merry eyes solemn. "Especially this close to the ocean; it's full of horrors. In my navy days, I knew a man who lost half his old crew to something that crawled inside the captain while the tide skimmer had the ship down an Echo. Came out of his mouth in a mess of tentacles back in Prime and killed them all."

Glory gave a polite little grimace; Vy put her hands over her mouth.

"Wouldn't *that* be convenient, to blame it on an Echo," Petras muttered.

"It's not impossible." Stars, I'd love nothing better than for it to turn out we had some horrible Echo wandering around murdering people. That would be a straightforward problem that I knew how to solve.

Vy shook her head. "I don't think it was an Echo."

"Oh? Why not?"

"Well...I have a tide skimmer on my ship. I've seen what Echoes can do." She'd gone a little green. "I'm the one who found him, and...this looked more like what humans do. It was...simple? It was done with a weapon. And you get a feel for it, when you go down an Echo so often—there's a tingle in the air, you know?"

I nodded. I knew.

"And there was none of that." She shrugged uneasily. "It's hard to pin down. I'm sorry. But if you go look, you'll see what I mean."

The last thing I wanted to do was look. I cleared my throat. "Does anyone else have anything they haven't mentioned yet? Noises, Echoes, people acting strangely?"

Glory laughed, not kindly, her voice molten gold. "Everyone in this house has been acting strangely from the start, Signa Thorne. How could I tell?"

"Good point." I drew in a breath. "All right. We know *some* kind of killer is on the loose. It could be an Echo, it could be a stranger hiding on the island, or it could be one of you. I don't want anyone to go anywhere alone. In fact, I don't want anyone to leave this room until the investigator gets here."

Jaycel drew herself up and glared around with tear-reddened eyes. "Whether the monster who did this hails from this world or another,

Kembral will find them," she declared. "If it was someone in this room...pray to the Void to take you, because it'll hurt less than what I have in mind."

Glory's stunning, liquid voice dropped into the tense pause that followed Jaycel's words. "Oh, I think we all know who did it."

Everyone turned to look at her. She sat rigid, eyes flashing, jaw taut with hurt or anger.

"Do we?" Vy asked, with evident surprise.

Glory lifted an arm with the precise, sweeping grace of a master performer and leveled it like a sword at Petras. "We have it from his own lips. He asked whether the last one alive would inherit the wish if he killed all the rest."

Petras stared at her in shock and naked anguish, like she'd run him through. Then his expression shuttered. His posture went stiff, his gaze icy.

"That's not what I said."

Willa leaped from her seat. "Close enough! Why would you ask that question if it wasn't to decide whether it was worth your while to murder us all?"

"Now, now." Amistead lifted his hands. "I'm sure there are many other reasons. The spirit of inquiry, perhaps."

"We are *not* going to jump straight to accusations," I snapped. "We're going to do this *right*."

Willa sank back into her seat with a sniff. "Do as you wish. Signa Glory is right, though—we all know what you're going to find."

"*I* am not going to find anything. The *investigator* is going to find the murderer. And *we* are not going to sling blame at one another, all right?"

It came out too angry. Petras looked miserable, still staring at Glory as if she'd ripped out his heart and was eating it in front of him. I didn't think he was the murderer—if *he* were going to kill somebody, he wouldn't give himself away by acting so suspicious, for one thing. But I couldn't jump to his defense while I was the Hound on duty. Until I handed this case off, I had to treat him like any other suspect.

The silence stretched. Everyone stared at one another, mouths sealed but accusations flying around the room in silence like invisible knives.

The door banged open on a stiff damp breeze, and the clunk of booted footsteps sounded in the foyer.

"Investigator Duran Camwell," came a tired bass voice. "I hear there's been a murder."

"Finally," I breathed. The watch was here.

LET THE WATCH HANDLE IT

Duran Camwell had a harried, rumpled look and about fifteen concentric layers of bags under his eyes. We'd worked together before; he was competent, and handing the scene off to him was a huge relief. There was nothing I wanted less than to be in charge of this investigation. Camwell had an assistant with him, a fresh-faced kid who couldn't have been more than twenty in a dripping camel-brown coat with sodden dark curls. I had a suspicion he was mostly there as muscle.

"All I've done is ask a few questions," I told Camwell after filling him in on the basics as he shucked off his coat in the foyer. "You got here fast."

"Not as fast as that woman who came to get us." Camwell shook his head in awe. "I'm a local boy, and let me tell you, I'd never dream of sprinting across Echo-infested waters with the tide flowing out across the sandbar at the rate it was going. We waited until it was ankle deep, and I still had to dodge some kind of fucked-up floating mouth orb from that hole in the Veil."

His assistant grimaced and nodded vigorously, presumably in case I had any doubt about the veracity of the mouth orb, which I didn't.

"The woman would be Vy," I said. "She's a local, too, but she was motivated."

"I'll say. Anyway, better get to it. Are you up for advising on this one? We could pay the usual rate."

"I can't take this job. Mareth is—he was my friend."

"Oh, shit. I'm sorry."

"Yeah." My throat tried to seize up, but I forced my voice to come out as close to normal as possible. "I can maybe look around, tell you anything I notice, but—"

"That'll be enough," Camwell said quickly. "Nothing official. Just let me know any thoughts or observations you have."

I wanted to help. I was willing and prepared to help. But I struggled with the idea of examining Mareth's body and seeing firsthand whatever violence had been done to him. Right now my delicate balance depended very much on not quite admitting to myself that he was dead. We were supposed to get lunch at the noodle shop in Guildhouse Square, damn it.

Camwell must have seen some of that on my face, because his expression softened.

"Listen, why don't you write up your report on everything you've got so far while we go look at the scene. I've got a team coming right behind us to take care of the body. You can come look when they've done their work and gone."

I nodded, grateful. "Thanks for understanding."

I knew the others were watching us through the open drawing room door, trying to overhear what we said. I could feel their eyes on me, anxious for some reassuring sign. But I didn't dare look back. If I caught Vy's gaze, or saw Jaycel's tear-streaked face, or glimpsed any sign that Petras was starting to crack around the edges, I'd lose it right here in front of Camwell. So I crossed to the music room instead, settling down to write my report on the lid of the pianoforte.

I sat there at the bench, staring at the blank paper, hands trembling too much to pick up the pen. *Mareth.* This couldn't be real. He'd been so alive just a few hours ago. Surely there was some mistake, and he was puttering around in the lantern room with the relics, excited about some new horrible discovery.

But no. I'd fallen asleep on the job, and he was dead.

Rika slipped into the room, like smoke sliding up a chimney, and closed the door behind her.

"Are you all right?" She came up behind me and put a hand on my back, which made me realize it was tensed hard as a rock.

"No," I admitted. "But thanks for asking."

She wrapped her arms around me as if draping a shawl tenderly around my shoulders, wreathing me in the scent of honey and cloves. The sheer gentleness of the gesture broke something in me. All of a sudden hot tears gushed down my cheeks in a messy, salty flood. Sobs tried to bubble up from my chest, but I throttled them, hunching over as if I could physically crush them back down into the overflowing bottle inside me.

Rika started to pull back, as if afraid she'd somehow burned me, but I held on to her in desperation. She leaned in then, her breath stirring my hair.

"I don't know what to do, Kembral." There was a suppressed note of panic in her voice, verging on wild, nervous laughter. "All I know about comforting people is how to do it insincerely, as a con artist, and that doesn't seem appropriate."

"You're doing fine."

We stayed like that a moment as I fought back the tears and my breathing steadied, her warmth and her scent around me. Finally, I let her go.

"It's...it's all right. I've got this." I scrubbed viciously at my face. *Later.* I was on the job. People were depending on me. I'd deal with it later. "Sorry."

"For what? Having feelings?"

"For wasting time we don't have on them."

Her warmth slid reluctantly away as she released me. That was fine; I needed to strap the job tight around me like armor, to protect every soft and messy and wounded part of me so I could function. I'd failed Mareth, too exhausted from taking care of Emmi to see any signs that could have saved him, or to be awake and alert when he needed me most; I wouldn't do it again.

I turned on the bench to face her and found her staring at me like I was some strange Echo that had appeared from the deep.

"It's all right," I told her again. "I can do this."

"I know you can. It's concerning, frankly."

"Talk to me about the case," I said, unable to keep the last remnant of a quaver from my voice.

"If you're sure." Her brow still furrowed, as if she wasn't convinced this was a good idea. "Who do you think did it?"

"It's too early for that. I need to gather evidence. Everyone's got a powerful motive, with a wish and their lives at stake. And there's our mystery squatter, too."

"Well," she said lightly, "at least you know it's not Jaycel. If she killed someone, the whole city would know about it."

"True." I dragged a sleeve across my eyes. "I really don't want to think it was *any* of my friends. It's been a long time since I've seen Vy or been close to Petras, sure, and they've changed, but...it's hard to believe they could've changed *that* much. I can imagine some of them killing a person in the right circumstances, yes, but not like this. And not Mareth."

Rika frowned. "Mareth is an odd choice for anyone. Ravens are well protected and potentially dangerous. If it was just a matter of eliminating competition for the wish, there are easier targets. Besides, he was the one with the best chance of figuring out how to keep everyone alive. He'd be my *last* choice."

The truth of that hit me with sudden, cold clarity. "Unless you didn't *want* him to figure out how to keep everyone alive. Because you felt confident you could get the wish...or because you wanted the game to play out."

"An Echo," Rika breathed. "Manipulating the game, keeping us from flipping the board."

"Or a pawn of one, yeah. We have to consider the possibility."

Our gazes locked, the words neither of us wanted to speak passing between us in silence. *Or an Empyrean.*

THE LAST SOUL AMONG WOLVES 119

As I finished writing up my report for Camwell, I tried to think through all my possible suspects in a rational manner. Even if there was an Echo—or, Moon forbid, an Empyrean—behind this, they probably had a human accomplice. There'd been no further sign of the mystery trespasser lurking around the island, so while that was a possibility, it was far more likely to be someone in the mansion.

Rika was right about Jaycel. I didn't feel bad crossing her off the list even if she was my friend. Same for Rika herself, for the opposite reason; she was a Cat, and when they killed it was done with absolute and consummate professionalism that simply wasn't on display here.

Vy...My instincts said no, both because of the sweet, fiercely loyal girl I remembered and the odd but seemingly harmless woman she'd become. But she'd found the body, which could be a warning sign, and she *had* been acting strangely. I couldn't imagine her doing it, but I couldn't rule her out, either.

The same went for Petras. It seemed impossible that one of my friends could have killed another, but I had little doubt he'd be capable of murder if he had a powerful enough reason. With his father's soul and his own at stake, who knew? His family might have some connection to the relics, or to Echoes behind them. His mysterious source might even be the mastermind behind everything, manipulating him to do their sinister will.

It was easier to think of the other three as suspects, without the cloud of childhood affection muddling things. Willa had made no secret that she wanted us all out of her aunt's house, and that she saw the wish as rightfully hers. Amistead's name had gotten entered in the book late, under suspicious circumstances, and as a former City Elder he was no stranger to deadly power struggles.

Glory had certainly made it clear that she'd go to dramatic lengths for her career—how much would she do to preserve her own life? Her accusation of Petras seemed to come out of nowhere, and might be a gambit to cover up her own guilt. Plus there was that desperate whisper I'd heard her utter on the stairs: *No, he won't do it. I won't let him.*

Right now she was seeming pretty suspicious. If I was being honest with myself, though, any one of them could have done it.

Camwell rapped on the music room door and poked his head in.

"They've removed the body. Do you want to come look at the scene?"

No. No, I did not.

I sighed. "All right. Let's get this over with."

Camwell took me up the stairs (which creaked quite loudly, on cue), then halfway down the hall of guest bedrooms. I braced myself, my whole body clenching around my spine, as he opened a door no different than the others—aside from the nightmares behind it.

I was spared the sight of my friend's lifeless body, at least. But the blood sprayed across the pillow was enough. The tangle of sheets and blankets as if he'd thrashed in pain, the pool of more blood on the tapestry rug...It was all more than enough. The antique display axe lying on the floor, crusted in yet more blood—now, that was too much.

I turned away from it, scanning the rest of the room first, forcing myself to note details. Mareth's silver jewelry and pile of amulets lay carefully arranged on the nightstand next to an overturned glass and a scrap of paper with a name scrawled on it: *Signa Zarvish, third floor.* There was a fat leatherbound book, too—*Realities as Chords: Jarlekin and Hodge's Theories of Harmonic Echo Working.* Some light bedtime reading. Oh, that was so like him.

I had to close my stinging eyes a moment. Damn it, I was a Hound. I tried to force on my usual professional calm, but it fit like a shirt that had shrunk in the washtub.

"No footprints in the blood," I muttered when I opened my eyes again. "Rug is rucked up. Probably jumped back out of the way and dropped the axe."

"Makes sense," Camwell agreed, too quickly. He was watching me all doe-eyed, like it was some great privilege to work with a senior Hound. Never mind that I felt far more like a sleep-deprived mother whose friend had just been violently killed than a sharp-witted investigator right now.

THE LAST SOUL AMONG WOLVES 121

"Also, that axe is for show. It did the job, but it wouldn't be the choice of a professional. It could easily have broken off the haft in the act."

I crossed to the window; it was open a few inches, letting in a knife-blade of cold air. Thick dust and a scattering of dead bugs coated the sill.

I grunted. "I can't imagine Mareth would have opened this before going to bed, with it so cold out."

Camwell came over to peer at the window. "So the killer opened it? To climb through from the outside, maybe?"

"No smudges in the dust, so unless they vaulted through without touching the sill, probably not."

I finally took a closer look at the axe. Blood stained the blade, and the handle as well. I tried really hard not to think about whose it was. Dust still clung to the antique showpiece in places, and specks of rust pitted the blade. I checked for the marks of fingers in the bloodstains.

There—not in the blood, but in the dust that remained on the back of the handle. Impressions of a short segment of bumpy line—a seam.

"Gloves," I muttered. "So much for an Echo being the culprit." Nice as it would have been to pin the blame on an actual monster instead of a metaphorical one, this crime was looking far too human. I could see what Vy meant.

An idea was forming in my mind. I rose, starting for the door.

"Signa Thorne?" Camwell asked uncertainly.

"Walk with me. I need to check something outside."

We walked down a dismal hall past the lonely remaining axe, crossed with an empty pale spot on the wall, before descending the stairs. The steps creaked again, loud and sharp. I led Camwell out through the solarium side door and into the overgrown garden. Briars tangled everywhere, leafless and hungry with thorns. I paced along the side of the house, squinting up to find Mareth's window.

There it was, just a few inches ajar. A bed of dead rosebushes sat beneath it. I poked through them, but didn't find what I was looking for. What I *did* find was a footprint in the wet ground. Nothing I could use to identify someone—it was in soggy grass, not mud, and far too soft and blurred to pick out details—but it told me enough.

I stood beside the footprint and scanned the grounds, lingering on the fancy stone garden house and the run-down potting shed, trying to imagine everything shrouded in night. Where would I—*ah*. There.

"What are you looking for?" Camwell asked, following close at my side as I strode over to an ancient rusted wheelbarrow full of moldering leaves.

"The killer threw something out that window, then came outside to retrieve it. I'm hoping they hid it in the garden instead of taking it back into the house with them or heading all the way down to the sea."

Sure enough, the wet scraps of leaves in the wheelbarrow had been disturbed, their decomposing undersides showing in a few places. It probably hadn't seemed nearly so obvious at night. I dug through the leaves until my fingertips touched something else: soft leather.

Everything was terrible, but the hot little thrill of discovery still felt so good. I'd missed it.

Carefully, I pulled my prize out of the decomposing leaves: a bloodstained glove.

Camwell sucked in a breath through his teeth. "Wow."

I handed the glove to him, then dug around until I found another. They were slim and finely made of good soft leather, but somewhat worn, starting to come apart at the seams.

And they were a distinctive powder blue—an exact match for the smart tailored jacket of Willa Lovegrace.

OPPORTUNITY DEMANDS ACTION

For an instant, all I felt was relief. Thank the Moon, the murderer wasn't anyone I liked. Close on its heels came a wash of shame for feeling that, mingled uncomfortably with fury at Willa for killing my friend.

But no. This wasn't proof. Anyone could put on a glove. It sure did look suspicious, though.

"These are Willa Lovegrace's gloves," I told Camwell. "I saw her take them off last evening."

He whistled. "That sorts it, then."

"Does it?"

"Of course." The energy of discovery lit his face. "Lovegrace wore the gloves to keep telltale bloodstains off her hands, then threw them out the window to dispose of them. Then she realized the color was a giveaway and came out here to hide them better."

It made sense—it was more or less what I'd been thinking when I followed the trail out here, in fact—but it left too many questions unanswered. Why would Willa bring up the creaking stair if she didn't want to draw attention to the evidence in the garden? Why choose Mareth as her target? I had no doubt she probably *wanted* to murder all the interlopers in her aunt's house and claim the wish, and it was temptingly easy to put the blame on someone so unlikable. But everything was pointing toward some clever manipulator who was working with Echoes, and Willa didn't seem the type.

"We don't know it was her. Not for sure—not on just on one piece of evidence." I grimaced and added, "Sorry. You're the investigator. Don't mean to tell you your job."

"No, you're right. The magistrate will want more. But I'd wager we've got our killer." He gingerly took the glove.

"Are you going to arrest her?" I asked, uneasy.

"Given the circumstances, and the likelihood that the killer will strike again, I'm inclined to. If it turns out she's innocent, we can release her."

I was about to agree when the full implications sank in. "If you take Willa Lovegrace out of this house, it's a death sentence." I explained to him about the relics, and how with all its other targets staying safe inside, the Deepwolf would come for her, kill her, and take her soul.

"Stars, that's sick." Camwell chewed it over for a moment. "Still, if we're reasonably sure she's the killer...do we really want to put innocents at risk to protect her?"

There would be a certain tidiness to it. Arrest Willa, and the Deepwolf would come for her instead of the others. My friends would all be safe for a while longer, giving us time to figure out how to break the curse. Mareth's murder would be avenged...maybe.

Or an innocent woman would be killed.

"We can't just say 'Oh, she's probably guilty' and haul her off to get her soul ripped out in jail. Even if she turns out to be the murderer, it doesn't feel right." I paused, then added, "I mean, that's my thought. You're the one in charge here. I'm just a Hound."

Camwell sighed. "A Hound with valid points. You're a woman of honor, Signa Thorne."

I blinked. That was a unique way to say annoyingly stubborn.

"I'll have her confined to her room, though," he added. "I don't want to take any chances."

THE LAST SOUL AMONG WOLVES

Willa, predictably, did not respond quietly as Camwell bent to murmur in her ear, his assistant flanking her with his hand resting near his sword.

"What?" She scowled at him. "On what grounds?"

Everyone in the drawing room went very still; only a few of them pretended not to stare. I stood awkwardly nearby, trying not to look like I was ready to tackle her to the ground if she tried to run, which of course I was. I might have my reservations, but there was a good chance she was guilty, and I'd be damned if I let Mareth's killer get away.

Camwell muttered something about gloves, and "just a precaution."

Willa crossed her arms, remaining stubbornly in her seat. "This is nonsense. I left those gloves in the foyer with my coat; anyone could have taken them. Someone is trying to kill us all! You should catch them, instead of wasting your time harassing me."

Camwell gave up trying to be discreet. "Nonetheless, given the circumstances, please come with us."

"Am I under arrest?"

"Not yet, but if you won't accept a temporary confinement in your quarters, you absolutely can be."

"This is outrageous!" Willa glanced around, realizing that no one was going to leap to her defense. Her face crumpled. "You believe him, don't you? You all believe him!"

Jaycel rose, putting her hand on her sword hilt. "I believe him enough to offer you an alternative to prove your honor, if not your innocence."

Willa drew away from her in clear alarm, eyes wide. "Excuse me?"

"Jaycel," I said warningly, "leave it to the watch. She could be innocent, and she's not exactly a duelist."

"I'll fight her left-handed."

Camwell cleared his throat. "For your own safety, Lovegrace. If you're innocent, we'll let you go with apologies."

Willa scrambled to her feet, putting the assistant's young muscles between her and Jaycel. He looked a bit alarmed at this development.

"Well, fine!" She dusted off her dress in an overly aggressive fashion. "I didn't want to remain in such horrible company anyway. I'll just sit in my comfortable room and read a book and wait for you all to *die*."

She swept off toward the stairs, leaving the investigators scrambling to catch up.

Jaycel whirled on me, fire in her eyes. "Did she do it? I won't let her cowardice stand in the way of justice if she did."

"I'll cheer you on," Petras growled.

Glory had turned her face to the window, studiously avoiding looking at Petras. But I could tell she was listening.

I lifted a hand. "We don't know for sure. We found some clues that point that way, and the investigator just wanted to be careful."

"That means she did it," Vy declared. Then, less certain, "Doesn't it?"

"It means we don't know," I insisted. "We may not know for a while, because we've got more important things to do right now than make an exhaustive search for more evidence. If that reset the clock, the Deepwolf could be back in less than twenty-four hours."

"I'd rather not have to worry about getting a dagger in my back in the meantime," Petras murmured, fingering his cuff in a way that made me suspect he had a knife up his sleeve.

"That's why Camwell is locking her in her room," I said pointedly. "He's using an Echo-worked lock, so she should be secure in there. But the murderer could still be free. Stay in groups for your own safety, and shoot the bolts when you go to sleep."

"Bah. We can sleep when we're dead." Jaycel waved off such trivial human needs. Having an antagonist seemed to have revived her spirits. "If someone tries to murder me, I'll be delighted to have a problem I can solve with violence. Sadly, this curse appears to be vulnerable neither to my rapier wit nor my actual rapier, which is deeply aggravating."

Petras caught my gaze and then glanced to Rika, brushing at his already flawless waistcoat. "Speaking of the curse, can I have a quick private word with you and Signa Nonesuch? It's urgent."

Amistead raised his eyebrows. "Aren't we supposed to stay in this room? Investigator Camwell was *quite* clear on that."

"We can talk in the foyer," I suggested. "It's close enough. If Camwell gives you grief about it, Petras, I'll take the blame."

The three of us stepped into the foyer, sliding the wood panel door to the drawing room closed.

"First of all," I murmured, "I can't believe she turned on you like that."

Petras's gaze flicked away. He knew I meant Glory's accusation. "I can. Or at least, I can believe she did it *now*. The Silena I knew wouldn't have, and I thought at first maybe she still..." He shook his head. "But then she started brushing me off, and now this. I swear I didn't do anything to upset her—I've been giving her space."

I frowned, my instincts pricking. "She told me last night that she wanted to make things right with you. Any idea why she's suddenly decided you're a villain?"

He shrugged, a listless, defeated motion. "I can't guess. I don't know her anymore. People change."

There was so much heartbreak in that *people change*. "Is there anything—"

"I'm not here to talk about that. I've learned something important."

Rika's brows lifted. "Does this mean your mysterious source got back to you?"

"Yes." He ran a weary hand along the beard edging his jaw, which looked a bit less neat and sharp than it had yesterday. His eyes, always deep-set, seemed nearly lost in pools of shadow; he couldn't have gotten much sleep at all. "And I'm feeling a bit less positive about said mysterious source, I must confess. But I have information."

"Wait." I gave him a narrow look. "Your source got back to you in the middle of the night on an isolated island? Before or after the murder occurred?"

"Around the same time, given that I was reading the message when I felt the Deepwolf come through, but don't get excited. He didn't come here in person. He sent it with a...carrier pigeon." He grimaced. "At least, that's the closest thing I can think of."

"An Echo?" Rika asked, voice tight.

Petras nodded. "Weird round thing with six wings and one big eye, sitting there on my windowsill, talking to me in this creepy squeaky voice. I almost screamed. And before you ask, no, this is not how we usually communicate, but yes, I knew it was a possibility."

"Petras," I said slowly, "I'm going to need you to tell me a little more about this source of yours."

He hesitated. "I really can't. If I tell you, my information dries up, and I can't risk that—not with my father's soul at stake. Suffice to say it's an independent, uh, supplier who I've worked with for years. He has an excellent reputation."

"Supplier?" I realized what he probably meant. "Oh. Echo booze."

"Rich customers will pay a *fortune* for it, and it lends a certain prestige to my gambling halls," Petras agreed, modestly buffing a cuff link. "But it doesn't matter. The point is, he's slipped me information before, and it's always been good. I've never had a reason not to trust him."

"Until now," Rika said, with weary irony.

"Yeah." Petras sighed. "Until now. He's holding back. It's not like him. He must have known about the curse, and after our last conversation about how maybe someone could be targeting my family, I was pretty angry. So I sent him a message demanding to know what was going on."

"I'm guessing by your face that the answer you got was not entirely satisfactory."

"Yes and no. He said he couldn't explain, but he was sorry, and to make it up to me he'd give me some valuable information."

"And?" I prompted.

"I know how to break the curse."

"Well, damn, you should have led with that."

"We need to destroy the lantern." The look Petras gave me contained a desperate hope that cut right to my heart. "He said it's the crux of the curse. If we break the lantern, the whole thing unravels. The wolf leaves everyone alone, and all the trapped souls from previous rounds are freed."

Rika gave him a deeply skeptical look. "If your source is unreliable, how can we trust his information?"

"I happen to know he can't actually lie. Leave stuff out, sure, but not flat-out lie. It's . . . Well, it's an Echo thing."

THE LAST SOUL AMONG WOLVES   129

Ah. We'd been suspicious that there might be an Echo behind this mess, and here was an Echo, pushing Petras into the middle of it. An Echo who clearly knew way too much. I exchanged a long look with Rika.

"What do you think?" she asked me.

"It makes sense that the lantern is the key, if the souls are the power source. And it fits with the general awfulness of the whole situation." So well, in fact, that I'd lay down cold money it was the truth. The key to breaking the curse was in the mouth of a Deepwolf, five Echoes down, because of course it was.

She nodded warily. "I rather doubt it's the *whole* truth, however."

"Oh, absolutely not."

"And we don't know this Echo's motives in sharing this information."

"Right. He could want the lantern for himself, or have ulterior motives for wanting it broken, or be trying to get Petras killed. We just don't know."

But none of it changed the simple, compelling fact that this was something I could *do*. Something I could do better than anyone else in the whole city, in fact.

"The one thing we know for certain is that this is the way to free the souls," Petras said softly. He started to reach out toward me, hesitated, then finished the gesture and clasped my hand. "Kem. I know I haven't always been the best friend. I know I said I couldn't trust you not to snoop around, because you're a Hound. But it's exactly *because* you're a Hound, and my friend, that I can trust you with this. To help free my father's soul, and to save my life, and to not be secretly screwing me over."

I squeezed his hand, my eyes suddenly damp. "Thanks. That means a lot."

Almarah always said that there came a moment when you'd done enough research, and it was time to act. The tricky part was knowing when that moment came.

I rolled my neck to loosen up. "All right, that settles it. I'm going in."

—◊◊◊—

I glared at the mirror like an enemy. Its cloudy surface shimmered with a faint opalescent sheen, the light across it shifting more than the flickering candlelight would explain. The portal was still open.

Beneath the mirror, the book lay on its table. A fresh red slash glistened through Mareth's name, the blood not quite dry. The sight galvanized me with a cold fury.

"Kembral." Rika stood half a step behind me, warning in her tone. "I don't think you should do this."

I met her reflection's gaze in the mirror, keeping my eyes fixed on its silvery surface.

"I don't see that I have much choice. It's going to close soon, and we need the lantern to keep anyone else from dying. I've got to track the beast, see where it goes, try to grab the thing."

Her eyes narrowed. "I know you Hounds love to charge right in, but there's got to be some other way to do this. One that doesn't involve jumping into an unknown Echo with no idea what's on the other side of the portal."

"That's literally my job," I pointed out. "It's the first step of any Echo retrieval mission."

"This isn't just any Echo retrieval mission." Her tone sharpened into exasperated urgency. "For love of the Moon, Kembral—"

"Rika." I turned to face her at last. "I already lost one friend because I didn't solve this thing quickly enough. I'm not going to lose another."

She stared at me, her expression guarded, unreadable. Her shoulders twitched, and for a moment I thought she might actually try to tackle me. But something seemed to drain out of her, and she shook her head.

"Hounds! No sense of self-preservation. Fine. If you're dead set on going in, I'm going with you."

"You *hate* Echoes," I protested.

"Believe me, I haven't forgotten." Her jaw flexed. "It's for the job."

I gave her a long, considering stare. Rika was one of the few people I'd trust to come with me into an Echo and actually be helpful rather than just causing more problems. But going into Echoes was one of the few things that truly terrified her.

"You could quit the job." I softened my voice. "Let someone else take it."

Her gaze flicked away. "I'm also not letting you go in there alone."

"I go into Echoes alone all the time."

"Not since the year-turning, you don't."

Ah. That was why she was pushing so hard against this—and she had a point. A chill of foreboding tickled along my nerves. If word got out that I was wandering around down there with my veins full of priceless hope, every Echo for miles would come try to bleed me dry. A year ago I might have shrugged that off, but I had Emmi waiting for me at home. Personal danger weighed much more heavily on the scale of my decisions.

"Most Echoes don't know about the year-naming." I was trying to convince myself as much as Rika. "And they won't recognize me by sight. It shouldn't be any more risky than a regular trip into the Deep Echoes."

"Which I seem to recall you once told me was obscenely dangerous."

"Fair." I rubbed my forehead, wishing things could be easy for a change. She was right; any time I stepped into a Deep Echo I was putting my life on the line, and for Emmi's sake I shouldn't take that chance. But Mareth was dead. I couldn't let Jaycel, Vy, and Petras join him because I didn't do my job.

And this *was* my job—more, it was who I was, and who I wanted to be. The one who went places no one else could and saved those abandoned as lost. I didn't *want* to give that up, even for Emmi. I'd done this plenty of times before; I'd be cautious, and make sure I came home to her.

I let out a puff of breath. "All right. Let's play this safe."

I drew my dagger and set its tip against the glass. Rika's hand fell lightly on my back as if she were worried I'd dive right in and wanted to be ready to hold me back.

"Here goes," I muttered, and pushed.

There was a soft, yielding resistance at first, like I was pressing my knife into a block of cheese. Then it slipped through all at once, the surface of the mirror rippling like water.

I stopped just before the cross guard went in, held it there for a second as the mirror surface shivered around it, then pulled it out.

No marks or residue marred the blade. I poked the flat of it; not any hotter or colder than I'd expect. It seemed totally fine.

"So it's not instant annihilation to go through, at least," I concluded.

"Lovely," Rika said faintly. "That's reassuring."

"With the Deep Echoes, I'll take what I can get." I sheathed the knife. "Right, then. With a portal like this, sometimes you can stick your hand through, and sometimes it takes you entirely if you try, so let's be ready. We may or may not be able to return the same way. Are you *sure* you want to come with me?"

"Stars, no. There's nothing I want less. This is the most absurd sort of Hound behavior." She looked absolutely disgusted with herself. "But I'm coming with you anyway."

"If you insist. I'll go in first, and I'll throw something back through the portal if it works both ways."

I felt in my pockets. Instead of the familiar array of various useful Hound things that would have been there a year ago, I found Emmi's ring of play keys, a cleanup rag, and a baby spoon. Well, good enough. I pulled out the spoon.

"Don't step through until you see this come out of the mirror," I told her.

"Fine. Ugh, I can't believe I'm doing this."

I shot her a sidelong glance. "Are you *sure* you're sure you want to—"

"Shut up, Kembral."

"All right. I'm going in."

I faced the mirror and rested my fingertip against the cool glass.

There was that less-than-solid feeling, the sense that the hard metallic reality of the mirror's surface was negotiable. I pressed harder. A cool tingling started on my fingertip, then rushed up to my knuckle as I poked my finger through.

All at once, the world turned inside out, and took me with it.

WHEN THINGS GO WRONG, GET OUT

I was standing in a domed alcove, its rough walls painted a rich midnight blue, tiny twinkling lights set into it like stars. My palm rested on the cold flat surface of a mirror; it was circular in this Echo rather than oval, with an ornate silver frame. The mirror reflected everything behind me—the alcove opening onto streets that only vaguely resembled Southside, with chalky white buildings under a sky the delicate lavender of a winter twilight—but it didn't show me.

The alcove had a simple elegance to it, with the quiet celestial beauty of a Moon shrine, except for the delicate spiderwebs spun across the domed ceiling. More webs obscured patches of the star-scattered walls. I searched them warily for spiders, every nerve alert—this far down, spiders were bound to be bad news. But nothing seemed to lurk in the silvery strands.

Then it hit me, with the sharp urgency of an ice pick to the brain. Stars. Webs. *Fuck.*

Stars Tangled in Her Web. Rika's manipulative, terrifying, deeply malevolent Empyrean mother.

This was a trap.

It had all been a trap, since the beginning. *She* was the manipulative force whose outline I had glimpsed. This sort of indirect, elaborate scheming was exactly her style.

This was all Arhsta's web—and Rika was about to walk right into it.

I pushed against the mirror, frantic to stop her before she could come through. But the glass stayed hard and impermeable beneath my hand.

"Shit, no, don't—"

It warmed and softened, and for a brief instant I thought maybe I could go back after all—but no, it was a slim hand pressed against mine, palm to palm through glass that thinned to nothing.

I tried to shove her back into Prime, throwing the full weight of my body behind it. But the mirror went suddenly solid again, the unyielding impact jarring up my arm, and Rika was standing beside me.

She took her hand away from the mirror and gave me a curious frown. "What are you doing?"

"Damn it! I told you to wait for the spoon!"

"I wasn't going to let you go alone regardless, so I just came through. What is it?" She looked around, her body tensing beside me. "Are we in danger?"

"Of course we're in danger! We're five Echoes down!"

I whirled to put my back to her, heart pounding, searching for signs that I might be overreacting, that we might not be totally screwed. Maybe, just maybe, the appearance of Arhsta's symbols was a coincidence—maybe her influence had always been everywhere in the Echoes, and I was just noticing it now. But I didn't think there were a lot of coincidences where she was concerned.

The mirror alcove stood on a low hill in the midst of the city. Small, bone-white buildings spilled down the hillside below us like tumbled vertebrae, vaguely following the same pattern of little plazas and connecting streets that Southside did in Prime. Except for one thing.

Several blocks from the base of the hill, a castle reared up where

Lacemaker's Row should be. A castle of black marble, swathed in a haze of mist and veined in silver that glittered like stars.

"Kembral, calm down and—" Rika's breath hitched in her throat. She stared at the castle like it was an old and terrible enemy, all the warmth draining from her face.

"Do you know it?" I asked, my gut knotting. "It's *hers*, isn't it?"

"No." Rika's voice was a hoarse shredded remnant of itself. "It's mine."

Oh, that was so much worse.

"What..." I swallowed. "What do you mean, yours?"

"It's the one she made for me, when I was a girl. The same one." She whirled back to the mirror. "I need to get out of here."

She started scrabbling at the glass, her nails scraping it with the sheer panicked fury of a trapped animal.

"The way is closed. *Rika*. Stop that. We have to find another way back."

She grabbed my arms, eyes dark with terror. "You don't understand. That's the castle she kept me in when she stole me, all those years ago. Except it was smaller then, and in the first Echo. She sat me on a throne and called me a queen. But when I tried to leave..." She choked off, the past too terrible to utter, but I remembered the faint weblike scars that only the light of Echoes made visible on her skin.

"So we won't go there." I carefully folded her in my arms, against my frantically beating heart; she was rigid as a drawn blade. "We'll stay the Void away from it. I promise."

"Is that usually there? Have you... Have you seen that castle in this Echo before?"

"No," I was forced to admit. "But things change all the time down here."

"Then it's for me again." Her voice was high and breathless. "It's a trap. Or a message. Or—"

"Don't think about it." I didn't like this any more than she did, but she couldn't break down now—I needed her at her best. "Answer me this. Does Petras always turn to you for jobs like this? Is that something his contacts would know?"

"I..." Some of the wild horror left her gaze; it sharpened, wary. *Good.* "Maybe. Probably. Why?"

"Think for a minute." I hated to say this, but Rika was an adult, and it would do her no favors to protect her from the truth. "If you were hired to get the lantern, and the only way to get it is to go through this portal, and Petras found out about it from his dubious Echo source, and the portal takes you to the creepy castle your mom built just for you..."

"She is *not* my mother!" Rika snapped fiercely, followed by, "*Fuck.* It was a setup."

"I hate to admit it, but yeah, it looks that way. The whole thing, all the way back to the Echoes that killed Auberyn Lovegrace." I was on high alert, scanning our surroundings for danger, ready to blink step at the slightest provocation. "So we're going to be very careful, and we're going to get you back to Prime as quickly as possible, and then you can drop this job like a hot poker and never have anything to do with it again."

"You know it's not that simple. But you're right." Her whole body was trembling; she closed her eyes and took a deep breath, and it stilled. "When the job goes bad, you leave. We can figure out the rest later. Let's go—I don't want to be here one second longer than I have to."

"Just give me a minute to look around."

I stretched all my senses, trying to get a feel for what was happening in this Echo right now—what the rules were, what might be prowling abroad, what strange eldritch weather might be rolling in. Down this deep, an action as innocent as taking a step forward could mean our doom.

It looked absolutely nothing like the last time we'd been to the fifth Echo, when the whole city had been inverted in bottomless chasms. The only similarities I could spot were narrow dark cracks marring some of the streets. That might mean everything had shifted over the intervening months, or it could still be like that over near Marjorie's house; this deep, space and time could both work dramatic changes.

The Last Soul Among Wolves

The little bone-white houses I'd seen were, on closer examination, in fact made from hollowed-out, colossal bones. A few of them were definitely skulls; another might be a couple of cobbled-together pelvises or something. Whatever creatures they'd come from had been absolutely massive.

Bone houses were fine. I was more concerned about the vultures soaring in lazy circles above, which now that I squinted at them were *substantially* larger than regular vultures. Their feathers, beaks, and talons all had a dull metallic sheen, like tarnished brass, and looked wickedly sharp. The few people I spotted moving in the streets spread out below us—and the term *people* applied only loosely—all bore parasols marked with a sigil that looked a bit like a closed eye with a slash through it. Possibly to keep the birds away, but it might also mean there was some other kind of danger in the sky—killing rain, perhaps, or the rising Moon itself. Scents of rosemary and decay-rich earth wafted on the breeze. Everything was eerily quiet.

I pulled a loose hair from my collar and dropped it onto the paving stones in front of the alcove. Nothing happened. The ground felt solid when I poked it with a cautious toe.

"Stay close behind me," I murmured, and stepped out onto the street.

I felt a little lighter than I should, my step holding a bit of extra spring, and what looked like paving stones gave a brittle crunch beneath my boots—but that was it. I risked a glance up at the vultures; they didn't seem to notice us.

So far, so good. I released a long breath, then started moving at a firm stride, trying to project a confidence I didn't feel. You never wanted to look vulnerable in any Echo, and certainly not in a deep one.

Shining clusters of eyes peeped out from the dark windows of the bone houses, watching us. Rika stayed so close she might as well have been glued to my back. I wished the crunching of our footsteps didn't announce our presence quite so loudly, but nothing immediately terrible was happening.

Maybe this wasn't a trap. Or if it was, maybe it was of a subtler nature than the kind where you wind up instantly dead or stuck in a dark hole. Given the fear in Rika's face whenever she glanced toward the castle, Arhsta's trap might operate largely in her daughter's mind—which made me mad enough I had to forcibly remind myself that I couldn't afford to focus on anything but the moment right now.

We passed another shrine-like alcove, this one painted pure black. A humming noise emanated from a jagged crack in its floor; the instant it hit my ears, a sharp pain lanced through my head. Rika made a muffled noise behind me.

"Cover your ears," I warned her, teeth gritted, and pressed the heels of my hands over mine. The pain and the noise both abated a little. As we hurried past, I noticed a scattering of dead bugs around it, and the thin twisted corpse of something that looked too human to be a rabbit, half-covered by a ragged cloak.

"How do we find a way back to Prime?" Rika asked. "You do this all the time, right?"

"The Veil's usually thinner down by the river. But if we're lucky, we might find a way up an Echo sooner than that. You get a feel for it." I scanned around for any sign of edges that didn't quite match up, shimmers in the air, places where the light bended off true. "We can ask around, if we need to."

Rika glanced dubiously at the clusters of beady eyes staring at us from the windows. "Ask the local Echoes? Is that safe?"

"Not this deep, no."

"Fantastic."

The path split, one branch heading directly toward the castle. I took the other one. I led Rika around a shiny patch on the flagstones that looked almost like a slick of ice and might have been safe but maybe not, and dodged a misty tentacle that reached for us from one of the cracks in the ground. A pair of skeletally thin lizard-like creatures passed us in the street, walking on their hind legs, dressed in antique doublets with cartwheel ruffs and sporting those parasols. They eyed us with wary hunger, forked red tongues flicking out to taste the air in our direction.

The road bent, and suddenly the castle was in front of us again. It definitely shouldn't have been.

Rika's breath hissed between her teeth. I held up a hand to stop her, staring at the castle like an enemy whose fighting style I needed to assess. The giant vultures circled overhead, a little lower now.

"All right," I said warily. "Let's see what happens if we turn around."

We did, retracing our steps past familiar bone-white houses.

The castle waited for us around the bend, looming silent and taunting, closer than before. *Shit.*

Looked like we'd found the trap.

"What now?" Rika's voice was flat and even, brutally suppressed. I hated to think what that control must be costing her.

"We've got to find a way up to the fourth Echo before it catches us." Which was an odd thing to say about a building, but we *were* five Echoes down. "We're going to have to ask directions."

I scanned the street. The buildings here had gotten a little bigger, cobbled together from multiple broken plates and curves of massive crack-webbed, sun-bleached bone. Some of them looked like shops. One bore a sign that read CRUNCHY and had stands full of different kinds of beetles out front, displayed at an angle like produce, some with legs still waving. Another store with PIP'S SKULLS scrawled above the door had a round eye socket of a display window full of a wide variety of skulls—mostly animal, but some apparently human, straggling hair still attached. A few paces down a cross street, a cobbled-together stall made of slivers of bone and a sheet of half-rotted leather bore no sign but was hung with strips of unidentifiable raw meat, ragged and dripping blood.

"We could go find the tea shop again," Rika suggested. "That was nice."

"Too far. We wouldn't make it."

I headed for Pip's Skulls. I've never been enormously fond of bugs.

I ducked in through a ragged blowing curtain into a dim, low interior; I had to hunch a little to fit beneath the ceiling, and I wasn't exactly tall. Shops were usually relatively safe, since the proprietors would get no business if they weren't, but I still gave the place a thorough once-over before waving Rika in after me.

The bone walls curved in odd directions, following the extinct cranium of some enormous ancient beast, and skulls filled every nook and cranny. Countless empty eye sockets gazed accusingly at me. Some had leering jaws still attached, with tusks or razor-sharp rows of teeth or disturbingly white human smiles. A few had been worked into drinking cups, helmets, or other household items. The warm glow of candles flickered from within a handful of them, casting light and shadow through the claustrophobic space.

A rail-thin man with hollow cheeks and deep-set eyes rose from a vertebra stool to greet us, spreading a toothy smile. His head could have been a skull itself if it weren't for his great mane of dusty hair. He had an excessive number of fingers.

"Welcome, welcome. Buying or selling?" His voice scraped like a spade on rock.

"Pip, I presume? And neither, actually—we're looking for directions."

"Yes, Pip. Pip is the name." His tongue flicked out, forked and slender, tasting the air. "*Ah.* Are you perchance from Prime?"

I ignored the question, which unfortunately was answer enough. "We're looking for a thin spot in the Veil, going up. Do you know of any?"

A cunning light entered Pip's hooded eyes. "What will you give me if I tell you, then?"

I didn't dare offer him a drop of blood. Not only was it a bad idea to start with that in case Echoes got greedy, but if he somehow could sense that mine was extra tasty year-namer blood, we might get swarmed by locals seeking to do a little prospecting in my veins.

"How about a hair?" I offered. "Or maybe a joke? You look like you could use a laugh."

"Not good enough." He edged forward, eyeing the pulse in my throat. "I think you know what currency I'll take."

"I think you'll find you can't afford it," I retorted, letting my hand rest openly on a sword hilt.

"Oh, stop it. I can pay." Rika stepped up beside me, wearing a harassed frown. "Just one drop, and you'll give us exact directions to a usable rift in the Veil."

Pip's tongue flickered into view again. He took a half step forward, then stopped himself. "You're far down from Prime. Very far. You must want to get back rather badly."

"One drop," Rika snapped. "That's the only deal I'm offering. Do you want it?"

I tensed, ready to move. It was a risky deal to make when we still had an unknown distance to travel through a Deep Echo, but it was Rika's choice. I'd probably have offered the same if I dared. Hopefully he'd take it instead of deciding he could get a whole lot more blood by ripping us to pieces.

Pip considered, his eyes hungrily tracing the veins in our wrists and necks, then lingering on my sword.

"Your deal is acceptable," he said grudgingly. "Pay first."

He held out a hand, waggling his many fingers.

"Very well." Rika pulled out a knife as easily as if she did this all the time, though I was pretty sure she never had before. She pricked the heel of her thumb with the tip of her blade, so delicately she barely parted the skin. A single crimson drop welled up.

Pip stepped forward, tongue eagerly lapping the scent of her blood from the air.

"Just one drop," I warned him.

Rika held her hand above his. With clear reluctance, she squeezed her fist tight until the single drop fell on Pip's extended, quivering palm.

Where it touched the Echo's flesh, it gleamed with sudden brightness. He screamed.

Rika backed up, alarmed; I had my sword half out of my sheath before I realized it wasn't an attack. Pip gripped his own wrist, staring at his hand; a tiny mote of light glowed where Rika's blood should be. A slender thread of smoke rose from it.

Well, shit. I forgot that her blood was special, too.

"What is it? What have you done?" Pip screamed again, and this

142 MELISSA CARUSO

time it sounded more like terror than pain. "Ah! No! Blood of the stars! *Empyrean!*"

Without warning, he flung himself down on his knees, cowering before her.

"Forgive me, Celestial One!" he howled. "I didn't know! Have mercy!"

Rika gave me a lost, haunted look. "I...I don't..."

I stepped forward, glaring at him, pressing our advantage. "Tell the lady what she asked."

"Of course! Of course!" Pip lifted his head eagerly, then cringed again as if afraid this dared too much. "Toward the sun two blocks, then left on the street of the severed spine. There's a gap in the Veil another block or two ahead on the right, in the shrine of the broken fountain. Please, Celestial One, spare me! Do not destroy me for my hubris! I didn't know!"

Rika had recovered her composure. "Tell me one more thing. Did a Deepwolf pass this way recently?"

He covered his eyes. "I do not gaze upon the lantern-bearer! I am no fool."

"So you know it." I stopped myself from advancing on him farther; he was frightened enough. "Do you know where it went?"

"No. I do not look. I turn my eyes away, so it will spare me."

"How about the lantern?" Rika asked sharply. "Has anyone ever seen the lantern *without* its bearer?"

"No, Celestial One. I have heard of the bearer without the lantern, but never the lantern without the bearer."

Well, *that* was interesting. It sounded like the wolf brought the lantern back and forth to this Echo, but put it down somewhere. If we could find out where, we could get the lantern without having to deal with the Deepwolf.

If we retrieved it now, no one else would have to die. We *needed* that lantern. But Arhsta's involvement changed everything. If this was an Empyrean's trap laid for Rika, with the lantern as bait, it'd be beyond foolish to walk right into it. Doing whatever it took to finish the job was all well and good, but you couldn't finish it if you were dead.

THE LAST SOUL AMONG WOLVES

143

Rika's gaze flicked anxiously to the window, through which the distant black spires of the castle loomed above the rooftops in quiet mockery, then to me.

She drew herself up, giving Pip a regally disdainful look. "Your information is useful. I will not destroy you at this time. Come, Kembral."

She turned on her heel and left. I followed her, putting my body between Rika and Pip's hysterical gratitude so I could block the sight of her trembling hands.

Once we were safely out of earshot of the shop, her face crumpled from arrogance to disgust. "Moon above, I hated that."

"You did great."

"I told myself it was just another con. But it wasn't, was it?" She wrapped her arms around herself. "The con is me pretending to have regular red human blood in the first place."

"Hey." I touched her cheek. "First of all, you shouldn't be ashamed of being half Empyrean. It's pretty amazing. And second of all, it *was* a con. Not because you were pretending to be an Empyrean, but because you were pretending to be some arrogant Empyrean bitch."

Her mouth twitched. "Why, Kembral. Are you saying I'm not a bitch?"

"No, I'm saying you come by your bitchiness honestly. It's not a divine legacy, it's just your defective personality—ow!"

She'd pinched me in a tender spot under my bicep, but I was so glad to see her looking vexed rather than haunted I didn't even mind. Besides, I'd maybe deserved it.

"You're the one with a defective personality, voluntarily taking on a career that involves going to horrible places like this." She turned resolutely toward the sun, her shoulders rigid. "Come on. Let's get out of here."

We walked in wary silence. Eyes tracked us from the windows of the bone houses. The vultures wheeled a little lower, close enough that I could hear the brassy scrape and squeak of their feathers rubbing against one another as they angled their wings to catch the wind. They might be watching us; I couldn't tell.

144   MELISSA CARUSO

A trio of skull-faced birds in long grey robes approached us in the road. They loomed about seven feet tall beneath their parasols, ragged trains trailing behind them. Their gimlet eyes fixed on us; their long beaks uttered dry tutting sounds.

I didn't break my confident stride, intending to walk right past them before they could decide we were interesting. But they spread out with quick swaying steps, moving in eerie unison.

"Krraaaaak," one uttered.

"Kraaaaaak," the others repeated back in a chorus.

I gave them a cautious nod. "Hello."

Purple sparks kindled deep in the black hollows of the middle bird's eyes. With a certain slow, almost ritualistic grandeur, it furled its parasol, staring at me the whole time. One by one, the others copied it, the same sparks flickering into being, parasols folding up.

Oh, here it came.

"Kembral," Rika breathed. "What are they—"

She didn't get to finish. The light in their eyes flared, and all at once, the birds attacked.

DON'T LET THEM SEE YOU BLEED

The Echo birds moved with terrible speed and coordination, lunging toward me on long hidden legs. Bone beaks stabbed at me in sudden, vicious jabs that should have punched deep into my chest and throat, leaving me impaled three ways.

I slipped into the Veil just in time.

It was like a sudden catch of breath, the startled reflex Almarah had drilled into me. I jerked *up* and *away*, except that those weren't the right directions at all. Everything went golden and thick as honey; everything around me froze, including the three razor-sharp beaks stabbing for my heart.

I stepped to the side through the illusion of space and drew my swords. My longer right-hand one—the featherlight, swept-hilted blade Marjorie had given me—I stabbed down at an eye; my shorter left-hand one I jabbed up under a chin. I popped back into reality the instant before they hit, color rushing back over my senses, Rika's cry of alarm ringing in my ears.

Both blades struck home, punching through the less-real substance of the Echoes as if they were made of condensed mist. I jerked them free and danced backward, the ragged energy of adrenaline coursing through my veins.

The bird-skull creatures collapsed in a puff of tattered robes. They fluttered to the ground, empty.

The remaining one let out a dry hissing sound and backed away, opening its sigil-painted parasol to hold it up defensively, like a shield.

"I suggest you step aside." I tried to keep my voice even despite my quickened breath and racing heart. "Better yet, tell me first—did a Deepwolf with a lantern pass this way?"

I was peripherally aware of a few more figures gathering in the street to watch, keeping their distance. If they jumped in on the other side, this could get bad quickly. Rika fell in beside me, tense and ready.

The bird's skull dipped down toward its grey-robed chest. "So unfriendly, it is. We just wanted its blood."

"Answer me."

The creature's beak clicked open and closed, showing rows of sharp teeth. "Why should we tell it?"

"Because you attacked us. I'll overlook the offense if you tell me."

"Our friends, our poor friends!" It gestured dramatically at the puddles of tattered robe on the ground.

"They'll be back to normal in a day or two and you know it." Too many watchers were gathering. I had to end this. "Will you tell me or not?"

"Ahhh, it's so bossy! Fine, fine! The lantern-bearer passed into the castle. It always goes to the castle."

Void take it. That was *not* what I wanted to hear.

"Thanks." I sheathed my swords, more as a show of strength than because I harbored any illusions that the danger was over. "Have a good evening."

"It has *ruined* my evening!"

I gave it a *what can you do* shrug, gathering Rika with a glance and striding past the bird and the empty cloaks of its fallen companions. A motley assortment of passersby watched us under their parasols, beady eyes assessing us, strange faces tipped toward one another to whisper. One almost human-looking figure licked far too many needle-sharp teeth with clear hunger.

The Last Soul Among Wolves

No one followed us, which was good. But I didn't like how they watched us go.

"The castle," Rika hissed, as soon as we were past them. "That confirms it. She's behind this whole thing, wolf and relics and all. I should have known."

Fury seemed to have replaced fear in her voice, which was good. Rika was supposed to be a ruthlessly competent force of nature; if she was terrified, I was terrified. Even if I'd learned at the year-turning how much of her poise was a mask, and how much fear seethed beneath it. Sure, we were all like that inside—I pretty much assumed everyone I met who seemed to really have their shit together was a disaster beneath the surface—but seeing that careful facade crumble made a jittery alarm flutter up inside me. By comparison her anger was more familiar, almost comforting.

"I don't see what we could have done differently," I told her, keeping my voice low and my senses alert. "It's not like we could have backed out of this and let everyone die. If this is her web, she put bait in it we can't resist."

"That's what this is, then." Rika dug her fingers into her arms. "She's showing us her cards on purpose—flaunting that castle in my face, making it clear that she's involved. Because she knows we can't escape."

"If it's only that, I'll count us lucky."

There was bound to be more. Arhsta wouldn't let us get off so lightly. But I knew one thing for certain: There was no way under the Moon or in the Void I was going to let Rika get anywhere near that castle. I'd get her out of here if I had to fight every Echo in this reality to do it.

We found what I assumed was the street of the severed spine (there was a severed spine impaled on a spike at the corner, anyway) and turned onto it, navigating a narrow curving path between dwellings shaped like jagged broken teeth. One bore a sign with a picture of a bleeding hand; another had a mop leaning out front that looked like it was made with human hair. All relatively normal stuff, for the fifth Echo. Maybe Rika was right, and this phase of Arhsta's plan was just a show of strength, and we'd get out of here without too much fuss after all.

A massive shadow and a metal-scented breeze passed over us. Rika swore, grabbed my sleeve, and yanked me down halfway to a crouch.

One of the great brass vultures swooped *far* too close, its gleaming claws skimming only a few feet over where our heads had been. It veered up to circle above; its bright eyes fixed on us, keen and cruel.

My heart pounded wildly, feeling fragile in the brittle cage of my ribs.

"This is such absolute bullshit," Rika hissed, her fingers digging into my arm. "The worst creatures I should ever have to deal with on a guild job are guard dogs, and they're easy to bribe."

I gave a shaky laugh. "You don't carry snacks for giant murder birds in your kit?"

"I'm pretty sure we *are* snacks for giant murder birds."

We rose on unsteady feet and started moving again, as fast as I dared let us go.

Rika shot an alarmed glance skyward. "It's coming around to dive at us again. Can you fight that thing?"

"I mean, I can *fight* anything. It's whether I can win that's the question."

"Ha, ha. Give me a real answer, vulture bait."

I thought it through: one blink step minimum to get above it, another to get safely to the ground—assuming I could kill it quickly, which was far from guaranteed. And I'd just used a blink step a few minutes ago.

"Probably I can defeat one. *Maybe* two."

"There are four of them up there—no, five. Bloody Moon." Rika increased her own pace, her long legs striding faster than I could go without breaking into an undignified trot. "Should we run?"

"No! That'll bring every Echo for blocks down on us. We're almost—"

The sky darkened. A rush of downward wind and the whistly rasp of air through metallic feathers warned me in time to tackle Rika out of the way of the massive claws that ripped through the air where she'd just been.

We rolled in the dust, Rika's softness alternating with the cobbled hardness of the street. A line of pain burned across my shoulder blades.

I jumped up, swearing. "Did it get my fucking *coat*? This is *brand new!*"

"Kembral!" Rika was already on her own feet, reaching out to touch my back, eyes wide. Her fingertips came away red. "You're bleeding."

The world went still. Everything around me took on a strange sharpness and brightness as all my nerves came alive. For an instant I wondered if I was hurt more badly than I'd realized—but no, the cut stung, but it wasn't deep. This was something else.

Something far more dangerous.

Purple pricks of light kindled in the dusky windows around us, one after another after another. Several blocks away, a wild cry went up, a hunting call between a hawk's scream and a cat's yowl; in another direction, voices rose in a sudden warlike chorus.

Every vulture in the sky swiveled its naked head our way.

"Oh, *shit*," I breathed.

"Your blood." Horror stretched Rika's voice. "They can sense it."

"Okay, *now* we run."

I didn't wait; I broke into a sprint. It was me they were after. Did my blood on that vulture's talons mean its hopes of ripping me to pieces were more likely to be fulfilled? I had some on my back, too— I hoped as hard as I could that I could make it to cover. Almost at once, I spotted another alcove, like the one we'd emerged from.

A shadow fell over me. A gust of wind from massive metallic wings ruffled my hair.

In midstep, I slid between layers of reality like a knife, plunging into the liquid golden silence of the Veil. I didn't stop running, pushing my way through the eerie stillness of this non-space, but I glanced over my shoulder.

A vulture hung frozen in midstrike, right above where I'd

been—brass talons extended, tail fanned, the terrifyingly massive span of its wings caught in the delicate complexity of a braking beat. Another vulture, higher in the sky, poised at the brink of its own dive, and a third was approaching.

Rika, a few steps behind where I'd been, contorted herself in midstride to dodge away from the stooping talons, mouth shaping some obscenity. Part of me wanted to shout at the vultures that they were carrion eaters and shouldn't be doing this—but then, birds and lizards didn't walk around holding parasols, either. The Echoes didn't care.

The shrine was a long way to go in one blink step, and I wasn't sure I'd make it. Pressure built in me with each pounding heartbeat, the increasing burning need to return to reality, my whole being craving it like air. Five more strides...two...

I flung myself beneath the alcove's protective roof and back into the world, gasping. The line of pain across my back erupted anew, and a brassy shriek filled my ears.

The vulture, confused by my sudden disappearance, swooped up and away. Rika sprinted to join me, her black hair flying. I held my breath, desperately hoping they wouldn't all attack her now. They circled hungrily, calling to one another.

I glanced around, trying not to panic. The shrine was open on one side; it hid me from the sky and limited their approach, but nothing more. I'd bought myself maybe the minute it would take the vultures to figure out where I'd gone. If I even had that long—a ragged assortment of figures walked and crawled and slithered up the hill, emerging from the houses and joining a growing mob. All of them after my blood.

This was really, *really* bad. But that hole to the next Echo had to be close. I could feel its tingle on my skin.

Ah. As Rika dove panting and cursing into the alcove beside me, I spotted it.

This shrine had a similar construction to the others we'd seen, with a domed roof and a starry evening sky painted on its walls and ceiling. But it went a bit deeper than the one we'd emerged from, and

THE LAST SOUL AMONG WOLVES   151

in the back of it was a niche, sealed off with an iron grille, that held a small broken fountain. A crack split its simple marble basin, shearing it in two; at that divide, the air shimmered slightly, reality not quite lining up properly on either side.

Something had slashed the Veil here, probably long ago by the rust on the grille, and the locals had sealed it off for safety.

Which meant we couldn't get to it, either.

I whirled on Rika. "Can you get us through this fence?"

She looked it over, biting her lip. "There's no door, no lock to pick. We'd have to unseat it. Chip it out of the wall."

"You're a Cat! Surely you've got some secret way to get through a simple iron grate!"

"Sure! I have several ways! They all take time we don't have!"

The mob was getting closer, a sea of approaching parasols crested with a foam of purple sparks gleaming in hungry eyes. But they recoiled suddenly as a gust of wind blasted the dust from the cobbles in front of them. One of the vultures was landing.

A sick, cold certainty settled into my bones: They were going to tear me apart scrabbling over me. They'd spill my blood across the stones and then lick them desperately clean.

My glance fell on Rika's fingers, still stained red. No. There *had* to be a way out. If I understood how this worked, our situation *couldn't* be hopeless.

I grabbed Rika's shoulders. "You're half Empyrean. They can shape the Echoes."

She pulled away, looking ready to slap me. "Void take it, Kembral—"

"No, *listen*. I know you hate your mom and all, but you're not like her, and using your power won't make you like her. If you can—"

"But I *am* like her!" Rika hissed. "You don't know what I had to do, when I was little—to stay human, to survive. If I touch that power, it could undo everything—which is *exactly* what she wants. *This* is her trap. Did you notice the castle left us alone once we started heading here? Don't ask it of me."

She meant it. She was shaking, her hands curled tight with rage and frustration. There was some danger here that I didn't understand, some terrible edge we were skirting that I couldn't see.

I understood the things coming to rip me apart just fine. I didn't have time to unravel what was going on in that labyrinthine mind of hers.

"I don't see a lot of other options! Can you at least *try* to do something to those bars? I'm about to die in a really unpleasant way, here!"

Brassy talons touched down on the street; vast metallic wings rasped and shrieked as they furled. The mob retreated from the vulture, the ones in front lowering their parasols to aim the closed-eye sigils at it protectively.

Rika shook her head, eyes dark with panic. "I can't! Even if I *could* do it, I don't know how!"

Beady vulture eyes fixed on me. The creature began pacing with its stately gait toward us, its tail feathers screeching across the cobblestones.

A shadow fell over the mob. *Another* vulture was landing. I could blink step through the grille, but that would mean leaving Rika behind to face them alone, and there was no way I was doing that.

"Just try, Void take it!" I didn't wait for her, but grabbed at the bars and gave them a vicious yank. They didn't budge.

"*Fine!* Get out of the way."

I stepped aside. Rika drew in a breath so sharp and high it nearly whistled in her throat. Squeezing her eyes shut, she laid a slim, elegant hand on the rusty iron bars.

Nothing happened. She just stood there, perfectly still, face scrunched as if in pain, sweat forming on her temples.

The second vulture had touched down. They were getting closer, hunched low to see beneath the roof of the alcove, heads tilting back and forth to watch me with one eye and then the other. Metal beaks as long as I was flashed in the sun. They could each eat me in one bite, and they'd be here in seconds.

I took a shaky breath. "Rika, if I say run, can you—"

"Shut up, Kembral. I'm concentrating."

I shut up.

THE LAST SOUL AMONG WOLVES
153

There were three vultures now, and the first was almost at the shrine entrance. I forced myself to relax into readiness. I let go of most of my terror and stood poised on the edge of existence, ready to tip over it into the Veil. If I could kill one right in the entrance, that might block it and buy us a little more time.

Rika's eyes opened a sliver. Scarlet light seeped out between her lids. *Holy shit.*

The lead vulture had reached the edge of the alcove. It snapped its beak at me; the razor-edged nightmare maw came *way* too close, its hot metallic breath blasting my face. I stabbed at its open mouth. It snatched its head back from my blade, glaring.

I couldn't keep quiet any longer. "Can you hurry?"

My only answer was a sharp popping noise, then another. The vulture had started to jab at me again, but it recoiled suddenly, making a startled sound like the scrape of metal on metal.

There came a great clanging crash. Rika jumped back with a squawk and nearly knocked me over. The iron grille toppled to the ground.

I didn't stop to marvel at what she'd done, or figure out how she'd done it. I grabbed Rika's hand and dove at the slit in reality, even as a great brass beak snapped the air behind us.

WHAT YOU DON'T UNDERSTAND WILL KILL YOU

We tumbled through onto some kind of balcony, girdled by a rickety-looking driftwood railing. Above us, an aurora of spectacular colors shimmered across the evening sky. The city looked a bit more like the one I recognized from Prime, save that the buildings standing cheek by jowl seemed to be cobbled together from scraps of sea-weathered wood, and black water shone in the streets below, reflecting the lights above. Boats cut streaky paths of radiance through the water, pulled by shimmering rainbow-finned fish. It was so beautiful I caught my breath.

I turned to make some comment to Rika, who had landed hard on her hands and knees. It died in my throat, impaled by a spike of worry.

She was panting, head bowed, her whole body hunched as if in pain.

"Are you all right?" I reached for her. "Did they get you?"

Before my hand could touch her back, she struck it away.

"I'm fine," she snarled. "I just need...a moment...*Ah!*"

Her body jerked. The shoulder blades I'd nearly touched rippled

THE LAST SOUL AMONG WOLVES   155

strangely. Rivers of darkness poured down over her shoulders, and for one terrified instant I thought it was blood. But no—it was her *hair*, if you could call it that anymore, black as the Void with tips that fanned out and floated like smoke.

I started to reach out again, tentatively. "Rika, what the—"

A blast of light knocked me onto my ass.

Rika cried out as luminous silver wings erupted from her shoulders, spreading in vast grandeur against the night. She threw back her head, and her eyes glowed crimson.

Noises of alarm and a few splashes sounded from the boats below. I could only stare. I had no idea what to do. I knew how to help a friend who was bleeding too much, or falling-down drunk and vomiting, or freaking out after coming back from a Deep Echo. Nothing I'd learned had prepared me for what to do when your girlfriend was suffering some kind of involuntary transformation into a divine celestial entity.

Glowing tears streamed down her cheeks, and her kneeling body shuddered as if in shock. I grabbed her hand.

"Rika. Rika! I'm here. It's all right."

"Don't look at me!" she cried. "Damn it, Kembral, get away from me!" But she clung so tightly to my hand the bones nearly ground together.

"I'm not going anywhere."

The memory came back to me, suddenly, of a very different-looking Rika—maybe five years old, with brown eyes full of frightened despair as she went translucent from the edges inward and began to fade away. I'd grabbed her hand before she could fall out of Prime altogether, urging her to stay, talking to her until she turned fully solid and opaque again.

This felt as urgent as that moment. As if she were slipping away from me, and if I didn't catch her, I could lose her forever.

I seized her other hand, too; they were both icy cold. "Listen to me, Rika. You can't get rid of me that easily. You know me, I'm stubborn as a rock. I'm here with you, and I don't know what's going on, but I'm going to stay with you until you seem like you're okay."

Her great wings beat the air as if in agony, and she made a strangled sound—but I could tell she heard me.

I kept talking, forcing myself to sound quiet and calm. "It's going to be all right. We're going to get through this together, and we're going to get back to Prime."

She murmured something that sounded like my name. Her whole body shuddered; her wingtips relaxed, just beginning to furl.

"Also, holy Void, woman, your hands are always *so cold*. What do you do, walk around wearing gloves full of ice?"

She let out a strange, choked noise that was mostly sob, but maybe just a little bit laugh.

The glow in her eyes started to fade. The shining wings drooped, shedding a brilliant feather or two, collapsing down over her shoulders. I hoped that was good.

"Kembral," she rasped, her voice hoarse as if she'd been crying or screaming. "You ridiculous...pigheaded... *Hound*."

"That's me," I agreed. "Someone's got to keep you grounded."

The crimson light drained from her eyes. They fluttered shut, and she slumped all at once into my arms.

I half folded under her suddenly limp weight, struggling to rearrange myself to support her. Was she unconscious? Maybe she was just...concentrating. I tried not to panic, tried not to remember holding her while she died only a couple of months before.

I had no idea what in the Void had just happened or what I was supposed to do. All I could think of was to cradle her warmth against me and keep muttering a string of what was supposed to be reassurances but came out mostly as swears.

Slowly, her wings faded and retracted into her shoulders. The river of unearthly darkness flowing from her scalp diminished to normal human-looking hair again. I brushed stray locks of it back from her face. The undoing of her transformation couldn't have taken more than a minute, but it felt endlessly long.

She didn't wake up.

"Rika," I whispered. "Come on, don't leave me like this."

It was only a matter of time until someone or some*thing* came to

THE LAST SOUL AMONG WOLVES   157

investigate the light. We were still four Echoes down, I had already blink stepped twice, and I was bleeding. If I tried carrying an unconscious Rika around looking for a way up to the third Echo, we'd be set upon in moments.

This was my fault. She'd warned me, but I'd pushed her to use her powers anyway. And now something had happened to her, some Empyrean thing I couldn't understand, and we were never going to make it home.

No. I set my jaw and hoisted Rika into a more comfortable position in my lap, nestled against my shoulder. It couldn't end like this— I wouldn't let it. I'd named this year, and it was mine. The Year of Hope. That had to be worth something.

"Hey." I gave Rika a little shake. "Wake up. Naptime is over. We have to get out of here."

A shudder traveled through her whole body. Her eyes flew open, grey and clear.

All at once, she lurched up out of my arms, dusting herself off as if she'd just taken an embarrassing fall.

"Ugh."

Thank the Moon. I cleared my throat. "Are you all—"

"Yes. And I'll kindly and lovingly ask you to drop it, Kembral."

Fine. So she didn't want to talk about it. I couldn't think of anything else, and my hands were shaking, but fine.

"Rika..."

She gave me a warning look. "Where do we go now?"

I stared at her for a moment. So that was it? All I wanted was to ask what just happened, and was she *sure* she was all right, and was there anything else I should probably know before we climbed back up through four more Echoes together. But there was a brittleness about her, as if she might shatter if I breathed on her too hard.

So I rose, waiting for my pulse to slow, and pulled myself together as best I could. There was no way she was okay, but if she wanted to pretend she was, I could respect that. I might be doing a little pretending myself.

We needed a way up. I closed my eyes a moment, and *hoped* we'd

158   MELISSA CARUSO

find one quickly. I felt the tickling urge to give a quarter turn to the right, so I did, and opened my eyes.

And there it was. On the roof of a building a couple blocks away, a shimmering gap flickered between two tall, slender chimneys.

"We...we got unreasonably lucky, actually. Look." I pointed it out to Rika, using the excuse to stand close enough to steady her.

She followed my gesture, then glanced down at the boats clustered below our balcony, whose oddly shaped occupants exclaimed and whispered and pointed up at us. She returned her gaze to the rooftop portal, her expression hardening with resolve.

"Time for me to take the lead, I think. Rooftops are my natural environment." She gave me a teasing, haughty mask of a smile, hard and fragile as glass. "Don't take this the wrong way, Hound, but you don't know how to move up here."

"I'm not arguing." I gestured grandly, playing along in this *pretend we're all right* game. "After you."

She picked out a route, then flowed nimbly up the wall to the roof. She moved with her usual grace, but I recognized the spare economy of exhaustion. I stood poised on the edge of a blink step, ready to catch her in the impossible event of a fall.

Whatever had just happened, it had taken a lot out of her. I couldn't begin to guess whether it was the manipulation of the Echo to get rid of that grille, or her transformation afterward, or stopping it and returning to her usual human form that had taken the toll. Either way, it didn't look like something she'd be eager to repeat. Guess we couldn't rely on Rika's Empyrean nature to brute-force our way back to Prime.

My worries that she could slip were groundless, though. She might be drained, but it didn't hold her back from climbing around as nimbly as her guild's namesake. I followed her on a shoulder-achingly, nail-shreddingly difficult course, clambering up to rooftops and leaping across alleyways, struggling along behind while she took everything with the casual ease of long practice. She steadied me or offered a hand a few times, always with a little biting quip; I had to blink step once to save myself from a bad fall. Which was getting close to too many blink steps in too short a time, and left my legs shaky and my head pounding.

We were doing it, though. Maybe there *was* something to this year-namer thing. The Echoes poling the canals in their long shining boats didn't look up, though sometimes they'd lift their heads and sniff the air. For whatever reason, they couldn't sense my blood from half a mile away—maybe because it hadn't been shed in this Echo.

When we arrived before the shimmering gap in reality at last, Rika suddenly grabbed my hand as if for balance. I glanced at her, alarmed; she'd squeezed her eyes tight shut.

"Everything all right?"

"Yes. Fine." Her breath huffed quickly in and out, as if she'd been running.

"If you don't tell me what's wrong," I began carefully, "then I can't—"

"If I think about it, it gets worse," she said sharply. "Talk about something else."

I cast around for a topic, desperate. "Uh...The sky is really pretty?"

She blinked her eyes open and looked up. A sheen of faint red glow covered them, but I clamped my mouth shut on any reaction I might have had.

Rika let out a shuddering breath, her shoulders relaxing. The colors of the aurora bathed her face, shifting from green to pink to blue.

"Yes," she said softly. "It's lovely."

She leaned her shoulder against mine. We looked at it together for a long moment, our heads tilting together, lending each other warmth.

"You take me on the worst dates," Rika murmured.

"Bah. You can't see *this* at the Grand Theater."

She slipped her hand into mine and squeezed it, then straightened. "I think I'm ready. We should go."

"Yeah." Worry wound itself through my chest—for Rika, for my friends back in Prime, and even for Emmi, which made no sense because she was far safer than any of us.

"Thanks for shutting up when I needed you to." The look Rika gave me was softer than her words, her eyes simply grey again, her face beautiful in the glowing night.

"Sure," I said, because I was no good at this feelings stuff. "Let's go through."

It was a huge relief to slide through the shimmering, nerve-tingling gap to the third Echo. Ravens argued about whether the fourth counted as a Deep Echo, but everyone agreed that the third was a shallow one. It was dangerous, sure, but more in ways that mortals came reasonably equipped to deal with. We should be able to make it home all right.

From there, it was all stuff I'd faced plenty of times before. A curving street tried to run us in an eternal circle until we closed our eyes and took a left with our hands skimming the damp stone wall. A stray cat demanded a secret before it would let us pass; I told it about the time I stole my sister's apple cake and blamed the neighborhood dogs, and it was appeased. We had to be careful to dodge the locals as much as we could, and a few times an individual or group started to follow us in a menacing sort of way, but Rika's skills as a Cat were more than adequate to shake them off.

She seemed fine. I watched her almost as closely as I watched the Echoes around us, searching for signs of distress, of any further transformation. She looked tired, and lines of strain bracketed her eyes, but she was very much herself. Thank the Moon.

"Rika," I began hesitantly, "why does Arhsta want you to—"

"Not talking about that right now," she cut me off with breezy finality, avoiding my eyes. And then, more softly, "Later. When it's safe."

Which was fair enough. But it left me with a certain anxiety over whether *when it's safe* meant when we were out of the Echoes, or whether there was some continuing imminent crisis to which my mortal senses left me oblivious. Was she on the brink of some strange Empyrean meltdown? Was her mother watching us, poised to strike the moment we got too complacent?

I was just barely smart enough not to push my luck and ask. If there was an immediate danger, she'd tell me. My job was to get us home.

We were halfway to the river when a woman in a red coat with bright blue hair and some kind of little squirrel-thing on her shoulder rounded a corner maybe fifty feet away and froze. Our eyes locked, recognition shocking between us.

"Shit," she said, with feeling. She turned back into the street she'd emerged from and strode quickly away.

Rika stared after her. "Was that...you?"

"Yeah." The woman's face stuck in my brain. My face, very nearly, except for the blue hair and a different pattern of freckles. My voice, my walk—though apparently I was missing out on a pet squirrel. A weird feeling tingled on my skin, a bit like being near Echo stuff, only more personal somehow.

"Why did she run away like that?"

"If someone from Prime touches an Echo of themselves, or even gets too near, the Echo usually gets destroyed. Prime overwrites all other reality." I shook my head. "It's best never to meet your own Echoes—for a whole bunch of reasons, but that's chief among them."

I couldn't help worrying about the hour, even as we found a door with edges that didn't match the surrounding reality and opened it onto the second Echo, then headed down to the river to find an easy path back to the first. I was getting a rather uncomfortable reminder from the fullness of my milk that time was passing. We didn't know whether Mareth's death had reset the clock, but at best we had a little over a day until the Deepwolf returned to claim another life.

And we didn't have the lantern. That failure gnawed at me with sharp teeth of guilt. Mareth's *soul* was in that thing now. We couldn't have stayed and searched for it—not with the castle a trap and the whole place after my blood—but we were short on time to make another attempt. Worse, with the mirror portal likely closed by the time we got back to Prime, we'd have to work our way down to the fifth Echo the hard way.

I, not we. That castle was a giant trap for Rika. Much as I'd love to have her help on an Echo heist, she couldn't take the bait.

At last, we stepped out into a perfectly normal street in the Tower district in Prime, blinking in the watery sunlight. It felt like we'd been down there for ages, but by the great clock looming above us, only a few hours had passed in this reality.

Some of the tension left my shoulders. Which was dangerous, because there were still too many hovering feelings trying to land the moment the crisis was over—but it wasn't over yet. Not really.

Rika let out a long, ragged sigh of relief. "Thank the Moon. Solid Prime streets under our feet again at last."

"Yeah." I eyed her sideways. "How are you feeling?"

"If you keep asking me that, I'm going to stick a knife in you. Speaking of which..." She reached toward my back.

"I stopped!" I threw up my hands. "I'm stopping!"

"Oh, hush, I'm not stabbing you. I want to get a good look at that cut now that we—oh!"

Well, now I was tense again. "What?"

"The slash in your coat is gone."

"Oh, good. I was really hoping it would revert when we got back to Prime. Sometimes stuff does."

Rika let out a rueful little laugh. "You were really hoping, were you? I guess your blood works as advertised. You certainly got some on the coat."

I wasn't sure how I felt about that, and about the suspiciously timed good luck I'd had in the Echoes. It wasn't as if I'd had any doubt that what I'd done at the year-turning was having real effects. I'd been following the news more than usual since then, and I couldn't pretend not to see the influence of the name I'd given the year.

Some of it was good, like treatments being discovered for chronic illnesses, droughts coming to an end, or Dona Vandelle finally getting worker protections passed through the council. Some of it was harmless, like underdogs winning horse races or people finally deciding to chase old dreams. But hope could be dangerous, too. There was turmoil in Cathardia, as the anti-royalists calling for the establishment of a senate suddenly sensed a real chance to overthrow the monarchy, and the monarchy prepared to crack down...But so far, hope for a peaceful resolution remained as well.

That was what I'd been thinking, in that desperate moment when I'd had to give the year a name—*any* name—before Rai did. If things were never entirely hopeless, the year couldn't be *too* bad.

But my blood being some kind of magic elixir now—that was just weird.

"How about your cut?" Rika asked, frowning. "Is that healed, too?"

"No. I don't have to go out of my way to hope about that. It's pretty shallow."

"We should treat it anyway." She glanced around. "I have a safe house nearby. We could stop there and get you patched up."

"I'm genuinely fine, and we need to get moving." *I* needed to get moving. If I stayed still too long, I'd start thinking about what had happened to Mareth, or how screwed we were now that we knew Arhsta was behind everything.

She closed her eyes. "Kembral. I could use a minute."

At her sides, her hands were shaking.

Ah. She was *not* all right. That was why I needed to stop asking. Stars, I could be dense sometimes.

I swallowed. "Sorry. Yeah, let's swing by your place before we head back."

—⟐—

Rika stopped at an utterly unremarkable spot in the street, sudden as if she'd hit an invisible wall. Mist beaded in her hair, but it was sweat that shone on her temples.

"Rika? What's wrong?" I started to reach out to her.

"Nothing." She let out a forced little laugh. "I'm not going to sprout wings, Kembral. You can relax."

"That's not what I...Never mind."

"The whole point of a safe house is that no one knows where it is, that's all. If I show you this one, it's compromised."

Questions crowded my mind, the kind with uncomfortable shapes and sharp corners. *What do you think I'm going to do with this knowledge, exactly? When was the last time you invited someone to any place of yours? Do you even have a home, or just a collection of safe houses?*

"We could go to a café or something," I said instead. "It's up to you."

"No, it's fine." She didn't meet my eyes. "I do realize that you're the most tediously trustworthy person in Acantis, Kembral. It's just hard to break old habits, that's all."

She strode with bright, false confidence down a dingy alley behind a shoe shop, and up to an extremely plain door with peeling beige paint. It had far too good a lock, but otherwise it blended in seamlessly. She drew forth a fat bunch of keys, her nimble fingers unerringly hooking the correct one out of the herd. I wondered exactly how many safe houses and bolt-holes Rika *had*.

She swung open the door, ducking her head in an embarrassed sort of way. "It's not exactly set up for entertaining, I'm afraid, but it serves its purpose. Come on in. Let's get this done."

For the first time in all the years we'd known each other, I stepped into a place that Rika at least occasionally called home.

KNOW WHEN TO SHUT UP

Whatever I might have expected, it wasn't this. The room was dim and windowless, with a cedary smell, as if someone had sawed raw wood in there once and kept it sealed up ever since. There was a neat narrow bed, a pump and washbasin, a clothes chest, and tidy shelves holding an assortment of tools and useful items. It was ruthlessly utilitarian, save for an extravagant black-and-silver gown that lay thrown across the bed, a heap of jewelry tossed next to it.

Rika grimaced as she locked the door behind us. "Looks like I haven't been here since I worked that Hillside ball last month." She bundled the gown and jewelry haphazardly onto a shelf, almost fumbling a necklace. Her hands were still shaking.

I touched her shoulder, and she jumped. "Hey. Why don't you sit down and breathe a little."

"No. I need to be doing something." She pointed at the bed. "Sit down. I'll get the bandages."

"I don't—"

I forced myself to stop. I didn't want to take the time for myself, when my friends were in danger. But Rika was in danger, too. I could see it in the strain she couldn't keep from her face, the trembling, the mere fact that she'd been willing to let me in here at all.

166   MELISSA CARUSO

She looked half-ready to pass out.

"Fine," I said instead. "But, Rika, I'm begging you to tell me what's wrong. I can't help you if I don't know."

"*Sit*, Hound, and maybe I'll tell you." She paused. "And take off your coat."

I obeyed, hissing as I flexed my shoulders. I ran a hand along the scarlet fabric as if to soothe it, but it was perfectly smooth. There was no sign of the slash.

"You must not be as emotionally attached to your shirt. It's still torn." Rika's gentle touch fell just below the base of my neck.

I flinched. "*So* cold. You must have the worst circulation in Acantis, woman."

"Oh, hush." Her voice sounded a little steadier. Good. "Now, let me see that wound."

I pulled off my shirt, wincing as it peeled away from the cut. The air held enough chill to raise goose bumps on my arms, now that I was down to my bandeau.

"See," I said, "I told you it wasn't bad. It's hardly more than a cat scratch."

"Oh, I don't know. Cats can scratch pretty deep."

It was an invitation to fall comfortably into banter, to pretend nothing had happened. But I couldn't. The terrible knowledge of the trap Rika's mother had set for her burned in my mind. We'd just almost died, Mareth was dead, and more of my friends might be about to join him because I'd failed to get the lantern. And there was the matter of whatever had happened on the balcony, and what might be happening to Rika right now. I couldn't bring myself to let it all go.

"So," I began cautiously. "I realize you don't want to talk about this, but if we're going to keep winding up in Echoes together, I should probably know—"

"Kembral." Her cold fingers curled around the back of my neck, a little menacingly. "Let me tell you how this is going to go. You're going to shut up and let me tend to your cut."

"But—"

THE LAST SOUL AMONG WOLVES   167

"You are going to *shut up* and let me tend to your cut," she repeated firmly. "Keep your back turned and don't look at me. It's easier to talk about this if I can't see your annoying face."

I closed my mouth on the protests I'd been lining up. "Mmph. Not talking."

"Perfect. Blessed silence. Now, let's see." Her fingers trailed down my spine, stopping just above the wound. "Ugh, I'd better wash this. I don't think those vultures were the most sanitary creatures."

I started to twist, to try to look. "Is it—"

"No looking."

"Fine." I clasped my hands in my lap and closed my mouth, trying to treat this like one of Almarah's exercises. Breathe. No questions. Just listen.

There came the sound of a pump, and the splash of water. Rika's voice was muted, muffled, as if she had her chin tucked down to her chest.

"If you must know, it used to happen like that all the time. When I was a little girl."

"Like . . . on the balcony?" Oops. So much for no questions.

"Yes. Especially if I got angry or upset. That's why I kept having to move." The rising pitch of water filling a basin. "But I've had it under control since . . . well. Suffice to say it hasn't happened in a long time. I thought it must be like losing baby teeth or having tantrums— something I didn't have to worry about as an adult." She gave a bitter little laugh. "Embarrassing to have it happen now."

"It looked a little . . . uncomfortable." I switched words at the last moment from *scary*.

"You could say that."

There came a light trickle of water, and then a wet cloth on my back. I grunted, but she was gentler than I feared, dabbing carefully at the wound.

"Oh, don't be a big baby," she murmured.

"Sorry. Wasn't expecting it." I forced myself to relax, to wait for her to continue. After a moment, she did.

"I think what happened tonight was . . . When we were in that shrine, trying to get through the grille to the next Echo, I..." Her breath huffed against my neck. "I didn't know what to do. I never tried to shape Echoes before. So I treated it like it was an illusion."

Ah. It made sense. Empyreans could shape Echoes, but not the stuff of Prime. When they used their power in Prime, the things they created or changed weren't truly real—just temporary, fading with time. Unless someone from Prime sealed it with a bargain.

"What you do was never properly illusion in the first place," I realized. "Was it?"

A long silence. "No. Apparently not."

She finished cleaning the cut with a rough swipe that elicited an "Ouch!" from me and no apology from Rika.

"I'm putting ointment on this next." Rika's tone held so much warning she might as well have threatened me with a knife.

"Okay. I'll shut up."

"Good." The cool damp of the ointment hit the hot fire of the line across my shoulders. I braced myself, but Rika rubbed it in so gently that it barely hurt. She moved slowly, methodically, her touch lingering featherlight against my skin.

"It wasn't even hard," she whispered. "But using that ability... set me off. Tipped me over the edge into that other form." Her fingertips dug in, a seemingly involuntary movement, and I swallowed a hiss. "Which is *exactly* what she wants. For me to become like her, powerful and cold and terrible. And if it were just that, maybe I could find the strength to keep my human heart while wielding my Empyrean power, or whatever other upbeat bullshit you might tell me to do—"

"Hey," I protested. "My bullshit is pragmatic, not upbeat."

"—but that's not the only problem. That other form...it's dangerous."

Now we were getting to the heart of it at last. "Dangerous?"

"Yes." She drew in a soft breath. "Do you remember what Laemura said when we were in her tea shop? About Empyreans being unstable?"

"Right. Because the blood of the Moon and the Void don't mix.

So the Empyreans each have to follow their equilibrium thread with human anchors to help keep their balance, or they'll turn into stars or trees or something." The implications for Rika began to seep in, and it was all I could do not to whip around and stare at her. Which I supposed was exactly why she'd wanted me facing away.

"It's not like that for me," she said. "What would my equilibrium thread even *be*? No, thank the Moon, I don't have to deal with that. Except..." Her hands stilled on my back, and she was quiet.

I waited. After a moment, she continued, her voice even lower. "When I'm in that form, I can feel it. The pieces of me straining against each other. Everything starts to fall apart. It's *horrible*."

"*That* was what was happening on the balcony? You were...what, cosmically destabilizing?"

I'd started to turn, horrified, without even thinking about it. Rika was ready for me and grabbed my shoulders, holding me firmly in place.

"Presumably." Her voice had gone brisk and businesslike. "I'm not a Raven, and I don't intend to ask one, so I don't know. But it felt very, very bad, and...I'm not sure I would have survived if it had kept going."

"Rika..."

"What you did helped." She slapped a bandage on my back with the brutal efficiency of a mother cat holding her kitten down for a bath. "The whole point of telling you all these painful and personal things—which you must never mention to anyone or I swear to the Moon I'll cut your throat and throw your body in the river—was so that if for any reason it ever happens again, you know what to do."

What *had* I done? I searched my memory frantically, alarmed at this responsibility. "I should tease you about having cold hands?"

"No, dimwit. You should hold on to me and talk to me." She smoothed the bandage in place, then straightened and stepped away. "This has pretty much stopped bleeding. You were right about it not being serious."

I stood and turned at last to face her, a thousand unsaid things clogging up my throat. I blurted out one of the more important ones.

"I'm sorry I pushed you into using your power like that. I shouldn't have—"

"It wasn't your fault!" She threw up her hands. "You couldn't miss the point wider if you were a first-year apprentice on the knife-throwing range. I *chose* to use it! What else was I going to do? Stand there and watch you get ripped apart?"

She was staring at me strangely; I was suddenly very conscious that I was just wearing a bandeau and some ointment on the entire top half of my body.

"I mean, I'm glad you didn't, but..." I broke off. She was shaking again. Blood on the Moon, I was bad at this. "What's wrong?"

"What's *wrong*?" She let out a disbelieving laugh. "They almost *killed* you! I thought I was going to have to watch you die in the most horrible way because I wasn't fast enough! And all because you stepped into a trap Arhsta set for *me*. Void take it, Kembral, I can't lose you. I *won't* lose you. I..."

She closed the distance between us with one unsteady step and caught me to her, close and fierce. The honey and clove scent of her perfume teased my nose as I folded my arms around her, one hand sneaking up to stroke the soft river of her hair.

"She turned half the fifth Echo into a trap for you, and you almost came apart into cosmic forces, and *that's* what bothers you?" I murmured. "I'm fine. Don't worry about me."

"*Someone* has to worry about you. You're not going to do it yourself, you infuriating creature."

She touched my cheek, her fingertips trailing down to my lips. And then she leaned in and kissed me with such sudden desperation she nearly knocked me over. I had to grab the bedpost for balance.

I had no instinct for kisses, but it didn't matter. Rika seemed more than happy to lead, her mouth seeking something from mine that she knew how to find. And the closeness—that, I understood. The feeling of her warm body against mine was such a strange miracle, the thunder of her heart like a fury of beating wings. All her messy contradictions and graceful subtleties held against me, the divine flame of starlight made wonderfully, painfully human.

When she came up for air, she murmured behind my ear, "I've watched over you for quite a while, Kembral Thorne, no matter how hard you make it. I'm not going to stop now."

I held her, trying to be something solid and steady, a rock in the center of whatever storm was swirling inside her right now.

"Yeah, well, you don't make things easy, either, but I guess I'll keep you around."

We stayed like that awhile longer, and it was good just to know we were safe. That despite the trap Arhsta had laid, we'd gotten out, at least for now. That despite the death haunting us, we were alive.

At last, I let go, opening enough space between us to meet her eyes.

"We've got to get you out of this," I said. "Petras might have meant to hire you in good faith, but you don't have to fulfill a contract once you know it's a setup. You can return his fee and—"

"Are *you* going to walk away?" she interrupted.

"Of course not. It's not a trap for *me*. And my friends' lives are on the line."

"I'm a Cat. Give me the credit to imagine that I'm capable of doing the job despite the complications."

"This is too big." I couldn't keep some of the fear I'd been trying to squash out of my voice. "Look at everything she's already done to get at you. She sent those Echoes to kill Auberyn Lovegrace, set off a curse that's already claimed two lives, manipulated Petras into hiring you, forced you to use your powers, built that whole damn castle just to get under your skin. She's deliberately showing you her cards, one by one, going to great lengths to display to you how screwed you are. You only do that when you're in a position of unassailable strength."

"Or when you want to rattle your opponent into believing you are." Rika shook her head, composed again, as if my arms around her had been all she needed to restore her stability. "The bigger and more grandiose the trap, the easier it is to avoid."

"So avoid it. Go hole up in your guildhouse, or relax on a beach in Cathardia—"

"I assure you, she'll have accounted for the possibility of running away."

That stopped me. It sank in that maybe we were *not* out of Arhsta's web. That her web might not have an edge at all, but stretch beyond the horizon and through all the worlds.

Strain still showed in the shadows of Rika's face. She wasn't all right. But she met my gaze with grim resolve.

"I'm not going to meekly step back and let her keep on killing people to get at me, and I won't let *you* get hurt trying to solve this alone. We're doing it together, Kembral. I won't back down."

"But—"

"Shh." She put her finger on my lips. "No buts. Just tell me what's next. You *do* have a plan, yes? You always do."

I sighed. "Fine, yes. I have a plan. I need to go to Guildhouse Square."

I reached for my bloodstained shirt; Rika tossed a new one at my head instead. I caught it, the fabric slapping around my arm.

"Stopping by the Hound guildhouse?" she asked.

"No." I pulled on the shirt, which smelled faintly of cedar and Rika's perfume. "The Ravens. This is most definitely Raven business."

CONSULT THE EXPERTS

The Raven guildhouse was the oldest and grandest of the buildings on Guildhouse Square, because it was the oldest and grandest of the guilds.

The Ravens started as an Echo working school near the heart of the League Cities, hundreds of years ago. From the beginning they'd been smart enough to swear an oath of political neutrality, so that the League Cities wouldn't see such a large concentration of skilled Echo workers as a threat. They'd sent out journeyman teachers to roam the world gathering local Echo-working techniques and taking on apprentices, and eventually the school had chapter houses all over the place; soon enough they became more of a professional organization that offered training than a school. Other guilds sprang up following their model, until by a couple hundred years ago the guilds were solidly entrenched in their current form, charters and all.

The Raven guildhouse still felt a bit like a school, or maybe a library. Apprentices scurried across its soaring, marble-pillared main hall with books under their arms; one ran through with a smoking vial held out at arm's length, grimacing in apparent alarm, but no one else seemed concerned. A few Ravens clustered around some diagram in a corner, making serious thoughtful faces and muttering

174   MELISSA CARUSO

to one another. Something that looked a bit like an opalescent bat fluttered up near the ceiling, but everyone ignored it, as if an Echo loose in the guildhouse were an everyday occurrence. And maybe it was—there was certainly enough of a prickle of Echo magic in the air. Grand archways led off the hall to multiple different libraries, endless tall shelves of books enticingly visible, as well as to corridors of classrooms, workrooms, and laboratories.

And the stairs to the vaults, of course. It was best not to think too hard about what was in the Raven vaults, or how far they might or might not stretch under the city.

Rika and I headed to the reception desk, which was longer and more complicated than the Hound one, with more people working it. Signs directed us to *Emergency*, *Appointment*, *Ravens Only*, and *Other*. A frazzled woman at the Emergency desk held her arm before her to show the nodding receptionist.

"So you see, purple fur, spreading very rapidly, and it's *itchy*..."

At the Ravens Only station, an exhausted-looking field Raven leaned on the desk. "...The whole spectrum array, I think. We need to figure out what came on board the *Breath of Dawn* while their tide skimmer had it down an Echo—and we can't ask witnesses, because there were no survivors."

We headed to the Other station, urgency driving my stride. A heavyset Cathardian man greeted us, wrapped so thoroughly in a sigil-embroidered turquoise shawl that his words came out muffled.

"Signas! What can I do for you this miserable, frigid day?"

Rika smiled, despite everything. "Still adjusting to Acantis weather, are we, Signa Ember?"

"In Cathardia, by Blood Moon the flowers are blooming," he mourned.

"My grandparents told me that back in Viger the snow didn't always melt by the end of Blood Moon, so I guess it could be worse," I consoled him. "And we need to see Signa Zarvish. It's urgent."

The note on Mareth's nightstand had held that single name. I was guessing they were a colleague he'd consulted on the relics, or planned to consult. Our time was limited and precious, and I couldn't

THE LAST SOUL AMONG WOLVES   175

afford to waste any chasing dead-end leads—but this was deep Raven stuff, and I wasn't arrogant enough to think I could fix it all on my own.

Ember looked me over. "Most people, if they came to my desk claiming they wanted to see a senior Raven on urgent business, I'd point them down the line and say to make an appointment. But you two, with *those* looks on your faces?" He shook his head and handed over a couple of blue-beaded necklaces. "Her office is on the third floor. These passes will get you everywhere that's not restricted access; just turn them in on your way out."

—⟋⟋⟍—

Signa Zarvish's office bore an alarming quantity of scratches on the bottom edge of its otherwise gleaming wood-paneled door. The reason became apparent as soon as we opened it, in response to a somewhat beleaguered call of "Come in."

There were cats everywhere. And all right, it only takes about two cats for there to be cats everywhere, and realistically there were probably only four, but they felt innumerable. An orange one twined our ankles the moment we walked in. A Void-black shadow of a cat lurked on top of a bookshelf, staring down at us with predatory intensity. A massive stripy greyish fluff cloud groomed itself on a cushioned chair covered in so much fur its original color was indistinguishable, ignoring us pointedly. And a yellow-eyed tortoiseshell sat in splendid magnificence directly on the open book that lay before Signa Zarvish, as if it were a platform designed solely to display her.

Signa Zarvish, whose office was otherwise exactly the cluttered collection of books and Echo relics and strange inexplicable objects one would expect from a senior Raven, lifted her exasperated stare from the tortoiseshell to offer us a gruff welcome nod.

"Close the door before the orange one gets out, will you? Thanks. Sorry, the others have free range of the guildhouse, but I got too many complaints about Pyrite stealing things—and when a student caught him carrying off the Eye of Abria in his mouth, well, the guildmaster put his foot down. Have a seat." She waved vaguely at an assortment of chairs, most of which were covered in books. I moved a stack onto another stack and took one; Rika turned, clearly marking all the objects of mysterious provenance she didn't want to accidentally touch, and then gingerly settled on the edge of a chair that held only a canvas bag of what appeared to be skeins of yarn.

"Thank you for seeing us without an appointment," I began.

Zarvish blinked. "You're not the couple with the night slitherer infestation? It isn't five o'clock?"

"Not that we're aware of," Rika said.

"No," I said carefully. "We're here because we're working on the same relic job Mareth...Signa Overfell was."

"Ah." Zarvish let out an explosive breath. "Stars! Poor Mareth. Such a damned shame. I heard, of course. I recommended to the city authorities all those years ago that those relics were too dangerous and they should confiscate them, but they said they reviewed Lovegrace's isolation plan and it passed regulations, so nothing they could do. I'm kicking myself for not hiring a Cat to steal them and throw them into the sea or something."

Rika raised an eyebrow. "Would that work?"

"Probably not, unfortunately. Cursed relics have a way of washing up on shore and getting found by kids. It's why there are laws against dumping them." She sighed. "I tried to talk Lovegrace into letting us stick them in the vaults, but we'd just had a rather messy and public containment issue that month, and she didn't trust us to keep them safe."

I leaned forward. "So you're the one who inspected the relics last time? Twenty-whatever years ago?"

"Ugh, has it been that long?" Zarvish shook her head. "I would've said ten. But yes, and I already heard about the current situation from poor Mareth—if you find out who murdered him, let me know, by the way, I'd like to put a curse on them—"

"Naturally," Rika murmured.

"Appreciated. So, I do know the basics."

"My job is to obtain the lantern so that it can be destroyed," Rika said, reaching down absently to pet Pyrite, who was rubbing up

THE LAST SOUL AMONG WOLVES

against her chair. "We're running into some...complications with that."

Zarvish snorted. "Like the thing being carried back and forth from five Echoes down by a Deepwolf?"

"Yes, that, among other things."

"I've been thinking about it," Zarvish said. "Obviously you don't want to go into the mirror after it, since no one in their right mind goes five Echoes down."

Rika gave me a Look. I shrugged.

"So I think we need to figure out a way to get the lantern from the wolf the next time it comes through," Zarvish concluded.

"We're not sure when to expect it next," I said. "That's another thing I wanted to ask you about—whether Mareth's death affects the timeline."

Zarvish nodded gravely. "Right. If someone tied to the relics dies for any reason, that triggers the portal and the Deepwolf. The book still records the death, and the calling enchantment on the book resets the moment it's recorded. So you're counting from Mareth's murder, unfortunately, and the interval is halved again."

My stomach sank. That wasn't the answer I'd wanted. "So... twenty-four hours after his death. We have until tomorrow morning."

"I have some ideas, but it'll take all night to prepare. I'll come over with a team about an hour before dawn to set up traps for the Deepwolf, and we'll see what we can do." Zarvish tried to take a pen from too near the tortoiseshell cat, got swatted for her efforts, and grabbed a charcoal pencil instead. She started scrawling notes on a scrap of paper. "I don't think I can finish before then, so it's going to be close—if this works at all. You might want to have a backup plan."

"If your team can distract the Deepwolf enough, I might be able to get the lantern by blink stepping in and out even if you can't force it to drop it." I didn't much like the idea, since it would involve sticking my hand into the wolf's mouth for a flickering instant, but if I was quick and careful, it could work.

"Sounds good," said the Raven who would *not* have to stick her hand into a Deepwolf's mouth. "One more thing. Be careful who gets ahold of the lantern, assuming we can get it away from the Deep-wolf at all. It's designed to absorb the souls of the people connected to it. For someone who knows how to activate it, that capability will work whether its targets are alive or dead."

I grimaced. "I'd like to think nobody would use it that way, but... with a wish at stake, yeah, let's not give anyone the chance."

"Once we've got the lantern, I imagine we'll have to break it quickly so the Deepwolf can't just take it back," Rika pointed out. "If throwing it in the ocean is a bad idea, how *would* you recommend destroying it?"

Zarvish set her pencil down, frowning. "That's the problem. I didn't get a chance to tell Mareth this, because he was so shaken up about the soul-stealing thing that he ran right back to the island." She paused, a cloud settling over her face. "His soul. *Stars.* Poor Mareth."

"All the more reason to destroy that lantern," I said quietly. "But Mareth wasn't having any luck with the mirror or the book. So unless you just have to break the lantern first—"

"I only wish it were as simple as that." Zarvish looked grim. "How much do you know about Echo relics?"

"Enough not to mess with them."

Rika's mouth quirked. "Enough to steal them."

"So there are fundamentally three ways they can be created, and they all look different to the trained eye." Zarvish frowned absently at the tortoiseshell cat, who had sprawled across her book and was now casually batting the contested pen closer and closer to the edge of the desk. "The first is that someone skilled in Echo working— Echo or human—can bind magic into an object. That's what poor Mareth was assuming those relics were."

"That's what I assumed, too," I said.

"The second kind," Zarvish went on, "is an object from an Echo that inherently has magical properties. That's actually the most common type. When relic smugglers bring things back from the shallow Echoes to sell on the grey market, or when mudlarkers find Echo flotsam down by the river, it's usually this type."

"But these relics are too complex for that," I guessed.

Zarvish nodded agreement. "Right. Now, few people ever see the third kind. I'm sure Mareth hadn't. They have a very distinctive look and feel, magically speaking, and once you've analyzed one it's impossible to mistake if you run across another."

I had a very unpleasant suspicion about where this was going. "And what is this third kind?"

"Relics created by an Empyrean."

Rika had gone very still. Her face was a blank mask, politely listening, with no sign of the turmoil that must be going on inside.

"And these three are that third kind." I didn't bother to make it a question.

Zarvish nodded. "Anything created from nothing by an Empyrean has a certain...structure to its magic. Almost crystalline."

I'd bet cold money that I could guess which Empyrean had made them. But these relics had been around for ages—so either Arhsta was reusing old tools, or she'd been planning this long before Rika was even born.

"How do you destroy a relic created by an Empyrean?" Rika asked, with pasted-on bright curiosity.

"You don't," Zarvish replied. "Only another Empyrean can do it."

"Well, fuck," I said, like a professional.

—◆—

Walking out into the misty grey light of Guildhouse Square and its busy afternoon crowds felt like coming out of a cave. I blinked, still stunned.

"An Empyrean. I don't want to work with a fucking Empyrean," I muttered. Then added without thinking, "Present company excepted, of course."

Rika looked as shaken as I felt. "We can't. We just *can't*. Even if we somehow get in touch with one who doesn't have a grudge against us, they'll twist it into some awful bargain that will only make things worse."

But I was staring at her, my own last words still hanging in my ears. "Maybe *you* could break it."

She recoiled. "What? Stars, no! I'm not..."

She cut herself off in midsentence and bit her lip, visibly struggling with the idea. People grumbled as they parted around us in the square.

"Not if it would be dangerous for you," I said quickly. "It's not worth risking you dissolving into chaos or whatever. But if you can just...smash it with a hammer or something."

Rika flexed her fingers like she was unsheathing claws. "That would be lovely, but I doubt very much that it's going to be that easy."

"The alternative is to start looking for a cooperative Empyrean." I hesitated, then suggested reluctantly, "I could try to get in touch with Tilting Toward Oblivion."

It was the last thing I wanted to do. They'd been far too interested in me, and I had concerns that they might have wanted to make me an anchor. To save my friends, however, I'd take that chance.

"No! I don't want you to put yourself at risk. I just..." She drew in a breath that shivered at the edges. She was hiding it well, but she was still not okay. "You saw what happened when I used that part of me for one brief moment. If this is all some elaborate scheme of Arhsta's, then it's no coincidence that it takes an Empyrean to destroy the lantern."

"You're right. That's probably part of her trap, too." I pushed a hand through my hair, frustrated. "But we *have* to destroy it. And we have to retrieve it. She's got us at every turn."

"I can't believe I took her bait." Fear kindled into anger in Rika's eyes. "She did this to me at the year-turning, too—leaking information in just the right places to lure me in. I should have realized this job was suspicious from the start."

"You can still walk away." I grabbed her arms, right there in the square, with pigeons stalking around us and people bustling by. "It's very noble of you to put yourself at risk to save the souls of virtual strangers and all, but—"

"Is *that* why you think I'm doing this?" She let out a strained, despairing laugh. "Oh, Kembral."

"If not that, why?"

She gave me an odd look. It turned into something soft, with half a smile, and she shook her head. "You really don't know, do you?"

"If I could read your thoughts, I assure you that my life would have been dramatically different."

"Let me put it this way. Are *you* going to give up and walk away from this job?"

"No, of course not!"

"Of course you aren't. Because you're Kembral Thorne, and you don't abandon people to die. And I..." She traced the line of my cheek, a haunted look in her eyes. "*I* won't abandon *you*."

A storm was gathering along the boundary of sea and sky as we returned to the Lovegrace house, clouds knotting themselves into distant grey mountains among the fiery remains of sunset. We barely made it across the damp crescent of the sandbar before it vanished into hungrily lapping water, still dotted with the faint glowing specks of those little Echo things Vy had shown me. I didn't remember seeing them when I was a kid; maybe they were new, or maybe they only showed up during a Blood Moon or something, when I'd never felt like mucking around by the frigid water.

I'd stopped at the Hound guildhouse to grab some supplies for a jaunt into the Deep Echoes, just in case, like some Echo venom antidotes and a portal tether to keep the mirror open both ways. I had high hopes that Signa Zarvish would come up with a way to get the lantern from the Deepwolf before it could collect another soul, but Almarah always said it was better to prepare for a contingency that never happened than *not* to prepare and have it bite you in the ass.

We ran into Camwell at the foot of the sandbar, heading home for the night. (How nice for him. *I* didn't expect to see my bed until tomorrow.) He assured us that his team had searched the island for trespassers and found nothing, and that Willa was still safely confined in her room. I tried not to show on my face that our little Echo journey and its various accompanying revelations had driven Willa almost completely from my mind. Mareth, never—but I'd started thinking of Arhsta as his killer, regardless of what mortal hand had done the deed.

"Things should be stable, so far as the case is concerned," he concluded. "I'll be back in the morning, and we'll see if we can scrape up enough evidence for an arrest. After a night to think it over, maybe she'll even confess."

I was less sure than ever that Willa was the murderer. But knowing what had set this curse in motion and why gave me new leads to follow, so I just nodded for now. No point arguing with the Watch until you had to.

"Sleep well," I called after Camwell as he headed for shore. I didn't think he caught the ironic edge in my voice, but Rika gave me a sympathetic look.

The Lovegrace mansion loomed above us, rising in dilapidated glory from the crest of the island against a sky violet with falling dusk. As we slipped through the gate and climbed the path through the overgrown garden, I spotted a splash of color. A tall, graceful figure in a dress bright as a candle flame slipped out through the solarium door and crossed, rapid and furtive, to the nearby garden house.

Silena Glory. *Well, now.*

Rika saw her, too. She touched my arm, and we ducked behind a row of thick pine bushes. We watched as Glory glanced around before slipping through the garden house door. It was a fancy little stone building with lots of windows—the kind of place built for having small garden parties without worrying about the weather. I couldn't think of any legitimate reason why Glory should be sneaking out there.

"What's she doing?" I muttered.

"She keeps leaving to meet with someone. You must have noticed."

"Maybe our mystery squatter. You think they're in the garden house right now?"

Rika raised an eyebrow. "I doubt she went in there to have a lovely evening picnic."

"Can we eavesdrop?"

"Have you forgotten who you're talking to? Of course we can

THE LAST SOUL AMONG WOLVES   183

eavesdrop." Rika scanned the house with professional eyes. "If we come around from the back, we can get to a window without entering her line of sight. This should be easy, even for a Hound. Come on."

She led me through a patchwork scraggle of trees to the far side of the garden house, where we crouched on the mossy ground beneath an elegantly scrolled stone window frame. Glory's voice sounded from within, highly trained enough that she was easy to overhear despite the muffling window glass.

"You've got to get me out of this." She sounded husky, breathless. Even directed at someone else, the power of her resonance stirred a protective instinct in me. "Before it's too late."

The voice that responded was harder to hear—lower, masculine, with a strange rich depth to it that settled into my bones. It was familiar somehow, in a way that set off alarm bells in my mind, but I couldn't place it or make out the words.

By the lazy warning edge to the tone, however, the speaker wasn't much impressed by Glory's urgency.

"I *know* I got myself into it," Glory replied, not sounding very chastened. "But you need me. I'm no good to you dead. So please—I will ask nicely if you like; I will ask humbly if I must—preserve my life, which neither of us can afford to lose."

This time, I understood the reply: "That was not our deal."

Rika's fingers dug suddenly into my arm, her eyes gone wide.

"It hardly matters what our deal was, does it?" Frustration marred the smooth perfection of Glory's voice. "It's in both our best interests for you to free me from this curse."

A contemptuous murmur.

"What do you mean, you *can't*? You can do *anything*!"

Oh, I had a bad, bad feeling about this.

"Not without the lantern." That disturbingly familiar voice grew louder, as if the speaker had turned toward the window. Its smooth, otherworldly sound coiled around me and through me, striking a cold note of fear deep in my belly. "Which means we have something to talk about with our...uninvited guests."

I recognized the voice at last.

The sharp energy of terror yanked me to my feet, and I stared in the window. It was too late to hide anyway; he knew we were here.

In the small room beyond the glass, Glory sat on one side of a little wrought iron tea table, her hand curled into a tense fist beside a lantern flickering with golden light. On the far side, a lithe and elegant figure lounged in an exquisite black tailcoat, his chair tipped slightly back. Curling black horns crowned his mane of silver hair, and a cape like a smoke-blurred wisp of starry night sky fell from his shoulders to the floor.

Rai's mirror eyes stared straight at me.

"Don't you think so, Kembral Thorne?"

LET YOUR ENEMIES TALK

I eased into the chair opposite Rai with the delicate caution of reaching out to touch a venomous snake.

His silver eyes commanded all my attention, piercing through the dusky light. I barely noticed Glory, stiff at the intrusion, her hands folded on the table, or Rika, who pushed the last remaining chair as far back from Rai as was reasonably possible. If I read the Empyrean's intentions wrong, I might not walk out of here alive.

Did the little garden house always have four chairs, or had he known we were coming? His face, predatory and perhaps subtly pleased, betrayed nothing. There was a leanness to the alien angles of it that I didn't remember from last time, a sharpness of starvation to his cheekbones. And there was an ancient exhaustion in the hollows of his eyes—*that* I remembered.

It was Glory who spoke first, reasonable and measured on the surface with seething tension underneath.

"I am somewhat distressed to find this conversation less than private."

"I'm somewhat distressed to find you conspiring with an Empyrean," I retorted.

Rai lifted one silver eyebrow. "Hypocrisy doesn't become you,

Hound. If an anchor counts as a conspirator, turn that disapproval on yourself."

My stomach sank. Ylti—Tilting Toward Oblivion, the Empyrean we'd bargained with to cure me of Rai's curse at the year-turning—had made some enigmatic comments at the time, but I'd maintained a desperate hope that they hadn't chosen me as an anchor. The confirmation came like a blow to the stomach. The last thing I needed was to be some Empyrean's cosmic balance rail.

Rika stirred uneasily. Right—she was her mother's anchor, too. I'd put both feet in it at once. This conversation was off to a great start.

I tried to keep Rai's success at needling me from my face. "So Signa Glory is one of your anchors."

"I am," Glory said, a firm reminder that she was sitting right there and could hear me.

Fair enough. I turned to her. "You should get out of that if you possibly can. He'll ruin your life and destroy everything you care about."

"On the contrary." The relaxed purr of Rai's voice suggested no concern of losing Glory. "I have ensured that everything she cares about is hers for the taking."

"You've always delivered on your promises," Glory agreed, her glance shifting from me to Rai. "I've never shrunk from pursuing my dreams, and you've been with me every step of the way. But to achieve my goals—and to sustain *you*, my patron—I must survive."

With a sinking feeling, I wondered exactly how long she'd been his anchor, and what kind of debts had accumulated between them. *People change*, Petras had said—but they changed faster with an Empyrean pushing them. I knew from bitter experience how quickly Rai could twist a rational, decent person into a murderer.

"I'm somewhat shorter on anchors than I once was." The edge in Rai's voice was all for me. "So yes, I'd like to preserve you, Silena Glory. Which brings us back to the lantern." He raised a brow in my direction. "I'm sure you can imagine how much I'd prefer to destroy you, but it seems we share a common problem."

THE LAST SOUL AMONG WOLVES   187

I crossed my arms. "So why not solve it yourself? I can't imagine a Deepwolf would pose you much trouble."

"Exactly," Glory murmured.

Rai bared sharp teeth. "The Deepwolf, and the lantern it bears, belong to Stars Tangled in Her Web."

Rika stirred uneasily at the name. I couldn't help a chill at it, myself.

"Is this some power struggle between you?" I asked. "Did she pull your anchor into this on purpose?"

"No." A weary irony infused Rai's voice. "My anchors are ambitious, and seek power wherever they can find it. Silena Glory sought a wish. She first tried to gain it by putting her name in that book, but when it didn't immediately yield what she wanted, she found me. I do admire her initiative."

Glory shifted uncomfortably, looking down at her hands. The flash of Rai's mirror eyes in her direction was not, perhaps, entirely admiring.

"So it's a coincidence?" Rika asked, sounding dubious.

Rai shrugged. "If you believe in coincidence, perhaps. In a crux year, we all seek to stake our claims on power for the next century, and I am less than pleased to find an anchor compromised by a rival Empyrean. But Stars Tangled in Her Web and I are not in conflict— yet—and I would prefer to keep it that way, for simplicity's sake."

I would also prefer that. The only thing worse than one Empyrean was two Empyreans, and the only thing worse than *that* was multiple Empyreans striving against one another. Their human pawns and the mortal bystanders always got by far the worst of it.

Still, there was an advantage here, if I was bold enough to take it.

I settled back in my chair. "So," I said, "you need our help."

"*Need* is not the word I would choose."

There were those shadows around his eyes, the hollows of his face. No, he didn't want to admit it, but right now he was *made* of need. He must be right on the edge of losing his equilibrium, after I'd stopped his year-naming gambit and lost him an anchor—and beaten him, which was not something he could tolerate, for his own survival.

Rika seemed to be thinking the same thing. She leaned forward, a deliberate reclaiming of the space she'd ceded to him at the beginning.

"Interesting that you should want to work with us," she said, "when someone's been sending Echoes after Kembral since the year-turning. Was that you?"

He turned his gaze on her at last. Feeling it leave me was a relief, like the too-hot summer sun going behind a cloud. Rika met it, uncowed.

"So protective." A strange little smile teased Rai's lips. "But that wasn't me. When I come to pay the revenge I owe you, Kembral Thorne, I'll do it in person."

Great. Nice to know I had that to look forward to.

"I'm going after the lantern regardless of what you do," I told Rai, determined to wring something useful from this wretched conversation. "But my understanding is that we need an Empyrean to destroy it. Are you telling me that if we get the lantern, you'll break it in order to free Signa Glory from the curse?"

Rai's eyes narrowed. "I'm surprised you'd seek a bargain with me."

"No bargains." I held up a hand. "Just common goals, like you said."

He laced his pale fingers together, slow and deliberate. Eyeing me the whole time as if contemplating whether to lunge across the table and rip my heart out right now. Then his gaze flicked to Glory, and weariness seemed to settle over him like the cloak of starry darkness that undulated at his back.

"The lantern is the key," he said at last. "Fetch it, dog. If you find yourself in trouble retrieving it from the Echoes, call out to me, and I may help."

Rika lifted a brow. "But not if it means direct confrontation with Arhsta?"

He turned his whole body to face her, leaning a casual elbow on the table.

"Do you know why we don't go up against each other directly, little sister? Why we always use human proxies?"

THE LAST SOUL AMONG WOLVES

189

Rika flinched at *little sister*, but then her expression went hard as stone.

"Because you're cowards, and you don't want to face someone who can actually hurt you?"

He gave a bitter laugh. "We survived the sundering of reality, in the moment of our infancy. We may be many unpleasant things, Rika Nonesuch, but we aren't cowards. No."

He moved closer to her, his voice dropping, soft and smooth as velvet over steel. "We don't strive against each other directly because our mother the Moon forbids it. Because our power is too great, and if we exert its full measure, we can tear at reality itself—just like our other mother the Void, when it attacked the Moon and sundered the world. You would do well to remember that."

Rika didn't shrink from him. She met his gaze with a cool calm that I was 90 percent sure was fake, but still, good job.

"Then I suppose you'd best not do anything to make another Empyrean angry."

She'd just *threatened* him. Every muscle in my body tensed.

But Rai only laughed, tipping his chair back again. "Oh, little sister. We make one another angry all the time. Do you know how we vent that anger?"

Rika's jaw flexed, but she didn't respond.

"We take it out on one another's pet mortals." Rai rose, a languorous signal he was done with us. "Perhaps you'd best remember that, as well."

—⟨⟩—

"Another Empyrean." Rika tried to keep a light tone, but her voice was unsteady as we made our way toward the front door of the Lovegrace house beneath a sky dark with clouds and dusk combined. "Just what we needed."

"Yes, but one of them is on our side!" I let my tone drip with sarcasm.

"He's not on our side, and you know it. He's opposing Arhsta, and we're in the middle, waiting to be crushed."

"At least we have an Empyrean who *might* be willing to break the lantern, if you can't do it. Though I'm not at all sure I trust him to do that."

"I sure as stars don't. He wants to *kill* you, Kembral." She shook her head. "I don't know how we get out of this. I should have known we wouldn't be safe, after the year-turning. Now we're caught in Arhsta's trap, with no way out without doing exactly what she wants, and Rai is waiting to finish you off if we somehow escape it."

Her shoulders had gone rigid with tension. I put a comforting arm across them. "Hey. It's all right. This is my year, remember? We'll find a way."

A shudder ran through her, and some of the stiffness in her posture began to ease. "You're revoltingly optimistic sometimes, did you know that?"

"It's not optimism. We have a plan. Another Empyrean being involved doesn't change anything. The Ravens will come in the morning, and—"

"It changes *everything*." She gave me a piercing look. "Do you really think Rai would happily let us destroy the lantern and upend the board when instead he could win the game? He's in this now, and he doesn't play to lose."

Before I could respond, a familiar voice called our names, a little out of breath. It was Glory, hurrying to catch up to us.

"Signa Glory," I greeted her, braced for this to be some play of Rai's.

"You know about being an anchor," Glory said, without preamble. Her dark eyes searched our faces.

Rika had her mask on, polite and a little amused. "More than we'd like to, yes."

"I...I'm hoping you can help me." Glory bit her lip, briefly— whether a genuine moment of vulnerability or a calculated one, I couldn't guess, but she at least seemed to be trying to keep her resonance in check. "I'm afraid I may be in trouble."

I grunted. "You've been his anchor for years, and you're only figuring that out now?"

"All the information I have comes from *him*." Desperation shone in her face, and I didn't think it was an act. "There's so much I don't know: how this works, whether it's permanent...He's given me a great deal, and I'm grateful for it. But I'm afraid it's all about to backlash in a way that could destroy me."

Rika and I exchanged the kind of glance that contained a whole conversation. She could be an innocent victim, someone we could help and save. Or she could be Rai's eager partner, willing to do anything to further her ambitions.

Maybe even murder a Raven who got between her and a wish.

"What has he given you?" Rika asked, in a soft, sympathetic tone that had inspired countless marks to spill their secrets. "If you want us to help you figure out whether you're in over your head, it's useful to know how deep you've gone."

Glory hesitated, and I tried not to read too much into that ominous pause. "You understand, the Acantis performing arts scene is highly competitive, and it's not easy to break in. But it was my only way out from a bad situation, and I was desperate."

My brain was already supplying horrible things Rai could have done to pave her way, from murdering competitors to mind-controlling directors to give her lead parts. Maybe she saw it in my face, because her eyes widened, and she hastily pressed on.

"Whatever you're thinking, it wasn't like that. I...Let me explain." Her voice fell into the mesmerizing cadence of a performance, her resonance swelling. "When I was a girl, my parents loved only three things: cards, dice, and tiles. Their daughter was just a way to get more money for gambling. They made me work several grueling, menial jobs at once, with never enough sleep or food. I was sick and injured all the time, and absolutely miserable."

This need for lengthy justification wasn't reassuring, and she still hadn't answered Rika's question. But sometimes the best way to get information from a source was to let them talk, so I made an interested noise and kept my mouth shut.

"I needed to be safe." Her beautiful voice trembled. "The job Petras got me wasn't enough. I needed to get out of Southside for good, to make sure I'd never have to go back to that life. Building a singing career that will give you that kind of security requires luck, connections, a Butterfly guild membership—but I didn't have any of that. No matter how well I auditioned, I couldn't get into the guild, couldn't get a role at the Grand Theater, couldn't even land a better job singing at a more upscale gambling hall."

"Until you met Rai," Rika suggested softly, her eyes locked on Glory's face.

"Yes." Glory lifted her chin, unashamed. "It was Rai who opened all those doors so I could walk through them, one after another. After I became his anchor, suddenly the guild accepted me. I got the roles I tried out for. I was able to cast off all that was holding me back, and everything went my way."

I couldn't help myself. "To cast off everything that was holding you back, huh? Like Petras?"

She had the grace to blush. "My patron made it clear that I couldn't triumph at my art if I was depending on other people."

That went against everything I'd ever heard about theater, but never mind. "So *Rai* told you to dump Petras?"

"Essentially. He...encouraged me to focus on my career. And it worked." Her shoulders lifted. "It may sound cruel to you, Signa Thorne, but I don't regret it. My patron's guidance has never led me astray. He gave me everything. What I am now, I am because of him."

I didn't doubt that. But what she was now was deeply, utterly alone.

"And now you're afraid the bill will come due?" Rika asked.

"No. I'm afraid he'll take it all away."

I stared at her. Rika murmured something very softly that sounded like *Oh, you poor fool.*

Glory wasn't in too deep. She was already drowned and lost. She regarded me so earnestly, her brown eyes worried, with absolutely no idea how she'd already ruined her own life.

I wanted to save her. To extricate her from Rai's grasp and show her that she didn't need him. But she had no desire to be saved, and it was ultimately her choice.

"What..." I licked my dry lips, tasting sea salt. "What do you want to know, exactly?"

"What he wants," she said immediately. "What he gains from me, so I know what leverage I have with him."

Fair enough. No matter how foolish she'd been, she deserved to at least know what an anchor was. What she had become.

"Empyreans are unstable by nature," I said. "Moon and Void don't mix. They need to latch on to some poor human who's following their equilibrium thread—their purpose, I guess. The Empyrean's guiding principle, their way of being, something like that."

"Ambition," Glory whispered, almost to herself. "Triumph. Destroying those who stand in my way."

"Right." I wished she sounded more distressed at the prospect of adopting that particular set of guiding principles. "So if you follow that thread, the momentum you create along it helps keep him balanced, like a wheel rolling in a track. If he loses that equilibrium thread and tips too far toward either his Moon side or his Void side, he...loses himself. Turns into something else, or ceases to exist."

A chill struck me as it hit that this had almost happened to Rika today. I studiously avoided looking at her.

Glory's brows pinched anxiously. "And if I don't follow that thread? Or if I try to follow it, but I fail?"

Ah. Understanding dawned on me. "Is this about that new alto? Signa Velar?"

"Velar! She's nothing." Glory's own resonance belied her, a flash of pure jealousy humming through her words. "She should never have gotten that part. It's only because since the New Year, suddenly everyone at the Grand Theater is talking about giving new voices a chance. Taking risks on fresh talent." She shook her head. "It's a passing fad, I'm sure."

"But you're concerned that Rai won't realize that," Rika said, all soothing sympathy.

"At first I blamed him," Glory admitted. "He'd always smoothed the way for me before. But he said something had changed—something about the year-turning—and that it would be harder to deny the hopes of the other singers looking to make a breakthrough."

Oops. So it was *my* fault she hadn't been cast, actually. I decided not to mention that.

"He said that I'd have to show him what I was made of and win some of my battles myself," Glory continued, twisting her hands together. "And now...I've failed. He despises failure. If I can't get him the victory he needs, what will happen to me?"

"If you're very lucky," I said, "he might decide you're no use to him anymore and drop you as an anchor."

"That would be a *disaster!*"

"Staying his anchor is much worse. He'll drive you to chase his equilibrium thread at all costs, without rest or diversion. He'll push you to reach for more and more, and to crush anyone in your way. To stop at nothing—even murder." I gave her a pointed look, just to see how she'd react. She was one of my top suspects right now, after all.

Her eyes widened. "Signa Thorne! Surely you aren't accusing me of Signa Overfell's murder. Willa was arrested for that."

"She wasn't technically arrested, but no, I'm not accusing you. I'm just saying that's exactly the sort of thing he'll drive you to do."

"For example," Rika suggested, with a touch of bite, "has he offered up any solutions regarding Irida Velar?"

Some emotion flickered across Glory's face. For a moment, she didn't speak, perhaps out of fear of what her resonance would reveal. I made a mental note to send Signa Velar a warning to watch her back.

"I see," Glory said, after a long silence. "I won't deny that he has... ideas and suggestions. But he can't force me to do such things, can he? My choices are still my own."

"Signa Glory." Rika touched her shoulder, the briefest brush of her fingertips, a gesture full of weary sympathy. "Trust a master con artist when I tell you that there are so very, very many ways to make people choose what you want them to."

"Believe me, I know that better than most." She laughed ruefully, and it was a beautiful music. "But I can't go back. Rai's patronage rescued me from a life of despair. I'm not willing to give it up."

"Even if it destroys you?" I pressed. "Being an Empyrean's anchor is one of the worst things that can happen to you. It's almost guaranteed to ruin your life."

Rika averted her gaze. Given our current shitty situation with her mother trying to pull her back into her web, that was maybe not the most reassuring thing I could have said, but it was honest.

Glory didn't seem impressed. "My life was already ruined. Becoming an anchor saved it...and will continue to do so."

That got my attention. "Oh? Did you make some new bargain with him to survive the curse?"

An evasive shrug. "He gave me a means to protect myself from murderers."

"I see." I chose my next words carefully. "And he hasn't encouraged you to use this means to take out the competition yourself?"

"Oh, he has." She met my gaze, a certain jaded irony in her lovely brown eyes. "You must understand that we have had this conversation before, over the years, and I always tell him the same thing."

"Oh?"

"That if there is some line that would compel me to commit murder, we haven't crossed it yet." She gave a wry sort of shrug, the shoulders of her gown shimmering. "I'm not so naive as to believe I'd never kill a person, but I hope to never find out what it would take to make me so desperate."

I was all too aware of what could make me that desperate. If anyone threatened Emmi, I'd gladly tear their heart out with my own teeth.

"I hope you never do," I said. I wished I had any certainty she was telling the truth.

Movement flickered in the twilight shadows of the woods beyond the garden.

I spun, reaching for my sword, ready to face the mystery trespasser or a hostile Echo. A figure exploded from the path that led down to the docks, her hair tangled, collar attractively disheveled—Jaycel Morningray.

"Kembral! Thank the Moon you're back. We have a problem!"

"We have so many problems already," I objected.

"Brace yourself. We've got another." She looked grim and wild, but fell into a dramatic pose out of sheer instinct. "I was looking out the window just now, watching the tide come in across the sandbar, and I saw a *ghost*."

Glory, Rika, and I all stared at her, nonplussed.

"A . . . ghost."

"Yes! All silvery and glowing, with trailing garments—I glimpsed it through the trees, moving off. I assume it was old lady Lovegrace." She waved a dismissive hand. "But that's not the problem."

"Excuse me, but a ghost seems like a problem," Glory objected, glancing around the deepening twilight of the garden in alarm.

My skin prickled. I'd seen that silvery light last night, down by the water. Given everything that had been happening, an Echo seemed more likely than a ghost. Or perhaps, if we were truly unfortunate, an Empyrean. It sounded a little like Arhsta, though with her preference for working indirectly I doubted she'd come here herself. It could even have been Rai, on his way to meet Glory—though Jaycel probably would have recognized him, given that they'd had a short-lived fling around the year-turning, a fact I regularly devoted significant mental resources to forgetting.

"This ghost—" Rika began.

I held up a hand. "We should definitely come back to the ghost. But what's the problem, Jaycel?"

"I went looking for the ghost, of course," Jaycel said, once again showing a terrifyingly casual disregard for her personal safety. "It was gone by the time I got outside, so I searched the island for any trace of it. But what I found was even more sinister."

"For love of the Moon, woman, just tell me."

Jaycel drew in a breath heavy with portent. I got the sinking feeling that her next words would hit like a brick.

"Someone smashed up all the boats at the docks," she declared. "We're trapped on this island until morning!"

ANTICIPATE THEIR NEXT MOVE

Jaycel was not indulging in hyperbole.

The storm we'd seen in the distance had crept closer under cover of the falling darkness. Lightning licked its forked tongue down on the horizon, and an ominous salty wind blew in from the sea, setting the trees to thrashing in the darkness. Waves slapped the rocks with heightened urgency. An early smattering of raindrops hit my face, fat and cold.

Not much light of Moon or stars made it through the thick clouds gathered overhead. But I didn't need much light to see what was wrong.

There were three boats at the docks. One was an old rowboat, hauled up on land long ago and flipped over to keep the rain out. Someone had staved a great hole in its upturned belly. The second rowboat had been tied up at the dock; only its prow was visible now, angling sharply up from the water that lapped over its sunken stern. The third, a small sailboat with room for maybe four people, lay with its mast tipped onto the dock, shreds of tattered sail trailing sadly from the boom where it had been furled. The entire back half of the boat was gone, jaggedly broken off, rudder and all; the current must have taken it.

Thousands of tiny Echo lights danced in the water around the wreckage, as if in celebration.

"Well, shit," I said.

Jaycel and Rika had come down to the dock with me, Jaycel showing off what she'd found like a dog with a dead rabbit, while Glory told the others. Vy had run to join us at once, catching up as we arrived at the docks.

Now she put her professional seal on our doom. "I don't think those look salvageable."

"Why would someone do this?" Jaycel asked, all traces of showmanship draining away as a lost bewilderment took its place. "I understand a dramatic gesture, but this hurts all of us. What could they hope to gain?"

"To keep us from calling for help," I said grimly.

An ominous silence fell as everyone digested that.

This was bad—catastrophically bad. Because this was a first move. Another was sure to follow, and with two Empyreans involved, it could escalate beyond mere human malice.

I didn't dare lose an instant.

"Jaycel, Rika, can you go check to make sure nothing terrible is happening in the house? Vy, I want to take a closer look at these boats. Figure out what happened, and whether that sunken one is smashed up, too, or just swamped."

Vy nodded; Jaycel gave me a flourishing salute.

Rika hesitated. "I don't want to leave you alone."

"She's not alone." Vy flashed Rika a fierce grin. "I'm with her. I'm an old hand at dealing with what comes out of the sea; I'll take care of her for you."

Rika gave her a narrow look, then nodded and went with Jaycel. It occurred to me as she left that it wasn't the ocean she'd been worried about. She didn't want to leave me alone with Vy.

I couldn't imagine little Vy as a murderer—but of course, this wasn't little Vy. This was adult Vy, who was at least half a stranger. I'd be a fool not to be on my guard, no matter how much my instincts said to trust her. Still, I was pretty sure I could take her in a fight, if it came to that.

I had a suspicion that Rika agreed, and that was why she'd been willing to leave.

Vy eyed the water, oblivious to our suspicions. "Be careful. That's a *lot* of little ones. Stuff must be washing in through that gap in the Veil as the tide comes in. There could be something more dangerous in there, too."

"I will," I promised, watching the dark water warily as I started out on the weathered planks of the dock. Vy's heavy boots clunked behind me. Shadows slipped among the lights—probably just fish, but I couldn't be sure. I kept my mind poised on the threshold of a blink step, just in case.

The damage done to the sailboat seemed vicious and excessive. Maybe a human with an axe could have chopped up the stern, but it would have taken a while, and they'd have come back sweaty from the effort. The shredded sail was what clinched it, though. Cutting sailcloth wasn't a trivial endeavor, and it wasn't necessary to disable the boat. This was almost certainly the work of an Echo.

The prow of the rowboat seemed intact, but I couldn't tell what it looked like below the restless, lapping surface of the black water. I knelt down on the dock, peering over the edge. More of those tiny glowing Echo fish swam near the surface, in and out over the swamped edges of the boat; some of them seemed to be sprouting stumpy tentacles, like a tadpole's baby legs.

"Can you see whether the hull is intact?" I asked Vy.

"No," she admitted, "but it'd be tricky to get it under like that without putting a hole in it. I mean, you could tip it enough for water to come rushing in over the edge, then sink the stern—that would work, but it might be hard to do alone."

I reached down to pull on the edge of the boat, hoping to get a feel for what shape it was in.

"Careful," Vy warned.

She'd barely uttered the second syllable when something lunged up out of the water at me, *through* the bottom of the boat, all teeth and teeth and teeth.

I swore and flung myself back, but Vy was faster. An oar came whistling down to crack the beast right in the snout, wielded with expert surety. It recoiled, uttering a terrible rusty-gate noise.

Then it reared farther out of the water, dragging the remnants of the boat with it.

It was like some horrid eyeless cross between a shark and an eel, with a great round mouth filled with endless rows of teeth. It had to be thicker than I was; it could probably dispatch me in a few quick bites.

I scrambled to my feet, but I barely had time to draw my swords before Vy hit it again and again, the oar coming around in sharp, vicious arcs.

"Back in the ocean with you, lout!" she yelled, without an ounce of fear, as if she were dispatching a cockroach. "You heard me! Get off! *Off!*"

With a roar of protest and a great splash, the thing dropped back into the dark water. The waves roiled and rippled over it for a moment. Then all trace of it was gone.

I stood there panting, staring in horror at the spot where it had disappeared, scanning the black waves for any further sign of it.

Vy shouldered her oar with an air of satisfaction. "We get those trying to come on board all the time, when the tide skimmer takes us down. You've got to have a firm hand with them."

I stared at her with increased respect. Maybe I couldn't take her in a fight after all.

"You could not pay me enough," I said, "to be a sailor."

The seaworm-thing Vy had beaten off might or might not be what had destroyed the boats, but I had no doubt in my mind that whatever hand or maw did the deed, it was on the orders of someone with a plan to trap us here. That thing hadn't writhed up onto shore to get the overturned rowboat just for fun. I could only think of a few motivations to strand everyone on the island, and they all led to more people winding up dead.

If Arhsta was behind this, and her goal was to get Rika into that castle, anything she did to make obtaining the lantern more urgent would feed into that. With Rai involved, he could be setting the stage to eliminate the competition so his anchor could win the wish. Not to mention that the way things were going, I wouldn't be shocked if there was some third party making their own play. Regardless, the most urgent thing right now was to make sure that whatever the Echoes were plotting, the humans didn't make it worse.

We returned to the house to find it in an uproar. Glory stood in the drawing room like a living flame, pointing in a grand operatic gesture at Petras. He slouched in a chair, cravat loosened, dangling a drink between his knees.

"It was *you*, wasn't it?" Glory's resonance was at full power, and for a moment my mind went fuzzy and it seemed like she could only be speaking the truth. "You're bitter about the past, and you trapped us here to get back at me!"

Petras gave her a withering look. "You're not worth that much of my time and energy."

"You seem awfully eager to make accusations," Jaycel said dangerously, "for someone who was outside for no good reason while the deed was done."

"I was nowhere near the docks!" Glory protested. "I was . . ."

She'd been meeting with Rai. Her gaze jumped to me, then to Rika, who leaned against the wall behind her client, arms crossed. Realization dawned on her face that maybe *I was meeting with my Empyrean patron* was not the most ironclad way to allay suspicions.

I was half-inclined to let her stew in it—I didn't like the way she kept trying to shift blame to Petras for things, and it made her look guilty as the Void itself. But this was exactly the sort of nonsense I needed to shut down before it could escalate.

"All right," I barked, "everyone calm down and listen up."

They all turned and looked at me. Good.

"First of all, stop slinging accusations. This situation is already dramatic enough without your help. Second, and most important, you should know that I talked to the Ravens. They're sending people to help us get the lantern from the Deepwolf when it next comes through the mirror, before it can kill anyone. Once we have it, we should be able to destroy it and end the curse." I felt a bit bad about exaggerating the certainty of the solution, but right now I needed everyone to calm down.

"Thank the Moon." Jaycel threw herself into a chair, her ire at Glory forgotten. "Much as I normally prefer to dashingly rescue myself, I'll make an exception when two-story invincible spectral wolves are involved."

Amistead raised his brows. "Does this mean we can all go home in the morning? Charming as this, ah, antique house is—"

"I think you mean moldering haunted wreck," Jaycel suggested.

"—I'd love to see my grandchildren. Allione sent over a courier message telling me she's been asked to play her violin in an upcoming recital."

"If all goes well, yes. We have to make it through the night first. And for that, we need to cooperate." I gave everyone a stern look, my friends most definitely included. "Echoes probably broke those boats, but they use human proxies in their games. Someone in this room is likely a murderer—or plans to become one, now that we're all trapped here."

Everyone eyed one another uneasily.

"I invite you to try it," Jaycel drawled.

"Nobody had better try *anything*." I let my voice sharpen. "I'm talking to the murderer right now when I say that destroying the lantern is your best chance of survival. You can't use the wish if you're dead, and you can't control this chaotic situation well enough to be sure you come out on top. If you won't make the right ethical choice, at least make the right strategic one. Let the Ravens do their job, and let's be done with this."

A pensive silence followed my words. I could only hope I'd gotten through to them.

I softened my voice. "I know we're all under a lot of strain. I know it's frightening to think that we're trapped here with a killer. But we only have to make it until morning. If we all stick together, and we all stay alert and keep our heads, we can do this. All right?"

THE LAST SOUL AMONG WOLVES 203

Wind rattled the windows, and a spattering of rain hit them as the edge of the storm reached us at last. A roomful of haunted eyes stared at me. There were scattered nods.

"Just let me know when there's something I can *do*, I beg you," Jaycel said, a restless edge in her voice. "I'm not built for all this waiting. I'm a woman of action."

She spoke lightly, but I could almost *feel* the tension seething under her deliberately relaxed pose. Jaycel had never been good at sitting around, and even less so in a crisis. She was doing her best to stay calm, but I knew an energy burned in her that without outlet inevitably turned to chaos. She needed a project, or she was going to start challenging people to duels or causing property damage out of sheer nerves.

Vy, who had been looking hunched and miserable, suddenly brightened. She leaned over and put an earnest hand on Jaycel's arm.

"It's all right," she said. "You're so strong, and you know how to be brave in a fight. But *I* know how to be brave when I'm helpless. Let's do something silly and fun, to prove to the world we're still alive."

"Like what?" Jaycel looked interested, which had me concerned because her idea of *silly and fun* could involve a wide assortment of civil and criminal offenses.

Vy clapped her hands together. "Let's go fishing!"

"Darling, I said I'm *bad* at waiting."

"When we were down at the docks just now, I saw a whole school of fish, come to eat the little Echoes in the water. They should be easy to catch while they're feeding, and then we can cook them for dinner!" Vy tilted her head, then added, "Oh, there was some kind of giant worm Echo, too, but I'm sure we can handle it. I left an oar down there."

Amistead rubbed his belly. "I wouldn't mind fresh fish for supper, if you catch enough to share."

Jaycel grinned. "Well, if they're biting, and there's a chance of a dramatic Echo battle to sweeten the deal, how can I say no?"

"That sounds perfect," I said. It sounded far more harmless than some of Jaycel's usual stress relief solutions, anyway. I turned to Petras, the person I'd come here to talk to in the first place. "While they're fishing... Rika and I need a little chat with you. About sources of information."

"Given what Signa Nonesuch told me while you were out looking at boats..." Petras grimaced. "Yeah. I'll bet you do."

—◁ꟽ—

"Your source set us up," I told Petras flatly as the music room door closed behind us. "It was a trap."

"I heard." Petras slumped into the nearest chair, looking stunned. "I don't understand. I've known him for *years*. He's always been reliable. I never thought he'd do something like this."

"Maybe he was under duress. Maybe he was manipulated and didn't know he was setting Rika up." I was talking about Petras as much as his source, and I couldn't keep the edge out of my voice. "But we barely got out of there alive."

Petras groaned and put his hands over his face. "This looks so bad. I *know* it looks bad. Here I am, with my mysterious information, sending you into danger, and it's a trap." His hands dropped, and there was pure misery in his eyes. "But, Kem, I hope you know I'd never do that to you."

I felt Rika's eyes on me, waiting to see what I'd say. I was the one who knew Petras best; she had to trust my judgment.

And I *did* know him. Sure, he'd changed, and the Petras of our childhood was only a memory. But he hadn't changed that much. He might set up a rich man to lose his wallet, but he'd never, ever set up a friend to die.

"Yeah," I said. "I know. And I hope *you* know that I'd never betray your trust for some stupid job."

A flicker of some emotion passed across his face, deep and old and yearning. "Yeah. I do know that."

"I'm sorry I left you all so suddenly," I blurted, before I could stop myself. "I didn't mean to. I just...I woke up after the kidnapping thing in the guildhouse, and it was like I'd fallen into an Echo. It didn't feel like I *could* go home. I should have slipped away and come to see you more often."

"Nah." Petras shook his head. "You did fine. I was a moody kid who missed my friend and decided to be hurt about it even though I could have walked over to Guildhouse Square just as easily. But you were always there when I really needed you, Kem. You still are. That thing with my bartender's kid, or the time you helped me figure out who tried to burn down my tile parlor, or now."

I'd forgotten about the tile parlor. On impulse, I reached out a hand. "Let's just forget about all the drama and trust each other. All right?"

He grinned, and it was the old smile, ready for trouble. "All right."

We shook on it. His hand was slim and strong and free of the calluses it had borne when he was a kid clambering around Southside.

"Now," I said, settling into my own chair. "I want every detail you can give me that might help us avoid another trap."

"That's fair, but…" He hesitated. "If I tell you about my source, he'll *know*. Echo business, you understand. We…may have had a pact."

I put a hand over my face. "You made a pact with an Echo."

"Look, I do business with him all the time. It's never been a problem before."

The thought of Petras making pacts with Echoes just to get fancy booze for his clubs didn't make me less twitchy, but it was done, and we had to move on. Fortunately, I'd run into this kind of problem before, and I knew a way around it.

"All right. So you can't tell us any details, or he'll know through Echo magic. But *I* can talk to you all I want. So I'm going to do that, and you just look at me."

He met my eyes, his own bright with memory and understanding, and gave a tiny nod. Long ago, when Petras was curious about my training with Almarah but I was sworn not to say a single thing about it, he'd make wild guesses out loud and watch my face. I was so bad at hiding my reactions that it was pretty easy for him to figure out when he'd hit the mark.

Petras was much better than me at hiding his expression—he always had been. But Hounds were trained at reading people, and he didn't *want* to hide anything from me now.

I glanced at Rika; she gave me a nod and gestured for me to go ahead.

"First of all," I told him, "you should know that your source is working for the Empyrean known as Arhsta, or Stars Tangled in Her Web."

"Holy Void." His eyes went wide. "I knew he was getting his information from other Echoes, but I never thought it was an *Empyrean*."

"Yeah, well, we're not happy about it, either."

He shook his head. "This is beyond me, Kem. I know my way around Dockside, but bring in the Echo stuff and I'm fresh as the first rube wandering in from Tower with money in his pocket and a passing familiarity with tiles."

"Maybe you shouldn't sit down at the table, then," Rika suggested, not without pity.

Petras passed a hand over his eyes. "Maybe I shouldn't. Damn it, this was always too convenient. I should have asked him how he knew, been more suspicious, said no."

It was like every time he'd gotten in over his head when we were kids, which admittedly happened less often for him than it did for, say, Jaycel. Unlike most of our friends, Petras could see with crystal clarity every single place where he'd gone wrong, and it haunted him. Jaycel moved forward proudly with no regret, learning nothing—but Petras lined up his failures on a shelf in his mind to take out and dust off and examine and brood over every now and then.

"So he approached you with this information," I said. "And he suggested you hire someone to steal the lantern, *knowing* you'd go to Rika, because you've worked with her before. Maybe even dropping hints that you'd need someone really skilled to pull off the heist of such a powerful relic."

Petras didn't need to nod. The self-accusatory despair in his face was all the confirmation I required.

"You got suspicious after the bequeathing and asked to know more. But he didn't answer until it became clear that Rika needed a nudge before she'd jump in the mirror. So he sent you that message about breaking the lantern being the solution to the curse, right during the brief window when we could immediately go into the Echoes after it."

Petras grimaced. "When you put it that way, it sounds so obvious."

"Yeah, well, I fell for it, too." I considered how to say the next bit. "I'm curious about the phrasing of that message. Whether it was vague, like he was hiding something, or weirdly specific, like he was trying to find a way to warn you."

He frowned. "I can probably tell you that, as best as I remember it, since I was supposed to pass it on. The Echo carrying his message said he was sorry, but he couldn't explain how he knew about the lantern. It said 'There are things I have to keep secret.' But to make it up to me, he'd tell me something new—'What I couldn't tell you before,' it said: how to free the souls and break the curse."

I exchanged glances with Rika. "That does sound a bit like he was under orders. Most Echoes can't resist an Empyrean's command."

"It's a shame the message was verbal and not written down," she murmured. "I would have liked to see if he might have hidden another message in there somehow."

"The Echo messenger said something about that," Petras remembered, straightening. "It said he didn't dare give me a physical note because other eyes were watching, and other hands might find it."

"Do you think he meant Arhsta?" I asked, dubious.

Rika's grey eyes had gone wide enough to drink in the whole world. "No. She doesn't need eyes or hands to watch us. He was giving us a warning."

It took me a minute, but then the full implications of what she was saying hit me.

"She's got another agent on this island."

———m———

Rika held me back in the music room with a look when Petras left. She shut the door behind him and turned to me, her face serious, all the play gone from her movements.

"Who do you think it is?" she asked.

I ran a hand through my already disheveled hair. "It could be the Echo that destroyed the boats. Jaycel's ghost, maybe—that silvery light. Or it could be almost any human here. Stars, they may not even *know* they're working for her."

"This job really has gone straight to the Void, hasn't it?" Rika shook her head. "All right, Kembral. You're the one who always has a plan. We're stuck on an island in the middle of Arhsta's scheme, along with one of her agents and a murderer, who may or may not be the same person. The Ravens won't get here until nearly dawn. What do we do?"

"That's a good question." I sank into a chair by a floor harp, thinking. "We can't let her get what she wants. But what *does* she want, exactly? Or more to the point, what does she want *from you*? Because I hate to rub it in, but this really does seem to be all about you."

"Ugh." Rika turned her head as if she couldn't look at me, the lamplight catching the angle of her jaw. "Broadly? She has some grand scheme about making me a queen."

"You'd think there'd be a less horrible way to accomplish that."

"Wouldn't you?" She let out a bitter laugh. "But it's never that simple for her. It's not just that she wants me to be a queen—she wants me to be a perfect little nesting doll copy of her, a power player with my own schemes that fit inside her schemes. To share charming mother-daughter bonding activities like world domination, which I'm sure would be quite wholesome if she intended to give me any free will or choice."

I remembered the weblike scars that showed up in certain lights in the Echoes. "So she wants you to be her puppet. Her toy."

"*And* a power source. Don't forget that part."

"Her own daughter." Anger simmered in my gut. I wished so much I could *do* something to Arhsta that she would actually care about—could force her to face consequences for hurting the woman I loved. But she was a divine celestial being, and I was an extremely mortal Hound. I'd be lucky if I could manage to get any of us out of this alive.

THE LAST SOUL AMONG WOLVES

Rika wanted me to have a plan. She was staring at me desperately, waiting for me to make this all right somehow. I drew in a steadying breath.

"She clearly wants you to go into that castle. Everything she's done points to getting you in there. So we make sure you stay away from it at all costs. That shouldn't be hard, with Zarvish's plan to get the lantern straight from the Deepwolf."

"Which she probably knows about," Rika pointed out. "You'll notice we're trapped here now. She's going to snip off our options, one by one, until the only road left for me is the one she wants."

"Then we make a new road."

"How?" Rika spread her hands despairingly. "Even if everything somehow goes according to plan and we get the lantern with no further mishaps—which, frankly, isn't going to happen with Arhsta interfering, and you know it—we'll still need me to draw on her legacy to break the thing. Which is exactly what she wants."

"We could get Rai, or Ylti—"

"No." She shook her head. "You know that's a terrible idea. I have to be prepared to do this."

I didn't like the edge of steely resolve in her voice. "How dangerous would it be, exactly?"

She gave a too-casual shrug. "You helped me before. If it comes down to it, I'm sure you can do so again."

"I helped you, sure, but you almost died! Or something worse! It's not worth risking your life."

"Kembral, you are an absolutely raging hypocrite, did you know that?"

I blinked. "What?"

"You'd jump back in that mirror without a second's hesitation if that was what it took to destroy the lantern, even knowing that one tiny cut is all it'd take for the whole Echo to be after you."

"Yes, but—"

"How is that any different? And don't say because you're a professional and it's a calculated risk. I can calculate my own risks, thank you." Rika glared at me. "Promise me you won't go back in there."

"Right now I don't have any plan to go back in there," I said carefully. "The Ravens—"

She threw up her hands. "You were thinking about it! I knew it! Promise me."

"You know I can't promise that. You heard Signa Zarvish—we need a backup plan. If something goes wrong, we might need to send someone after the lantern. I have no intention of going in at the moment, but if I *did*, I'd be careful, forewarned, and much better prepared."

Rika didn't look convinced. She grabbed the collar of the shirt she'd loaned me, releasing the lingering scent of cedar as she gave me a little shake.

"You're not listening to me. You *can't* go back in there. I need you to be safe." Her voice dropped to a whisper. "I won't lose you."

"You're not going to lose me." I brushed a thumb along the worry line between her brows, trying to erase it. "I'm the safest person on this island, right now. No one's after me."

"Except for a variety of crunchy Echoes, according to Achyrion! Did you think I'd forgotten?"

"All right, sure, but that's unrelated."

"Kembral..." Her gaze dropped from mine. She released my shirt, fingertips trailing down to my collarbone and then away. "I realize this sounds ridiculous. But I have a bad feeling that if you go into that mirror alone, I'll never see you again."

All right, that was a little disconcerting. I tried not to show the chill slithering up my spine.

"Look, it's a moot point at the moment anyway," I said. "The mirror is closed, and we need a different plan. But we don't know what Arhsta's next move is going to be, so it's hard to make one."

Rika rubbed at her arms as if she were cold. "Do you really think it was *her* doing that we're trapped here? I can't tell if I'm just seeing her in every shadow now."

"Given her nature, she probably *is* in every shadow," I growled. "Half the people here might be doing what she wants without even knowing it, like Petras. Whether they're serving her deliberately or

THE LAST SOUL AMONG WOLVES   211

not, it comes out to the same thing in the end. Which means..." I
trailed off, the implications hitting me. "*Shit.*"

"What? I hate it when you say that."

I started for the door, heart pounding. "If what she wants is to get
you to that castle, and the only way to get into the Echoes right now
is through that mirror, and the mirror only opens when someone
dies..."

"She's going to make sure someone dies," Rika breathed.

THERE'S NO SUCH THING AS SAFE

We burst from the music room like an ill wind, seeking signs of disaster.

I headed for the docks first, banging the door open and striding right out into the storm without bothering to grab my coat. All I could think of was Jaycel, going fishing alone with Vy when I *knew* there was a murderer around—especially since I'd just learned Vy was more dangerous than she looked or her friends remembered. I should have told them not to go. I should have made everyone stick together in a group, with no exceptions, instead of treating it like we were still a bunch of kids playing together down by the river.

The rain fell cold and miserable, soaking through Rika's shirt and trickling down the back of my neck, but I didn't care. Rika came up behind me and threw my coat over my shoulders, muttering something about Hounds. I barely noticed as we hurried along the path toward the shore, my nerves sparking with worry.

"Are they even going to be out here in this weather?" Rika demanded.

"The elements hold no power over Jaycel Morningray. And Vy likes the rain."

As we emerged from the trees onto the stretch of sloping lawn before the docks, I was terrified of what I might see: one friend dead

THE LAST SOUL AMONG WOLVES

213

and the other with bloody hands, or both laid out by some silvery Echo striking at Arhsta's command. A strange sound hit my ears, and for a panicked instant I heard it as anguished cries.

It was laughter. Great wild peals of laughter, thank the Moon.

"He almost pulled you in there, Morningray!"

"Good quick grab, Vy! Thank you for saving the tatters of my dignity."

"That worm would have eaten more than your dignity!"

Jaycel and Vy were not only fine, but they appeared to be having the time of their lives. Someone—probably Vy—had attempted to rig the tattered sail into a makeshift canopy. Beneath it, Vy and Jaycel leaned together, Vy's arm over Jaycel's shoulders, while Jaycel held up her line with a large, thrashing fish. Vy's oar lay near to hand. The canopy seemed ineffective, and they were both drenched, but neither of them seemed to care in the slightest.

Something in my chest eased. It was so good to see them smiling. And they were clearly taking care of each other. Any Echo that tried to bother Jaycel and Vy was going to have a nasty surprise.

I hated to break up their fun, but knowing there was an Empyrean bent on killing someone changed things. We couldn't protect everyone if they were scattered all over the place. I told them there was an imminent threat and I was gathering everyone at the house; Jaycel, eyes bright at the prospect of danger, promised they'd gather their things and follow close behind us.

Rika and I hurried ahead to find the others. I dripped a trail of rainwater into the foyer that would have earned a scathing condemnation from my sister, but human lives were more important than the mansion's questionably maintained floors.

The storm picked up as we swept into the drawing room, wind rattling the window glass and lightning flickering in the distance. Glory stood in a corner, back stiff as a spear, pretending to look out the window at the rain; Petras and Amistead seemed to be having a surprisingly engaged conversation.

"Yes," Petras was telling him, "they distill it from apples grown one Echo down, or something *like* apples anyway..."

He broke off as we stormed in. Everyone turned to look at us, surprised at our sudden entrance, bracing for more bad news.

"I'm gathering everyone together," I told them. "Wait here. I'm going to check on Willa."

She should be the safest of them all, with an Echo-worked lock between her and anyone who might wish her harm. But we'd left behind *should be* long ago. So as thunder shook the house, I climbed the creaking stairs and arrived at her door.

She didn't respond to a knock.

I exchanged a meaningful glance with Rika, who'd followed me up, and knocked again. Still nothing.

Something was wrong, even aside from Willa not answering. The air seeping through the crack beneath the door to curl around my ankles was too cold and damp, the room too utterly silent.

"Rika..."

"I'll take care of it." She swept her hair back from her face and knelt in front of the lock.

"It's Echo worked," I felt obliged to point out. "You're not supposed to be able to pick or break them, and they magically reinforce the door as well, so—"

"Yes, strangely enough, I know about Echo-worked locks. Now shush, I'm working."

I'd seen Rika's lockpicks before, when we'd cooperated on jobs. The tools she produced now (from apparently nowhere) were different: one looked as if it were made of thin red crystal, and another of some strange metal with a purplish sheen. She muttered to herself as she worked; the crystal one occasionally emitted a note, which she listened to and hummed softly back before proceeding.

It only took her about a minute and a half to open the lock. So much for them being unpickable.

She rose, making the lockpicks disappear. I expected some smug quip, but the look she gave me was serious, verging on grim. Which drove home what I'd been trying not to admit to myself: We'd made too much noise for Willa not to have heard us. Nothing good waited on the far side of that door.

I reached out and touched the handle. Thunder boomed outside as the door swung open.

I was braced for a corpse, but the room was empty. Loose papers blew off the desk, and mildewed curtains flapped in gusts of cold, rain-flecked air from the open window.

"She's not here," I breathed.

Rika frowned. "Do you think she escaped through the window?"

Before I could answer, the lamps in the hall flickered, and an all-too-familiar tingling crawled across my skin. I swore; my breath puffed misty in the suddenly frigid air.

A bone-chilling howl lit up my nerves and went straight through into my soul, mournful as the wounding of the Moon.

"*Fuck!*" I whirled to face the stairs, filled with the desperate urge to run down there and try to stuff the wolf back in the mirror somehow. "It's here. That means..."

A bluish glow bathed the hall, and a smoky fog engulfed us. The Deepwolf, too big to see properly and surrounded with mist, passing through walls on its way to collect its prey.

"She's dead," Rika finished softly.

Where in the Void *was* she? I ran to the window, half expecting to look down and find her broken body on the ground below, discarded as casually as her gloves had been.

Lightning flashed, lighting up the garden bluish white for one brief flicker of an instant.

Willa's body hung in the fork of a tree, her arms hooked over its branches, as if someone had lifted her corpse up and stuck it there for later. Blood drenched her chest and throat, streaking down from a wide slash beneath her chin.

SEEK TRUTH EVEN WHEN IT HURTS

Another murder. I'd been *right here*, on alert, and I still hadn't been able to stop it. We were so close to getting the curse broken. Everyone just had to wait one more night until the Ravens came. Nobody needed to die.

But of course, that was probably why they'd done it. To stop the night from ending without tragedy—Arhsta's plan come to nothing, the deadly wish unwon.

I was past hoping that no one here was a murderer. Once again, the physical evidence at the scene suggested a human hand: the kitchen knife used to cut her throat lay at Willa's feet, and faint impressions of boot prints marked the grass. We hadn't seen any indication that the trespasser had remained on the island after we'd all arrived, and by now we probably would have; whoever they'd been, they were gone.

I stalked into the drawing room and closed the door behind me, Rika sticking to my side like a bodyguard, and took in the shocked and frightened faces of the survivors. It had to be one of them: Petras, Vy, Amistead, Glory, or Jaycel. Maybe more than one, if there were two different killers. It was the people under the curse who had the motive, and an Empyrean would use the pieces already on the board.

THE LAST SOUL AMONG WOLVES · 217

I had five real suspects—three of whom were my friends.

"All right," I growled. "Let's do this. Did anyone see or hear Willa Lovegrace alive after Camwell did his final check on her before he left?"

Silence. A couple of headshakes. That meant she'd been killed sometime in the past hour or two. She could have been murdered right after Camwell left and been hanging there in that tree the whole time, invisible from the docks and the sandbar on the oceanward side of the mansion.

"Tell me where each of you were from when Camwell left until now. Jaycel?"

She lifted her head, tired but alert. "Looking for the ghost, along the riverward side of the island. Then I found the boats and came to get you. And then I went fishing with Vy."

"I went to my room to write up a certain message," Petras volunteered, with a significant look that made me think he'd been trying to get in touch with his Echo contact. "I came downstairs when I heard the commotion about the boats being smashed. Then we had that conversation."

Great. They both had a gap at the beginning where no one could vouch for their whereabouts. "Dona Amistead?"

"I'll admit I was intrigued by this ghost sighting, so I followed young Morningray outside," Amistead said. "But only just barely outside, mind you. She started bounding off down the hill through the forest and I decided that my old knees and I weren't up for it."

"After that?" I prompted him.

"No one was left in the house that I could see, so I poked around in the kitchen for a snack and poured myself a bit of brandy. Then came the commotion over the boats, and since then I've been chatting in the drawing room with various of our fine companions."

I nodded. "Vy?"

"Well, first I walked Investigator Camwell and his assistant to the sandbar, to look out for Echoes and make sure it was safe to cross. Then on the way back I saw Jaycel disappearing into the woods to look for her ghost, and I went after her—but couldn't find her, so I

218   MELISSA CARUSO

gave up and came back to the house. Dona Amistead and I had just
started trading tide skimmer stories when Glory gave us the news
about the boats. After that, well, you were with me, and then Jaycel
and I went fishing."

Glory shifted uncomfortably. "You know where I was. After that,
I've been with people the entire time."

I did in fact know—but there was still the window of time after
Camwell left the mansion, when he'd been crossing the sandbar
and talking with me. Maybe half an hour all told before Rika and
I arrived on the island and saw Glory sneaking out to the garden
house, which was perhaps enough time to commit a murder.

So they all had a motive, and no one had a complete alibi. Lovely.

I closed my eyes, then opened them again. "Rika and Jaycel,
can I ask you to keep an eye on everyone? I want to talk privately
to—"

Glory rose to her feet. "Why do you assume they're innocent? Just
because they're your friends? How is this fair?"

"Let me be clear," I said, unable to keep the edge from my voice.
"I'm not acting as a Hound right now. I'm far too close to this case
for that. It's *not* fair. I've given up on being fair and professional. Now
I'm just trying to keep you all alive."

"Do you have an issue with keeping everyone alive?" Petras asked,
watching her with glittering dark eyes. "The Silena I knew wouldn't
have."

She whirled on him. "I don't want to hear about the Silena you
knew! I'm not that person anymore!"

"Apparently." He shook his head, a sadness in his gaze. "I barely
recognize you."

"Good!" She took a step toward him, fury in the movement, then
stopped herself. "I *hate* the Silena you knew. I *love* who I am now—
Signa Glory of the Butterflies, star of the Grand Theater! Not some
pathetic little *nothing.* This is why I don't want anything to do with
you, you know—because you insist on reminding me of *her!*"

Glory's resonance crashed over the room like a wave. Rage and
despair and a desperate panic flooded me, hot and vibrant and far too

THE LAST SOUL AMONG WOLVES   219

real. Vy cried out and put her hands over her face; Petras reeled back as if she'd struck him.

Glory whirled to stalk from the room, but Jaycel stepped casually into the doorway, blocking her.

"Signa Glory," I said, as gently as I could manage as the dregs of her resonance drained from me. "As I was about to say, can I have a quick word with you in private?"

———ᨒ———

We didn't sit down. Glory stood by the harp in the music room as if she planned to accompany it, her posture regal; I faced her, too tired for this, but ready to do it anyway.

"You realize," I told her, "that you're making yourself look incredibly guilty."

She froze. That wasn't what she'd expected. "I am?"

"You fed me that whole line about wanting to make amends with Petras, but the moment Mareth died you immediately started taking every opportunity to accuse him and start fights with him. The only reason I could think of at first was that you were trying to scapegoat him for the murder because you'd done it yourself."

She stared at me, eyes wide and shocked. "But I didn't."

"You want that wish. You've got an Empyrean backing you who will insist that you win at all costs. You're already terrified of losing his favor. You're easily smart enough to think of stealing Willa's gloves to frame her. You've been using your resonance to try to get me on your side. Can you think of one good reason I *shouldn't* suspect you?"

"I . . . No. I can't. Not under pressure like this, on the spot." She bit her lip.

Luckily for her, I could think of one reason: She was working for Rai, and the timing of this move made it more likely Arhsta's doing. But it was a flimsy piece of evidence at best. He had plenty of reason to push her into action, too.

"Do you have some other motive for being an asshole to Petras, besides framing him?"

220   MELISSA CARUSO

Her cheeks reddened, and she dropped her gaze. "I know you won't believe me, but I truly wish him well."

"You certainly haven't acted like it."

"He...I need to prove to my patron that I'm focused on my goals. I can't let him compromise that. I have to show that he doesn't mean anything to me."

Which meant that he did. Blood on the Moon, that was the saddest thing I'd heard all day.

A knock came at the door.

"Who is it?" I snapped.

"Tylar Amistead." He slid the door open a crack, blue eyes peering in, more subdued than usual. "Sorry to interrupt, but when you have a moment, I'd like a word."

"I believe we're finished," Glory said, voice smooth as caramel once more. "Please, go right ahead."

She slipped out of the room with the speed of a child dodging punishment, the door nearly closing on her fluttering bright skirts. I let her go.

Amistead moved across the room much more slowly, easing down into a chair and arranging his joints and bones with the care of a Hillside grand lady arranging her dress. I pulled up a seat opposite him, since standing would have been awkward.

"Something troubling you, Dona Amistead?"

He sighed. "More than you can perhaps imagine. This may sound foolish, but it's a long time since I've been truly afraid, Signa Thorne."

I raised an eyebrow. "You don't seem like the kind of man who'd be coming in here just to ask me for reassurances. But I'm happy to give them, if that's what you want."

"No, no. You're quite right. The truth is, I can do the math. With the interval halving each time, I know how quickly a single hand could tip the balance and ensure none of us make it to sunrise." His mouth twisted in the nest of his beard. "Well, all but one of us, at any rate. And faced with the possibility that I might not survive, I find myself unexpectedly eager to ensure that certain relevant secrets don't follow me to my grave."

THE LAST SOUL AMONG WOLVES

221

Vague, half-formed suspicion slid into certainty, with the satisfying feeling of a key turning in a lock.

"Certain relevant secrets, huh?"

"Perhaps you already know them." He met my gaze steadily.

"Twenty-five years ago," I said slowly, "someone up in Hillside tricked a bunch of people in Dockside and Southside, mostly kids, into putting their names in that book. Someone who knew how the relics worked and thought they had a foolproof plan to win the wish."

Amistead nodded, his head heavy. "It was my brother."

"Did you know?"

"No. Not until later." His voice came out rough; his face fell into haunted lines. "I was off in the navy. Angling for admiral, in those days. I knew we had some ancestral relics, but only the heir got told how they worked. When my brother died of the curse, my father called me home and explained. And I..." Amistead shook his head. "What could I do? My brother was dead. My father was dying. The relics were gone. I was horrified, of course—but it wasn't my secret, wasn't my crime. And still, ever since, I've been doing everything I can think of to make amends."

"That fund for widows," I realized. "You just wanted an excuse to give money to Petras and his mother, didn't you?"

"And the other affected families, yes. I know it's not enough. But it was an easy place to start."

"I'm not here to dig into your moral reckoning." I leaned forward. "I'm here to save lives. Tell me everything you know about the relics."

Amistead looked relieved. "That's why I'm here, too. I assure you, I'm not dragging my family's ugly past into the light for my own entertainment. So...yes. The relics. They've been in Amistead hands for generations. My understanding is that some ancestor of mine made a deal with an Empyrean for them. He wanted the benefit of a wish without the consequences of a bargain, and he was clever enough to suggest making it a game."

That would work, given how much they liked games. "Did this same ancestor of yours come up with the idea for the ward that repels the wolf, too? So that your family could keep the relics in your own house up on Hillside, safe and sound behind the ward, while the Deepwolf rampaged around killing poor people no one would ask too many questions about?"

There was a silence. Amistead shifted in his chair, gazing at the rain streaming down the night-dark windowpanes. "Yes," he said at last. "But to the best of my knowledge, my brother was the first one who thought of recruiting children. May his soul be banished to the Void for it."

"If he died of the curse, that's not where his soul is."

Amistead grimaced. "No. I suppose it isn't."

"So he put his name in the book, planning to kill a bunch of kids and get the wish." It was all I could do to force my jaws to unclench around the words. "But then...Auberyn Lovegrace."

"Yes." His eyes kindled with something like awe. "My family had been doing this for hundreds of years; my brother had all the advantages. But she beat him at his own game."

"How?"

"She was too sharp for him. She looked younger than she was, you know—a tiny thing—and my brother mistook her for a child. Auberyn was suspicious from the start about being bribed to put a drop of blood in a book, and she found out where he lived somehow." He spread his hands. "Followed him, overheard his name, who knows? One way or another, whether by eavesdropping or cunning, she learned what was going on."

"And then?"

"She broke into the house and made herself a little nest in a hidden spot in the cellar, right underneath where the relics were kept. My family didn't find it until it was far too late. Since my brother thought he had full range of the house and grounds, he wasn't bothering to glue himself directly to the mirror. Auberyn was closest when it was finally down to the two of them and the Deepwolf came." He shook his head. "He got what he deserved, frankly."

"You sound like you almost admire her."

"Oh, I do. She was dreadfully clever."

"So you knew she had the relics, but you left her alone?"

"Because she was wise enough to lock them away, and clearly had no intention of using them. I want those relics destroyed as much as you do, Signa Thorne. Maybe more."

"You're not trying to get the wish yourself?" I pressed. "Dreaming about reclaiming it for your family?"

Genuine repugnance twisted his face. "My family stopped needing a wish to guarantee our success long ago. No, those relics are my family's great shame. And that's why I wanted to talk to you, Signa Thorne. If there's any way I can assist you in getting rid of them forever, I want to help." His eyes crinkled in something sadder than a smile. "And, well, if I don't make it to my granddaughter's violin recital...I want to be sure this curse won't pass to a new generation."

When Amistead opened the door to leave, Rika was waiting outside it like a sentry. She slipped in and closed the door behind her.

"I assume you were listening," I said.

"Naturally. Do you think he's working for Arhsta?"

"I don't think she's giving him orders, no. But I don't think she needs to. She's almost certainly the Empyrean his ancestors made the deal with for the relics in the first place. She's got the full measure of him, and she knows what he'll do. Her plans have taken him into account."

"Her plans have probably taken *everyone* whose names are in that book into account." She bit her lip. "Do you think he's the murderer?"

"It's hard to imagine him manhandling Willa's body out a second-floor window and up into a tree. For that matter, it's hard to imagine anyone doing that." I frowned. "I hate to say this, but I need to go outside and look at that wall under her window."

"I'll come with you," Rika said immediately.

I tried not to give her an odd look. She'd been sticking to me like my shadow since the fifth Echo. She was trying to hide it, but strain still showed in her body and her face, if you knew where to look. I doubted very much that anyone else would notice, but she was not okay right now.

But bringing that up wouldn't help. I understood about needing to leave certain things unexamined to hold it together until the job was done.

"If you like getting rained on, sure," I said lightly. "Come along."

The raw salty wind whipped my tangled hair into my face, and thunder rolled across the bay. The rain was steady and stinging cold now; I pulled my coat up, tenting it over my head. Lights glittered along the banks of the river, north and south, and the great harbor lights burned steadily to guide ships coming in and out of Dockside—though I sincerely hoped none were out in that storm.

Rika balked at the door. "This is miserable."

"You could stay inside."

She flipped up a deep-cowled hood on her wool coat and stepped out into the rain. "So could you."

I squelched my way through the garden to the seaward side of the house and found Willa's window. I peered up at it, blinking against the rain, trying to pick out a route up the wall as my eyes adjusted to the darkness.

"How long would it take you to climb that?" I asked Rika.

She barely glanced up. "That's easy. Less than a minute."

I grunted. I suspected anyone fit and modestly skilled at climbing could manage it, but it would certainly take me a lot longer. Jaycel, Vy, or Petras could do it. Glory...hmm.

"Could you do it in a dress like Glory is wearing?"

Rika considered. "Yes, if I tied up the skirt. It'd be trickier to do it without chipping those long painted nails she's got."

I eyeballed the window frames and drainpipe I'd use if it were me. "Amistead seems unlikely. Not to say he *couldn't* do it—I'm sure Almarah could, and she's about his age with arthritis to boot, and he must be a decent climber if he was in the navy—but I can't imagine this method would be his first choice."

THE LAST SOUL AMONG WOLVES 225

"Remember," Rika said, "the question isn't whether any of them could do it. The question is whether they could do it carrying a body."

"I assumed they just threw the body out the window and then climbed down. But the thing that gets me is why they bothered at all. Why not leave her body in her room? Why go to all the trouble to wrestle it out the window and up into a tree?"

Rika frowned. "Maybe she was escaping out the window when they killed her, and they were never in her room at all."

"Maybe." I remembered something, then. "Her corpse—she wasn't wearing shoes or a jacket. She would have put on something if she were going to run away in this weather."

I poked around at the rosebushes beneath the window. A few branches were broken and a bit squashed, as if something heavy had fallen on them. A strand of brown hair had caught on one of the briars, slick with styling cream.

"Looks like she *was* chucked out the window, alive or dead. Or else she was leaning out and fell, I suppose."

I stared off into the rain, thinking. Her throat had been cut, but something about the angle bothered me. It looked like it had been done while she was lying down, but there was no blood in her room, and the knife was left by the tree. Like they'd brought her there alive but unconscious, then cut her throat and stuck her in the branches. I shivered.

"Kembral, are you even listening to me?" Rika demanded.

"What? No," I admitted.

She glared at me, rain running off the edge of her hood. "I said if you're done looking and we're just thinking about this, we should go inside."

"Right," I agreed, still distracted. "Yes, let's."

We stepped back into the light of the foyer, our coats shedding copious rain on the marble tiles. As we shook them off and hung them up, Rika shot a glance at the closed drawing room door.

"So Amistead has a connection to Arhsta through his family, and Petras does through his source," she murmured. "And Glory is Rai's."

How about Jaycel? Does Rai have any hold over her? They had that fling."

"Ha! No." I shook my head. "That's over—though I gather she enjoyed it, and I nearly had to strangle her to keep her from telling me the details—and *Jaycel* barely has any control over what Jaycel does, let alone any third party. Rai's absolutely a concern, but he's not the sneaky and manipulative type. When he makes a move, we'll know it."

"That fits. So we've got two meddling Empyreans, at least three human pawns, and a murderer or two—not to mention five desperate people who know their time is running out—and we're all trapped here on an island swarming with Echoes until morning." Rika shuddered.

She wasn't going to like what I had to say next. I licked my lips.

"There is...one way off the island."

Her eyes narrowed. "I don't like that look on your face, Kembral."

"Everyone is readying their next moves, Empyreans and murderers alike. If they *make* those moves, more people are going to die. We've got to end this game now. Bring in Camwell and the Ravens, shut down any Echo nonsense or further murders, take control of this place back from Arhsta."

"And how are you planning to get them? Swim through the Echo-infested water? Or..." Her grey eyes went suddenly wide. "No. You promised."

"I actually was very careful not to promise."

"Kembral, you *can't*."

"It hasn't been that long since Willa's death. The portal should still be open. I already know the route to work my way back up to Prime, so I can do it quickly. And you know as well as I do that we're not making it to morning otherwise."

I didn't wait for her answer. I started out of the foyer and down the hall, heading for the relic room. Rika followed on my heels.

"Have you lost your mind?" she snapped. "We barely got out of there alive!"

"I'm prepared this time. I brought a portal tether to keep the

THE LAST SOUL AMONG WOLVES

mirror from sealing behind me, and all my usual Deep Echo gear. I'll be careful."

"Being careful would mean waiting for the Ravens!"

I stopped in the hallway and turned to face her. "Somebody's already decided they're not going to wait for the Ravens. Someone who's acting out Arhsta's will, knowingly or not. They were pretty slick about smashing the boats and murdering Willa, and I don't know if I can catch them before they kill again. They cut us off from the mainland for a reason, and it wasn't because they wanted to spend a little quiet bonding time together."

"You can't go down there!" To my shock, there was real fear on Rika's face, naked beneath the slipping mask of her fury. "This has got to be part of her plan. You *know* the mirror is a trap."

"Yes. A trap for *you*. Which is why I'm going alone, and I'm not going anywhere near the castle. I can navigate the Deep Echoes safely; this is my job. It won't be too dangerous."

"You don't know how dangerous it will be." She grabbed my shoulders. "I told you I've never had an *us* before. I refuse to go back to a *me* just because you have some inexplicable urge to go get yourself ripped apart by a hundred Echoes."

"I won't get ripped apart."

"You can't guarantee that!"

She was right. I couldn't, and not least because Prime blood was one of the strongest tools and most useful currencies I had in the Deep Echoes. Not being able to spill so much as a drop of mine safely made going that deep far more complicated and dangerous. But without Rika around to protect, I could blink step out of almost any trouble. I was pretty sure I could do this, so long as I didn't make any mistakes.

"Look. I can't just sit back and trust that things will turn out fine. Not with Arhsta three moves ahead of us making sure they don't."

"No." Rika's grey eyes shone with wild ferocity. "You can't go back in there, Kembral. I won't let you."

She'd had so little sleep, and it had only been a few hours since she'd nearly ... well, whatever had almost happened when she'd transformed. Unraveled into the Void, become a star, something beyond my mortal understanding. There was nothing rational in the look she was giving me, just an instinctive panic at the thought of either of us going back there—and to be fair, sticking my hand into the same fire that had so recently burned it might not be completely rational, either.

But there was too much at stake. I didn't have time to talk Rika down until she felt better about letting me go. A little rill of impatient anger made it through my concern for her.

"I'm not going to stand here and argue with you until the portal closes. I've got to do this." I softened my voice, because I didn't want to leave with an argument. "I'll be right back."

I turned toward the relic room door.

Something sharp bit my neck, a sting like a wasp.

"Ow!" I spun, expecting some insect—and instead found Rika, tears spilling from her eyes, a needle-thin little blade in her hand. "What the *fuck*, Rika? What did you..."

"I can't risk losing you," she whispered.

A numb tingling crept from the tiny wound on my neck. My legs already felt unsteady. No drug worked this fast—she'd wasted an Echo poison on me.

"This isn't..." My words ran together, blurring at the edges, but shock and fury helped me force them out. "You don't just *drug* people when they disagree with you."

"I can't let you go. I just...I'm sorry, but I can't do it."

It hit me, through the numb dizzy fog descending rapidly over my mind, that there was something strange about her tone. A buried anguish in the way she looked at me. She was hiding something—a whole extra layer to her motivations that I knew nothing about. It set off warning bells far beyond the outrage of betrayed trust.

I can't let you go. Not won't, but *can't*—and three times she'd said it, like an Echo.

It wasn't like Rika to relinquish control, to allow another force to bend her will. But she spoke as if whatever tied us together was beyond her, and she was helpless to resist it.

Oh. Oh, shit. I knew what was going on, and it wasn't the power of love.

The Last Soul Among Wolves

I grabbed a wall to steady myself against the drag of the poison, staring at her in horror.

"Blood on the Moon," I breathed. "I'm your anchor."

Rika flinched, a jerk of her whole body as if I'd slapped her.

"I thought I might be Ylti's, but I'm not." It all made too much sense. "I'm yours. I've always been yours."

"No!" She took a step back. "I... Maybe. I don't know."

"Come on, you can lie better than that." I should be angry, but my rage was gone. Only a despairing, awful shock remained, pulling me under like a cold tide. I slid down the wall, head swirling.

Rika reached to catch me. I swung out a clumsy arm to keep her back.

"Stay away!" I couldn't bear for her to touch me. Not now. "I can't believe... all this time, when you stayed with me, when you protected me..." The hallway was spinning and fading, but I managed a few more words, my better judgment fleeing along with consciousness. "I thought it meant you loved me..."

Everything went dark.

"I do love you, idiot," Rika's voice said, a thousand miles away. "This would be so much easier if I didn't."

I hit the floor.

DON'T BE A LITTLE DIVA

I woke with eerie suddenness, snapping from a deep and dreamless sleep to fully awake in an instant. I was lying on a divan in a dusty study near the relic room; someone had left a single glass lamp kindled on a small table beside me.

I sat bolt upright, heart thundering with a feeling that it would be refreshing to call fury, but it was too wild and complex for that. Paper crinkled on my chest, and a note slid to my lap.

She hadn't poisoned me after all, not quite. I felt far too good, and besides, I recognized it now. The Ravens made a very expensive Echo potion they had some fancy name for—Something Something of Restorative Slumber—but which the other guilds called Nap on the Job. It was completely safe, put you down for an hour, and then you woke up as refreshed as if you'd had a full night's sleep. Needless to say, it was in high demand—I was lucky if I got my hands on some once a year. And Rika had somehow *weaponized* it and wasted a dose knocking me out.

The note in my lap bore only two words, in Rika's handwriting.
I'm sorry.

Oh, screw that. She was *sorry*?! For stealing a precious hour of the limited time I had left to save my friends? For taking away my choice?

THE LAST SOUL AMONG WOLVES 231

For binding me to her on a cosmic level without my consent, admittedly probably not on purpose, and then being weird about it?

Her *anchor*. I buried my face in my hands. I should have seen this—should have figured it out ages ago. The very fact that I'd been able to keep her from destabilizing in her Empyrean form was a dead giveaway. Those uncomfortable faces she'd made when we talked about how awful it was being an anchor weren't because she *was* one—they were because I was hers.

All the desperate lengths she'd gone to in her attempts to protect me, all the things she'd said about me grounding her—she just needed me to survive. Like a *meal*.

I do love you, idiot.

What in the Void did it even *mean* that I was her anchor? She'd said she didn't have an equilibrium thread, so she couldn't need to drive me along it the way Empyreans usually did. Apparently it included being weird and overprotective, to the point where she had a plan in place to knock me out rather than let me take a perfectly rational risk that I took all the time for my job.

I tried to take a step back and ask myself if I could possibly be overreacting, if this was normal—but no, she'd fucking *drugged* me. *Again.* I still wasn't entirely sure I'd forgiven her for the first time, and you'd think she'd have learned after how badly that went—though I supposed waking up laid out comfortably on a divan was better than under a pile of stinking garbage in a cellar.

I crumpled the note, stuck it in my pocket, and stomped out into the hall. I could hear muffled voices; they didn't sound like they were raised in fear or anger, so hopefully everyone was still alive this time.

The bitter irony was that everything suddenly felt a lot more solvable, now that I was rested. That had been the closest thing I'd had to a full night's sleep in four months. If Rika had just *given* me the Nap on the Job, instead of *stabbing* me with it, I'd be crying with gratitude.

Light glowed down the hall, voices and the clink of glasses coming from the drawing room. I paused in the shadowy corridor, my whole body tensing. I didn't want to see Rika right now, especially in a room full of people. I was too angry and shaken. I needed to go kick rocks and swear for a few minutes until I calmed down, or I'd immediately make the situation worse.

The rain seemed to have tapered off to a light drizzle while I was out, so I veered into the foyer and stepped outside.

The raw, salty night air enfolded me like a mood. Oh, this was exactly what I needed. I stomped around the garden in the dark, cursing and kicking the occasional thornbush, misty rain beading in my hair.

She'd known I was her anchor. She'd *known*, I could tell. And then instead of telling me and working out what to do about it together, she'd knocked me out and stuffed me in a box to keep me safe. Sure, she was under a lot of stress, but blood on the Moon, there were limits.

"Kem? Are you all right?"

I turned, heart speeding, to find Vy behind me, her eyes big and round with concern. Her hair was straggling free of its brown braid, and the wind tugged at the skirts of her royal-blue coat.

"What are you doing out here?" I demanded, my voice too uneven. "Bloody Moon, is everyone just scattering to the four winds all over the estate to make things easier for murderers?"

"No, everyone's gathered together. I just came out here to make sure you were okay." Vy gave me the sort of look you might give a spooked animal that snapped at you, sympathetic but a bit wary. "Signa Nonesuch had told us you were napping, but in kind of a weird voice. And then when you went straight outside without saying hello to anyone, well...I thought I should check on you."

"I'm fine," I said gruffly, buckling my control together as best I could.

Vy tilted her head. "You don't sound fine, and Signa Nonesuch didn't look fine. Did you have a fight?"

That was none of her business, but I swallowed the words before I could say so. Vy was my friend, and this was the sort of thing I would have told her about, once. We would have chucked rocks into the river together until I felt better.

"Yeah, sort of," I admitted.

"Oh dear. What about?"

The Last Soul Among Wolves

233

There was so much I couldn't tell Vy. That Rika had bound me to her with a magic neither of us understood, with consequences neither of us could predict, in a way that usually ended in tragedy. That I didn't want what lay between us to be magical—that it felt false, forced somehow, messing up something I wanted to be true and simple and human.

I couldn't breathe a word of that great, awful ache sitting in my chest. But I *could* talk about the anger burning in my throat, already right behind my tongue.

"She *drugged* me. I didn't take a nap—not on purpose, anyway. She drugged me to keep me from going through the mirror."

"Oh." Vy bit her lip. "Well, that's not good."

"No, it isn't! Thank you!"

"Because it's not nice, of course," Vy said almost pensively, "but also because it ruins everything. You *needed* to go into that mirror, to save everyone, and now you can't."

"Exactly! Blood on the Moon, I'm glad *you* get it, anyway."

Vy patted my arm. "You'll get another chance, I promise. But Signa Nonesuch shouldn't have done that. Have you talked to her about it?" Seeing my expression, Vy hastily added, "That's what people do when they make mistakes and hurt each other, isn't it? I'm no good at this."

"Jabbing someone with knockout poison is a pretty big mistake. It's not like she forgot my birthday or spilled wine on my favorite shirt."

Which reminded me that I was wearing Rika's shirt right now. Some of her perfume still clung to the collar, despite the rain that had soaked the fabric until it stuck to my skin.

"Oh, definitely," Vy said. "But maybe she doesn't understand how bad it was. Like...well, you know I've been at sea for a long time, and I keep making mistakes, myself." She bit her lip, her eyes going distant, as if she were reviewing old memories. "On the *Breath of Dawn*, the crew would play pranks on one another, especially putting wet slimy things down people's shirts. Or live fish, or crabs. But I think most people on land wouldn't take that well."

"Are you suggesting that Cats poison one another to show affection?" I demanded, incredulous. Then I thought about it. "All right, that probably tracks for the Cats I know."

"They probably don't think it's as big a deal as we do, anyway." Vy lifted her hands. "Which doesn't mean she should do it! But friends are such a precious thing to have, Kem. It's not worth losing one over a single fight without even talking about it."

It wasn't that simple, of course. Rika knew damned well how I felt about getting knocked out for my own alleged protection. That wasn't some harmless prank like on Vy's ship. But still...

Wait. Vy's ship. That name tickled at my memory. I'd heard something about the *Breath of Dawn* recently. What was it?

A voice, deep and masculine, rose up in my mind—a Raven in the guildhouse entry hall, requesting some kind of equipment from the desk.

We need to figure out what came on board the Breath of Dawn *while their tide skimmer had it down an Echo—and we can't ask witnesses, because there were no survivors.*

I stared at Vy. Sweet, innocent Vy, my old friend, her brow furrowed with concern for me, earnestly trying to help.

Vy, who should be dead.

"What happened," I asked slowly, "to your ship?"

Something flashed in her eyes—not grief, but naked alarm.

The world went slow and still, as if I'd just stepped into the Veil.

Vy had been acting strange. She'd run across the sandbar before the tide went out, while the current was strong and full of Echoes, which anyone so familiar with these waters should know not to do—unless they had no reason to be afraid. She thought baby Echoes were cute. She'd said all that stuff about being at sea, and forgetting what it was like on land; I'd thought it was sailor talk, but now I wasn't so sure.

Amistead's words floated to the top of my memory: *In my navy days, I knew a man who lost half his old crew to something that crawled inside the captain while the tide skimmer had the ship down an Echo.*

"It...had an accident, but I'm fine." Vy flashed me a tentative sort of smile. "What did you hear?"

When I'd chased the silver light the first time, I'd found Vy; it had appeared again right around the time the boats were destroyed. Vy hadn't seemed overly surprised by either the condition of the smashed boats or the appearance of the sea worm. And Willa had fallen out of her window—maybe because she glimpsed something she shouldn't have, and was leaning out for a better view when something killed her to keep her from revealing it.

Like someone coming up to the house the long way around to avoid being seen after smashing some boats, perhaps. Or someone who looked less human than they should.

"Just rumors." I let my hand drift toward my sword belt. "It sounded pretty bad, though. Were you there when it happened?"

"I...Yes." Vy braided her fingers together, seeming distressed. "I don't like to think about it."

"Sorry. Let me ask you a different question, then."

"Yes?"

"Do you work for Stars Tangled in Her Web?"

Her eyes went wide with horror, and her hands flew to her mouth. She made a strangled noise.

There was no reason Vy should react to that name. An Empyrean's name was not a commonly known thing, and I'd never mentioned it to her.

I drew my sword in a swift, fluid movement, pointing it at her chest.

"You're not Vy," I said flatly.

Her face twisted in distress. "I am! Don't say that!"

"What did you do to her?" I snarled. "Who are you?"

"No!" Tears streamed down her cheeks, and she lifted pleading hands. "Don't say it, because...because I really like you! I like *all* of you! I remember everything, all her thoughts and feelings, and I *love* you, Kem. You're my friend."

I couldn't help it; I recoiled in horror, stepping back. But my sword tip stayed pointed firmly toward the spot between her eyes.

"But if you say I'm not her..." The thing that wasn't Vy was shaking now. "If you *know*...I have orders, and I have to...I have to..."

Blood on the Moon. Here it comes.

She squeezed her eyes shut, drawing a great breath as if to scream. Tentacles exploded out of her mouth.

BEWARE TREACHERY

Writhing white tentacles spread wide like the petals of a flower from Vy's mouth, reaching and straining into the night air—but where an octopus would have suckers, these tentacles had *eyes*. Hundreds of eyes, surrounding one great central eyeball ringed in sharp shining teeth.

"Fucking *fuck*!" I shrieked, all other words gone from my brain.

The eyes all opened and glowed red. Their light fell on me, bathing me in scarlet—and at once, a strange lassitude stole through me. It robbed the strength from my limbs, numbing my mind.

I tried to back away but stumbled to one knee instead. Everything besides those red eyes began to darken, as if they were consuming my vision.

Blink step, I told myself. *Come on, blink step away.* But my mind was too scrambled and fuzzy to reach the Veil.

Vy stepped closer, tentacles reaching toward me. This was how Willa must have died—stunned by those glowing eyes so she fell out the window, then finished off while she couldn't fight back. And now I was going to die the same way.

"I don't want to do this," a voice said that was not at all like Vy's—completely inhuman, thrumming in my bones more than my ears. "I can't resist her orders. I'm so sorry, Kem."

THE LAST SOUL AMONG WOLVES 237

A tentacle circled my wrist, with alarming gentleness. Another brushed my face. I was staring straight into that central glowing eye, which had begun to swirl with a slow fire. I tried to move, to look away, but I couldn't so much as twitch. *Shit, shit, shit.*

The Echo suddenly gave a violent jerk. The red light winked out, and the tentacles slithered back into Vy's mouth; she staggered forward with a strangled cry, nearly falling on me.

Two knives protruded from her back. Behind her, drawing two more, stood a radiantly furious Rika Nonesuch.

I could immediately move again. I rose, bringing my sword up, ready to fight. But instead of attacking, the thing wearing Vy's body made an anguished sound and ran.

She sprinted off, far faster than a human should move, heading into the shadows of the woods. Toward a steep, forested slope that plunged straight to the ocean—an ocean, I realized with rising horror, from which she probably came.

I couldn't let her escape. I started to launch after her, but Rika caught my arm, jerking me back.

"Don't follow her! You *know* that's exactly what she wants!"

I whirled on her, because it was better than thinking about Vy.

"Will you *stop* that?!" I yelled, too loud and too wild and too close. I yanked my arm from her grip, fury boiling from me so hard I should be smoking with it.

"Would you rather I let you run after the Echo that's trying to kill you?" Rika snapped, sheathing her knives. "Be reasonable, Kembral."

"Yes! *Yes*, I'd rather you let me! It's not your job to decide what's safe for me to do!"

"Well, if you weren't so bad at it yourself—"

"No, you listen to me!" I was too angry, too upset at what had happened to Vy, too shaken by the Echo's attack. "You've gotten *weird* about this, Rika. This overprotectiveness— How did you even know I was in danger just now? Because you were *stalking* me!"

"Yes, fine, I was following you! Because there are Echoes after you, and it's not safe for you to wander off alone. As we just saw!"

"That doesn't make it any less creepy! Although I guess I know why now, don't I?" My voice went bitter, much sharper than I meant it. "Because you need your anchor."

She stepped back. "That's not why."

"Oh? Are you *sure* about that?"

She didn't reply, her face shuttering like a slammed door.

"Look, I know you don't care about my free will—you've made that abundantly clear—"

"Of *course* I care!" She threw up her hands. "Damn it, Kembral—"

"But how in the Void am I supposed to have a relationship with someone who knocks me out and stuffs me in a cupboard every time she thinks I'm in danger?"

"Maybe if you put yourself in danger less often!"

"I *haven't* been! I've been careful. I just have a risky job. One I like and want to keep doing!"

Thunder rumbled, loud enough to shake the ground beneath my feet. The light drizzle stepped up to a hard rain, hissing through bare branches and withered leaves. Raindrops trickled under my collar with miserable cold fingers; dark hair straggled pathetically into Rika's face. We stared at each other, both too furious and upset to run inside, to say anything, to fix this.

Finally Rika made a frustrated noise, turned on her heel, and stalked off toward the house. The rain bounced off her so hard it gave her a silvery nimbus in the light from the windows.

I stared after her, too angry to follow. Standing in the rain like an idiot, alone in the dark, trembling all the way down to my feet.

Vy. *Vy.* She was dead, eaten from the inside out by something that digested her memories and wore her skin.

And yelling at Rika had only made everything worse.

I stood in the rain and darkness until I was drenched and shivering. The house loomed over me, a great black shadow, wind moaning past its turrets. I couldn't go inside, because that would mean accepting that everything that had just happened was real. I was stuck in this awful moment, sure as if I were in the Veil.

The Last Soul Among Wolves

Vy hadn't been Vy this whole time. The last time I'd seen her alive had been ten years ago, and now I'd never see her again. She was dead, horribly dead. Little Vy, the sweet and fiercely brave kid who'd followed us everywhere, been willing to try anything, who'd gone to sea chasing a dream. It was only her body that was still alive and walking around.

Unless it had been left behind in the ocean just now, a discarded skin with some tentacled Echo horror swimming out of her mouth and heading back to the rip in the Veil, its mission aborted. If that were the case, would the Deepwolf come? Her name hadn't had a line through it, so the book must only know that her blood was still living, since that was what had forged the link. What would the wolf do if it found her corpse already empty of a soul?

I needed to get moving. I needed to take charge of this situation and come up with a plan to counter whatever Arhsta was going to try next, now that I'd uncovered her hidden pawn.

Blood on the Moon—I needed to tell Petras and Jaycel.

All this time, we'd been chumming around with Vy's murderer. I'd *hugged* her, for Void's sake. She was some mind-eating tentacled eyeball monster, and I'd hugged her and laughed and cried with her. She'd saved me from that ocean Echo she'd beaten off with the oar, and gone fishing with Jaycel to cheer her up.

She'd said she loved me. What was I supposed to do with that?

She was some horror from a Deep Echo who'd killed my friend and puppeted her body—but it was Arhsta who'd made her do that, and Echoes couldn't usually resist Empyrean commands. She'd been so wistful, so eager to experience a stolen friendship. So starved for affection and approval, like wherever she came from, she'd never gotten any before.

Now I was crying over my friend *and* the Echo squid-thing that killed her. Bloody Moon, this was too much. Why did I care about the feelings of the monster who had killed Vy, and probably Willa, and maybe Mareth, too?

No. My brain—despite itself, despite everything—lurched into sudden motion. Not Mareth.

Arhsta was the one giving this Echo orders, and if she wanted to kill a random person to open the portal and put pressure on Rika, she wouldn't have picked our only Raven. She *wanted* us to know how the relics worked, so she could use the lantern as bait. After Mareth's murder, she'd had to funnel information to us through Petras instead, with a greater chance of it getting traced back to her.

No, whoever picked Mareth to kill out of all the names in that book wanted to *stop* us from learning about the relics. And the only reason I could think of to do that was if that person already knew how they worked and wanted to keep that advantage to help them gain the wish.

I started walking back along the wall of the mansion, thinking it through, desperate to focus on something that wasn't Vy or Rika. An irregular silhouette caught my attention, half behind a rosebush—the rusted wheelbarrow that had hidden Willa's gloves, still full of leaves sodden from the rain.

Those gloves—something wasn't right about them. They'd been new enough not to be rubbed shiny with use in the fingertips, but their seams had been strained to the point of tearing.

Not from use, but from someone shoving too-big hands into them.

One thing after another that had been fuzzy in my mind became crystal clear, my brain following a formerly twisted path suddenly laid out straight before me. Who put on their extremely distinctive gloves to do a murder, anyway? And then, having realized their mistake and thrown them out the window, went to all the trouble to sneak out of the house to move them, only to chuck them in a nearby wheelbarrow instead of, say, *the ocean*?

For that matter, if you were going to do a murder in a house you knew well, that you'd been visiting for your whole life, would you really step on the extremely loud creaky stair? Twice, if Vy was to be believed, going both down and up.

Besides, most damning of all, there was the timing of that telltale breeze from the opening door.

I knew who had killed Mareth.

CONFRONT YOUR ENEMY

I strode into the house with a new sense of purpose, sloughing off my soaking coat in the foyer. Muffled voices greeted me from the drawing room. I threw the door open to find a handful of people pouring themselves drinks from the sideboard—not Rika, thank goodness. I wasn't ready to face her. Avoiding Petras's and Jaycel's eyes—I wasn't ready to face them, either, for entirely different reasons—I fixed my gaze on my quarry.

"Dona Amistead, do you mind having a word aside with me? You said to let you know if you could help destroy the relics, and I've thought of a way."

"Of course, of course." He gathered up his brandy, gave a cheerful nod to the others, and followed me into the music room.

I slid the door shut behind us.

"So," he asked, as he settled into the same chair he had before, "how can I help?"

"By telling the truth." I took a few paces toward him. "If all you want is to destroy the relics, why did you write your own name in the book?"

He froze, his brandy halfway to his lips.

"When you broke in to do it, you left that glass of water by your bed," I continued, relentless. "Because your mouth gets dry when you sleep. You slept here to make sure you'd be near the mirror when the Deepwolf came through—you probably got the idea from Auberyn Lovegrace. And then once the rest of us arrived, you took that room on the first floor not because of your joints, but because it's right next to the relic room."

Amistead slowly set his glass down. He rubbed his forehead with fingers and thumb, as if he were fighting off a headache.

"Yes, well," he said wearily. "If you really want to know why I added my name...I did it because I'm a damned selfish fool."

"Care to elaborate?"

"You understand, I came here with the best intentions. But we all know where *those* lead." He shook his head. "I'd heard the news of Auberyn's death, and I was at once deeply concerned about what would happen to the relics. I didn't know she'd failed to keep people away from them, you see. Would someone find them and accidentally activate them? I thought if I got here first, before they disposed of her estate, I could whisk them away and get rid of them. Throw them in the sea, maybe."

"I'm told that's a terrible way to try to dispose of cursed relics, but go on."

"Well, as you can guess, I showed up and found the book full of names, and the relics immovable since they'd been activated. I stared at that book a long time." He lifted his gaze past me to the window, and beyond into the black rainy night. "All those names were already as good as dead, save one. It was horrifying to think about. And that one survivor would possess the relics—their magic ensures they can pass to no other—and might choose to do what my family did, continuing the cycle of death. Or they might be careless with them, like Auberyn Lovegrace, with the same result."

"I wouldn't call her careless," I said.

"No, I suppose not. The relics probably call people to them. I'm told it was always surprisingly easy to convince people to add their names to the book. And, well...I may have felt that pull myself." He took a sip of brandy. "I stood staring at it and found myself thinking, if they were all going to die anyway, why not add my name? If I had the chance to guarantee my children and grandchildren healthy, happy lives, how could I not take it? If I could ensure the relics would pass to someone with the intent to destroy them, wouldn't that be a worthy goal?"

I eyed him. "And did you believe that?"

"My dear Signa Thorne, it's remarkably easy to make yourself believe things."

"So you entered your name in the book. And then you took every step you could think of to make sure you'd win."

"Well, once I'd added my name and what I'd done sunk in, I admit I wasn't eager to leave the protection of the mirror ward. So I camped out in the house, which seemed harmless enough."

At last, I loosed some of the tight chains I'd had on my anger, letting it burn in my eyes.

"I wasn't talking about that."

Amistead went very, very still.

"If you were so focused on destroying the relics, Dona Amistead, why did you kill Mareth Overfell?"

For a moment, the silence stretched between us, taut to the point of ripping. Then he laughed, too heartily.

"You really had me going for a moment there! Stars, Signa Thorne, have mercy on an old man's heart." He took another, longer sip of his drink.

"I wasn't joking."

The brandy glass descended, slowly. His merry blue eyes went cold. "That is a dangerous accusation to fling around."

"You're the only one with a motive to kill Mareth rather than an easier target—to keep him from undoing the advantage your superior knowledge of the relics gave you. You're the only one with hands sufficiently larger than Willa's to damage her gloves when you forced them on. And you're a former City Elder, canny and devious enough to hide the gloves, knowing people question information less if they have to work for it."

He shifted in his chair. "This is all surmise and circumstance."

244 MELISSA CARUSO

"If it were only that, I'd agree with you." I'd been standing a couple of sword lengths from him; I prowled closer. "It was the creaking stairs that clinched it. Vy heard them twice, up and down, but Glory didn't hear them at all—even after a draft from the door opening awakened her. Anyone else would have creaked again *after* going outside to hide the gloves, as they headed back upstairs to their room. Someone sleeping *downstairs*, on the other hand, would have stepped on that treacherous stair for the last time on their way outside after killing Mareth. But you commandeered the only downstairs bedroom, didn't you?"

For a long moment, there was silence, punctuated by the faint ticking of a mantel clock. Amistead and I stared at each other, the air between us electric. The expression on his face was neutral, wary, a player who knew how to hide his thoughts.

All at once, it crumpled into a desperate, anguished despair.

"It was for my granddaughter, Signa Thorne," he whispered. "Surely you must understand that. She was so ill, and it frightened me more deeply than anything else I've ever experienced in my life. I'd face the Void itself gladly, so long as I never again have to feel that fear. I'll stain my soul with the vilest of crimes, if it keeps my children and their children safe."

My heart stirred briefly in sympathy. I knew that fear, and the immense relief of finding a way to hold it at bay. But his grandchild had already recovered from that fever. He'd built himself a slippery path to the Void with his own hands and then skidded right down it.

"I've met Mareth's parents," I said coldly. "I doubt they would be impressed by your logic."

Amistead winced. Thunder growled outside, its echoes ricocheting back and forth across the river. For a moment, I thought he would break down and weep and beg forgiveness.

Then his face hardened into classic Hillside arrogance, all vulnerability melting away.

"You," he said, "are out of line."

"Am I? I think I'm doing exactly what needs to be done."

"You'll need better evidence than *that* if you want to bring an

Amistead before the magistrate. Why, there's a street named after us not two blocks from the courthouse."

I considered how to reply to that. It might be satisfying to point out his hypocrisy, or to remind him that while his ilk might rule the city, they did not rule the Hounds. But we were trapped here on this island, and above all else, I had to choose the words most likely to get everyone through till morning alive.

"Let me be clear, Dona Amistead. Right now, I don't give a damn about bringing you before a magistrate."

He blinked, then frowned, like a man trying to figure out whether he was being solicited for a bribe.

"What I care about," I said, "is keeping everyone here alive. Part of that is making sure there are no more murders. Are you going to make that harder for me?"

"No, no, of course not." He shook his head. "I meant what I said earlier. I stand behind your attempts to destroy the relics, and I won't get in your way—or do anything that would speed up the timeline. I've made decisions I regret, and I must live with those stains on my soul for the rest of my life. But I'd like that life to last more than a day. I *do* want to live to see Allione's violin recital, after all."

He rose, knocked back the rest of his brandy, and headed for the door.

"Good evening, Signa Thorne. Think on what I said, and do call on me if there really *is* some way I can help."

I let him walk out of the room. It wasn't like he could go anywhere. It would be easy enough to collect him and lock him up in his room—or maybe one farther from the mirror, just to make him sweat. The question was whether it was worth it.

I didn't honestly think he'd kill again. I was certain he hadn't killed Willa; not only was I pretty sure that had been the creature wearing Vy, but it would have been foolish to kill his own scapegoat and make people look for another murderer. At this point, he still thought he could weasel out of consequences for Mareth's death— which only went to show that he didn't know the Raven guild—and he'd be inclined to be cooperative, to make sure he didn't hand me

246 MELISSA CARUSO

anything a magistrate could use. He might even be genuinely help-ful. Holding him prisoner, on the other hand, would take resources and cause problems down the line, since I didn't have the authority to lock up a former City Elder without a clear and imminent threat.

On the other hand, I didn't feel like letting Mareth's killer walk around free.

"I should feed you to Jaycel," I muttered, and followed after him.

I crossed the foyer to the drawing room and stalked in, not sure what I was going to do but sure that I at the very least wanted him watched. That need overrode even my overwhelming desire not to face any of my friends right now.

Jaycel and Petras crouched before the hearth. Jaycel appeared to have impaled a fish on a poker and was holding it over a fire. Glory sat in the far corner, face turned toward the window, studiously ignor-ing them. The smell of burning fish filled the room.

"This is a terrible idea," Petras was saying.

"It's a *brilliant* idea," Jaycel countered. "Kembral said we have to stay here, so we can't go to the kitchens, but that doesn't mean we can't cook!"

"Oh, for love of the Moon, you can go to the kitchens if you all go together. Just don't get overly excited by the abundance of knives and do anything we'll regret." I looked around, and unease prickled at me. "Where's Amistead?"

Jaycel frowned. "I thought he was with you."

"He didn't come in here?"

She cocked her head. "No, but I did feel the draft from the door opening. I assumed it was Rika and Vy coming back, but I suppose they would have made it in here by now."

My heart plummeted down to the Void itself. "Where's Rika? She's not back?"

Petras gave me an odd look. "Not since she went out looking for you and Vy earlier."

I spun on my heel without a word and headed for the door.

Why Amistead had gone outside I could only guess. Maybe he was hoping to escape, or maybe he didn't want to be publicly called out

THE LAST SOUL AMONG WOLVES   247

as a murderer in front of someone as impulsive as Jaycel Morningray, or maybe he just wanted some fresh air. Either way, he was in danger, but I didn't much care—only one thing mattered right now.

Rika was out there alone, looking for a dangerous Echo whose sole mission was to lure her into a trap.

"Kem!" Petras called after me. "Is something wrong?"

"Yes!" I tossed over my shoulder. "So many things! I'll explain later, but stay here, and if you see Vy or Amistead, don't trust them!"

They deserved a better explanation than that, but I was too afraid for Rika. And much as I hated Amistead, I couldn't let him die, either. We couldn't let the timeline accelerate any more; the Ravens would barely arrive before the Deepwolf as it was.

Arhsta would know that, too.

I threw the front door open and hurled myself out into the thorny garden.

The rain had slacked again, sparing my poor borrowed shirt another drenching, but everything around me was dripping and sodden. The tangled bare branches and wilted leaves hissed and thrashed in the stormy wind off the ocean. Shadows filled the garden with nightmare shapes, all bramble claws and the hunched figures of bushes and crook-necked reaching trees.

"Rika?"

The wind swallowed my call, shaking spattering cold drops off the trees. I shivered as it cut through my damp shirt. Lightning forked down a slender tongue across the river, silent in its distance as the storm moved away.

An eerie red glow caught my eye. At the far end of the garden, something writhed in the shadows, a pale figure struggling weakly against it. My heart jumped into my throat, and I started running.

The clouds thinned over the Moon, and silvery light pulled details out of the darkness. Vy stood with her head tipped back, braid bedraggled with rain, tentacles reaching from her mouth to wrap around the collapsing form of Tylar Amistead.

"Vy!" I called, because I didn't have any other name for the creature who wore her skin. "Stop!"

Dozens of glowing red eyes whipped around to look at me. The tentacles withdrew at once into Vy's mouth, quick as a guilty secret. Amistead tumbled to the ground. I couldn't tell if he was dead or alive, but he wasn't moving.

"Oh, Kem." It was the same voice I knew, uneven with heartbreak. "I didn't want you to see me like this."

"Don't do this!" I stopped a couple sword lengths away, heart pounding. "There's been enough death already."

"I never wanted to hurt *anybody*." She sounded so sad. "Not him, not Willa, not the people on the ship. Well, maybe Willa a little, when I thought she killed Mareth, but now I know that's not true."

I had to keep her talking, in case Amistead was still alive—and to keep her from remembering that she had orders to finish me off, too.

"Why are you doing this? What does Arhsta want?"

"The portal needs to be open." Vy dragged the back of a trembling hand across her mouth. "This is the only way to open it. I'm sorry, Kem. I'm so sorry."

Some hundred feet behind me, the mansion doors banged open, spilling a bright path of yellow light down the hill.

"Kembral!" Jaycel's voice called. "What's happening?"

I whirled to find a cluster of silhouettes in the doorway, peering down into the darkness at me. Jaycel had her sword out, ready to back me up.

"Stay there!" I shouted. The last thing I needed was more people storming into this delicate moment. I spun back to face Vy.

She was gone.

Amistead lay sprawled on the grass alone, the handle of a knife sticking straight up out of his heart.

I stared at Amistead's corpse, a bad feeling pooling in my gut like blood. This fucked *everything*.

Jaycel, Petras, and even a hesitant Glory came down the hill to gather uncertainly around me. Rika appeared out of the darkness like a wraith, probably having been there all along.

THE LAST SOUL AMONG WOLVES 249

She gave me a grim look, our fight washed away by shock. *She* understood.

"What does this mean?" Glory asked, her voice smaller than I'd ever heard it. "How long do we have now?"

"Six hours," I said. "Which means the Deepwolf will get here before the Ravens do. We're screwed."

It was too blunt, but I was beyond any kind of softness. That same inescapable arithmetic had sentenced Amistead to death. The thing pretending to be Vy was Arhsta's agent, and everything she'd done was precisely calculated to force Rika into her trap: smashing the boats so we had no other escape, then murdering Willa and Amistead to advance the timeline and make retrieving the lantern swiftly a matter of life and death.

She'd served her mistress well. Even if I could get a message to the Ravens, they wouldn't be ready. We had no choice now but to track the wolf into the mirror and try to get the lantern. Or rather, *I* had no choice—Rika shouldn't go anywhere near that thing. But without Rika's help, I was going to have the Void's own time getting the lantern out of wherever the wolf stashed it, especially if that bird Echo was right and it turned out to be locked up in that terrible black castle.

Rika was watching my face, through the light remnants of rain. She looked like she was about to say something—probably some maddening thing about how she wasn't going to let me do this that would start a fight again.

Before she could speak, the house itself seemed to shiver against the deep mottled black of the stormy night sky. Thin wisps of fog drifted from its windows, and the air grew colder.

"Here it comes," I breathed.

A great smoky shadow enveloped the Lovegrace house. And then it detached and stepped forward from it, opening two glowing blue eyes.

The Deepwolf had arrived.

We all scrambled back to the open door, out of its way. I barely dared to breathe as the monster paced forward, its limbs all fluttering tethered shadows and roiling mist, its tail streaming into the darkness. The lantern in its jaws glowed with golden swarming lights; it hurt with a deep, searing pain to know that one of those bright specks was Mareth's soul.

If it noticed us, it didn't care. It approached Amistead's body and bent low over him, the lantern drooping to nearly touch his still chest.

A droplet of light coalesced over Amistead's heart, beside the dagger. It began, slowly, to collect itself and rise.

Petras made a smothered sound, staring at the lantern in anguish. His father was in there.

"This is *wrong*," Jaycel whispered. "I don't say that often, but this is beyond even my limits."

"Yeah," I agreed, hoarse and low. Whatever you believed about where souls were supposed to go after death—whatever fate you imagined for those motes of consciousness, the final spark of self contained in those bright points of light—this was obscene.

The spark floated up from Amistead's body into the lantern. The Deepwolf's muzzle wrinkled in a ripple of shadow; it threw back its head and let out a deep, terrible howl that resonated through my bones, all the way down into the earth beneath my feet. I'd been braced for it, but I still shuddered.

It loped toward the house, lantern in its jaws, ghostly fire burning in its eyes. In a moment, it vanished through the dilapidated walls, smoke and darkness swirling in its wake. And then it was gone.

I was out of options. I had to go after it, and *fast*, or someone was going to die.

I whirled on the group. "Right! I'm going to go into the mirror and get the lantern. Jaycel, I'm trusting you to keep everyone safe."

She nodded, straightening. "Good luck, Kembral."

"If...if you see Vy..." I had to tell them, but there was no time. "If you see Vy, it's not Vy. There's an Echo pretending to be her. I'll explain later—I'm sorry. For right now, if you see her, try to lock her up or something."

Well, that was terrible, but there was no time to do better. Before

THE LAST SOUL AMONG WOLVES   251

anyone could stop me, I plunged into the house, closing my ears to the inevitable exclamations and questions. If I took the time to answer, the Deepwolf would get away. I ran through the bright space of the foyer and into the dim hallway that led to the relic room, bouncing off the wall on the corner rather than slowing down.

The hard patter of running feet sounded behind me. "Kembral, wait!"

I spun, jabbed a finger at Rika, and snarled, "Don't you dare try to stop me."

She looked offended. "If I wanted to stop you, you'd never have heard me coming. I've thought it through the same as you have, and it's necessary this time. I'm going with you."

That blindsided me, though maybe it shouldn't have. "You can't. You *know* what's waiting for you in there."

"What I *know* is that you have no idea how to execute a heist. I won't let you go in there alone."

I felt something go hard in my face. "You won't *let* me?"

She grimaced. "Look, I'm sorry about the—"

"I don't have time to argue with you now. Let me make this as clear as I can: You don't control me, Rika. You shouldn't, and you can't. You have to let me go."

Hurt blossomed across her face for a fleeting instant before her expression shuttered. I didn't wait to hear how she'd reply, didn't stay to soften words that had come out harsher than I'd intended. The moment was too urgent. Wounds could heal; death was forever.

I turned and ran down the hallway, following the last fading wisps of mist from the Deepwolf's passing. This time, I didn't hear anything behind me.

I nearly broke my key in the relic room lock wrenching it open. The cramped, eerie chamber with its flickering lamps remained the same as always, with no sign of the Deepwolf—save for the mirror's surface, which rippled with its passage like water.

The book lay open on the table, bloody lines drawn through four names now. I couldn't help but notice that Vy's name remained unstricken. The shimmering mirror hung there like a challenge, the light dancing madly across its surface from candles guttering in an otherworldly wind.

For all I'd said to Rika, I knew too well this was dangerous. The Deep Echoes always were, even without the hand of an enemy preparing the path before you. I had no margin of error, and if I so much as gave myself a paper cut I faced a grisly death. Emmi was waiting for me at home; she needed her mother in one piece.

But the alternative was to stand by knowing with absolute certainty that the Deepwolf would kill someone and harvest their soul. For better or worse, it just wasn't in me to do that.

I fished the portal tether out of my pocket: a small ball of red yarn that made my fingertips tingle with magic. I tied one end around the table leg, then straightened to face the relics with the unraveling ball in my hand. The silver eye of the mirror stared back, clouded with more than tarnish.

No one else had to die. I could do this. Just so long as I didn't fuck up.

Clutching the portal tether tight, I smacked my palm flat against the mirror glass. For a moment it felt hard and cool, as a mirror should. Then it warmed and softened beneath my touch, like melting ice.

"I'm coming, you bastards," I whispered, not sure who I was talking to.

A tingling rushed over my hand and up my wrist, as if I'd plunged it beneath the surface of warm, slightly effervescent water. A lurch of instinctive panic in my gut cried out that this was a terrible idea— and yeah, maybe it was, but sometimes terrible ideas were still the most reasonable ones left. I closed my eyes before the silver wave passed over my face.

For the second time, the mirror swallowed me whole.

STICK TOGETHER

On the far side of the mirror, a wind stirred the shrine, coaxing whispers from its gauzy webs. Beyond the arch of its entrance, cold silver stars spattered a low and deeply velvet night sky. The thick swirl of their shimmering bright flecks formed a shape like an eye, a fathomless blackness at its center as if the Void itself gazed down on me. That didn't seem like a good sign.

The portal tether trailed through the surface of the mirror, a strand of red yarn emerging from a silvery pool. I didn't see anything to tie this end around, so I tucked the little ball of yarn into a corner. So long as no one yanked on the far side, it should be fine, and it would hold the way open behind me, a quick escape if I had to flee up to Prime.

I turned to survey the city. Darkness transformed the bone-walled buildings beyond the shrine to a senseless jumble of giant's blocks. A dusty scent rode the wind, with a note of decay, like old leaf litter or ancient bones. No lights shone in any windows—none save in the distance, where that damned castle reared up its sharp towers to the sky, waiting, watching.

A shimmery feeling crawled across my shoulder blades. *No.* It couldn't be.

Rika Nonesuch stepped through the portal to stand at my side.

"Where's the wolf?" she asked, clipped and businesslike. "Do you see it?"

"What in the Void are you *doing* here?" I exploded, fear for her spiking through my chest with an intensity that pierced even my frustration.

"Kembral, I'm sure you would never dream of being a raging hypocrite."

"I don't see how—"

"So I'm *sure* you aren't about to tell me that I can't do something because it's too dangerous, and you're *certainly* not about to make some kind of grand statement about how you won't let me take the risk."

"You walking straight into your mother's trap is different than—"

"And," she added, her grey stare incisive, "I know we don't have time to argue. Which is why I didn't."

"You're absolutely infuriating. Did you know that?"

"Know it? I count on it. Now, where's the wolf?"

"*Fine.* Help me look for it."

She faced the city, wincing at the looming presence of the castle.

"Please tell me I'm only imagining that it's closer this time."

"You're imagining it," I lied.

From our vantage on the hilltop, I scanned the darkened city for a telltale light moving through the streets. There was no sign of the bustling life we'd seen here last time, during the day. Eerie silence blanketed everything. I supposed the Echoes who lived here knew better than to be out on the streets in an hour this quiet and hungry.

There. A ghostly gleam of blue light, moving away from us. It passed between the shadows of intervening buildings and was gone.

A jittery thread of excitement and fear laced through my tired muscles, giving them a bright false energy.

"Let's go," I breathed.

"Should we run?"

"In a Deep Echo? Never." I started after it at something between a stride and a lope, with Rika close behind.

THE LAST SOUL AMONG WOLVES   255

The fifth Echo had changed from our last visit. I didn't like how dark it was; I could hardly see our footing, let alone what might be crouching in ambush. I only spotted a jagged black hole in the road in time to step around it because of the muffled hissing sound that came from deep within it.

"I shouldn't have drugged you," Rika said abruptly, once we were clear. "But *you* need to be less damned sure you're right all the time."

Were we really doing this *now*? I couldn't help a thin rill of anger. "Well, *you* need to get over this weird controlling thing and let me do my job."

"Don't call me controlling," she hissed. "That's what *she* is."

"Well, maybe you should be less like her, then!"

I regretted the words the moment they left my mouth. Rika recoiled from them as if they burned.

"Rika, I..."

"I did warn you," she said, and her voice was hollow. "I told you— I already *am* like her. And I'm terrified that it'll get worse."

All my instincts urged me to brush it off, to tell her it was all right. But she *had* been controlling. It was entirely possible that her urge to disregard my free will and stuff me in a nice, safe box came from the same place as her mother's urge to disregard Rika's free will and stuff her in a castle. Empyreans were always weird about their anchors.

I should be saying something reassuring. I should be telling her she wasn't like her mother. But instead I was staring at her, and whatever was on my face, I could tell it hurt her. I swallowed.

"Well, let's make sure it doesn't get worse, then."

It was a botched and feeble reassurance, and I knew it—but now wasn't the time. I glanced away, up ahead in the direction I was *supposed* to be looking, where the wolf had gone. I couldn't let myself be distracted, couldn't be thinking about what exactly it meant to be her anchor and how much it might screw me over and how to fix that awful sadness in her face. I had to be completely focused and alert for danger.

Something skittered between two buildings, a click of legs or teeth. Behind us came a huff in the darkness, and then another, like a heavy breath.

Rika heard it, too, and went deadly silent. I eased my swords into a good drawing angle as we walked, poised and ready, pulse pounding. Ahead, a faint reflected flash of blue light lunged between buildings, beckoning us onward, along with an elusive flicker of gold.

"There it is," Rika whispered. "It's still got the lantern."

The thought of what fueled that golden gleam made me sick and drove my footsteps faster. But not too fast—the stakes were too high to get reckless now. And the wolf was heading straight for the castle.

"We could let it go," I said reluctantly. "Head for the portal in that fountain shrine and work our way up to Prime. Get the Ravens and bring them to the island, and hope they can distract the Deepwolf enough for me to get the lantern with a blink step."

"Do you think that would work? *Without* you getting killed, or your arm ripped off?"

"No," I admitted. "Without Signa Zarvish having time to prepare? I'm pretty sure I'd get my arm ripped off."

She gave me a sharp look. "What would you do if I weren't here?"

I considered lying, to try to get her to safety. Every step she took closer to that castle set my nerves to screaming. But she'd know, and she deserved better.

"I'd follow the wolf."

"Then we follow it."

I gritted my teeth. "It's totally different with you along. It's you Arhsta's after, and I can blink step out of almost any trap, so—"

"Are you implying that I'm holding you back?"

"That's not what this is about!"

Our voices had cut the silence with too sharp an edge. Something shifted in the night; I could feel it. I lifted a hand, and Rika swallowed whatever retort she'd been about to deliver.

A faint sound teased my ears, a liquid slither. I slowed my stride, nerves screaming, fingers curling around the hilt of my Echo sword.

"There's someone in the road ahead," Rika whispered.

As if her words had conjured them, my eyes pulled a figure out of the darkness: tall, narrow, leaning in an oddly lopsided way.

"There you are," it said, its voice a metallic rattle like a spill of nails. "We've been looking for you."

I drew my swords, moving in front of Rika. In almost the same instant, the thing exploded into a thousand filaments of darkness, all of them reaching for us.

Almarah had trained the instinct to blink step out of danger into me first, when I was young and likely to make the kind of rash mistakes that could get me swiftly killed. Then she made me spend years learning the much more difficult and nuanced skill of making a snap decision every time on whether to blink step out of sudden danger or save it for later. Making the wrong choice *might* prove fatal, but being paralyzed with indecision and making *no* choice almost certainly would.

Rika was behind me. I stayed where I was and brought my sword up in a sharp, vicious arc.

I caught the filaments of shadow barely in time, slicing their tips off, and followed with a half step forward and a clearing sweep with my off-hand blade in case any got through.

The creature responded by collapsing into a roiling puddle of shadow, emitting a furious seething noise. More whips of liquid darkness writhed from it, clawing through the air at us. I'd fought something like this in the fifth Echo before, and I'd had no idea how to kill it then, either.

I swung wide around it, keeping my blades pointed at it; Rika stuck close by my side.

"Keep moving past it," I told her. "We can't lose that Deepwolf!"

A few more quick, defensive cuts kept its reaching tendrils off us, but the creature didn't seem to care that it kept losing bits of itself; more flowed out of it to take their place. We maneuvered around it easily enough, but then it started *pouring* after us along the ground, flowing like a great spill of black ink.

This was not great. I'd try fire if I had any, but blades clearly weren't enough, and I didn't dare turn my back on it to run. We could continue backing up and maybe keep it at bay, but we'd lose our quarry for sure.

"Kembral, watch out!"

Rika suddenly slammed into me, shoving me to the side with her hip. I staggered and almost fell. A dozen snaking arms of inky darkness lunged for me, snatching wildly at the opportunity. I barely got my blades up in time, too off-balance to stop them all; something viscous and burning lashed around my wrist.

Out of the ragged-edged hole Rika had just saved me from falling into, a massive tongue suddenly reared up. It lashed around the shadow creature, quick and neat as a cat lapping water, and yanked it down into the abyss.

A wild nest of thin dark tendrils flailed briefly at the air for an instant, then disappeared below. I scrambled back from the hole, swearing.

Hissing and grinding noises sounded from its depths, and then silence.

"Thanks, Rika," I gasped.

"I knew you shouldn't go alone," she said, insufferably smug, and in that brief moment everything was right between us.

She pointed down the road, where a dim flicker of blue shone between the jumbled shadows of the buildings. "Come on, we're going to lose it if we don't hurry."

I watched the ground a lot more closely as we pursued the elusive lights through the bone-strewn midnight city. I made sure to go first, too, since being grabbed and pulled into a hole by a giant tongue was exactly the sort of thing a blink step was great for getting you out of.

We had to dodge around several more of the gaping cracks as we hurried along. Movement stirred in the shadows, and once or twice glowing eyes blinked at us. The stars in their swirling formation glared down relentlessly from above. I had the chill certainty we were watched, and marked, and tracked. It was only a matter of time until the next attack; more likely than not, something was setting up an ambush for us even now.

I lifted my gaze in the direction the wolf was heading, scanning the dark road ahead for danger—and swore instinctively.

THE LAST SOUL AMONG WOLVES

Maybe they weren't setting up an ambush, because they didn't need to. Maybe we were already hurtling straight toward the biggest trap of all.

The castle loomed much closer than it should be—terrifyingly close—its towers massive dark claws raking a deepest purple sky. As we rounded a final corner, chasing the ghostly blue light, its walls reared stark and sudden above us. Silver veins glittered against glossy black marble.

There was nothing between us and the castle but a stretch of open plaza...and the Deepwolf.

Its massive, shadowy hulk paused, its shoulders ragged with the hunched suggestion of fur. There was no door on this side, only the thick trunks of towers and the elegant pointed shapes of arched windows that began far higher than I could reach from the ground. The firefly sparks swarming in the lantern cast a swaying warm sweep of light across the slick gleaming stone.

The Deepwolf looked back over its shoulder at us. Great pools of blue fire stared down at me, striking a chill straight through me like a lance of ice.

I froze where I stood, drowning in its aura of dread. All I could do was try to block Rika's line of sight with my body. But I could tell by the sharp intake of her breath that she had seen it, too. Any small protection we might have had if we'd looked away was gone.

It turned its great head, shaggy with shadow, back toward the castle. The lantern still clamped in its jaws, it took a few loping paces forward—and with a shimmering ripple, it passed straight through the wall.

"Damn," I whispered. "It just went right through."

I started forward. Rika grabbed my arm.

"Where are you going?" she demanded.

"We can't lose it. I've got to follow it and see where it puts the lantern."

"It went through the *wall*, Kembral."

"I can go through walls, too."

She glared at me. Her breath made faint puffs of steam in the chill air. "I can't, in case you hadn't noticed. I have to climb over them, or pick a lock, like a normal person."

"You shouldn't go into that castle under any circumstances." I hated the idea of splitting up here, even briefly—but if we lost the wolf now, this was over, and someone would die. "Look, I'm just going to peek in there, see where it takes the lantern, and blink step back out. Will you be all right for a few minutes? Can you hide? I don't want to leave you alone."

"I'm a *Cat*. Of course I can hide. That's not the issue! Don't you dare..." She broke off, stopping herself from whatever command she'd been about to give with a noise of inarticulate frustration. "Fine, then. Go. But don't you dare get hurt."

"I'll blink step out at the first hint of trouble. Leave me guild signs if you have to move out of this area so I can find you."

We were out of time. But the thought of leaving her like this— after an argument and without any warning, all by herself at her mother's castle five Echoes down—twisted at my heart. I gave her a quick, fierce kiss, hoping it would somehow convey what I felt despite my lack of fluency in this language. One precious second, two, and I pulled away.

"Be safe," I whispered, as her fingertips trailed off my cheek. "Don't let her catch you."

"You are the *worst*, Kembral Thorne," she murmured, like an endearment.

I pulled myself away and ran toward the wall that the Deepwolf had disappeared through, my eyes suspiciously hot. She'd better be all right. But nothing in any world was as elusive as a Cat, and I'd only be gone a moment.

I let my fingertips brush the black marble, just to make sure we weren't being needlessly dramatic about some illusion-hidden door. It was cold and hard and real, solid stone. There was no way in.

No way except one.

I closed my eyes, slid between layers of reality like a knife's edge, and followed the Deepwolf into the castle of my enemy.

CHECK FOR TRAPS

No one lived in the castle. That much was immediately clear.

In the frozen instant of the Veil, I passed through its outer wall of impressively thick stone, gliding through gold-washed darkness with a couple of quick steps and coming out in a vast empty space.

I braced myself for danger: to face an array of traps, or a packed court of lethal and beautiful Echoes, or a bewildering maze that would snare my mind. But what I saw through the blurred, honey-tinted lens of the Veil was a long pillared gallery with impossibly high vaulted ceilings, all of it in the same silver-veined black marble as the exterior of the castle—and all of it utterly empty.

I slipped back into reality, ready for the floor to vanish under my feet or shock me with lightning. My boots tapped down onto regular glossy marble. A pale light glimmered from the veins of silver in the walls, but shadows swathed most of the cavernous room—except for at the very far end, where the last flicker of a blue glow abruptly dimmed.

I'd come out of the Veil just in time to catch sight of the Deepwolf's tail and haunches disappearing through the far wall.

"Shit."

I poked the floor with my toe to make sure it was safe. It seemed ominously fine.

262 MELISSA CARUSO

Fuck it. I broke into a run.

Almarah wouldn't have approved. But this place was clearly far bigger on the inside, this one room stretching to almost the size of the city hall, with no apparent doors or windows—if I lost the lantern now, there was a very real chance we'd never find it. And with so few features, there wasn't much to test besides the floor anyway.

My footfalls echoed past pillar after pillar; I peered into the shadows between them as I ran. If anything lurked there, it knew I was here now—but the place had a profound hollow absence that left me sure there was no one. This was not a space that anyone had ever used.

It made a certain eerie sense. This whole castle was a shell, its imposing size for show alone. It was a colossal, silent, mocking message for Rika.

I didn't slow down as I reached the far wall and the smooth expanse of marble that had swallowed the Deepwolf's fog-and-shadows tail. I slid between one reality and the next, leaving space and time behind once more, and followed after.

The far side of the Veil revealed another cavernous hall, this one done in shades of purple and black speckled with tiny glowing lights. It was dead empty like the first, with no sign any living creature had set foot here before me, and once again I arrived just in time to see the Deepwolf's misty form lope through the far wall.

I was agonizingly aware of Rika, left behind in danger, and the possibility that Arhsta wanted to separate us and leave her vulnerable. But it had only been a couple of minutes, and I had faith in Rika's abilities—not to mention that most of the things I'd personally be worried about five Echoes down weren't a threat to a half Empyrean. So I chased after the wolf.

This place was so big and fake and *creepy*. It had an eerie unfinished quality to it, like a placeholder concept sketch without any details filled in. As if Arhsta had created it in a slapdash fashion, on a whim, intending to complete it later. The idea that Rika's mother could just *half-ass* something on this scale was frankly terrifying.

What kind of inhuman obsession would it take to make all this

THE LAST SOUL AMONG WOLVES 263

just to mess with her daughter? Whatever waited for Rika here, the thought of her falling victim to it set a deep, unreasoning dread in my soul.

At the far end, I didn't hesitate, but flung myself between one world and the next and followed the wolf through the wall.

Surprise, surprise: another giant room. I wobbled a little on landing back in reality, but I didn't break stride, my boots sending echoes ricocheting around the vast dim space as I chased the smoke-trailing hindquarters of the Deepwolf and the elusive golden flicker of the lantern. I was all too aware of the passage of time—about five minutes now—and of my dwindling capacity for blink steps. These were very short ones, barely a heartbeat, so I could do more than my usual handful, but I had to make sure I'd be able to get back out.

In the shadowy distance, at the far end of the room, the Deepwolf paused. The glowing blue pits of fire that were its eyes swiveled for a moment to regard me. The lantern, golden lights swirling desperately within it, swung tauntingly from its jaws.

Then it passed through the wall and was gone. Again.

"All right, *fine*," I growled. "One more."

I made myself the promise that it would be only one. After this blink step, I would stop, no matter what. Even if it meant losing the lantern. I had to get back to Rika before anything could happen to her.

Bracing myself for an unsteady landing, I started my next step in one reality and finished it in none at all.

The Veil broke over me as if I'd plunged underwater, its silence roaring in my nonexistent ears. I took one long stride through the darkness of solid stone, then another.

This time, when I broke through into reality on the far side, I stumbled, my legs giving out under me, and caught myself on one knee.

The leading edge of a headache pressed at my temples, and my heart pounded in rapid, angry protest. I was immediately aware that something was different—that this wasn't another great empty hall like I'd expected. I laid a palm flat on the stone beneath me to steady my trembling limbs and looked around.

I'd tumbled back into reality onto a stone causeway barely wider than a chair above a lake of unknown black liquid. I'd come within a few inches of flinging myself straight into whatever glassy black substance flowed beneath this narrow bridge. Five Echoes down, I'd bet it was something nastier than water.

The room that stretched around me was even more cavernous than the previous columned halls, and just as unpopulated. A lapping black lake filled it completely, with only the one narrow stone path running about a foot above its surface.

It led to a sort of architectural island on the far end—an expansive stepped platform sitting like a stage against the wall. It was framed with decorative arches and impossibly tall, slender statues of gowned figures worn so smooth they had no features or faces. A great round skylight of stained glass in a spiderweb pattern filtered blue and violet light down onto the platform.

Now, *this* place looked like a trap.

The Deepwolf stood on the island, smoke roiling off its shoulders and streaming from its tail, the lantern still clasped firmly in its jaws. If it went through that far wall, I didn't dare follow it, no matter how much was at stake.

It looked over its shoulder at me. The blue flames of its eyes pierced into mine; a shudder of pure fear shook me down to my bones. I'd never had any doubt that it could kill me if it wanted to, but when those pits of fire gazed into me, I could *feel* it, like icy claws closing on my heart. All I could do was kneel there, panting, and hope it passed me by.

It turned to face a raised block of ornate marble at the center of the platform, like an altar. Carefully, it bent its great shadowy head and placed the lantern in its exact center.

Then it loped off through the wall, trailing smoke and shadows behind it.

The lantern stood in its place, casting golden light on the pillars and statues around it. The arches and stonework framed it perfectly; it made such an ideal focal point that I had no doubt this whole place had been designed to display it. Flecks of the light of souls danced on the black water. The faint noise of lapping wavelets and my own slowly steadying breath were the only sounds.

There it was, glowing and beckoning, mine for the taking. It might as well have a massive sign hanging over it saying TRAP.

Right. Time to stop running around in a panic and act like the professional I kept claiming to be.

I rose, running my fingers through my hair to collect a couple of loose strands. The first one I let fall on the walkway in front of me; it lay there in a perfectly normal way.

Great. The path was probably safe. I dropped the second hair over the edge, into the black water.

It hit the surface and hissed, releasing a thin trail of smoke. Writhing like a dying thing, it curled in on itself and shriveled into ash in an instant. The black liquid sucked what remained under, consuming it.

Okay. Extremely not safe. *Don't miss your step, Kembral.*

I made my way along the causeway, slow and careful. No doors in this room, either, so far as I could tell, though if they were across this inky death water it was a moot question. I supposed if the only beings using the castle were the Deepwolf and Arhsta, neither of whom needed doors, she just couldn't be bothered to make them. I wondered whether even a legendary burglar like Rika could find a way in.

For all that I absolutely didn't want her in this giant trap, I couldn't help wishing I had Rika at my back as I reached the end of the causeway and contemplated the stepped platform of glossy silver-veined marble rising up before me to the lantern's plinth. Her absence felt wrong, a vulnerability, like being unarmed.

Maybe I only missed her because I was her anchor, and we were connected. But I doubted it. This was more like how I missed Emmi, an absence of an important piece of me, a person who had become so integral to my life that the idea of living it without them felt hollow.

When I got out of here, I had to take the first quiet moment we had to patch things up.

All right. I tapped the lowest stone step with my boot. Nothing.

This couldn't possibly be so easy. Disquiet grew in my belly as I carefully made my way up another step, and another, and nothing continued to happen. I reached the top of the island, a mere handful of paces away from the lantern, and still everything seemed disturbingly fine.

Oh, I didn't like this one bit.

The sparks trapped in the lantern seemed to dance faster, as if they could tell I was coming to rescue them. There were dozens in there, more than I could easily count. The Amisteads must have kept performing this horrible rite of passage, reaping souls to power their family's success, generation after generation, until the light they shed through the lantern glass was bright enough to bathe my skin in their warm glow.

"I'm sorry," I whispered to them, though I doubted they could hear me. "Someone should have saved you before now. I'm so, so sorry this happened to you."

The lantern looked simple enough, like something you might hang over your door or from a carriage, but larger. It sat on a round raised stone in the center of the plinth, which seemed awfully suspicious, directly under the center point of the spiderweb skylight above.

Well, I could always blink step if everything turned to flying blades or the floor dropped away the second I touched it.

No sense getting cocky, though. I examined everything as thoroughly as I could, from the floor around the plinth to the slab of stone itself, to the statues and columns surrounding me, to the skylight above. I wasn't sure why I bothered; this was an Echo. There didn't have to be telltale gaps or scrape marks for a stone to move, or clockwork for a statue to come to life, or a hidden spout for the walls to start spewing poison or lava. An Empyrean had created this place, and the deeper you went, the more easily they could shape Echoes to their whims. The whole castle could turn into cake or spiders if I said the wrong word, for all I knew.

Nothing left to do but go for it.

Poised on my toes, ready to run or duck or blink step, I tapped the lantern with one finger, quick and tentative as a cat taking its first cautious bat at a strange object.

The Last Soul Among Wolves

The lantern abruptly shrank, diminishing in a brief burst of light from Deepwolf-sized to human-sized. I jumped back in alarm, stifling a curse, but nothing else happened. It had just made itself conveniently portable.

I waited for my racing heart to calm, then tapped the top of the lantern again. No reaction this time. It felt like perfectly normal metal.

I grabbed the lantern by its ring.

It was a little heavier than I expected. Not much—about what it would have been if there were a sizable candle in it—but somehow I'd thought it would feel empty and light, buoyed by the weightless flickering of the entrapped souls. But perhaps souls had a heft to them after all, or else whatever metal the thing was made of was denser than it looked; it came up slowly in my hand.

The round stone it had rested on was worn as if with age. An inscription marked it in bold, deeply carved letters, previously hidden by the lantern. Three words, the edges softened as if by the erosion of time.

Three words that made my heart drop down another seven Echoes to the Void below.

HELLO, KEMBRAL THORNE.

RUN

O h, *fuck*.

My heart clawed its way up my throat and halfway out of my mouth. I stared at my name, carved in seemingly ancient stone, feeling like a blade had just run me through. I'd made a fatal mistake, and it was too late.

This place wasn't a trap for Rika. It was a trap for me.

No one could make it to this doorless room unless they could blink step. The Deepwolf had led me here, making certain I never quite lost sight of it. I'd followed its bait like a fool, too sure of my own unimportance. And now I was caught.

All at once, the blank faces of the statues looming above me opened shining black eyes.

I stared up at them in horror, my heart racing. I felt like some small animal in a trap that has no idea what's happening to it, only that it's about to die. My mind was a blank slate on which I furiously scrawled obscenities; the lantern full of souls hung useless from my hand.

The terrible eyes overflowed. Black liquid poured down smooth marble faces in great rivers of inky tears, rushing in waterfalls to join the rippling deadly lake below.

Shit. I spun and ran for the causeway.

THE LAST SOUL AMONG WOLVES 269

Before I could set foot on it, it began to sink into the murk. Black water lapped across it, swallowing the stone into its darkness, and it was gone.

I was trapped on the island, and the waters were rising.

I ran to the back wall, frantically testing it for any sign of a hidden door. I checked the floor, the statues—anything I could think of.

There was nothing. The window above mocked me with its vague, diffuse light, but there was no way to climb up there—and even if I could, it didn't look like it opened, and I might not be able to break it.

The shining black pool was filling far faster than it had any right to, its little waves lapping higher and higher. They swallowed the first step, the platform shrinking around me. That mocking stone with my name on it would be the last part of it above water. I could climb a statue or a column, maybe—but it would only delay the inevitable, and I wasn't sure I could do it holding the lantern. *Shit, shit, shit.*

I was going to have to blink step out of here. There was no other way.

I had no idea what lay beyond the wall that backed the island—it could easily be another trap, or solid stone. I peered across the length of the vast hall, back toward the empty room I'd come from. *That* one was safe, at least. Could I make it all the way across the wide black stretch of lethal water in one blink step, when I'd already done four to get here?

I'd never tried to blink step that far before. The most I'd done in one go was about half that length, and that had been a strain.

I couldn't screw this up. Rika needed my help to get back to Prime. My friends were counting on me, Emmi was waiting for me, and I literally held dozens of *souls* in my hand. If I made the wrong choice, I'd let them all down.

Given what I knew about Arhsta, she'd probably gone to great lengths to try to ensure there were no right choices. The one that looked impossible was likely my best chance.

I took a few steps back, to give myself a running start. Clenching the lantern handle so tight my knuckles turned white, I sprinted toward the edge of the platform and hurled myself out over the water in a great leap.

At the peak of my arc, I slipped into the Veil.

The rush of black tears pouring from stony eyes went abruptly silent, and the vast room filled with a sourceless honey-colored light.

I sprinted across the black pool, not quite touching its surface, leaving no splashes in the frozen moment. The lantern swung in my hand, the souls within it stuck in place like insects in amber. Their motes glowed more faintly here, as if they hadn't quite made the leap to the Veil with me even though I'd dragged their receptacle along.

A pressure built in me: the desperate need for reality, sure as my lungs needed air. My headache surged in an overpowering wave— except my head was merely notional here, so it hit my whole body. It was the familiar ache of pushing myself too far, of overexercising a muscle of the soul that I didn't truly understand.

At last I hit the wall, and its darkness passed over me with sweet relief. Now I just had to make it through into the empty hall on the far side and—

Light hit my face. The twisted, tattered forms of flame frozen in mid-writhe filled my vision.

The entire hall was on fire. *Fuck.*

I pushed myself onward, past my own straining limits, sprinting as fast as I could through the flames. The urgent, drowning need for reality consumed me. I was one striving, desperate, thwarted gasp after something far more vital than air. Pinprick black spots formed in the edges of my vision, slowly growing; if I stayed here much longer, I would unravel into them and cease to exist.

I had to make it. *Had* to. I forced myself faster, farther—into and through the merciful darkness of the far wall, beyond the flames.

The next room broke over me in light and a blessed lack of fire. I exploded back into reality like a swimmer desperately cresting above the water, sucking in a great gulp of air.

I was falling.

The ground I expected beneath my feet was simply gone, stretching into a vast, fatal nothingness whipping up at me from below.

THE LAST SOUL AMONG WOLVES

Pure instinct took over. I don't think I could have done it otherwise. I yanked myself immediately back into the Veil.

It felt like I'd ripped my own soul in half. Everything went unsteady, the Veil seeming to surge in time with my faltering pulse. The black pinpricks waited for me, already there and yawning wider, ready to swallow me whole. I clutched the lantern close with hands I couldn't feel and drove myself forward with legs I was losing the sense of.

No. I had to hold it together, keep my concept of what was *Kembral* clear, no matter how much it hurt or how thin I'd stretched myself. No matter how desperately every tiny bit of my mortal body screamed against this unnatural place, thirsted ravenously for reality, dying in slow agony for lack of it.

I glanced down as I started moving; a floor covered in sharp killing spikes waited for me below, filling the entire vast room. If I wanted to live, I had to make it to the far side.

This was how you killed someone who could blink step out of any danger. This was how you tricked an arrogant fool who thought there was no reality so deadly she couldn't just slip out of it and get away. My enemy had thought this through, and laid her trap, and I had fallen right into it.

And now I was shredding into nothingness, forcing myself out of existence with my own stubborn will.

It was too far. I'd blink stepped too much already; I'd used myself up, already hovering at the brink. But no—it *couldn't* be too far. There had to be hope.

Because this was the Year of Hope, and I was the year-namer. I would not be so easily erased.

I pushed on, past the point where on some level I knew I should have fallen out of the Veil or died, even as the spots of Void-black darkness gaped wide all around to devour me. At last I stumbled heedlessly out the far side and into reality, not caring what I fell into this time—if it was a pit of snakes or a cloud of poison, I was just going to have to make my peace with that, because I couldn't stay in the Veil so much as a fraction of a second longer.

Pain split my skull, blinding me utterly. I was dimly aware of hitting the hard marble floor, limp and graceless, the impact jolting through me. The lantern skittered from my hand.

I gasped after air—and more, after reality itself—convulsing and shuddering on the floor. I couldn't tell what was happening around me, or the state of my own body—I could have been impaled or on fire for all I knew. Everything hurt, but that meant I was *real*, and I sucked in the sweet return of time and space like it was fresh spring water.

I still existed. I had fucked up horribly, and I was in a world of trouble, but I was alive.

Consciousness, however, was too much. It slipped out of my numb grasp like the lantern had, and I tumbled into darkness.

CUT YOUR LOSSES

I fought my way back toward consciousness. It didn't matter what I'd done to myself, or how badly I was hurt; I had to wake up. Every second I was out was a second I was completely helpless, deep in the heart of Arhsta's power, unable to stop whatever it was an Empyrean had wanted to do so badly that she was willing to construct such a grand and elaborate trap to incapacitate me for it.

Of course, this was Stars Tangled in Her Web. Intricate traps were bread and water and air to her. She made them to live. She probably set up something this devious and complicated every time she wanted breakfast. Right? Maybe I wasn't as screwed as I thought. Maybe I'd wake up and find myself simply lying in an empty hall, able to take the time I needed to recover, pick up the lantern, and go reunite with Rika before she got in any trouble.

Something hurt. A sound, abrading my raw brain like every other sensation. A voice, unfamiliar, echoing down to the bottom of the dark well my mind was lost in.

"Here it is, my lady, like you wanted. I'm afraid it's in poor shape."

An impact jolted through me—my body hitting a hard floor. Someone had been dragging me, and they'd dropped me. Voices spoke overhead, blurring into incomprehensibility as my awareness swam desperately back toward the surface.

Light stabbed through my head. I opened my eyes a slit, letting in a cold silvery radiance. A vague pinkish blur obscured half my vision—oh, that was my hand.

I was lying curled on my side, shivers sweeping through me, one hand trembling against the stone in front of my face. My nails dug divots into the marble—no, that was wrong. It should feel unyielding, not strangely soft. I blinked everything into focus.

The floor was perfectly normal-seeming silvery stone, polished to a high shine. It was my fingertips that had become unsettlingly permeable. The last joints had gone translucent, the tips transparent, almost invisible.

Oh, this was bad.

Almarah had warned me about this. *Reality shock.* I'd spent too long in the Veil, and I hadn't come back quite in one piece. I needed to get back to Prime, where my proper reality would reassert itself, as quickly as possible. Until then my very existence was doing the equivalent of slowly bleeding out, and I'd fade and fade until I was gone.

"Are you sure this is the one you want?" the same voice asked, sounding dubious. "It doesn't look like much."

"She's more dangerous than she seems." The voice that replied was rich and beautiful, resonating strangely almost like Glory's had, as if it bridged multiple realities. It was bloodcurdlingly familiar.

Something slithered all around me—something thin and strong and whippy, like fine thread. It hooked me under my arms and hauled me to an approximation of my feet.

Two icy cold fingers beneath my chin tipped my face to meet another. A face like the night sky in all its terrible beauty, dusted with a faint speckling of stars in place of freckles. The eyes that stared into mine glowed with the bright, merciless radiance of the Moon.

"Aren't you, Kembral Thorne?"

Stars Tangled in Her Web. Rika's mother. The most dangerous Empyrean I knew. A cold, awful feeling gripped my stomach. This had gone wrong beyond my worst imagining—I was well over the

THE LAST SOUL AMONG WOLVES

cliff and falling, and the only thing remaining to discover was how far before I hit the bottom.

"Maybe not...at the moment." My voice came out a bare, dry whisper. I struggled to sort through the painful, shattered fragments of my returning senses to figure out where I was and what was happening.

Rika. Arhsta had gotten me, but what about Rika? I forced myself into enough awareness to look around.

The hall was unfamiliar, its stone silvery and shining, far more detail worked into its high vaulted ceiling and soaring columns than in the other rooms of the castle. I wasn't about to waste precious brain space focusing on the particulars, but they involved clusters of twinkling lights and sculptural details and soft ethereal clouds of faintly glowing mist hovering near the ceiling, surrounding another great stained glass skylight. It was a beautiful, airy, celestial space, fit for the majestic, divine being who stood before me. Stars shimmered in her gown at the slightest movement, and her hair fell in a river of pure moonlight.

But there was no sign of Rika. Something in me relaxed. She was still free.

The slithery threads I'd felt scooping me up and putting me so helpfully on my feet—all that supported me now so I didn't just collapse in a boneless pile again—were fine strands of black webbing that wound around my chest, my arms, my waist. They stretched up and out to connect at several points to the columns that flanked me and the arch vaulting over my head.

Caught like a bug. I curled my fingers with their transparent tips in frustration. It was a struggle to pull myself to sufficient consciousness to think clearly, but I had to be unspeakably clever now, or I was never going to make it home.

A sudden realization hit me in a spike of panic. There was no sign of the lantern. Whoever had brought me here—and my money was on the lean, angular Echo standing a few steps behind Arhsta, looking like a collection of javelins in a tailcoat—must have left it where it fell.

I returned my gaze to Arhsta's terrifying, beautiful face and tried again. My voice came out a little stronger this time.

"You seem to have gone to a great effort to bring me here."

"And you, mortal, seem to have gone to a great effort to arrive. You are nearly spent." She tipped her head slightly, her hair falling in a wave of light. "Cooperate, and I will preserve your life."

"I can't imagine anything we'd want to collaborate on," I rasped, working my arms to see how much give there was in the webs. Plenty, until I made the slightest motion toward slipping free, and then they jerked taut.

"On the contrary. We want the same thing." Arhsta stepped back, turning as if to graciously include the rest of the room in our conversation. "We want what's best for my daughter."

Her movement revealed what her presence had blocked. The focal point of the hall, the radiant center of all its ethereal magnificence.

An empty throne.

It was a thing of soaring and delicate beauty, formed of stone wrought like fine lace, glowing softly from within. All around it, the same black webs that bound me radiated to the walls and ceiling and seemed to pass through them, as if they continued outside. As if whoever sat on that throne would be the spider in the center of a net that stretched into infinity.

Except that the heart of the web was empty, and all the inner points of those strands looked wickedly sharp, ready to pierce and cut. I remembered the faint scars on Rika's skin, visible only in certain light in the Echoes, and a shiver of pure fury passed over me.

"Together, you and I will persuade her," Arhsta said, soft and compelling, "to take her throne."

I wanted to curse at her, but I wasn't quite that much of a fool. I contented myself with flexing my fingers, letting them contemplate the violence they'd like to unleash.

"You and I have different ideas about what's good for Rika."

"Do we? I only want her to stop making herself smaller than she is. I want her to come into her true power, accept herself, and be what she was always meant to be." Those glowing eyes fixed on me, and there was a strange yearning in them. "Surely you would not want her to live but half a life. Surely you, too, wish for her to reach her full potential."

"Maybe, but not like *that*." I gestured weakly with my head toward the throne, since I couldn't move anything else. "I won't help you convince her."

"Oh, you will," Arhsta assured me. "You will be instrumental."

I didn't like the sound of that at all.

She turned to the Echo who waited attentively behind her. "Linnaeus. Guide my daughter here."

He bowed his blue-maned head. "As my lady commands."

I could see the future as if I were an oracle: She would torture me until Rika agreed to ascend that awful throne and become hers forever. The moment Rika walked into this room, everything would get infinitely worse for both of us. While we were separate, there was a chance that one of us would think of something clever; together it would be far too easy for Arhsta to use us against each other.

I had to think of a way to stop it from happening, and fast.

The Echo Linnaeus strode off on long, mantis-like legs, the tails of his coat fluttering behind him, out through the hall's massive arching doors. It was hard to think with fear pulsing through my veins in time to the stabbing of my headache, and my very reality trickling away from me.

"Why do you care if she sits in some fancy chair anyway?" I asked, desperate for any kind of angle. "If she's your anchor, I'd think you'd be better served with her out there being devious, furthering your equilibrium."

"She is more than just my anchor." Arhsta's rich, musical voice thrummed with pride. "She is my daughter. Part of me and not; human enough to be an anchor, and Empyrean enough to be divine. Her human side connects her to Prime in ways impossible for me. It took me centuries to succeed in creating her, all for this moment."

She swept toward the terrible throne, her hair and garments trailing behind her. She *had* to explain her machinations when prompted, just like Rai couldn't turn down a direct challenge; it was too central to her equilibrium. But this time, she seemed pleased enough to lay everything out for me.

"You know the feeling, I trust, of wishing your child to exceed you. To become greater than you could ever be. Behold the place I have prepared for her—a throne worthy of all she is and all she can become."

"I presume it's more than just furniture." I dreaded the answer, but if I wanted to save Rika from it, I needed to know.

"So much more." She laid a graceful hand on the arm of the throne, fondly, as if it were a pet. "The threads of this web run through every nation of your world, all through Prime. When she ascends to her place at its center, she will be able to directly manipulate her world in ways that I can only dream of. She will be the power behind every throne, the voice in every ear, the eye gazing upon the hidden secrets of every heart. My child deserves no less."

Arhsta turned back to me, moonlight glowing in her eyes. "And because she is mine, all the world will feed my equilibrium. With my daughter and anchor as its secret empress, I need never fear losing my balance again."

The most horrifying part was that there was true pride in her voice. As if on some level, she *cherished* Rika—but only as an extension of herself, a sign of her own power. An accomplishment rather than a person. A finely crafted vessel, to be displayed on a shelf when not in use.

"You need her to agree to it." That was the only part that gave me any hope, and I clung to it. "You can't force her, or you wouldn't need me."

The pressure in the air seemed to shift, becoming electric as if a storm threatened. "I do not *need* you, mortal."

"But I must play some role in your plan, or you wouldn't have bothered to collect me."

She bared her shining teeth. She knew what I was doing, forcing her to reveal more than she wanted, but she couldn't stop me.

"I made her ascend a different throne once, when she was small. But she has...changed." Arhsta's expression didn't alter, but the whole room darkened slightly. "You must understand that it is vital for my daughter to embrace her true nature. The more she comes into her power, the more control she will have over Prime when she accepts her fate as its ruler." She moved closer, a dangerous prowling drift toward me; I could tell that her patience with my questions was growing thin. "But as with any move in a game, there are trade-offs. I am forbidden to wield my power directly against a fellow Empyrean, and now...she qualifies. So she must choose this herself—which is where you come in, little mortal fly."

The webs wound tighter around me, their touch stinging my skin. All right, maybe annoying the Empyrean who could rip me in half with a flick of her will wasn't my best idea.

"Luckily, I took steps long ago to draw you into my web, to have my daughter's only anchor under my control. Though you surprised me seventeen years ago by refusing my bait and letting your friends take it instead."

"Seventeen years..." I stiffened. *The Lovegrace relics.* She'd been planning to capture me for that long. She'd pointed Jaycel at the relics, sure she'd invite me along, because she always did. But I'd said no, and now Mareth and Vy were dead and Petras and Jaycel cursed in my place, all because I'd unwittingly evaded a trap Arhsta had set for me.

Only to fall into one now, years later, when I was an adult and should know better.

Arhsta tilted her head, as if listening. "And now the moment comes when all my planning bears fruit at last."

The throne hall's intricately carved doors swung open with a slow, dramatic grandeur any Butterfly would envy. Linnaeus entered, bowing and stepping aside, his whole body folding in invitation to usher the guest of honor into the room.

Rika stood framed in the doorway, frozen, with the poised, elegant terror of a deer that has spotted a predator. This had to be a scene from her worst nightmares. Her wary grey eyes flicked to her mother, then the throne, then me.

Our eyes locked, and a connection thundered between us. Whole wordless conversations poured across the expanse of the hall in an instant. Chagrin, fear, apology, anguish—I could almost hear her making some sharp comment about where all my supposed professional expertise had gotten me, the barb a thin bandage over a gushing wound. Void's teeth, it was too much. I couldn't take it.

And the urgent question in the foreground: *What under the Moon do we do now? How are we going to play this?*

Arhsta spread her arms wide. "Welcome home, my daughter."

Rika didn't acknowledge her—didn't take her eyes off me. Something within her stilled. Her face became a mask of arrogance, her posture disdainful.

"*You,*" she said to me, dripping scorn.

Whatever clever gambit I might have tried turned to dust on my lips. That one word slid between my ribs like a knife.

She turned to her mother, stiffening. "Is *this* why your servant invited me here? To return this pathetic creature to me? I'm not interested. She argues too much, she's a hypocrite, and she's made it clear she'll leave me behind in a heartbeat for her precious job. I don't want her."

My whole body tensed, drawing the webs taut. *She's just saying that,* I told myself. *This is her angle, and you have to play along.* But there was too much truth in it—and her words hit me right in the sore spot Beryl had left when he'd unceremoniously dumped me.

If Arhsta was at all disappointed at her daughter's reaction to the tableau she'd so carefully arranged, she didn't show it. If anything, she seemed...excited. She moved toward Rika, her moonlight hair and the stars in her gown glowing even brighter, the Void of her skin seeming ever darker, the night sky incarnate.

"You have grown stronger, child," she purred. "I am pleased to have underestimated you. I applaud your resistance of my will. But come now. You know as well as I do that you are far from indifferent to this one's fate."

I didn't like where that was heading. All right—I had to follow Rika's lead, and never mind how much her words cut. Better yet, lean into that and let them hurt me, so I'd sound less like a liar.

"No," I growled. "This is the truth, coming out at last. You never *did* care about me, did you, Rika? I was just useful to you. A convenient tool you could cast aside at will."

Rika's piercing grey eyes fell on me, a look that went straight through my soul like an arrow.

"It was an enjoyable pretense," she said coolly. "But it's over now." She turned to her mother. "Spare me your offers and your threats. If you have nothing of interest to me, I'm leaving."

Without waiting for a reply or glancing back, she started toward the door. Which was exactly what I wanted, and shouldn't hurt at all.

"Are you?" Amusement danced in Arhsta's voice. "Even if I do *this*?"

Oh shit. I barely had a chance to brace myself before the webs that entangled me wound tighter and *twisted*.

I smothered any sound I might have made and struggled to stay loose, to bend with the pressure yanking my limbs in painful directions and crushing the wind from my lungs. The slender filaments burned like the touch of ice on bare skin, and they wrung me like a rag. I kept my teeth clenched and tried to wriggle away from the worst of it—*not my knee, Moon help me, don't wreck my knee*—but above all, I knew I *must not* cry out.

Rika stopped, fists clenching at her sides.

"Don't you *dare* turn around," I gasped. "Don't you dare show me your face!"

Webs looped my neck and squeezed a warning. The strands on one leg gave a hard jerk, and something in my ankle snapped.

"Fuck!" The expletive burst out of me; I couldn't hold it back. Rika flinched.

A jagged stab of pain went through my lower chest next—a rib giving way. She was going to crush me into splinters. Fear formed ragged frost along all my screaming nerves.

Wild at the edges now, I snarled, "For Void's sake, get out of here!"

Rika stood there, frozen, her shoulders rigid.

"You can't leave, can you?" Arhsta's voice was soft, almost compassionate. "I know what she is to you."

A visible jolt went down Rika's spine at her mother's words. Then she lurched into motion.

Her boots struck a vicious rhythm from the marble as she walked away toward the throne room doors. I strained to look after her as the webs squeezed away my breath, willing her to leave with all my might. Desperately afraid she'd do it, and abandon me here alone.

Rika paused in the doorway and spoke, her voice cold and distant, as if it came from another reality.

"I can always get another anchor."

And then she left me to die.

HOUNDS DON'T GIVE UP

It shouldn't have hurt. Rika had done exactly what I needed her to do—the only thing that might get at least one of us out of this mess. She'd found a strength I wasn't sure I could have mustered in order to do it.

Or else she'd simply discovered that I was, after all, something she could cast aside.

The moment the door closed behind her, I sagged in the webs that held me, unable to keep up the pretense of being remotely all right any longer. My ankle stabbed in blinding pain with every movement, and more shot through my rib with each shallow breath. The ends of the hair hanging past my face had gone transparent, fading into nothingness. And as the icing on my cake of woe, my head still throbbed like a bastard.

I was completely screwed.

It was the ankle that did it. Never mind being wholly in the power of a terrible enemy; I could work with that. The awful, simple truth was that I needed to get back to Prime within a couple of hours or I'd die... and I couldn't walk.

It was all too much. I'd failed Mareth, I was still in shock over what had happened to Vy, and now I'd managed to fall into the hands of an enemy Empyrean. My only redeeming victory was the fact that

Rika had been willing to abandon me. Which did not feel great, as victories went.

"Interesting," Arhsta murmured. She was staring after Rika, nothing about her tone or posture suggesting that she'd been handed a setback—more like an opportunity. "She has grown strong indeed."

She was always strong, I thought, but I wasn't going to waste any breath on pointing out the obvious.

Arhsta turned toward me, then. "And you will make her stronger still. She will come back for you; she can't help it."

"No she won't," I rasped. "You heard her."

"Please. Spare me your theatrics. I have been manipulating your kind since they came into being; I am not so easily deceived." She considered me. "Or do you believe it yourself? That she has embraced her true nature enough to lose her weak mortal fondness, so that you truly *are* nothing more than an anchor to her?"

My mouth had gone dry. "It...seems that way."

"Only to a fool." Arhsta drifted closer, and I didn't like the way her glowing eyes fixed on me at all. "No. So long as I have you, she is mine."

And that would be worse. Much as it would be terrible to die here alone, fading out of existence while Arhsta waited for a daughter too smart to look back, it would be so much worse to live out whatever remained of my life as bait.

Well, to the Void with both those possibilities. I needed to get back to Emmi. I'd carve out some other path to return to her if I had to do it with my own fading teeth.

Arhsta had given me an edge to pry at. She needed me. I might be stuck in her web with a broken ankle, but without me, all her convoluted plans to trap Rika fell apart. I could use that.

"You won't have me for much longer." Every breath hurt; I had to gather myself between sentences. "If I don't get back to Prime soon, I'll die."

She tilted her head slightly, regarding me. "This is true."

I dared feel a small surge of hope. If she brought me to Prime, I could escape and—

"In that case," she continued, "I should get all the use I can from you in the meantime."

Well, fuck.

Arhsta made a casual gesture, and a table appeared beside me—a pretty little thing, all wrought of silvery filigree shaped like fanciful spiderwebs. On it stood a handful of pale, lightly frosted glass bottles with decorative stoppers, about the size of large wine bottles. It looked like a drink table at a fancy party, except that there were no cups and they were all empty.

"Linnaeus." She began to move away with the absent disregard of someone whose mind is already fixed on her next task. "Take as much blood as you can without killing her."

He bowed. "Yes, my lady."

The sharp, slender Echo started toward me.

"Wait," I protested, in rising panic. "Wait, I already told you I'm...I'm not exactly in the best condition for this!"

Linnaeus sneered in distaste. "It *does* look rather damaged, my lady."

"She's tougher than she looks." Arhsta didn't slow or glance back. "And, Kembral Thorne...just think how much you'll help my daughter by making all my hopes for her come true."

Something in my brain snapped. I went into a pure, feral panic—I *could not* let her use my blood against Rika. I threw myself against the webs that bound me, heedless of the jabs of pain from my broken bones, and sank my teeth into Linnaeus's reaching hand.

He let out a yelp of pain. I tasted anise; pale green light bled down his wrist.

At once, the black strands yanked me backward and up. They wound tighter and tighter, no matter how hard I thrashed against them. One squeezed my throat until the pounding in my head spiked and the fight went out of me. I could only hang there, dazed and exhausted and hurting, tangled in enough threads for a whole troupe of broken marionettes. I could barely breathe, let alone move; spots seethed in my vision as my head swam.

The webs pulled my left arm out from my body, stretching it taut. Something sharp stabbed all the way through it.

That jolted me alert again. "*Ow!* You bastard, what are you—*ah!*"

A needle-thin, sharply angled spear of web pierced my arm near the elbow, going in one side and out the other. My stomach twisted at the sight of it. Linnaeus, grumbling and favoring his injured hand, uncorked one of the bottles and slipped it over the end of the slender black spike just as crimson drops began to run down its length, one after the other. They hit the bottom of the bottle in a rapid patter, like rain.

"What a boring job," Linnaeus complained. "I can't even steal any—she'd know. Moving unconscious humans and holding bottles, *ugh*. I could do so much more than this tedious, menial work."

I stared at him in numb disbelief. What did he expect me to do, commiserate? I tried to wriggle my arm free somehow, but the instant I moved, pain shot through it and the flow of blood increased. A surge of dizziness swamped me.

"Oh, hold still, you uncooperative thing." Linnaeus glared at me from three narrow, silvery eyes, then sighed. "As much as you can without killing it, she says. I don't have the faintest idea how much that is."

"Not a lot." I tore my eyes away from the horrible fascination of watching my blood leave my body. "Not much at all, in this state."

"Of course you'd say that. But she gave me *all* these bottles." He frowned at the collection on the table. "Maybe two-thirds of them?"

My heart lurched. "That will absolutely kill me."

"Quiet, human. I'm not asking *you*."

After everything I'd been through tonight—the Deepwolf, the flood and the fire and the pit, reality shock, snapped bones, Rika walking away—it was going to be this Echo's lack of understanding of human physiology that finished me off. My throat burned with the sheer wretched irony of it.

I had to *think*—quickly, at the rate the crimson froth crept up from the bottom of that bottle—and figure out some clever way out of this.

Rai. He'd offered his assistance if we got in trouble in the Echoes. I hated the idea, but maybe I could call on him. But no—this would

The Last Soul Among Wolves

definitely count as going directly up against Arhsta. And besides, I didn't want his help. I doubted I could pay what it would cost.

At least Rika had left. Thank the Moon, she'd had the strength and wisdom to walk away. She'd followed my urging and let me go.

Why did that feel so terrible?

I closed my eyes. I should be *happy* she'd left me here, damn it. It wasn't as if she'd known she was leaving me to die—I'd actively tried as hard as I could to hide it from her. She probably thought I had some clever plan to rescue myself. Which was exactly what I needed to come up with, right now.

Any time now.

Fuck.

A strange, warm, queasy dizziness came over me. I dragged my eyes open and looked at the bottle. It was getting full. Oh, that was no good.

"Hey," I said. It came out slurred. "Hey, you should stop. That's too much."

Linnaeus snorted. "Please. It's only the first bottle."

"No, if you don't stop..." I searched for something, but my brain was too fuzzy, wrapped in fog. At least the pain had faded a little. "If you don't stop..."

There came an enormous, terrible sound, like rock grinding or crumbling or maybe melting into lava. Impossibly loud, and as sudden and unexpected as a summer storm.

A large patch of the wall shimmered, swarming with glowing sparks, and fell away into a cloud of dust and steam. Harsh, wild light poured through the gap where it had been.

Rika stood in the smoking hole, shoulders heaving with rage. Her hair lifted around her, black as the Void, streaming on an unreal wind. Her eyes blazed with scarlet light. And great glowing wings spread in vengeful glory from her shoulders.

"...my girlfriend will be mad," I finished, in a bare, rough whisper. My vision blurred with the sudden threat of tears, as if I hadn't lost enough fluids already.

She'd come back for me. Damn her for a fool, she'd come back.

IF THERE'S NO WAY OUT, MAKE ONE

Linnaeus let out a terrified, metallic screech. He jammed the stopper into his precious bottle, quickly set it on the table, and raised his hands, as if disavowing all connection with it.

"I'm only following orders! My lady, have mercy, I'm not—"

There was no trace of mercy in Rika's radiant, inhuman face. She reached out toward him, teeth bared in a snarl, and clenched her fist in the air.

His back arched. Light seeped from his joints, his three eyes, his fingertips. The terrible sound of tearing metal burst from his screaming mouth. He lifted slightly off the floor, as if an invisible hand to match Rika's gripped him.

All at once, he exploded into a thousand scattering motes of light. Only a thin cloud of bluish smoke remained of him.

She could do *that*? No wonder Echoes were terrified of her.

"Rika," I croaked, torn between wonder and worry. "Be careful, it's a..."

I didn't have a chance to get any more out. Rika flung herself across the hall at me like an arrow, spouting a stream of sizzling

THE LAST SOUL AMONG WOLVES 289

curses, wings tucking away behind her back.

There was something downright surreal about the contrast between the shining divine radiance of her Empyrean form and the profane language pouring out of her mouth. But then, everything felt surreal right now, like the edge of a dream.

"Kembral!" She grabbed my face, her searching eyes bathing me in scarlet light. "You look terrible. Oh, I'm going to *kill* her."

Before I could point out that it was literally impossible to kill her mother, Rika made a violent, furious gesture. The web piercing my arm dissolved, followed immediately by those binding me. Which had been all that was holding me up.

I couldn't even make a doomed attempt to take my own weight; my head had gone light and distant, and my body wouldn't respond. I collapsed against Rika, loose as a rag doll. She caught me with a grunt of effort, squeezing me tight in a fierce hug.

"*Ow!*" I protested. "Broken rib! Broken rib!"

Her arms loosened at once. She dropped to her knees, easing me down half in her lap with one arm supporting my shoulders, staring anxiously into my face with those glowing red eyes. It was embarrassing that I couldn't do much to help—and more than a bit worrying that my limbs weren't responding properly—but also strangely comforting. Like she was in charge now, and I could rest.

"I'm sorry," she said, with the stubborn air of someone continuing an argument, "but I can't let you go. That's not who I am. I can respect your free will and let you make your own choices. If you tell me to get out of your life, I will. But I am never, *ever* going to be normal about you. And there's no way under the Moon or in the Void I can walk away and leave you in a place like this."

"Okay." The word came out with enough rough edges to sand down a board. I managed to reach up and touch her face; she was trembling, her breath heaving in and out as if she'd run the whole way here. "Are you all right?"

"No," she said. "You?"

"No."

She gave a firm nod, as if to say, *We're agreed, then.* "Let's get out of here. Can you walk?"

Oh, that was funny. I sifted through the various reasons I couldn't walk—the swooning nausea of blood loss, the unraveling reality of my toes—and settled on, "Broken ankle."

She let out a sharp, frustrated breath, as if I were being unreasonable. "Fine. I'll carry you."

She scooped me up as if I weighed no more than a child, rising to her feet in the same motion. I'd had to carry plenty of people in my years of doing Echo retrievals, and it shouldn't have been that easy. Clearly her Empyrean form didn't care about little details like how heavy an adult human body was—at least not this far down below Prime.

"The lantern," I said urgently, remembering. "I had it, but I dropped it when—"

"Fuck the lantern. I'm getting you out of here."

She started moving, but I grabbed her shoulder. "Wait! The bottle. Got to take it with us."

"You mean the one that's *full of your blood*? Have you lost your *mind*?"

"I'm not leaving it here for Arhsta," I said grimly. "She wants to use it against you."

"Ugh. Fine, but you have to carry it. My hands are full."

The exasperation in her voice was good, human, familiar. Maybe the way I anchored her was by annoying her. I felt a loopy, light-headed sort of smile cross my face.

Rika stepped close to the table; I scooped up the bottle, trying not to think of what was in it or why it was so sickeningly warm. I worked the stopper in as tight as I could and cradled it against me.

A sound had begun to build at the edge of my senses. At first I thought it was the surge of my pulse, but no—it was coming from beyond the smoking hole Rika had made, and past the throne room doors.

Footsteps. A great many of them, approaching quickly and forcefully, with no attempt at stealth—along with other, more unnerving sounds: scraping, slithering, humming. Arhsta must have noticed we were escaping, and now an army of Echoes was coming for us.

THE LAST SOUL AMONG WOLVES 291

All at once the loose dangling ends of the webs Rika had destroyed stirred into life, writhing toward us, splitting and reaching with ends that curled into sharp, piercing hooks.

Rika cursed. Her vast glowing wings snapped open, shedding a feather or two of pure light. She tightened her grip on me enough that my rib stabbed in protest, her knees flexing, gaze lifting upward.

My breath caught. "Are you going to—"

She launched up from the ground, wings beating with a powerful thunder. My stomach seemed to stay below, my head swimming dizzily. Holy shit, yes, she was *flying*.

Webs strained after us, hundreds of filaments snaking through the air from every corner of the hall. My pulse did faltering acrobatics. I was all too aware that I couldn't do a damn thing to help fight or flee—that my job was to be very, very still and not unbalance Rika in any way.

She glared up at the skylight above us, eyes blazing with red light, and it shattered. Shards of colored glass rained down around us, sliding away from Rika as if an invisible parasol protected her.

It was all too much for my battered body, no matter how stubbornly I tried to cling to consciousness. As we rose into the light, my mind slipped down into a waiting darkness.

—⚬—

I was dimly aware that I needed to be awake, that if I couldn't stay awake that was pretty bad, that Rika needed me. But everything was too far away. I was struggling deep underwater, already drowned.

I knew things were happening, sometimes felt Rika's heart beating wild and panicked against me, dimly heard cursing and other, more alarming sounds. Just little flashes, bits of light or noise or a sudden panicked lurch, and then a thick soft nothingness, like being swallowed.

I woke at last to the sound of a door banging open, warm light hitting my face, and the enfolding scent of herbs. Rika's breath sounded in ragged gasps by my ear. She lurched as she carried me, which didn't seem good.

292   MELISSA CARUSO

With enormous effort, I dragged my eyes open.

I couldn't quite get them to focus properly, but I recognized where we were immediately. The shelves upon shelves of shining tins, the soft shifting of glowing lights in the ceiling, the handful of little tables and the gleaming polished wood of the counter—but it was the smell that gave it away. That and the sense of peace and safety that surrounded us the moment Rika staggered in the door.

Laemura's Curious Tea Emporium. A rush of gratitude and relief swamped me. *Rika, you brilliant woman.*

"Help us," she gasped. "Please."

Laemura bustled out from behind the counter, wiping her hands on her apron. In this Echo, she sported tall tufted ears and a swishing tail.

"Welcome, Signas! My, you're both in quite a state." She looked us over critically. "I suppose you'll be wanting medicinal teas *again*. Really, Signa Thorne, this is becoming a habit."

"Sorry." I barely mumbled the word, nudging the bottle still cradled in my arms. "Can pay."

Laemura's eyes widened, her hands stilling in her apron. "For that, you could buy my whole shop and then some. Top shelf it is, then." She took down a CLOSED sign from a nail on the wall, hung it on the door, and locked it. "Sit down, and we'll see what we can do."

Rika all but dumped me into a chair, clearly unable to carry me any longer, and collapsed against me into an adjacent one. We leaned on each other; she was shuddering and glowing, and I was transparent around all my edges and barely conscious, with my ankle swollen enough to make me dimly anxious about my Damn Good Boots. We made quite a pair.

Laemura pursed her lips. "You first, Signa Nonesuch. Your situation is a bit less dire, but I can't have you destabilizing in my shop and ripping reality to shreds around you. It's bad for the tea."

She started pulling canisters off shelves, using a stepstool to get most of them, muttering to herself. "Let's see, a nice earthy black tea to ground you as the base—lightly smoked, I think—and something of Prime to stabilize you . . . Signa Thorne, give me that bottle, won't you?"

THE LAST SOUL AMONG WOLVES 293

I couldn't lift it, but I let her take it from me. Rika raised her head from my shoulder in alarm.

"I don't want to drink her blood!"

"Oh, hush, it's just a drop. Prime blood is the very best stabilizer, dear, and your anchor's will be particularly potent. You won't even taste it. Now, hmm, a touch of lemongrass for clarity, and some crystallized moonlight to steady your divinity..." Her muttering trailed off into incomprehensibility as she collected more and more ingredients. It was a nice, safe sound. I started to slip away again.

"Kembral," Rika said sharply. "Talk to me."

There was an edge approaching panic in her voice, and I wanted to tell her it wasn't that bad, I was just sleepy. But right—she needed me to talk to her not just so I'd stay awake, but for herself. I had to ground her, so she wouldn't unravel into opposing cosmic forces.

"Uh. I like your wings." My words came out slurred. "They're pretty."

She made a sound that I wasn't sure was a laugh. "You're nicer when you're semiconscious, did you know that?"

I searched my brain for something else to say, but my thoughts ran like rainwater. Somewhere in me was a core of urgency—things we needed to do, terrible things that could happen if we didn't—but I had to fumble around in my own mind like I was wearing mittens.

"Need to get to Prime," I mumbled. "I...overdid it a little."

"I *tried*." Her whole body trembled. "There were too many of her forces between us and the mirror. I had to run in another direction, so I came here."

"Good thinking."

"I didn't know where else to go." She laced her fingers through mine. They didn't feel cold, for once, which was heartening for a second, until I realized it probably meant mine were even colder. "I don't...I don't feel good, Kembral."

Her wings hung bedraggled and glowing behind her, in some transitional state not quite folded away into invisibility and not quite out. The glow in her eyes brightened and dimmed unevenly, and she couldn't seem to stop shaking.

"You...shouldn't have done this to yourself for me."

"Oh, shut up. I had to get in there somehow, and the main doors were too heavily guarded. Besides, I was angry."

"When we're better...the lantern..." I felt my words starting to slide together in my mouth; my eyelids were getting heavy again. "I know where it is, unless they moved it. We could..."

"Let's not get ahead of ourselves. You can't even walk."

I let out the dry ghost of a laugh, then regretted it immediately as a sharp stab of pain went through my rib. "You haven't seen...what Laemura's top-shelf teas can do."

"Have you tried them before?"

"Me? No. Could never afford them." Now my eyes closed. It felt good to be slumped against each other, Rika warm at my side. Her hair still smelled like her hair, even if it was a river of pure darkness. Her hand in mine was nice. A wing curled around my shoulders, soft and comforting. We were together, and terrible things might be happening, but we were in good hands. Maybe, just maybe, we could still salvage this.

"You'll see," I whispered, and passed out again.

SOMETIMES YOU HAVE TO START OVER

There was a time of distant voices and heavenly scents, of a blessed numbness creeping over me and taking away all the pain I'd grown so weary of. Then Laemura's voice, distinct and annoyed:

"It's too hot, and it won't taste right, but it can't be helped—we're losing her."

Then scalding liquid in my mouth. I sputtered and swallowed, and it burned all the way down my throat.

After that was an interlude of darkness, and then a series of far more delicate and delicious sips, one after another, each different from the last. I wished I were awake enough to properly appreciate it. Someone held my head up each time; by the gentle elegance of the hands, I knew it was Rika. Someone else put the cup to my lips, and by the fact that they didn't pour boiling hot tea all over my face, I suspected it was Laemura.

At last the candle of my mind rekindled, and I found myself blinking up at the glowing creatures twining in the ceiling beams—snakes, in this Echo, with beautiful jeweled patterns of scales like stained glass. I seemed to be lying on an exceedingly soft and sumptuous pallet on the floor of the tea shop, with Rika sitting cross-legged next to me. She looked exhausted but entirely human, with weary grey eyes and no wings whatsoever. An assortment of empty teacups sat all around us on tables, chairs, and the countertop. Laemura stood behind the counter, brewing up yet another cup and humming to herself.

Rika brushed a strand of hair out of my face. "How do you feel?"

"Alive?" I tried to sit up, but Rika stopped me with a hand on my shoulder just as a surge of dizziness swept over me.

"Not yet. She's making you a few more. Apparently reality shock is tricky."

My eyes were suddenly welling up with tears for no good reason, except maybe that we were alive.

"I lost the lantern," I said hoarsely. "I had it, but I lost it. You were right, Rika. I shouldn't have gone in alone."

"I'm going to have that engraved on a golden bracelet and wear it constantly," she murmured. "*You were right, Rika.*" She squeezed my hand, and her voice dropped low. "But don't be foolish. This was entirely my fault."

"I don't see—"

"Because I made you my anchor."

"Oh." My head was still foggy, but a tired flare of resentment rose up, like some final bubble from the deep buried murk of my soul. But like a bubble, it broke and vanished almost at once. "Were you ever going to tell me about that?"

"I swear I didn't know. I was starting to suspect, but..." She sighed. "I didn't want to admit it. Especially to myself."

"So you didn't make me your anchor on purpose." That hit me in such a huge wave of relief that I had to close my eyes for a moment.

"No!" Rika sounded appalled. "No, I think...I think it happened a long time ago."

I blinked, looking into the depths of her grey eyes, and suddenly I remembered them brown. Sad, *so* sad, giving up all hope as she lost her hold on reality and began to fade...

Reflexively, I caught her hand, an echo of that long-ago movement. It had been cold even then, I realized, though much smaller.

"When we were kids," I whispered. "Was it then?"

Rika bit her lip and nodded. "It was an instinct, I think. I was slipping away, and you...you caught me. I can never tell you how much that..."

She looked away suddenly. With a curse, she rubbed the back of her free wrist against her eyes.

"Anyway," she said, her voice rough, "I think I was like a drowning swimmer, grabbing at a branch. That was when it happened. I didn't even know what an anchor *was* until the year-turning, but looking back...Whenever I started to lose myself, whenever I felt my humanity slipping, I thought of you. Your warm, strong hand. Your voice."

"Rika..."

Silent tears spilled onto her cheeks. Her brow wrinkled in vexation. "And later, all the maddening things you do. I'd think of how annoying you were, and that would ground me."

"Thanks," I said dryly. But my eyes were stinging, too.

"I know you didn't ask for this." She looked down at our joined hands. "I know you didn't have a choice. And now it's put you in danger and gotten you so badly hurt."

"No." I found the strength to put iron in my tone. "Your horrible monster mother did that."

"Technically, I suppose, but—"

"The only unpleasant things *you've* done to me as a result of making me your anchor have involved being weirdly overprotective and knocking me out. Assuming that's some strange Empyrean instinct and not just you being irrational on your own."

She looked half-ready to snatch her hand back, but then her expression turned worried. "It probably is. Empyrean instinct, that is. I've felt...different, since the year-turning. When I had to...come back to life like that. And it got worse after we went through the mirror the first time."

"I noticed."

"I think the more I use that side of me, the stronger those instincts get. So you're right, I've definitely been getting weirder about you—much as I do despise the idea of being ruled by my baser urges." She said the last airily, a desperate attempt at humor.

"Then don't be. If there's one thing I know about you, it's that you're too stubborn and contrary to let anything dictate what you do."

Before Rika could reply, Laemura came bustling over with a steaming cup. "Oh, good, this will be much easier with you awake. Here's another, dear. Then you have to rest a bit longer to let them work, and I can give you one last tea to finish things before you go."

I sipped a cup that tasted like burnt apple and lightning, the deep golden liquor tingling as it crossed my tongue. I let out a long sigh.

"Delicious as always," I murmured.

Laemura beamed at me. "It's been a while since I needed to brew quite so many teas for one person! You really were a mess. Now, this one should finish stabilizing your reality shock, but that's only temporary. You'll have about half a day to return to Prime, so long as you don't do anything foolish like blink step again—which you *must not do* before getting back to Prime under any circumstances, or it'll all be undone."

"How about the broken bones? I know in the past you've told me to go easy on them for a couple weeks, but—"

Laemura raised an eyebrow. "My dear, you *did* pay for top shelf. You should be fine to walk or even run on that ankle now; just rest and elevate it when you get home. And blood loss is easy to fix, but do be sure to hydrate. Plus I gave you some ginger lemon black tea to refresh your energy and a bit of soothing lavender chamomile blend to take the edge off, because you looked like you needed it."

"Thanks. Do I...do I owe you, or..."

"Don't be ridiculous, Signa Thorne. If you're truly giving me that whole bottle, you'll have an unlimited tab here for the rest of your life."

I shuddered. "I don't want to ever look at that thing again, so I'll take that deal. Just...don't use it for anything regrettable."

"My dear, I am a professional," Laemura said, somewhat reprovingly. "It's hardly the most dangerous substance in this shop."

THE LAST SOUL AMONG WOLVES   299

I almost asked what was, then decided that maybe I didn't want to know.

"Thank you," I told Laemura, with feeling. "I don't want to think about what would have happened if we hadn't come here."

"Nothing good. Come more often when you're *not* in dire trouble, Signa Thorne."

"I will."

She returned to her brewing, humming busily again. I found Rika watching me, her eyes soft but also oddly calculating.

"So," she said, subdued. "What do we do now?"

"That's the question." I exhaled a shaky breath. "The minute we walk out of here, we're pretty fucked."

"But you have a plan." It was as much a plea as anything.

"I have more of an intention, at this point."

Rika gave me a long, inscrutable look. "You want to go after the lantern."

"Yeah. If we can come up with a way that has a decent chance of success. It's that or just accept that someone is going to die, and I don't want to do that."

I braced for the inevitable argument that we should go back to Prime, that it was too dangerous to stay, that we were both hurt and I couldn't blink step—

"All right," she said.

I stared at her. "Really?"

She waved an airy hand. "It's a heist. I've successfully burgled far more difficult targets. I found about a dozen ways into that castle while you were busy being captured."

"But Arhsta will be expecting us. We could fall right back into her hands."

"Kembral...let's not deceive ourselves. That could happen anywhere."

I opened my mouth, then closed it again. She had a point, and the implications chilled me to the bone.

"She's just as powerful outside her castle as inside it," Rika went on quietly. "I'm sure she's got another trap set for us—stars, she probably has dozens of traps. They could be right outside this door. They could be in the castle. They could be on the mirror, or anywhere in this Echo, or back at the Lovegrace mansion, or on the door to your house, or in our guildhouses. All the worlds are her trap, and we can never escape it."

"Well, that's grim."

"It's the truth." She shrugged. "So we may as well try to get the lantern. At least there we know there's *bound* to be a trap, and we can be on high alert and hope to avoid it."

I considered this. "You're the expert here. She's an Empyrean, and she has ways of just *knowing* things. How can we get in and out without her noticing?"

Rika hesitated. "Well...there *is* an advanced Cat technique for hiding your presence from Echoes, which I suspect might work. The most senior Cats use it to get past Echo wards. But I can only use it on myself, and only for a limited time—and for that matter, I can't be sure she couldn't overpower it."

"Sounds like I should be the distraction, then."

"Are you delirious from blood loss? If we split up and you draw her attention, what's to stop her from scooping you up again and putting us right back where we started?"

"Her own nature." It came to me in a clear surge of satisfaction. "That's our one advantage over the Empyreans. They *have* to act according to their equilibrium threads. She can't just send some minions to grab me by force. There has to be a devious plan involved."

"That army of Echoes we heard converging on us when I rescued you might disagree."

"That extremely loud and obvious army? I'd bet cold money that was meant to herd us into some trap. She just didn't expect you to fly out through the skylight." I shook my head. "No, she's got to either act indirectly through manipulation, or through clever traps, or as the result of some complex scheme."

"And by that very nature, she'll have something in place to catch us if we come back!"

"Right. But you're a Cat, and you're too smart and elusive to fall into her traps."

THE LAST SOUL AMONG WOLVES

Rika looked dubious. "And you?"

I grinned. "I'm going to be too stupid."

—⁓—

The problem with this plan was that it required me to wait and trust that Rika would handle everything.

It was my plan, but I hated it.

Sure, she was extremely competent, and knowing that her mother couldn't act directly against her made me less overwhelmingly worried than I might have been. But still, I'd been a senior Hound for ages; it had been a long time since my job was to sit back and let the other person do the important things, let alone in circumstances dangerous enough to leave my nerves constantly on fire.

I liked even less that the place I had to wait was the fantastical landscape of the castle's roof, all peaked gables and turrets, with slender towers rising above like trees. It felt a bit like clinging to a steeply sloped and forested mountainside, if the mountain were tiled in some shining black substance. The roof fell away far too sharply under my feet, vanishing over the edge into a long drop to the streets below.

It was my job to look like I was hunting for a way in, so I couldn't just crouch there and cling to the shingles. I clambered around, carefully as I could, allowing myself to be puzzled by the utter lack of relationship between the castle's outside and the inside that I'd seen. Turret windows yawned invitingly into darkness; I peered at them, visibly dithering over whether they might be in the right place to get me close to the lantern. I wandered through a forest of intricately wrought chimneys that could serve no possible purpose in an empty Echo castle that lacked apparent fireplaces, eyeing them as if trying to determine whether they were large enough to admit me (they absolutely were, probably by design). I deliberately failed to see an ornate arched door that opened from one tower onto a little balcony just in reach of the rooftop, meandering in the other direction and muttering to myself about how *if only* I could find a way in.

It was as if the castle, formerly featureless and so completely without portals as to require a blink step to enter, was suddenly desperate to show me a dozen possible routes to break in. I had no doubt that every single one of them was a trap. Now I just had to buy enough time pretending to scout around to let Rika do what she did best.

It'd be easier if I weren't in constant terror that at any moment a pit would open under me or something. Worst of all was lacking the usual comfort of knowing that I could blink step out of danger if it did. Playing bait was all very well, but I hated being so genuinely vulnerable. And I couldn't stop worrying about Rika. She could be hurt, or captured, or dead, or—

"Kembral."

Or standing right behind me. "Holy *Void*, Rika, I almost fell off the roof."

I turned around to find her giving me such a grim look that my whole chest clenched tight around my heart. I nearly didn't notice what swung from her hand.

The lantern. The lights of souls swirled within it, agitated, casting a golden glow across her arm.

"You got it," I breathed. "You really got it."

"I tried to break it, but I think I'd have to be in my other form, and Laemura made it very clear that I shouldn't do that again before I get back to Prime." She held the lantern out to me, the lines of her face tight and wary. "Take it."

I did. The smooth ring of the handle felt cool in my hand as its strange weight settled over me.

"What's wrong?" I asked, heart pounding with an increasing sense of dread. I could almost feel the electricity of Rika's nerves firing, she was so on edge.

"It was far too easy." She crossed to a turret window she must have emerged from to retrieve some silver cord from its sill—probably enchanted to bypass traps or wards. "There were protections on it, but nothing like there should have been. No sign of guards, no sign of *her*. This isn't right."

"That means we're probably still in the trap right now."

She gave a sharp nod, slipping the silver cord into some hidden pocket. "Let's get out of here before it closes."

THE LAST SOUL AMONG WOLVES   303

"I'm afraid," said a terribly familiar voice, deep and resonant, "it's too late for that."

From the other side of the tower, a long, lean figure detached from a shadow, a shred of night sky fluttering behind him. Mirror eyes flashed in the darkness as they fixed on us.

Rai.

TAKE THE RIGHT RISKS

Rai was back in his form-fitting armor, his jagged black sword riding on his shoulders. He paced closer, as surefooted on the sharp roof ridge as if it were level ground, putting himself between us before I could close the gap and get to Rika's side.

"I was hoping you'd call on me for aid. That would have been more convenient. But you're annoyingly self-sufficient, so I had to go to the trouble of waiting in ambush." He turned toward me and held out his hand. "The lantern, please."

Rika went sharp and ready as a drawn knife. "I thought you said we were on the same side in this."

He glanced back over his shoulder at her. "We had a shared goal, for a while. That's hardly the same thing."

I retreated along the slope of the roof, testing my footing carefully, working my way up to the ridgeline where I could have better balance. "If I give it to you, will you destroy it?"

"Come now, Kembral Thorne." He matched me step for step, silver gaze intent. "You know me well enough by now. Do you think I would cast aside a tool that would feed my anchor's ambitions so perfectly?"

"I thought you couldn't steal it yourself. I thought that would be going up directly against Stars Tangled in Her Web."

"How convenient, then, that you stole it first, so I can take it from you."

He paused with an air of something strangely like politeness, and I realized I'd come to the gable edge. A sheer drop waited a couple of feet behind me. I stood rooted with one foot on either side of the ridgeline, feeling incredibly precarious, the lantern swaying from my hand.

Rika met my eyes past his shoulder. She had a hand on her dagger, but frustration vexed her face. She gave me a tiny shake of her head— she couldn't attack him, for the same reason her mother couldn't attack her, not that it'd do much good if she did.

"We're still on the roof of her castle," I said. "This is her territory."

"She has made it quite clear that she only cared about the lantern as bait for you two. So if she has you, well, the lantern is mine for the taking."

"But she doesn't have us," I pointed out. "And you don't have the lantern."

"A situation I'm here to remedy."

He reached back over his shoulder and drew his sword. It gleamed in the starlight like a long shard of black glass.

Without my blink step, I couldn't hurt him. Standing up on a roof where he had the perfect balance of a cat and I had to worry about falling to my death if I made a mistake, he had all the advantages. This was not going to go well.

I drew my sword anyway—my slim, swept-hilt Echo blade. The other stayed in its sheath for now, since my left hand was full. Looked like I was fighting sword and lantern.

Rika's voice rang out from behind him, cold and powerful as the Moon. "Don't you dare lay a finger on her."

"I'm forbidden to fight *you*, little sister," Rai said, without so much as turning around. "There's no rule against killing each other's anchors. You could even call it customary."

With slow, liquid grace, he fell into a reactive stance, poised to counterstrike the instant I moved. His eyes dared me to come at him.

I didn't have a lot of choice. I was backed up against the edge; it would be child's play for him to push me off. Presumably he didn't only because he couldn't be bothered to go collect the lantern from my shattered corpse on the ground below. But my normal tactic when facing an opponent with longer reach—get inside quickly and stab the living shit out of them—wouldn't do me much good when he was invulnerable to my blade.

The best thing I could think to do was try to knock him off the ridgeline. If I could unbalance him enough to get past him, I could give the lantern to Rika, who by his own admission he wasn't allowed to beat up to take it back. It was probably why his first move had been to put himself between us.

I dropped to a low, forward stance, keeping my center close to the roof to make it harder to fall. He adjusted the angle of his blade and shifted his feet. We stared at each other for a long moment. He was taking me seriously, after last time, which was bad news for me.

I realized I couldn't see Rika anymore; she was probably doing something devious. All right—time to make sure he didn't start wondering where she was.

I launched myself at him, fast and low. My ankle twinged, but held. His sword came at me in a vicious sweeping arc; I swung up the lantern to intercept it.

It was a gamble. The lantern was slow and unwieldy, but I had a suspicion—and *yes*. He cursed and twisted his blade aside at the last instant, scrambling back a couple of steps. He didn't want to hit it.

"Worried you'll break it?" I held the lantern aloft in front of me, elbow tucked in line behind it, angling sideways to give him very little target area that didn't require him to go through the lantern first. "Good to know that there's no special trick to it."

"If you truly wish to lean on such an awkward defense, be my guest."

Rai launched into a series of quick, controlled attacks—no more great sweeping strikes, but delicate twisty cuts at my wrist that threatened to take my hand and the lantern with it, and sneaky thrusts beneath my guard at my midsection. I kept the lantern moving, swinging it into line again and again to force him to abort his strikes, parrying with my blade when the lantern wasn't fast enough. It was all harder because I had to move my feet as little as I could get away with to avoid risking a misstep and fatal fall.

Rai landed a light cut on my forearm. I cursed. It was a shallow thing, not remotely dangerous—but it meant I wouldn't be able to keep holding the lantern up and waving it around for a prolonged time, and he knew it.

I hated being on the defensive anyway.

On his next strike, I knocked his blade aside with the lantern and closed. His sword came back around quickly at me in a tight arc; I dropped under it, angling my own blade up to parry as I launched a kick at his legs.

It was too similar to how I'd taken him out last time. He was ready for it. Rai sprang back, landing lightly on his feet, and I was down here half on my ass.

"Kembral!"

It was Rika, calling with what sounded like a *do it now* kind of urgency rather than an *oh no he's going to stab you* urgency, from somewhere off to my right.

Hoping I hadn't read her wrong, I surged to my feet, swinging the lantern up with the same motion in the direction of her voice—and yes, there she was, braced against a turret at the edge of the roof, hands spread and ready. It would leave me wide open, but I could toss it to her, in the desperate hope that Rai would be too distracted to stab me and she could catch it.

It was the Year of Hope. I let the lantern go.

It sailed from my hand in a graceful arc, glowing against the night sky like a comet. Rika stood poised to catch it, determination in her face. Rai swore, which was incredibly satisfying.

And then he lunged with inhuman speed. The tip of his great black sword—still stained with my blood—just barely caught the ring at the top of the lantern.

Shit.

With a terrible scraping noise, the lantern slid down the length of his blade as he returned it to a vertical line before him. It came to rest with a discordant chime against the hilt, casting its golden light up into Rai's face.

His cheeks looked less hollow than I remembered. His silver eyes practically glowed with victory.

He offered me a mocking bow. "My thanks."

"Destroy it," I urged, tensed to move, sword still ready. "It threatens your anchor's life—surely you don't want that."

"On the contrary." He lifted his sword, holding the lantern aloft to marvel at its light. "This is the prize in a game. One that with the lantern in her possession, my anchor is guaranteed to win. What could I want more?"

"What are you going to do with it?"

"I'd say you'll see, but alas, I doubt you'll make it back to Prime." His cloak lifted and spread behind him, splitting into great wings black as the Void and speckled with distant stars. "They're all yours."

It took me longer than it should have—a full second as he lifted from the ground, his vast wings sending a cool lightning-scented breeze into our faces—for me to realize his last words hadn't been directed to us.

"Oh holy Void," Rika breathed.

All around us, with a terrible groaning noise, the slender black towers started to grow.

They sprouted bare stony branches like winter trees, which split rapidly into more branches, reaching and crossing. Above us, Rai rose up into the night sky, the lantern a golden star in his hand.

"Damn it!" My whole body wanted to strain instinctively upward, as if I could fly after him, but it was too late. "We've got to stop him somehow!"

Rika seized my arm with rigid fingers. "We have other problems."

The intersecting branches of the towers around us were forming an intricate latticework, like a web—or a cage.

Already, the gaps had closed too small to wriggle through. Once Rai cleared the tops, more branches spread out to form a bare carceral canopy, starker black against the velvet night sky. Stars twinkled in the branches, tiny shards of light like broken glass. Some of those motes of light began to drift down toward us, little gleaming specks falling like snow.

A sense of presence smothered us. A heavy clarity that gave the air a wintry crispness and made every crack and ping of the shifting stone go through me like a knife.

I turned, careful on the shuddering roof and my weak ankle, to face the source of the power that burdened the air.

Stars Tangled in Her Web had arrived.

ALL BLUFFS CAN BE CALLED

Arhsta floated a couple of inches above the roof ridge, her hair streaming into the night sky, her star-shimmered gown stirring slightly in a breeze I couldn't feel. Her eyes shone like the Moon, and her face drank in the light. My heart pounded wildly, all the memories of what she'd done to me far too fresh and vivid in my mind.

The rooftop flattened beneath our feet, easing down into a more level plane; Rika and I grabbed each other for stability as we dropped with it. Arhsta drifted down, surrounded by falling stars, until her toes touched the tiles and gravity seemed to gently, gracefully reassert itself upon her, hair and gown falling around her like wings folding.

"Welcome back." Her voice was honey and thunder, the radiance of dawn and the oppressive fall of night.

Rika stepped in front of me, her back rigid, arms outstretched protectively. I drew my second sword, well aware that without my blink step, I had no means to hurt an Empyrean, and no way to defend myself.

Arhsta let out a rich chuckle. "There's no need for that. Come. Let us talk."

She made a beckoning motion, a rising lift and curl of her fingers, and a table and chairs of more black latticework grew from the roof-top. Candles sprouted from its surface like flowers, opening blooms of flickering flame.

The specks of light falling around us accumulated on the ground, twinkling, like a dusting of snow. A few clung to Rika's hair, shimmering; the ones that hit my mortal skin went out at once.

"I don't have anything to say to you." Rika's tone was icy.

"Perhaps not," Arhsta said, amusement dancing in her voice. "But it would still be wise to sit and talk. The alternatives are far less pleasant."

I let out a breath like a last prayer to the Moon. Then, before Rika could deliver some retort, I sheathed my swords and stepped past her.

"All right," I said. "Let's talk."

Rika gave me a warning look but gathered herself and fell in beside me. Together, all three of us sat down at the table—Rika and I on one side, and Arhsta, enthroned in radiance, on the other.

Between one blink and the next, the table was suddenly full of food, as if it had always been there. Shimmering golden fruit formed artful, decadent heaps on platters with what might be cheeses, nuts, and some strange crumbled substance I couldn't identify, all of it in different hues of gold from champagne to honey. Tall flutes of a pale, shining liquid stood in front of each of us. My mouth went suddenly dry.

"It is safe to eat and drink," Arhsta assured us. "I have no need to taint your food when I can turn the air you breathe to poison on a whim."

Well, that was a thought I hadn't needed. Suddenly I became far too conscious of the act of breathing. Of all the ways she could hurt me with a flick of her will, just to get at Rika. My appetite vanished.

"This has to be quick," I said, aware of the rough bluntness of my dull mortal voice after the music of her celestial one. "We have urgent business back in Prime."

"Ah. The lantern." She gave a gracious nod. "You are concerned for your friends. You should be. In a very short time, they will all be dead."

312 MELISSA CARUSO

I gripped the edge of the table, my knuckles whitening. "Because you let Rai take it. Which seems out of character for you, frankly. Don't you exist to gather power to yourself?"

"It has served its purpose as bait. I hardly care what human uses it now, or what souls fuel it." She took a small sip from her glass of glowing starlight. "It's far more useful to me out in Prime, where I can use it to twist mortals to my will. Having your friends' souls in it will only increase its value to me."

Suddenly all I could think of was what Signa Zarvish had said, about not letting the lantern fall into the wrong hands. Because *any-one* could use it to draw out the souls of its targets, living or dead.

Jaycel. Petras.

"I have to stop him," I breathed, and leaped to my feet.

Or I tried to. Fine webs bound my legs to the chair, keeping me in place.

"We are not done speaking," Arhsta said.

Rika's jaw flexed. "They have nothing to do with any of this. They're Kembral's friends, not mine."

"And yet you have made it amply clear that by controlling her, I can control you, my daughter."

A tiny spark of furious red light kindled deep in Rika's eyes. "I am *not* your daughter. There's no connection between us. You gave up all claim on me when you dumped me on the streets of Acantis after I was born."

"No connection?" Arhsta's glowing eyes narrowed with amuse-ment. "I *created* you. I am half of what you are."

"It's the human half that made me who I am," Rika said through her teeth. "It's my human life that has shaped me."

Arhsta laughed, the sound pealing out across the city. "Oh, child! Your *human* side? I *consumed* your father to create you. He was noth-ing, a mere source of materials, and he is gone. Your human face is a false mask you change at will. Your human life is a role you play, a juvenile entertainment."

Rika flinched. I laid my hand against her back, where her mother couldn't see it, lending her what support I could. Something rustled

THE LAST SOUL AMONG WOLVES   313

beneath my hand like feathers, but at my touch, it smoothed out into rigid muscle.

"It pleases me greatly that you have embraced more of your true nature." Arhsta reached across the table and laid a hand like a tear in reality on Rika's cheek. "You should never have suppressed it. You have always been so much more than human. I look forward to seeing what you can yet become."

Rika jerked her face away from her mother's hand. "I'm already everything I need to be."

"Oh?" Arhsta smiled, a slow and terrible smile radiant with starlight. "You've made it quite clear that you'll embrace whatever powers you must to protect your mortal toy. And now, my daughter, you have a choice before you."

"*You* do not give me my choices," Rika snapped. I couldn't help a surge of pride.

"You face one nonetheless." Arhsta remained cool and distant as the Moon, flecks of starlight falling around her and pooling at her feet. "You can determine what your future looks like. Ascend your throne, and you become the secret ruler of all the world, with power reaching to every corner of Prime, to be echoed down through every reality. You can do whatever you like with your anchor—make her part of your court, keep her as your consort, let her go about her life as she sees fit. I would even be willing to let the souls free from the lantern, if you like."

The webs that bound my legs snaked up around me, rising past my waist, wreathing my arms, caressing my face. I caught a sharp breath, expecting pain, but they whispered gossamer-soft across my skin—not constricting yet, not burning or breaking, but teasing the promise of all the damage they could do to a fragile mortal body.

"Stop that," Rika snapped, an edge in her voice.

"I think you know what the other choice is," Arhsta said, as if Rika hadn't spoken. Her lips curved into a smile. "There is no escaping my web, little fly. It stretches across all the worlds. If you value your anchor, your decision should be simple. Take the place and the power that await you."

314 MELISSA CARUSO

And that was the terrible, despairing truth of it. She was divine, and she was everywhere. No matter how we ran, we couldn't escape. I was doomed to be her hostage forever, tormented anytime she wanted leverage over Rika, and there wasn't a damned thing we could do about it.

Wait. That couldn't be true. I'd named this year for a reason.

And once I realized that a way out must exist, it opened before me like a secret road wending ahead through the starry night.

I met Arhsta's unearthly gaze. "Or else what?"

Arhsta spread her hands. "I have no desire to delve into the gory particulars. Suffice to say, daughter, that if you walk away from this table, your anchor remains in this castle, under my power, until you change your mind."

Ah. Wild satisfaction surged through me, too bitter to be elation. There it was. I had her.

"Say no," I told Rika, without taking my eyes off Arhsta's ethereal face.

"It's not that easy, Kembral," she began, her voice low and full of anguish.

"No. It is. Say no, and she's lost." I was sure of it. "It's not great for us, granted—she can crush me like a bug and there's nothing I can do about it—but it's worse for her."

Arhsta's glowing eyes moved slowly from her daughter's face to mine, fixing on me with a malevolent radiance. "You seem unusually eager to suffer, mortal."

"You're not good at threats, are you?" I picked up my flute of mysterious glowing liquid, a heady tingle running through me that could have been a side effect of blood loss or reality shock, but felt almost like victory. "Because they're not in your nature. Your equilibrium thread is complex, delicate manipulation. Using force isn't just crass to you—it's anathema."

Her gaze narrowed to white-hot slits. "It's not a matter of force. This moment is the culmination of years of planning. Centuries, given how long it took me to discover how to create a child with a human—our dalliances with mortals do not result in offspring, as

THE LAST SOUL AMONG WOLVES   315

yours do. You scarcely could comprehend all of the threads that have converged in this moment."

"But that's the problem, isn't it?" I took a deliberate sip of the glowing stuff. It was delicious, with notes of champagne, peaches, and honey. "You're not like Rai; it's not victory you feed on. You win by playing the game. Now that those threads of yours have finished converging and we're in the crucial moment, if Rika says no, all that complexity has nowhere to go. All those threads are cut off."

Rika was watching me, lips slightly parted, like I was a revelation. Arhsta's nails came down on the table, one after another, in a series of sharp raps that set the roof beneath us to trembling, but she said nothing.

I leaned in. "Sure, you could torture me or kill me or whatever you like. Rika might be very sad, and I certainly wouldn't have a good time. But that's not cunning manipulation, is it? It's brutish force. You'd be breaking your own equilibrium thread."

"You know nothing of such things, mortal." Arhsta's tone had a vicious edge.

"But I do. It's the only thing I know about your kind that matters." I took another sip of sweet starlight. "It's why you let us escape, isn't it? You could have stopped us easily, but you didn't. Better to let us get away and then catch us again, like a cat releasing a mouse so it can keep playing with it. Because if you catch the mouse and kill it, the game is over, and you lose."

"And yet," Arhsta said ominously, "that still leaves you very much a dead mouse."

The trembling in the floor beneath my feet hadn't stopped. Arhsta's face remained remote, celestial, and unreadable as the Void itself, but something strange had begun to happen. The dusting of stars across her cheeks glowed more brightly, more sharply; those in her gown did as well, taking on an edge of piercing clarity. Maybe it was just because she was angry, or it was an aesthetic choice, but I suspected there was more to it than that.

She was losing control.

"Sure," I agreed. "Very dead. But where does it leave *you*?"

She didn't answer. Her fingertips remained clawed against the tabletop; her eyes blazed calamity at me.

Rika deliberately pushed back her chair and rose. She stood among the falling stars like a queen, fully human, entirely beautiful.

"No," she said. "I will not take that throne. Not now, not ever. No matter what you do."

She was lying. I knew it, because I knew Rika. She was strong, absolutely—but she was brittle, and I had no doubt that with enough pressure, Arhsta could break her.

But her mother didn't know her like I did, and Rika was a con artist. She knew how to be believed. How to shape herself into whatever the person she was talking to most expected, or desired... or feared.

An Empyrean's fear, it turned out, was dangerous to behold.

The glittering motes in the air froze, as if time had stopped. Then, slowly, they began to drift upward. The ones on the ground, too, lifting up into the air and rising back toward the branches from which they'd fallen. It looked utterly unnatural, and it filled me with a cold, unreasoning dread.

Arhsta's freckles of light began to spread into hair-thin fractures, as if her face were cracking to reveal a terrible radiance within. An oppressive sense of awful power gathered in the air, titanic and malevolent as the spreading ash cloud of a volcanic eruption.

Arhsta rose, flinging out her arms and throwing back her head.

"*Fools,*" she hissed, and the castle trembled with her fury. "You don't know what you're tampering with."

Reality *rippled,* warping out from her in a wave.

It slammed me out of my chair and would have flung me back twenty feet if Rika hadn't caught me. She stood as if braced against a heavy wind, her hair streaming—was it longer and darker than usual? Was that a gleam of red in her eyes? Oh, we were in trouble.

"Let's get out of here," I gasped, grabbing on to her for balance as the world shook around us.

The floor—roof?—was changing under our feet. It sprouted silvery grass, which bloomed into flowers with eyes for centers, which in turn opened into mouths and launched more motes of light at the sky as the petals withered and fell. The towers around us flickered rapidly from stone to trees to columns of ice to pillars of fire, shivering from one to the next, all in a few seconds as the cracks in Arhsta's face spread.

"*Run, then,*" Arhsta bellowed, and the sound was a hundred different voices crying together in discordant harmony, the words shuddering through us in a way that I suspected shook more than one reality and resonated through the Veil. "*Run, little mice.*"

I didn't need to be told again. Grabbing Rika's hand, I ran, dodging between towers as they changed shape and shook to their foundations, threatening to fall. I expected to get to the edge of the roof and find ourselves trapped—but a tower tumbled before us, shaking the world beneath our feet, and in its collapse, changed into suspiciously convenient stairs of rough-hewn stone.

"*Run as far and fast as you can,*" Arhsta's agonized divine chorus of a voice called after us. "*You will never, never escape my web.*"

Clenching each other's hands hard enough it was a wonder our bones didn't shatter, we fled down the stairs into the convulsing world below.

TIMING IS EVERYTHING

You should never run in the Deep Echoes. But we ran.

You should especially never run in the Deep Echoes when you have a cut on your arm and are bleeding liquid hope that everyone for a hundred yards can smell, and it's too dark to see where you're going, and there are people-eating cracks in the road. But everyone else was running, too, fleeing the grandiose collapse of the castle, and they were too busy to worry about us.

The reality-warping waves that rippled out from the castle affected the panicked Echoes, too. A thing like a scaly horse that galloped past us in terror shifted in midstride to a sort of antlered cat; it stumbled, let out a feline wail, and kept going. A family in long robes with heads like ants chittered in distress as a ripple passed over them, leaving them with iridescent blue feathers. The buildings around us shifted from bone to glass to tangled roots as whatever was happening to Arhsta shook reality like a blanket.

We alone remained unchanged, because Prime meant stability. It was a good thing everyone around us was too distracted to notice; if they figured out what that meant, they'd fall upon us for our blood in an instant to make it all stop.

"What's happening?" Rika gasped as we ran, her eyes wide.

THE LAST SOUL AMONG WOLVES   319

"What did we do?"

"She's losing her equilibrium. Or she's on the brink of it, anyway."
I dodged a narrow crack in the ground that sizzled with subterranean
lightning, letting go of Rika's hand to avoid pulling her into it in the
process. It was a bit silly to hold hands while running anyway. "I took
a gamble that if you said no, and she believed it, she couldn't resort
to force. That thwarting such a huge, involved scheme of hers would
mean she'd have to let us go and convince herself it was all part of her
master plan in order to stabilize again."

Rika shot a glance back over her shoulder and shuddered. "Do you
think…Do you think she'll recover?"

"I have no idea, and I'm not going to stick around to find out. But
if she does, I'm sure she'll let us know."

A building stretched suddenly upward, like the growth of a tree
sped up hundreds of years. It loomed several stories above us, tilted,
and fell, toppling dark and final toward the street below. We dodged
into an alley to avoid it, along with a stream of the screaming crowd.
I didn't slow down, just reoriented and kept sprinting up the hill
toward the shrine.

"Are we going to make it in time?" Rika asked, and I knew what
she meant.

Before Rai and Glory sucked out my friends' souls and killed
them. It could already be too late.

"I'm going to hope as hard as I can that not much time has passed
in Prime."

And to seal it, I grabbed the cut on my arm, which had stopped
bleeding, and gave it a good, hard squeeze. Maybe too hard; I let out
a hiss of pain.

"Kembral, what the Void?!"

My palm came away red. I wiped half of it onto Rika's shoulder
before she could stop me.

"You're ruining my shirt!"

"Sorry. But we've got a much better chance of making it back
before anything terrible happens now."

An Echo running beside us with a tangle of snakes for hair eyed the blood greedily, but before he could do anything, a larger Echo built like a cross between a bear and a house obliviously ran him over.

And then, all at once, we were there. The shrine had changed along with everything else, settling for the moment on something between a gazebo and a giant box kite. We ducked in, away from the throng of fleeing Echoes and the shuddering ripples of destabilized reality. The inside felt quiet and still, as if it were waiting for us.

There, on one of the pale airy walls, hung the mirror. The red yarn of the portal tether still trailed from it, despite all the madness surging around us. *Thank the Moon.*

I didn't so much as slow down. I grabbed Rika's hand, stretched mine out before me, and plunged through.

—⁓—

As I emerged from the shimmering liquid portal of the mirror, a tingling feeling rushed over and through me. My edges immediately felt a lot more solid. Laemura's tea had kept me going, but it was a huge relief to breathe in real Prime air, with Prime earth beneath my feet, bolstering my own reality. Rika looked relieved, too, shuddering and flexing her shoulder blades as if to reassure herself that they weren't about to sprout wings.

Still, I was spent. Laemura's top-shelf teas were incredible, but I didn't think she'd meant for me to fight an Empyrean and run through the city without resting. My ankle and ribs hurt, I felt light-headed and terribly thirsty, and exhaustion dragged at my limbs as if I'd tied sandbags to them.

There was no time to rest and recover. I threw open the door and charged into the hall, my heart clawing its way up my throat in fear that we were too late.

"Come on, stay out of trouble without me for once," I muttered. "Please be alive."

Muffled shouts and commotion greeted my ears, but at least no screaming. *Not yet.* We ran for the drawing room; I bounced off the corner rather than slow down. And then we burst out into the light.

Petras lay crumpled on the floor, not a mark on him—but I saw

The Last Soul Among Wolves

his chest rise and fall, and he stirred weakly. A thunder from the steps suggested someone was running upstairs.

I dropped to my knees beside Petras, heart in my mouth, and gave him a shake. "Are you all right? Wake up!"

He blinked his eyes open, dazed, and struggled to lever himself up onto an elbow. "I'm fine. Silena...did something. Stunned me somehow and ran off. Jaycel's chasing her."

Of course she was. I cursed and sprinted after without another word, Rika on my heels.

We followed a trail of Jaycel's shouts and clamoring footsteps up the creaking stairs, through the bedroom hall, and up another flight to the dark and dusty servants' level. A door swung ajar on creaking hinges, beckoning us upward yet again, to the steep, narrow stairs to the roof. My ankle twinged with each step now, and I had a vicious stitch in my side, but the vision of Jaycel at the mercy of a lantern-bearing Glory pushed me onward.

At last, we broke out onto the widow's walk, an open platform with an iron railing rising from the roof of the mansion. Glory stood with her back to the rail, heaving for breath with dramatic vulnerability. Jaycel faced off with her, hand on her sword hilt in a hero's pose—they were playing two different scenes. Lightning flickered in the distance beneath a dark and roiling sky.

"Explain yourself!" Jaycel demanded. "Or let events give their account uncontested—but I warn you, Signa Glory, it's not a flattering one."

Glory lifted her hands in a pleading gesture—and they were empty. No sign of the lantern. A wave of relief almost buckled my knees. We'd beaten Rai here. Passage through the Veil must have given us a time advantage over him; maybe being the year-namer gave my hopes an edge.

"I only came here to meet someone who can help." Glory's voice thrummed with resonance; she would have sounded perfectly reasonable if I didn't know the truth.

"You knocked out Petras," Jaycel said. "That seems a strange act in service of so innocent a motive."

"He was trying to stop me from coming up here! I didn't hurt him."

I stepped past Jaycel, just within conversational distance.

"Signa Glory. The person you're meeting is Rai, isn't he?"

Jaycel dropped her confrontational pose, blinking in shock. "Wait, what?"

Glory's dark eyes slid sideways. "He promised me...things."

We probably only had minutes before he showed up. I had to talk fast. "I'm sure he did. What matters is that you're in a position to save everyone."

"Forgive me, Signa Thorne, but I fail to see how."

"He's going to give you the lantern. Isn't he?" I didn't wait for her to reply. "You tell him thank you, and then you turn around and give it to us. We destroy it, the curse is broken, and the souls are freed. You're the hero, and no one has to die."

Glory was already shaking her head. "I can't," she whispered, and there was genuine distress in it, with only the faintest vibrations of resonance. "Maybe once I could have, but...things have changed."

"You told me that you hadn't found anything yet that would make you resort to murder," I reminded her.

Her dark eyes were haunted, deep pools of shadow in her lovely face. But her jaw firmed into a line of unwavering resolve.

"You were right about him." *Now* the resonance crept into her voice, washing through me in a warm wave, stirring my heart to sympathy. "He won't let me turn aside from the path we're walking. He could tell I was faltering, becoming more concerned with survival than winning, and...he raised the stakes of the game."

Petras stepped out onto the widow's walk, tugging his jacket straight from any disarrangement it might have suffered during his brief incapacitation. Whatever she'd done to him, he seemed to have recovered quickly.

"Forgive my interruption, Silena," he said, "but as a gambling professional, I can tell you that when the stakes get too high, it's time to walk away from the table."

Her eyes locked on him, and there was genuine anguish there. "Petras," she breathed. "I don't want to hurt you."

THE LAST SOUL AMONG WOLVES

323

"But you have," he said bitterly. "And you will."

"No, I..." She swallowed. "I still care about you. I always have. I know I never deserved you, but please believe me when I say I never truly stopped loving you."

Petras swayed in the wave of longing that poured through her voice. But then he shook his head. "I loved you, Silena. And maybe you loved me, in your own way. But if the best love you can manage is a twisted kind where you're willing to cast me off again and again, try to get me arrested for murder, and now plan to kill me...well, I hope you can understand if I want no part of it."

Glory's eyes gleamed with tears. "I understand. But I still care about you, nonetheless."

"Then don't do this." He took a step forward, holding out his hand. "Do what the old Silena would have done, before you lost the heart I loved. Walk away."

"I'm so sorry, Petras," she whispered. "But it's too late."

That didn't sound good. I took a half step forward, ready to move if I had to.

Glory wheeled to face me.

"*Stop.*"

Her voice hit me with the power of an ocean wave. My feet rooted in place. For an instant, my breath froze in my lungs; my heart stumbled and missed a beat before it kept going.

I'd never heard of resonance doing anything like *this*. Rai must have given her something more.

"Kembral," Rika murmured from beside me, so soft I almost couldn't hear. "She's not going to listen. Hold her attention while I move into place."

"I don't want to—"

Lightning flashed over the ocean, and thunder cracked across the bay.

A figure hung in the sky, silhouetted against the clouds. One with wings like rips in reality, stars shining through their undulating darkness.

Rai began to descend, his silver eyes glowing with malice, the golden light of the lantern held aloft in his hand.

"Behold!" he called, spreading his arms wide. "The final act has come, and the brightest star of Acantis must take center stage at last."

Glory lifted her head as if hearing a familiar call. She leaned over the rail, flinging up an arm to reach for him; the motion was pure artistry, the graceful angle of her body perfect.

Rika swore and took a half step back. "I'm going to disappear," she told me. "I can't do anything while he has it, but I'll be ready to move."

"Understood." I didn't draw my sword, not yet—if Rai was grandstanding rather than stabbing people, I'd rather keep it that way.

"You again!" Jaycel stepped forward, hands on her hips, eyes flashing with something alarmingly like appreciation. "You just can't stay away, can you, darling? But it's bad manners to upstage someone else's show."

"Three of them," Petras muttered, and my heart lurched in alarm before I realized he didn't mean Empyreans, he meant scene-stealing drama hounds.

Rai's gaze lit on Jaycel. "Alas for the price of victory. I do wish I could spare you, Jaycel Morningray. But we must play out the hand we are dealt."

His wings fanned gusts of salt-laden wind at us; we instinctively scrambled back as he descended to the widow's walk, the searing power of his presence clearing a space. He landed perfectly beside Glory, whose upraised hand met his on the ring of the lantern.

"Take it, my anchor," he breathed, eyes glowing. "Take it, and claim your victory."

Glory's hand closed on the lantern as Rai's relinquished it, the weight of souls settling into her grasp. The golden light of the whirling sparks bathed her face; she gazed at them in wonder.

"Signa Glory," I said sharply. "This is your last chance to make the right choice."

"Indeed." Rai's lips curved in a wicked smile. "Seize the prize that is yours by right, and ascend to become the greatest singer the League Cities have ever known. Or else cast aside your ambition, and by the terms of our bargain, lose your resonance with it."

Glory's cheeks flushed, and the truth buried in Rai's words hit me all at once. When I'd said she must have trained hard to learn resonance, she'd replied, *It came to me more easily than most.*

"You never learned resonance," I breathed. "You never earned it through training and hard work. He *gave* it to you."

"Because I deserved it!"

Her voice rolled over me with the power of sweet thunder, and in the moment she uttered it, I believed it wholly. Yes, of course she deserved it—she was special, a rare talent, the jewel of the Butterfly guild.

It passed the moment the sound of her words died from the air, leaving me with a skin-crawling feeling at having fallen so completely under her sway, even for an instant.

"My own family used me, mocked me, said I was *worthless.*" Her voice rose, ringing out clear and strong, full of a conviction that shuddered through me. "They forced me to work until my body was worn and broken, and told me I could never be anything more. But I had something they couldn't understand, couldn't dream of: I had a *voice.* And I will not give up everything I've striven for, all I am, everything I can yet become—not for anything."

"Ha!" Jaycel scoffed. "A performer who needs magic to hold her audience is no performer at all. If you truly believe yourself nothing without your resonance, brand yourself a hack and sing chorus for someone with *real* talent."

Glory whirled on her in a sudden fury. *"Silence."*

Jaycel's mouth moved, but no sound came out. Her expression twisted in scorn, and she made a gesture that eloquently conveyed her meaning without any words at all.

"Enough," Rai growled, and the sound vibrated in my bones. "Silena Glory, it is time."

I tensed, ready to move. I didn't know where Rika was hiding, but I suspected she did the same.

Glory bit her lip. Her gaze went to Petras, anguished.

"You've thrown me aside once already to dwell in the empty house of fame," he said, voice dripping contempt. "I only wish I thought well enough of you to expect any mercy now."

326   MELISSA CARUSO

Outrage kindled in her eyes, and she lifted the lantern.

Light blazed forth, but it didn't come from the lantern in her hand, and it wasn't the golden radiance of souls. A spot in the air opposite her shone with piercing silver light, as if a star had fallen to earth. It waxed rapidly, with feverish intensity, and I had to cry out and avert my eyes.

"*I have come*," said a terrible voice, "*to reclaim what is mine.*"

I blinked fiercely against the light, and a figure came into focus—a form made of jagged glowing cracks in the air, with darkness leaking out of them like blood. It was an aberration, a wrongness, a wound in the firm reality of Prime that dragged claws across my mind.

It was Rika's mother.

KNOW WHEN YOU'RE OUTMATCHED

Arhsta extended a limb crackling and buzzing with unsteady light toward Rai.

"Give me the lantern, thief. I require it as bait for my web, to begin again."

He recoiled a step, watching her with fascinated horror. "I won it by conquest, and you did not contest my victory. It belongs to my anchor now."

Glory withdrew behind him, eyes wide with fear, like a child hiding behind a parent. She clutched the lantern close against her chest. I held my breath; there was no way in the Void I was going to interfere in an argument between Empyreans if I didn't absolutely have to.

"And I am going to take it back." Arhsta's voice reverberated unpleasantly in my bones. "Stand aside."

Rai stared at her, that hollow desperation returning to his face. He glanced up, inexplicably, at the cloud-darkened sky. And then he spread his arms, his starry cloak unfurling halfway to wings behind him, shielding Glory.

"I cannot spare this anchor. I'm afraid you'll need to find some other bait."

"Do not trifle with me, Laughing As He Rises. Not ever, and especially not now." Lightning crackled around Arhsta. The wind picked up, howling across the widow's walk. I had to brace myself against it. Petras dropped to a knee, cursing.

"I cannot cede you this, Stars Tangled in Her Web." A glowing nimbus grew around Rai, hair-thin tendrils of starlight reaching out from him like the corona of an eclipse. "By my nature, I can never cede anything."

The air warped with power, wavering like heat rising from paving stones on the hottest day of summer. My skin tingled with electricity in a way I usually only felt near an opening in the Veil. I backed farther, reaching for Jaycel and Petras as if I could somehow gather them away from harm; they gave me wide-eyed looks, begging me silently for guidance.

If those two started fighting, there was nothing we could do. Rai's words about why Empyreans were forbidden to engage in direct conflict came back to me: *Our power is too great, and if we exert its full measure, we can tear at reality itself.*

This was not a good place to be. Void below, all of Acantis might not be a good place to be right now.

The stones beneath the feet of the two Empyreans began to glow a sullen red. Lightning flickered in multiple places on the horizon, and thunderclaps rolled one into the next, the great voice of the sky roaring across the ocean. They glared at each other, the air crackling with power. Glory had backed up to the far railing with the lantern, trembling.

A rift opened suddenly in the clouds. Their dark muffling blanket boiled abruptly aside to form a hole to the clear sparkling sky beyond, like the lid of a great eye opening.

And there, shining whole and furious, its pupil: the bloodstained Moon.

The moonlight slammed into me like a physical force. I dropped to my knees, dizzy with the pressure of it. Awe and terror flooded me in a bright, drowning wave.

THE LAST SOUL AMONG WOLVES   329

She was *looking at us*. The Moon was *looking at us*. Holy fuck, we were all going to die.

Every mortal on that widow's walk cowered, overcome by divine radiance. Even the Empyreans flinched away from the light of their mother's gaze. But they still stared hate at each other.

A small, high voice cried, "Wait!"

A voice I knew, brave and sincere and ferocious. I looked up in shock at the new person who had somehow appeared on the widow's walk, her braid blowing wild in the divine wind, her tattered blue coat streaming in the gale.

Vy. Or rather, the Echo who wore her. My heart twisted like a fish on a hook.

She bowed before the lightning-clad ruin of Arhsta. "Mistress, you don't need to do this! Celestial Ones, you have us—your proxies, your pawns! There's no reason to incur the wrath of your mother!"

Arhsta turned to regard her. Her edges flickered like flames in the wind, but her shape seemed to coalesce somewhat from its jagged, crumbling chaos. Once again I could make out long trailing hair, the outline of a gown, bright glowing eyes.

"Yes. Through...pawns." Her shoulders lifted—she had shoulders again—and black webs extended from the hem of her gown and receded, like an exhalation. "Of course."

Rai watched her warily, still standing with his wings spread before Glory. But some of the terrible, crushing pressure of power in the air eased.

"I've told you," he said. "I cannot lose this anchor, nor cede this fight."

Arhsta's voice smoothed out, sweet and rich as dark honey, vibrant as starlight. "Surely your anchor is strong enough to stand on her own and achieve this victory for herself."

Rai twitched at that. Arhsta's outline grew clearer, the light shining from her steadier. She had stopped bleeding darkness, though cracks of jagged light still webbed her form.

"Surely," she continued, "no anchor of *yours* would decline a challenge from a mere servant of mine, and turn to you for help in winning a game when you have already brought her to the very cusp of victory."

Rai hissed like an angry cat. But his wings eased down, collapsing back into a cloak that fluttered like a trail of smoke in the darkness, showing ragged glimpses of stars.

"Very well," he said grudgingly. "We will do this as we have always done. Your agent against my anchor. But if you think your little pet will find her a weak target, think again."

"Perhaps we could place an additional wager on the contest." Arhsta's voice and form strengthened. I could almost see her throwing out the first strands of a web to catch Rai, stabilizing herself in the act. "A prize to whoever's agent or anchor wins the lantern in the end. Come, let us discuss it elsewhere, to avoid drawing the wrath of our mother."

Rai eyed her uneasily, but nodded. "Very well. The eleventh Echo?"

"It is acceptable. The eleventh, then."

She winked out like a candle flame, as if she'd never been there in the first place. Rai glanced warily up at the Moon, then back at Glory.

"Earn me a victory worthy of both of us," he told her. And then he, too, disappeared—as if reality blinked, and he was gone.

The clouds closed back over the Moon, plunging the night into darkness once more.

Everything went deadly silent except for our breathing, all quick and tense, as we mortals stared at one another. I felt very, very small and fragile. In the distance, thunder growled, moving away.

"Vy?" Jaycel reached out a tentative hand, then dropped it.

The Echo that wasn't Vy shook her head, tears standing in her eyes. "I'm sorry, Jaycel. I remember being Vy. I . . . I *want* to be Vy. It's nicer than being me. But . . . I'm not."

"Then where is Vy?" Petras demanded, his voice rough.

The Echo shook her head. "I'm so sorry. She's . . . she's gone."

"Because you killed her!"

"I didn't want to," she said softly. "There was a time . . . hundreds

THE LAST SOUL AMONG WOLVES   331

of years ago, when I was young. I didn't know any better, and I'd devour humans who came down into the Echoes at sea, if I could. I loved their memories, so bright and full of color, and laughter, and... and love." Tears streamed down her cheeks now. "I loved being human. I loved walking on land. But... but I came to care too much about humans to want to hurt them, so I stopped doing it. I stopped for so many years, no matter how I missed it all—being up in the sun, talking, touching, smiling. It's very dark and cold where I come from, and everyone is always eating one another, and no one has friends."

My eyes stung. I didn't know what to think, how to feel—how to reconcile my aching sympathy with the fact that this was a monster who had killed my friend and taken her skin. A cold, alert part of me kept watching Glory, who was standing very still, staring at Vy with wide eyes and clearly absorbing all the implications that an Echo had been among us all this time.

"But you killed her," Petras growled. "No matter how you try to dress it up, you killed Vy."

"I don't deny it." She hung her head. "My lady—Stars Tangled in Her Web—she ordered me to, and I don't have the power to resist her commands. I knew this moment would come, when you would find out, and you'd hate me. But I want you to know that I still love you, Petras. And you, Jaycel, and you, Kem. I remember being such very good friends. They're bright memories, ones I'll treasure in the deep for the rest of my life."

"Damn," Jaycel whispered. "You have accomplished what the greatest wits of our era never could: I don't know what to say."

Vy turned to Glory, her back straightening. "And now," she said, "I have to ask that you give me the lantern."

Glory wrapped her arms tighter around it, shaking her head.

"Signa Glory." I put as much surety of command into her name as I could. "There's nothing good at the end of this road. Choose the side of humanity and life, and give the lantern to me."

Her face went still, all trace of pain and conflict gone, replaced by a regal, aloof beauty.

332 MELISSA CARUSO

"No. I stand by my patron. I will not cede to you, either."

She raised the lantern. Its glow began to brighten, the trapped souls giving off more and more light until I couldn't see individual specks anymore, but only an intense golden radiance filling every inch of the glass.

I didn't wait to see what the lantern would do. I drew my second sword and sprang into motion, closing in an arc that would put me between her and my friends.

"*Stop*," she cried again.

I stumbled over my own feet, staggering to a halt halfway there no matter how much I willed myself forward.

Vy seized her moment. She made a sudden lunging movement to grab Glory's attention—and as soon as the singer's head whipped toward her, tentacles burst from her mouth, spreading wide in a pale, writhing flower.

Jaycel and Petras did some very creative swearing and scrambled back in horror. I couldn't blame them, really.

The eyes on those pale tentacles glowed red, and Glory swayed on her feet. The lantern drooped in her hand. Whatever powers Rai had granted her, she had no defense against this.

Just as she seemed about to fall, she opened her mouth and uttered a single word, thrumming with resonance powerful enough to draw an answering chime from the metal railing.

"*Sleep.*"

Her voice smothered me like a blanket, pressing down on my consciousness. It resonated through me with a pure note of weariness, accentuating my own natural exhaustion a thousandfold, making my mind and body cry out to collapse on the floor and rest.

Jaycel dropped in a boneless heap, her sword clattering against the stones. Petras followed half a blink later, barely managing to roll with his fall, landing curled up as if he'd lain down for a deliberate nap. And the thing that wasn't Vy...

The red light went out, the tentacles drooped, and they slithered back inside her mouth. Her human body swayed and fell.

The pressure of Glory's command dragged at my eyelids, but I forced them open. The guilds trained their own to resist this sort of thing, and I'd faced similar attacks from Echoes more than once on my retrieval missions. But just as much, there was another kind of training and experience that made it second nature to shrug off weariness and press on, to remain conscious no matter how much my body cried for rest.

Glory turned to face me, frowning. "*Sleep,*" she said again, with a touch of tentative confusion this time, and once again immense weariness washed over me. My knees nearly buckled, but they held.

I laughed, a harsh and bitter thing. "Oh, you're going to have to do better than *that*. I've got a baby at home who never fucking sleeps. This is *nothing.*"

Glory gritted her teeth. "No matter. I'd hoped to keep this in reserve, but..."

Oh, I didn't like that. I tried to lunge at her, but while her earlier command to *stop* was fading, my feet still moved too slowly.

She threw back her head and let out a long, rising note that started low and climbed up to a piercing pitch that set my bones to shivering. It was pure and beautiful, and it reverberated through the night until the air in front of her seemed to shimmer with the sound.

No, it *was* shimmering. The distortion in the air rapidly coalesced into a shining figure—an Echo. Blood on the Moon, she'd summoned an Echo with her voice.

The creature looked as if it had been delicately sculpted from ice or glass. It was vaguely human-shaped, but crests of spines or feathers bristled from its shoulders and formed a hackled mane that ran all the way down its back to its lashing, tufted tail. Its eyes gleamed an opalescent blue, and it held what looked like a glass sword in one hand and a sword-sized icicle in the other.

"Hello," I said cautiously, because you never knew.

It hissed at me, displaying a jagged mouthful of icicle teeth, and fell into a low, feral stance.

All right. Not here to talk. And another two-blade fighter. I loosened up my shoulders and dropped into my own ready stance, one foot back and both blades forward, knees flexed, weight centered, ready to spring in any direction on an instant's notice.

334 MELISSA CARUSO

The Echo's shining eyes darted around, looking for other threats. For all I knew, it could sense Rika, a strange Empyrean in the area. I launched an aggressive attack, forcing it to give me its full focus.

The thing about fighting with two swords is that the line between attack and defense is thoroughly blurred. My parries are attacks on my opponent's blade, trying to force it out of line to give my other sword an opening. My strikes sweep a protective arc in front of me to make it harder for my opponent to sneak a cut through. And of course parry becomes riposte and attack returns to guard, each move flowing into the next in the ancient grammar of swordplay.

When you put a couple of two-sword fighters up against each other, well, there are a lot of blades spinning around doing a lot of things. It's exciting, it's dynamic, and it's *messy*. You're either standing back taking cautious little cuts, trying to draw each other out, or you're all in—and if you're all in, it's fast and furious and someone is going to get hurt. Probably both of you are going to get hurt.

I would have really preferred to be cautious, because I don't like getting hurt. But the Echo was all in, so I was all in.

The Echo was *fast*, and it liked to fight in close. We became a snarl of flashing blades, eye to eye and at times almost chest to chest. The Echo could only thrust with the icicle sword, which lacked an edge; it fought with its point angled down and forward to protect its body and take sharp jabs at me that were difficult to parry. Its glass sword was light and quick, but rigid, without the flexibility to do sneaky arcs around my guard like I could with the Echo blade. Not brittle enough to shatter, though—any hopes I might have had to break one of those fragile-looking weapons with a good hard parry didn't last beyond our first furious exchange.

When we stepped back from each other to catch our breath, panting, I had *another* cut on the same forearm Rai had injured, which wasn't great—that was going to slow me down and could lose me this fight. The Echo was leaking bluish icemelt from a slash along its ribs and grinning like this was the best day of its life.

"You're pretty good," I said.

Hhhhhhhhhheeeeehhhhhhhhh, it hissed at me, in a complimentary fashion.

Behind it, Glory lifted the lantern, and it began to glow. *Shit*. I couldn't get past this Echo to stop her—not without blink stepping, anyway, and I wasn't at all sure it'd be safe to do that yet—and there was still no sign of Rika.

All at once, Jaycel Morningray rolled to her feet. She took two springy bounds toward Glory before the singer stopped her with another resonance command. Petras climbed upright more slowly and moved to her side, knives drawn; Vy was still on the ground, but she was stirring.

Jaycel held her blade in a close, vertical guard, watching Glory analytically. I suspected she was calculating whether she could reach her on a single lunge, and possibly trying to draw Glory forward a step to come within her range.

"You can see things aren't going to end well for you," Jaycel said conversationally. "You're outnumbered, and you can't keep us all at bay forever. But you haven't done anything unforgivable yet—it's not too late to hand over the lantern, have a drink, and forget this happened."

"You're right," Glory said, and her voice was so riveting that even her Echo had to look over its shoulder at her. I should have taken the opportunity to attack, but she'd claimed my attention, too. "I *can't* hold you at bay forever, and it's pointless to try. I've been putting it off, but it's time to end this now."

She raised the lantern, fixing her gaze on Jaycel. Its glow intensified until it was hard to look at.

A shaft of light shot from the lantern directly to Jaycel's chest.

PROTECT YOUR FRIENDS

Jaycel screamed. It was an awful, terrified sound, nothing like any noise I had ever heard her make.

I screamed, too, and started toward her in a panic. The Echo stepped between us, blocking my way.

Jaycel's back arched with apparent agony. Her sword clattered to the floor. A spot of liquid golden light began to gather on her chest, right where the beam struck her, as if starting to seep up out of her skin.

A great, anguished cry shattered the air: "*No!*"

It felt like it came from my own throat. But it wasn't me—or Jaycel, or Petras.

It was Vy.

She was up off the floor, and she hurled herself between Glory and Jaycel.

The beam struck her chest instead, instantly turning blue. She let out a terrible shriek, but took a step forward, pushing into the beam as if against a hurricane, teeth bared, sweat instantly beading on her face. Jaycel dropped to her knees, heaving great desperate gasps, both hands clutching her chest.

"*Vy!*" I cried instinctively.

THE LAST SOUL AMONG WOLVES 337

I couldn't think of her as a murderer, or an enemy Echo. I saw the last vestige of my friend, the determined little kid who would do anything to keep up with us, pushing herself past what someone her age could reasonably have been expected to do. And I saw the desperate love of a creature of the deep who had never known any friendship save what she had stolen.

I tried to rush past the ice-and-glass Echo, but it stopped me with a flurry of fierce attacks that I barely parried, distracted by what was happening to Vy. I had to dance back out of range.

Petras threw a knife at Glory. It sank into her shoulder, and she let out a cry and staggered, but the lantern's beam remained unbroken.

It was enough, however, to keep Glory from noticing Rika in time.

She swarmed up over the railing, coming from below where she'd been clinging to the side of the mansion, and landed silent as a shadow directly behind Glory. With a delicate twist of her wrist, she plucked the lantern from the singer's grasp.

"*Drop it!*" Glory gasped, clutching at the knife in her shoulder.

Rika cursed as the lantern slipped from her fingers—its blue beam still connected to Vy, who had dropped to her knees. Glory lunged for the lantern as it fell.

I couldn't just stand here and watch Vy's soul get sucked out—even if she wasn't Vy at all. Bracing myself for pain and consequences, I ducked out of reality and into the Veil.

It hurt about as much as I'd expected, which was to say a lot. Now that I was back in Prime and some time had passed, I was less worried about my reality unraveling from one blink step, but there was a very real chance that I'd pass out the moment I popped back into Prime. This was a big gamble, but I had to try.

I sprinted through the honey-tinted, blurry form of the glass Echo, whose intense fighting stare remained fixed on the spot where I'd been. The lantern hung in the air between Rika's reaching hand and Glory's; the ray of light connecting it to Vy had inverted to black in the Veil, dark as the Void. Vy was frozen in mid-collapse, her eyes rolled up, her body falling inevitably to the floor—but I couldn't

338 MELISSA CARUSO

think about that. I had a single job to do, and by the Moon I was going to do it.

I hooked my fingers through the ring of the plummeting lantern and ducked back into Prime.

Noise hit my ears—screams, chaos—and the cool metal ring hit my fingers. I was collapsing, but I'd expected that, and had angled myself to turn it into a roll, tucking around the lantern to make sure Glory couldn't just grab it again. Waves of red and black surged behind my eyes, threatening to drag me down. I managed to roll to my knees, gasping, the lantern raised in my unsteady hand.

"Rika!" I called.

Glory cried out in a voice that shook the house beneath us, "*Give it back!*"

My arm moved to hold it out toward her, against my will. But I couldn't get up to bring it to her, and Rika was a Cat, faster than any Butterfly. She snatched it out of my grasp.

Vy gasped, "My lady...we've won."

And she collapsed to the floor.

Glory opened her mouth to shout at Rika again. Before she could utter a single syllable, Petras wrapped an arm around her throat from behind, and Jaycel pricked her chest with the tip of her sword.

"Not a word," she warned her. "Not a note from you."

The glass-and-ice Echo looked at Glory, clearly defeated and with a sword at her throat. It looked at Rika holding the lantern, a subtle red spark flickering deep within her eyes; a shiver ran visibly through the feathery spines on its shoulders.

All the fight went out of its stance at once. It gave Rika a deep bow, offered me a friendly sort of hiss, and vanished in a swirl of shimmering light.

I couldn't get up. I knelt there, headache slamming through me in red waves, struggling not to pass out.

"Rika..." I gasped.

"I know," she said grimly. "This can't wait. Be ready to catch me."

Before I could ask her what she meant, or protest that I was in no shape to do anything of the sort, a cloud of fluttering moths burst up

The Last Soul Among Wolves

out of the floor. They swirled thick in the air between us and Glory, a curtain of tiny flashing wings. It took me an instant to realize—it was illusion, of course, a wall to block the others' view in a desperate attempt to preserve her secret.

Which meant she was about to transform. Right here, right now, trusting me to pull her back before anything could spiral out of control.

"Wait!"

Too late. She threw back her head, and rivers of glorious Void-black darkness poured from her scalp, cascading out into the air. Her eyes blazed with red light from lid to lid. In one bold, sweeping motion, great silvery glowing wings sprang from her shoulders, stretching out against the darkness. The moths swirled thicker, thousands upon thousands of them in ghostly shades of pale green and lavender, their wings making a soft shushing music, fluttering all around us and rising to the sky.

I grabbed Rika's free hand, holding it tight enough to crush, hoping that would somehow help. She lifted the lantern, let out a great furious cry—and brought it down in a swift, merciless arc to smash it on the stones.

Glass shattered, flying everywhere. Light and a hot wind with a scent like scorched metal blasted from it; even in her Empyrean form, Rika reeled back, dropping the lantern's ring and shaking out her hand. I had to squint against the glare.

But I had a job to do, and I had to do it quickly—before anyone noticed, before the moths all fluttered away. I flung myself at Rika, not sure I could stand but trusting her to catch me.

Her arms went around me, convulsively tight. She was shaking, her eyes glowing bright scarlet. I had to ground her somehow, call up her human side.

Well, I knew one thing that always got her attention. I kissed her.

I was all too aware that I didn't know what I was doing, that I didn't know what people wanted from kisses. Rika usually led with these things. But I tried to pour everything I felt for her into it— how much I cared about her, how much I needed her, how empty the space at my side felt when she wasn't there. All the admiration and frustration and affection, all the teasing energy with which we'd danced around each other on the job for so many years.

Her lips moved against mine in response, at first as if she were waking from sleep, then with the desperate focus of a drowning swimmer seizing an outstretched hand. I ignored twinges from my rib and held her as tight as she held me, until our bodies seemed on the verge of blending together; we sank to our knees in each other's arms.

I whispered her name against her lips like a prayer: "Rika Nonesuch."

A shudder went through her at the sound of it.

I added, tenderly, "Stop being such a big diva."

"Kembral," she gasped, "you are *insufferable*."

Her wings folded in a rustle of silvery feathers behind her back. As the great cloud of moths thinned and fluttered away, her hair was still a bit long and overly dark, but I hoped no one would notice. She'd closed her eyes, so no more than a trace of red light seeped out between her lashes as she struggled to master herself.

I whirled to face the broken lantern. The flare of light and heat faded, and it lay cracked open on the floor like an egg with a glowing yolk. The last jagged pieces of glass fell out of its metal frame, tinkling onto the stone.

Glory dropped to her knees and screamed as if we'd ripped her heart out. It was a strangely flat, empty sound, for all its emotion— the scream of a normal human woman, without any trace of resonance to it.

Dozens of golden sparks floated up from the shattered remains of the lantern, dancing and swirling around one another. Dozens of golden sparks—and one blue one. For a moment, they surrounded Rika and me in a cloud.

Petras reached a trembling hand out toward them, his eyes full of pain and wonder. A tiny golden light separated from the swarm and briefly, delicately, lighted on his fingertips. Tears overflowed his eyes and cut trails down his cheeks.

The Last Soul Among Wolves 341

The blue spark danced in front of me for a moment, flickering.

"Thank you," I murmured. "You were a true friend in the end."

It flared brightly in response.

And then all the lights swirled up all at once like sparks up a gusting chimney, in one wild, exultant rising, and were gone.

CLEANUP IS ALWAYS MESSY

I caught myself on my hands and knees, pulse pounding, breath coming hard. We'd done it. Blood on the Moon, we'd actually done it.

All I wanted was to go home, hold Emmi, and curl up in a ball and sleep. But chaos was erupting around me, and things relentlessly refused to stop happening, no matter how the pulsing waves of my headache crept down my spine into my entire body, or how my arms trembled to hold me up, or how my heart clenched in a hard knot of barely suppressed grief.

Glory bolted for the stairs immediately. Petras tackled her to the floor and put a knee in her back, while Jaycel pointed her sword at her neck. Glory kept trying to command them to let her go, but her voice held no power. Jaycel responded to each attempt with one of the stock insults she'd memorized for times when she was too overwhelmed to come up with a fresh one.

Meanwhile, I squeezed Rika's hand, murmuring whatever came into my head to try to stabilize her, as she took deep, sharp breaths with her eyes closed. She had regained enough control to obscure who exactly was helping who by bending over and making a big production of assisting me to my feet—which, to be honest, I needed.

I was so focused on her—on watching for the smallest sign of red

THE LAST SOUL AMONG WOLVES   343

light leaking between her lashes, of monitoring the tiniest shifts of her facial structure that might hint she was slipping toward or away from human—that I barely registered Jaycel and Petras declaring they were going to lock Glory in a storage closet and marching her off. By the time they returned to the roof, Rika's trembling had steadied, and her eyes were clear grey again.

And then the crisis was past—crises, really, I couldn't even keep count—and it was just Jaycel and Petras and Rika and me, alone on the widow's walk.

And Vy.

She looked peaceful as she lay there, eyes closed, her familiar face marked with less-familiar lines added by the years. The wind stirred the loose tendrils of her hair, giving it the semblance of life—but her body was still, so still. The ocean sounded endlessly below, its waves breathing on long after all the life that dwelled in and on and under it ceased.

The three of us remaining from the old crowd knelt around our friend. Rika stood behind me with her hand on my shoulder, anchoring me for a change. Something twisted sharply in my chest, but I forced it down, down—I'd have to unpack that bottle soon, but not yet.

"So...it wasn't Vy, the whole time?" Jaycel asked, sounding lost.

"It wasn't."

"And the real Vy is..."

"This is her. Or her body." I swallowed back a tight knot. "She's dead."

Petras bowed his head, pressing his knuckles to his mouth.

Jaycel lifted bright brown eyes to me that overflowed with tears. "I'm mourning two friends, then. One old companion of many shared adventures, whose heart took her away to the sea. And one new one, given to us by the sea in return, who I only drank and laughed with for a day and a night—but who valued my friendship enough to give her life for it."

"Your heart is more generous than mine, Morningray," Petras said. "I can't forget she took Vy from us. But she did save you, so I suppose I'll call the scales even."

"Do you..." Jaycel swallowed. "Do you think the Echo will reform, Kembral? They do that, don't they?"

I shook my head. "Getting her soul ripped out by an Empyrean's relic is a bit different than getting run through with a sword. I don't know. It's a question for the Ravens, if anyone."

"You can ask them," Rika said, gazing out across the river. "I think they're coming now."

I was not expecting the Ravens for another couple of hours. But I supposed I should have anticipated that a pair of Empyreans having a dramatic confrontation on the roof would attract some attention from the city, especially once it escalated to the point where the Moon herself visibly became involved.

The boats that arrived at the docks disgorged *multiple* crews of senior field Ravens, led by Signa Zarvish, all weighed down with various excitingly dangerous artifacts. They came ready to seal off the mansion with barriers or blow it up—or, if necessary, to lay out enticing offerings and beg assorted enraged celestial beings for mercy. They seemed incredibly disappointed to find the situation dealt with already, and peppered us with questions.

"Moths?" one of them asked as Jaycel described what had happened, sounding bewildered. "Why moths?"

"An illusion," I jumped in, as Rika tensed beside me. "Signa Nonesuch needed to keep Signa Glory from interfering while we destroyed the lantern."

"Ah!" The Raven nodded. "Of course. I'd really love to know how you do such quick and detailed illusions someday, Signa Nonesuch."

Rika gave him her most mysterious smile. "Trade secret, I'm afraid."

That excuse wouldn't hold up with Signa Zarvish, who knew that destroying the lantern required an Empyrean; but she was across the room talking to a colleague, so I'd have to hope she didn't poke too deeply into how exactly we'd managed to break it.

The Ravens had some answers for us, as well. Yes, the magic was gone from the book and the mirror as well as the lantern, though they still would make fascinating objects of study. Yes, the freed souls would have gone on to whatever rest or rebirth the lantern denied them. No, they didn't have any real idea what had happened to the Echo that wasn't Vy. They were excited (and somewhat alarmed) to resolve the *Breath of Dawn* mystery, though.

Camwell arrived a little later, to take Glory into custody and summon a crew to deal with the bodies. I gave him my report, so exhausted I could barely stand, my head pounding in cruel punctuation to each phrase.

At long last, with Rika at my side, I staggered home. And I held Emmi, and Rika held me, and I cried for a long time.

—ɱ—

Jaycel, Petras, and I held the traditional League Cities farewell feast for Mareth and Vy, where we set empty places for them at the table and told stories and made toasts. We only spoke of the real Vy, but I noticed a little silver pin in the shape of an octopus glinting near Jaycel's collar. We laughed and cried and said our goodbyes three times, and three times *May we meet again.*

We also all swore to get together with the three of us more frequently, to not let time make us strangers. Farewell feast promises were notoriously unreliable, but I hoped to the Void we could do better...And maybe I snuck my dagger out of my sheath and pricked my finger to bind that hope, because I wasn't above cheating a little.

While the blood was still wet, I raised my glass in a silent toast to the Echo that had sacrificed herself for Jaycel, hoping as hard as I could that wherever she was, alive or dead, she would find friends and be happy.

A couple days later, Camwell told me that someone had broken Glory out of jail. Not just any someone, in fact, but an Echo with silver hair and horns.

Rika, Jaycel, Petras, and I met up to discuss this news at one of his clubs. Jaycel informed us that the gossip was that Glory turned up in Rainnes. She was trying to make it in the opera scene there, and

346 MELISSA CARUSO

there was a whole furor about whether the king of Rainnes would send her back to prison in Acantis or whether as a great patron of the arts he'd choose to shelter her instead. Either way, she was out of the Butterfly guild for good, which limited her prospects.

Petras swirled his glass broodingly. "I hope she finds some kind of happiness," he grumbled.

"I don't," Jaycel said. "I want her to face consequences. She tried to rip my soul out, and it *hurt*."

"She's already facing consequences," I said quietly. "Silena Glory is a woman who has carefully crafted her own punishment, and now she's going to dwell in it."

I suspected that with no resonance, no friends, an all-consuming ambition, and a starving Empyrean riding her heels, Glory wouldn't last long. It was sad, except she'd chosen to take every step along this path herself.

"Poetic," Jaycel said admiringly. "I'd still like her to fall into a pit full of bees, though."

Rika and I stopped at Laemura's on the way home for a cup of tea. Regular tea, this time, to the degree that Laemura's tea was ever regular. Not medicinal, anyway. I'd brought Emmi along on the outing so Petras could meet her (Jaycel had made jokes about starting her on a life of vice young, but whatever, she didn't know it was a gambling club), and she was getting restless in my arms. She kept reaching toward my teacup, and I kept having to move it farther away.

It felt natural, sitting here with Rika and Emmi, together. I'd been so worried that everything would be strange, now that I knew mere mortal feelings weren't the only bond between us. But she was still Rika, and I was me, and we were *us*.

"Rai must be pretty desperate, if he was willing to personally break such a failed anchor out of jail," I said, with some satisfaction. "He invested a lot of effort and power into Glory, and now she has to start over."

"Good. Let's hope it keeps him busy enough to leave us alone." Rika swirled her spoon in her tea, a little moodily. "And . . . let's hope that goes double for the other one."

"You think she's alive, then?" I dropped my voice instinctively, as if that could somehow stop Arhsta from overhearing us.

"I'd know if she were gone." Rika scowled at her tea. "I've thought about it, Kembral, and I think I *saved* her."

"How?"

"You saw what she was doing with Rai, setting up that wager, and how that helped stabilize her a bit. He was thinking it was a contest between Glory and Vy, but she said agent *or* anchor, which includes me. So I accidentally won that bet for her, through cunning and deception on both our parts." She shook her head. "And then I had to use my Empyrean form to break the lantern, which played right into her long-term plan for me. Everything I did there strengthened her web just as it was falling apart around her."

"I don't see what else you could have done." I handed Emmi a saltshaker to keep her busy, then immediately thought better of it when she lifted it toward her mouth. "You saved everyone from horrible fates. Not to mention that I don't know what a completely destabilized Empyrean does to the world, but given what was happening to the fifth Echo as we left, I'm going to guess it's nothing good."

Rika sighed. "I suppose so. But still... Well, suffice to say I hope it at least set her back enough that we don't have to worry about her for a while."

"We can hope," I agreed. It'd be nice when this year was over and I could say that word without feeling weird about it again.

There was one thing I might want to take care of while it was still my year, though. I cleared my throat.

"Where do you think you'll go after we're done with our tea? Back to your place?"

Rika gave me an exasperated look. "You've seen one of my safe houses now, Kembral. You don't need to keep fishing around for hints about where I live."

"It's not that. I was just wondering..." Emmi started fussing, and I had to pause to hand her my teaspoon, which she received with as much awe and fascination as if it were a magical scepter. At once she began flailing it around so vigorously I was worried she'd smack herself in the head.

"Yes?" Rika smiled. At me, at Emmi, because the tea was so good—I couldn't guess. After all we'd been through, she remained a creature of mystery to me.

"Well, I was wondering whether you might like to, you know." I waved a vague hand. "I have all this spare room in my house, and it's close to the guildhouses, so it's pretty convenient. You're over at my place all the time anyway, and it seems silly, if you have rooms all over the city, for you not to have one here. I mean, in my townhouse. With me."

Wow, could I possibly have botched that more spectacularly? My face burned.

Rika went very still. "That's... nice of you to offer, but..."

My heart started to sink. I'd moved too fast, and she was going to back off. Like Beryl.

"...Are you sure that's a good idea?" Rika's voice dropped down low and soft and serious. "We don't know what will happen if you and I keep getting closer. I would think you'd want a certain amount of distance, to be safe."

It took me a moment to realize what she meant. "To be safe... from you?"

She averted her gaze. "Yes. So I don't get too controlling, or obsessive, or anything like that."

She carefully didn't say the words *anchor* or *Empyrean*, but I could see them in her eyes, the set of her shoulders. The worry, and the guilt.

"You've been pretty good about that lately," I said lightly. "I think you can keep it within reasonable bounds now that you're on the watch for it."

"But, Kembral, we don't know what I'll do to you." Her grey eyes met mine, anguished. "We don't know what kind of effect I might have on you."

I let out a bark of a laugh. "Don't be ridiculous. Of course we're going to have an effect on each other. That's what..."

THE LAST SOUL AMONG WOLVES 349

Uh-oh. I caught the word before it could escape my mouth, like grabbing a dog by its tail before it could run out the door. I'd almost blurted it right here in Laemura's, for Rika and the world to hear.

Rika tilted her head, giving me an uncertain look, waiting for me to finish my sentence. My very dangerous sentence.

I swallowed. All right, why not, we were doing this.

"That's what love is," I finished, my voice husky.

Rika closed her eyes. A small smile teased at her lips, as if she had a really good secret she wasn't going to tell me.

"Well, in that case," she said, "sure."

Heedless of all the dangers of fate and Empyrean malice and Emmi's spoon waving alarmingly near our eyes, she leaned across the table to kiss me.

The story continues in...

**Book THREE of
the Echo Archives**

Acknowledgments

The thing about achieving your dream of having a creative career is that said career—fed by all your fevered passions and wild imaginings, your ambition and desperation, your sheer stubbornness—can grow to consume your life, until it gets in the way of everything else, like a large, contrary, variably affectionate cat. Thus, first and foremost, I must thank my family and friends for their unflagging patience and support as I struggle to manage the demands of this career-animal (not to mention those of our actual pets—looking at you, Lupa). All my gratitude and love forever and always to my wonderful husband, Jesse, and my amazing daughters, Maya and Kyra. You're the best.

The Orbit team continues to be fantastic, and I consider myself so lucky to have such talented people working on my books. Huge thanks to my US editor, Angelica Chong, and my UK editor, Emily Byron, for all they've done for this book and this series. I am immensely grateful for all the time and love and wisdom and effort you've given this story. My awe and gratitude goes out to Lisa Marie Pompilio for lending her witchcraft to *yet another* mind-bogglingly good cover. Thank you once again to my excellent copyeditor, Kelley Frodel, and to my ever insightful and competent production editor, Bryn A. McDonald. I'm also immensely thankful for the work of Ellen Wright, my US publicist, and Nazia Khatun, my UK publicist, for all they do to help spread the word about my books. Thank you to everyone at Orbit who lent their efforts to this book—it feels so good to know it's in such excellent hands.

Acknowledgments

This is my eighth published book (somehow!), but there are a few people who've been in my corner helping my writing for longer than that. Thank you to my wonderful agent, Naomi Davis, who gave me the nudge to write this series in the first place. And my warm and heartfelt thanks to my faithful friends and beta readers of lo these many years, Deva Fagan and Natsuko Toyofuku.

Writing can be a pretty lonely profession, and community makes such a huge difference. Thank you to all the amazing authors who've shared their support, wisdom, commiseration, pet pictures, and company with me on assorted Discord servers, as well as in person at various events and conventions when I've been so lucky. I consider myself incredibly fortunate to have made such good friends in a career that can be very isolating (but has somehow proven the opposite for me).

And finally—thank you, my readers, for letting me tell you this story. It wouldn't be complete without you.

extras

meet the author

Erin Re Anderson

MELISSA CARUSO was born on the summer solstice and went to school in an old mansion with a secret door but, despite this auspicious beginning, has yet to develop any known superpowers. Melissa has spent her whole life creating imaginary worlds and, in addition to writing, is also an avid LARPer and tabletop gamer. She graduated with honors in creative writing from Brown University and has an MFA in fiction from the University of Massachusetts Amherst. Melissa's first novel, *The Tethered Mage*, was shortlisted for a Gemmell Morningstar Award for best fantasy debut.

Find out more about Melissa Caruso and other Orbit authors by registering for the free monthly newsletter at orbitbooks.net.

if you enjoyed
THE LAST SOUL AMONG WOLVES

look out for

THE LAST VIGILANT

Kingdom of Oak and Steel: Book One

by

Mark A. Latham

Shunned by the soldiers he commands, haunted by past tragedies, Sargent Holt Hawley is a broken man. But the child of a powerful ally has gone missing, and war between once-peaceful nations is on the horizon. So he and his squad have been sent to find a myth: a Vigilant. They are a rumored last survivor of an ancient and powerful order capable of performing acts of magic and finding the lost. But the Vigilants disappeared decades ago. No one truly expects Hawley to succeed.

extras

Then, in a fabled forest, he stumbles upon a woman who claims to be the last Vigilant. Enelda Drake is wizened and out of practice, and she seems a far cry from the heroes of legend. But they will need her powers, and each other, to survive. For nothing in their kingdom is as it seems. Corrupt soldiers and calculating politicians thwart their efforts at every turn.

And there are dark whispers on the wind, threatening the arrival of a primordial and powerful enemy. The last Vigilant is not the only myth returning from the dead.

CHAPTER 1

Lithadaeg, 23rd Day of Sollomand
187th Year of Redemption

Holt Hawley hunched over the reins, the wagon jolting slowly down the track. Sleet stung his face, settling oily and cold on his dark lashes and patchy beard.

The whistling wind had at least drowned out the grumbling of his men, who sat shivering in the back of the wagon. Their glares still burrowed into the back of his head.

It mattered not that Hawley was their sargent. The men blamed him for all their ills, and by the gods they'd had more than their fair share on this expedition. Twice the wagon had mired in thick mud. On the mountain road, three days' rations had spoiled inexplicably. Now their best horse had thrown a shoe, and limped behind the wagon, slowing their progress to a

extras

crawl. They couldn't afford to leave the beast behind, but risked laming it by pressing on. Whatever solution Sargent Hawley came up with was met with complaint. He was damned if he did and damned if he didn't.

Tarbert rode back up the track, cutting a scarecrow silhouette against the deluge. He reined in close to the driver's board, face glum, still mooning over the hobbling horse that was his favourite of the team.

"V-village ahead, Sarge," Tarbert said, buckteeth chattering. "Godsrest, I th-think."

"You see the blacksmith?" Hawley asked.

"Didn't s-see nobody, Sarge."

"Did you ask for him?"

"Not a soul about."

"What about a tavern?" That was Nedley. It was only just dawn and already he was thinking of drink.

"No tavern, neither."

"Shit on it!" Nedley grumbled.

"That's enough," Hawley warned. He pulled the reins to slow the horses as the wagon began to descend a steeper slope.

"Typical," Beacher complained.

Hawley turned on the three men in the back. Beacher was glaring right at Hawley, face red from the cold, beady eyes full of reproach.

"What is?" Hawley said.

"Three days with neither hide nor hair of a living soul, then we find a deserted village. Typical of our luck, isn't it, *Sargent*?"

Ianto sniggered. He was an odd fish, the new recruit. A stringy man, barely out of youth, yet his gristly arms were covered in faded tattoos, symbols of his faith. His hair showed signs of once being tonsured like that of a monk, the top and rear of his scalp stubbled, fringe snipped straight just above

extras

the brow. He'd proved able enough on the training ground, but would speak little of his past, save that he'd once served as a militiaman in Maserfelth, poorest of the seven *mearcas* of Aelderland. He'd bear watching; as would they all.

Hawley turned back to the road, lest he say something he would regret.

"*Awearg*," someone muttered.

Hawley felt his colour rise at the familiar slight. Again he held his tongue.

The men mistrusted Hawley. Hated him, even. Bad enough he was not one of "the Blood" like most of them, but even Ianto was treated better than Hawley, and he was a raw recruit. For Hawley, the resentment went deeper than blood lineage. For his great "transgression" a year ago, most men of the Third agreed it would've been better if Hawley had died that day. They rarely passed up an opportunity to remind him of it.

These four ne'er-do-wells would call themselves soldiers should any common man be present, but to Hawley they were the scrapings from the swill bucket. Hawley's days of fighting in the elite battalions were over. Now his assignments were the most trivial, menial, and demeaning, like most men not of the Blood. Beacher, Nedley, and Tarbert served under Hawley in the reserves only temporarily—it was akin to punishment duty for their many failings as soldiers, but their family names ensured they'd be restored to the roll of honour once they'd paid their dues. For those three, this was the worst they could expect. For Hawley and Ianto, it was the best they could hope for. Command of these dregs was another in a long list of insults heaped on Hawley of late. But command them he would, if for no other reason than a promise made to an old man.

extras

The words of old Commander Morgard sprang into Hawley's mind, as though they'd blown down from the distant mountains.

What you must do, Hawley, is set an example; show those men how to behave. Show them what duty truly means. But most of all, show them what compassion *means. When I'm gone, I need you to lead. Not as an officer, but as a man of principle. Can you do that?*

Hawley had not thought of Morgard for some time. He reminded himself that the old man had rarely said a word in anger to the soldiers under his command. He had trusted Hawley to continue that tradition when he'd passed.

He'd expected too much.

From the corner of his eye, Hawley saw Tarbert cast an idiotic grin towards Beacher. Then Tarbert spurred his horse and trotted off down the slope.

The dull glow of lamps pierced the grey deluge ahead. Not deserted, then.

They'd travelled two weeks on their fools' errand, as Beacher liked to call it. And at last they'd found the village they searched for.

Godsrest.

*   *   *

"Godsrest" sounded like a name to conjure with, but in reality was a cheerless hamlet of eight humble dwellings, a few tumbledown huts, and one large barn that lay down a sloping path towards a grey river. The houses balanced unsteadily on their cobbled tofts, ill protected by poorly repaired thatch.

Two women summoned their children to them and hurried indoors. That much was normal at least. As Hawley knew from bitter experience on both sides of the shield, soldiers brought trouble to rural communities more often than not. There was

extras

no one else to be seen, but though the sun had barely found its way to the village square, it was still morning, and most of the men would be out in the fields. There was no planting to be done at this time of year, especially not in this weather. But it was good country for sheep and goats, for those hardy enough to traipse the hilly trails after the flock. In many ways, Hawley thought soldiering offered an easier life than toiling in the fields. A serf's lot was not a comfortable one, not out here. Here, they would work, or they would starve.

Hawley cracked the thin layer of ice from a water trough so the horses might drink. Tarbert unhitched the hobbling gelding from the back of the wagon and led it to the trough first.

Beacher spat over the side of the wagon. "I can smell a brewhouse." He looked to Nedley, hopefully, who only snored.

The yeasty scent of fermenting grain carried on the wind. A late batch of ale, using the last of the barley, Hawley guessed. It'd be sure to pique Nedley's interest if the man woke up long enough to smell it.

"We're not here to drink," Hawley said.

"Why *are* we here? There's nothing worth piss in this wretched land. You know as well as I there's no Vigilant in those woods. Not the kind we need."

"If they've got his ring, stands to reason he exists."

"Pah! Dead and gone, long before any of us were born. More likely the merchant found an old ring and was planning to sell it, but when he lost his consignment, he invented this fairy story to save his neck. Face it, he had no business being this far north. The only people who use the old roads are outlaws and smugglers. Mark my words, we're chasing shadows. There's no True Vigilant anywhere."

Hawley had been ready for this since they'd left the fort, but it made him no less angry.

extras

"So what if there isn't?" Hawley snarled. "You reckon that frees you from your duty?"

"My *duty* is to protect the good people of Aelderland, not travel half the country looking for faeries."

Ianto leaned against the wagon, watching the argument grow. Nedley stirred at last, peering at them from the back of the wagon through half-closed eyes.

Maybe Beacher had a point, but this wasn't the time to admit it. Hawley took a confident stride forward, summoning his blackest look. Beacher shuffled away from his advance.

"If there's a True Vigilant, he'll be able to find them bairns. It's them you should be thinking about."

"There's only one child Lord Scarsdale cares about—that Sylven whelp—and only then because his bitch mother wants to start a war over him. That's what you get, putting a woman in charge of an army."

Hawley waved the protest away tiredly. He'd heard it all before.

"Besides," Beacher went on, growing into his tirade, "even you can't believe they still live."

Even you. Beacher's lack of respect was astounding. He'd barely known Hawley at the time of the sargent's great transgression. His animosity was secondhand, but seething nonetheless. Men like Beacher needed something to hate, and in times of peace, that something might as well be one of their own. Sargent Holt Hawley, the Butcher of Herigsburg, bringer of misfortune: "awearg."

"Then we'll find the bodies, and take 'em home," Hawley snapped. "If you can't follow orders, Beacher, you're no use to me. Leave if you like. Explain to Commander Hobb why you abandoned your mission."

Beacher looked like he might explode. His face turned a

extras

shade of crimson to match his uniform. His hand tensed, hovering over the pommel of his regulation shortsword.

Do it, you bastard, Hawley thought. The sargent had taken plenty of abuse this last year, maybe too much. Some of the men mistook his tolerance for cowardice instead of what it really was: penance. It made them think he would shy from a fight. It made them overreach themselves.

"They say a True Vigilant can commune with the gods." The voice was Ianto's, and it was so unexpected, the tone so bright, that it robbed the moment of tension.

Hawley and Beacher both turned to look at the recruit, who still leaned nonchalantly against the wagon, arms folded across his chest.

"Commune with the dead, too. And read minds, they say. That's how they know if you're guilty of a crime as soon as they look at you. Such a man is a rarity in these times. Such a man would be...valuable."

"Speak plain," Beacher spat.

Ianto pushed himself from the wagon. His fingers rubbed at a little carved bone reliquary that hung about his neck, some trapping of his former calling. "Just that the archduke sent us, as the sargent said. The Archduke Leoric, Lord Scarsdale, High Lord of Wulfshael. Man with that many titles has plenty of money. Plenty of trouble, too—we all know it. The Sylvens could cross the river any time now, right into the Marches. Might even attack the First, then it's war for sure."

"The First can handle a bunch of Sylvens," Beacher said.

"Maybe." Ianto smiled. "But maybe there's a handsome reward waiting for the men who find the True Vigilant and avert such a war. I don't know about you, brother, but I think it would be not unpleasant to have a noble lord in my debt."

"And what say you, *Sargent?*"

extras

Hawley almost did not want to persuade Beacher to his cause at all. Part of him thought it would be better to throw the rotten apple from the barrel now, and be done with it. There was a saying among the soldiers "of the Blood"—something about cutting a diseased limb from a tree. But for all his faults, Beacher was liked by the others. Hawley was not. That would make harsh discipline difficult to enforce.

"I say if by some miracle we turn up a true, honest-to-gods Vigilant after all this time," Hawley said at last, "they'll be singing our names in every tavern from here to bloody Helmspire. But if you don't follow your orders, we'll never know, *will we*?" Hawley added the last part with menace.

"And if... *when*... we don't find the Vigilant?" Beacher narrowed his eyes.

"Then we return to the fort, and be thankful we've missed a week of Hobb's drills." Hawley held Beacher's contemptuous glare again.

In the silence, there came the ringing of steel on steel, drifting up the hill from the barn.

Hawley and Beacher looked at Tarbert as one.

"No blacksmith?" Hawley said.

Tarbert laughed nervously.

"There you go," Ianto said. He came to Beacher's side and patted the big man on the shoulder. "Our luck's changing already."

Beacher finally allowed himself to be led away, still grumbling.

The sargent stretched out his knotted back, feeling muscles pop and joints crack as he straightened fully. Only Tarbert matched Hawley for height, but he was an arid strip of land who barely filled his uniform, with a jaw so slack he was like to catch flies in his mouth while riding vanguard. By contrast, Hawley was six feet of sinewy muscle, forged by hard labour

extras

and tempered in battle. He shook rain from his dark hair, and only then did he remember he was not alone.

Nedley was still on the wagon, watching. For once, he didn't look drunk. Indeed, there was something unnerving in the look he gave Hawley.

Hawley shouldered his knapsack, and hefted up Godspeaker—a large, impractical Felder bastard sword. Non-regulation: an affectation, a prize—a symbol of authority. The men hated that about him, but Hawley could barely care to add it to the tally.

"Make yourself useful, Nedley," Hawley said, strapping the sword to his back. "Find some supplies. And bloody *pay* for them. Show the locals that we mean well."

Hawley snatched the reins from Tarbert, who still looked forlorn. He cared more for the gelding than for most people. Baelsine, named for the blaze of silver grey that zigzagged up its black muzzle. He talked to it like a brother soldier.

"Help Nedley. I'll go see the smith."

* * *

A small forge blazed orange. A stocky, soot-faced man with a great beard and thick arms tapped away at a glowing axe-head.

"A moment, stranger," the man said, without looking up from his work.

Hawley basked in the welcome warmth of the bloomery, indifferent to the acidic tang of molten iron on the thick air.

The smith gave the axe-head a few more raps, before plunging it into a water trough, creating a plume of steam with a satisfying hiss. Only then did he look up at his visitor. Only then did he see the crimson uniform. "My apologies. I . . . I didn't know."

Hawley waved away the apology. "We need your services."

extras

The smith squinted past Hawley. "How many soldiers?" he asked, suspicion edging into his voice.

"Five."

"Expectin' trouble?"

"No more than the ordinary." It had become standard wisdom that five men of the High Companies were worth more than twenty militia, and no outlaw of the forests would dare confront them. Fewer than five, and there'd be insufficient men to perform sentry and scouting duties. More importantly, there would not be enough to adopt the fighting formation favoured by the companies. The wall of steel. In full armour, every High Companies soldier clad their left arm in pauldron, gardbrace, and vambrace of strong Felder steel, adorned with an ingenious system of five interlocking crescent-shaped plates. When the arm was locked, a spring-loaded mechanism within the soldier's gauntlet would push the plates outwards, forming a rough circle of steel petals, almost like a shield; but when the arm was straightened, the plates retracted, leaving the arm free of any burden. Some men of the High Companies even had the skill and speed to trap an enemy's blade within the plates, snapping it in twain with a deft movement. In the press of battle, the soldiers would stand with their armoured left arm facing the foe, right hand wielding the short, thrusting blade, attacking in pairs with one man free to protect the rear and pick off the stragglers. That man was usually Hawley, whose heavy Felder sword needed room to do its grim work.

"This horse threw a shoe a few miles back." Hawley pointed to Baelsine, tethered near the barn.

The smith squeezed past his anvil to the horse. He lifted the hoof, and sucked at his teeth.

"Won't be fit for ridin' today. I'll shoe him. He can go in the paddock with my dray."

extras

"Our own drays need feed and water."

"Ye planning on staying long?"

"Not if we can help it." Hawley didn't need consent to bunk in the village, but didn't like to flaunt his authority. "Perhaps we can be on our way today...with your help."

"I'm no miracle-worker, sir. That horse'll go lame if—"

"We can travel on foot from here. But I need you to point the way."

The smith's expression grew guarded. Hawley wondered if the man had cause to be suspicious of soldiers, or whether it was the custom of such isolated folk to be wary of strangers.

"Don't know what help I can be," the man said, wiping his hands on a rag. "Nor anyone else here, neither. We're simple folk. We keep to our own."

"Three weeks ago, perhaps more, an ore merchant passed through Godsrest. He'd been set upon. Beaten, nearly killed. You remember?"

"Aye, I remember."

"Men from this village helped him fetch his belongings. And among those belongings was a silver ring. You remember that?"

"Something of the like."

"Someone saved that merchant's life. We think it was the same man who owned the ring. We need to find him."

"Don't know nothing about that. Some o' the lads brung him to the village. I mended his wagon, he stayed a couple o' days while he recovered his strength, then he left."

"Fair enough." Hawley took out his map and unfolded it. "You can show me where he was found?"

The smith squinted at the map. "Old map," he said. "Them roads aren't there any more. Forest claimed 'em, and nobody in their right mind would travel 'em. Exceptin' your merchant, o'course."

370

extras

"Show me, as best as you can."

The smith pointed at a spot in the woods, near to a road that supposedly was no longer there.

Hawley circled the spot with his charcoal, and frowned.

"How did you know?" he asked.

"How'd you mean, sir?" Was that nervousness? A quaver of the voice; a twist of the lip?

"You said you brought him here. But how'd you know to look for him?" Hawley studied the map. "No shepherd of any sense would graze his flock north of the river, let alone enter that forest. Unless he's particularly fond of wolves—or bandits."

"Had a bad season. Some o' the younger lads were out hunting the game trails. Heard the commotion. When they got there, they found an injured man and an empty wagon."

"Poaching in your lord's woods?" Hawley said.

"Nobody lays claim to the Elderwood, sir. Not our lord, not nobody else. Them woods is cursed, they say. Them woods is . . . *haunted.*"

"But your hunters aren't afraid of ghosts?"

"They've the good sense not to stray too far." The smith eyed Hawley carefully. "You're not a soldier born," he said at last.

Hawley glowered.

"I mean no disrespect. All us folk of Godsrest abide by the king's law, and serve the king's men when required. It's just that . . . well . . . you try to speak proper, sir, is what I mean. But your roots are clear. It's like working a bloom that don't contain enough iron, if you take my meaning."

"I'm a sargent of the Third Company, that's all that matters."

Footsteps squelched loudly along the muddy path. Ianto appeared, that thin smirk upon his lips. He looked at the smith with keen eyes—*mean eyes*, Hawley thought.

"I told you to stay with the wagon," Hawley said sharply.

371

extras

"I thought you'd want to know there's some...trouble."

There was something almost lascivious about Ianto's manner, and it sent a cold, warning creep up Hawley's spine.

"What kind of trouble?"

"The kind that gives soldiers a bad name."

* * *

Hawley followed the sounds of shrieking, pleading. The odd obscenity. The pained bleating of some animal. Hawley rounded the cob wall of a cottage to see three women of middle age remonstrating with Nedley. The soldier was stood near the largest hut, foot resting on a keg, sloshing ale down his throat from a flagon. Two more kegs lay on the track nearby. One had cracked open, dark ale foaming into the dirt. Behind Nedley, Beacher played tug-of-war with a red-headed boy, over the rope around the neck of a nanny-goat swollen with kid. The beast bleated pitifully as the noose tightened about its neck. Tarbert stood near, clapping his hands in joy at the unfolding chaos.

The woman doing most of the shouting rushed to Nedley, shrugging aside the half-hearted attempts of the others to hold her back. She pounded her fists against Nedley's chest. The soldier belched in her face, and shoved her away roughly. She spun into the arms of her companions as Nedley drained his flagon.

"Nedley!"

At Hawley's shout, Nedley narrowed his eyes in an insolent glare, the likes of which Hawley had never seen from the man. He wiped ale foam from his beard, but he did not answer.

As Hawley drew near, Nedley's hand moved just an inch towards the pommel of his sword.

That was everything Hawley needed to know. He lowered his head like an angered bull, and didn't so much as check his stride. Nedley thought better of drawing steel. Hawley shoved

extras

Nedley away from the hut. The drunkard shot Hawley another glare, but did nothing.

The boy cried out. The three women wailed and cursed.

The boy was in the mud now, holding his face, sobbing. Beacher had slapped him to the ground. But the boy cried not from pain but from sorrow. The goat was dead, blood spilling onto dirty straw from an ugly wound in its throat. Beacher had his sword in his hand, a grin on his blood-flecked face. Tarbert laughed like an imbecile. His laughter died on his lips when he saw Hawley.

Hawley kicked open the gate of the animal pen.

Beacher hadn't even noticed Hawley. At the interruption he said only, "Nedley, I told you—"

Hawley grabbed Beacher by the ear, twisted hard, and pulled him away from the goat with all his strength. Beacher squealed like a stuck pig as Hawley dragged him to the gate. Hawley spun the man around, and gave him a kick up the arse that sent him face-first into the dirt, his shortsword skittering from his hand.

Tarbert had taken a step forward, slack-jawed face more agawp than usual. Hawley slapped him hard across the side of the head for his trouble. Tarbert cowered like a kicked dog.

Hawley took one look back at the weeping boy and the dead goat. The animal was worth far more alive than dead to these people. The family's meagre fortunes may well have depended upon the creature. And now they would struggle, for the simple greed of a soldier. Hawley stepped onto the track, Beacher in his sights.

Nedley had picked up his flagon again, more concerned with saving the last undamaged ale keg than helping his brother soldier. The villagers could scarce spare the ale either, Hawley thought. But one thing at a time.

One of the women pushed past Hawley to see to the boy.

extras

The other two, realising Nedley was no longer standing in their way, came to scream at Beacher.

Ianto reappeared. He stood over by the cottage, leaning against the wall, watching. Grinning.

Now the smith appeared, hammer in hand. That was the danger. Hawley had to deal with Beacher before any villager got involved. Otherwise, he'd be hard-pressed to stop even this band of good-for-nothings taking vengeance on the peasants.

Beacher rolled over, scrambling away on his elbows. "Don't you touch me!" he snarled, blinking away mud from his eyes. His hand found the pommel of his shortsword in the dirt. His fingers curled around the hilt, and his expression changed at once. He clambered to his feet and spat, "You filthy *mongrel*!"

Mongrel. Not one of "the Blood," who could trace their family back through five or more generations of military service. Looking at the state of the men around him, Hawley couldn't take it as much of an insult.

Hawley advanced another step. "Sheathe that sword," he said quietly, almost in a growl. "Sheathe it, or I'll kill you." He held Beacher's gaze, saw the man's eyes falter. Beacher believed him. He was right to.

Beacher pleaded with his brother soldiers left and right for support. Hawley heard Tarbert behind him, but the dullard was of little concern. Nedley... now there was an unknown quantity. Up until now, Hawley hadn't taken the drunkard seriously. That could have been a mistake. Nedley was staring at Hawley with utter detachment, like a butcher appraising which cut of meat to take next. But he didn't make a move. When Beacher looked to Ianto, the recruit gave only the merest shrug of his shoulders, as if to say, "This is not my fight." He may not have been a friend to Hawley, but nor was he one of the Blood. He'd wait and see which way the wind blew before committing himself.

extras

Beacher stood alone, and he knew it. He took a moment to weigh up his chances against Hawley, and found them lacking. He sheathed the blade and spread his palms.

Hawley marched to Beacher, loomed over him, pressed his forehead into the bridge of the man's nose. Beacher averted his eyes, like a wild dog that had just lost a pack challenge. Hawley reached to Beacher's belt and took the man's sword away with no resistance.

Other villagers arrived now. Seven or eight men and youths tramped up the hill, pointing, chattering. Their approach was cautious. There weren't enough men in this village to cause the soldiers real problems, but enough that they might try. And die.

Any sense of decorum was lost. Any chance Hawley's reserves had of looking like proper soldiers was gone.

"Ianto, Nedley. Get him away," Hawley said. "To the bridge. Wait for me there."

Neither man moved. Nedley gazed at the flagon, weighing up the order.

"I said get him away. *Now.*"

Ianto exchanged looks with Nedley and shrugged again. Nedley finished his dregs, tossed the flagon aside, and weighed in. Together they led Beacher away from the gathering villagers, down towards the river.

Tarbert staggered from the pen at last, nursing his sore ear. Hawley jerked his head in the direction of the others. Without a word, Tarbert followed.

Rightly or wrongly, Hawley had done the men an insult— one that might yet come back to bite him on the arse. As king's men, they had the right to claim whatever they wanted from a serf, and by denying them their perceived due, Hawley had only deepened their loathing of him. He might even face more punishment back at the barracks, once Beacher had made his

extras

inevitable complaint. Hawley was past caring. What he needed to do right now was make amends with the villagers.

"Master Smith—" Hawley ventured.

"Godsrest is a peaceful place," the smith interrupted. "Apt named, for we honour the gods here and invite no trouble. You've brought trouble to our door."

The other men drew nearer. Hawley weighed up his chances of regaining the smith's trust before they took exception to his presence.

"They're soldiers... not good ones, I admit. But you'll have no more trouble."

"No?"

"No. Look, Master Smith—"

"Gereth. My name is Gereth. And that boy over there is my son."

Hawley turned to see the dishevelled lad on his feet at last, being comforted by a woman. From the mane of red hair that tumbled from her bonnet, Hawley guessed she was his mother—Gereth's wife. She held her son close, and glared accusingly at Hawley, who cursed Beacher's name under his breath.

"Gereth, then. You know the law. You know the power of the High Companies. I would choose not to exercise that power. Let's come to an arrangement instead. See to our horses as agreed, and I'll pay you fairly."

"That much I'll do, sir, as duty to manor and king dictates."

"You don't have to call me 'sir.' My name's Hawley. Holt Hawley. You were right before, I am a common man, from a place much like this. I chose this life 'cause I was tired of seeing common folk—people like us—downtrodden and uncared for."

"Then you chose poorly, Holt Hawley."

"Maybe. But there's no leaving the companies once your bunk is made, unless it be on a pyre, an enemy's blade, or the

extras

end of a noose. So I do what I can, and I'll at least talk straight with you."

The others gathered around. Hawley didn't know how much they'd overheard, and it didn't matter. As a craftsman, Gereth was of a higher station than they. Gereth was the one he needed to convince.

"You had little reason to trust me before," Hawley went on, "and even less now. But I'll tell you why we're here. This past year, six bairns have been taken from their homes. Six—that we know of. One of them is a lad of wealth, a foreigner. You've no reason to care for such a boy, why would you? But the others... they're from villages like this, poorer than this. Boys and girls of Aelderland. Boys younger than your own. They're lost, and nobody can find them. Not the high lords, not the companies, and certainly not the bloody Vigilants. But it's said that there's somebody in these parts who could help. A *True* Vigilant, of the old order. If it's true, then maybe he can find those children, where others have failed."

Gereth shook his head. "Fairy stories, Holt Hawley. There's nobody alive who's ever seen such a man. Not many who've even heard of one, neither."

"That merchant," Hawley persisted, "said he was helped by a mysterious stranger. Didn't get a good look at him, but he did find his ring. A Vigilant's ring."

Gereth waved a dismissive hand. "As I've said, there's nowt in them woods but trouble. If you want to go chasing shadows, that's your affair. All we can offer you is food and water for yer horses and a dry place for yer wagon."

Hawley sighed. He reached to his scrip and took out a few silver pieces. "For your trouble."

"Keep it."

"Come on... you've lost livestock, supplies. Let me compensate you."

extras

Gereth looked Hawley square in the eye. "Keep it, and go in peace."

The villagers stared at Hawley. Women had come out of their homes to scowl at him. Hawley put the money back in his scrip and nodded ruefully.

He went to the wagon and retrieved two packs, heaving them one on each shoulder. "I'll come back for the rest," he said.

"No, we'll bring 'em," Gereth replied. He didn't want the soldiers in the village a moment longer than necessary, and Hawley couldn't blame him.

Hawley walked past the assembled villagers, down the hill to the bridge where his men idled, doubtless cursing his name still.

Gereth followed, a couple of young lads in tow, with the rest of the packs. They weathered the sullen glares of the reserves just as well as Hawley. Hawley was impressed, but then he'd always thought the northerners were a tough breed.

As the villagers piled the supplies at Hawley's feet, Gereth leaned in.

"Just don't stray far from the trails," he said. "The Elderwood has no end, and it's easy to get turned around. You're like to get lost...or worse. Cross the bridge, then head north. You'll pass a trapper's shack after a few hours, so you'll know you're on the right path. It's near enough a day's walk to the old trade road."

"You really don't know any more?" Hawley tried once more to plead with the man. He still felt like the smith knew more than he was letting on.

"All I know is, you're more likely to find a witch in them woods than a Vigilant."

With that, Gereth and the youths returned up the hill, leaving Hawley to weather the glares of his men, and their whispered accusations of giving up the secrets of their mission to a commoner.

if you enjoyed

THE LAST SOUL AMONG WOLVES

look out for

HOW TO BECOME THE DARK LORD AND DIE TRYING

Dark Lord Davi: Book One

by

Django Wexler

Davi has done this all before. She's tried to be the hero and take down the all-powerful Dark Lord. A hundred times she's rallied humanity and made the final charge. But the time loop always gets her in the end. Sometimes she's killed quickly. Sometimes it takes a while. But she's been defeated every time.

extras

This time? She's done being the hero and done being stuck in this endless time loop. If the Dark Lord always wins, then maybe that's who she needs to be. It's Davi's turn to play on the winning side.

PROLOGUE

Life #237

It takes me two weeks to die, locked in my own dungeon.

Not for lack of trying on my part, mind, but orders have come down from the Dark Lord that the Princess isn't allowed to pop off early. I found a bit of chicken bone in my soup once, but the spoilsports got to me before I could choke on it.

On the plus side, to the extent that there is a plus side to being tortured to death, I don't have to see what's happening out in the city. I assume it's bad. It's usually bad. If I got into therapy and unloaded half the shit I've seen, Dr. Freud would take a running leap out the nearest window. So not having to actually watch is kind of a relief.

I hear Artaxes coming, the *clank clank clank* of his rusty iron shitkickers. When he opens the door, I give him a little wave with my fingers. This is all I can manage, since I'm manacled to a wooden contraption that raises my arms like I'm in the middle of a cheer routine.

"Morning, chief!" I sing out. "What's the haps?"

I keep hoping being cheerful will annoy him, possibly enough to rip my throat out, but so far no joy. It's hard to tell

extras

how anything lands with Artaxes, since he wears his iron armor like a second skin.[1]

"How do you poop?" I ask him. "Just between us. I won't tell anybody."

He gives a grunt and steps aside. There's someone else in the doorway. Tall and gaunt, black robe hanging limp from her bony shoulders, mouth full of long curving teeth. Sibarae. She looks me over and raises her scaly eyebrow bumps.

I'm naked at this point, modesty provided only by a crust of dried blood and matted hair. For all that matters to Artaxes, I might be a side of beef on a hook. I mean, maybe he has a raging hard-on inside his rusty codpiece, but I doubt it. I've seen Artaxes serve as the right hand of the Dark Lord more times than I can count, and he always goes about his business with the dumb brute efficiency of a buzz saw. You get exactly what you expect with him. It's comforting, in a way, although obviously not when he's tearing my fingernails out.

Sibarae is a whole other kettle of snakes. She's practically drooling at the sight of my gory tits. Her tongue comes out, long and forked, to taste the air. I briefly contemplate what it would be like to get head from a snake-wilder,[2] but I have let's say a premonition that this is not on the agenda.

"Look, clanky," I tell Artaxes, "I realize you're worried about not...you know, getting the job done anymore, but you can't just introduce a third wheel into our relationship without talking to me about it. We have something special together, I don't want to spoil it."

---

1 He seriously never takes it off. How does he poop? *I have to know how he poops.*

2 The tongue would be fucking weird, right? Dunno. Maybe I'm into it.

381

extras

"My master worries that you may become accustomed to the conditions of your imprisonment," he says. His voice is as cold and dead as his armor.

"And I *begged* him to be allowed a turn," Sibarae says. "I've always wondered what a princess tastes like."

This is *not* a sex thing, trust me.

"Sorry, scaly. I only date girls with tits."[3]

"Those bulbous mammalian things?" She glides forward. "So soft and . . . vulnerable. Like the rest of you. *Skin.*" She pronounces the word with a contemptuous flick of the tongue.

"Remember our lord's instructions," Artaxes admonishes.

"Oh yes," Sibarae hisses. "I'll be sure to show . . . restraint."

He clanks out, shutting the door behind him. She gets on with the business at hand. Which, let's not put too fine a point on it, fucking sucks. You think you'd get used to this shit after a while, but nooooo, when someone bites your finger off, your body's gotta be all like, oh no, someone bit my finger off, pain pain pain! I know, okay? I was fucking there, you don't have to remind me.

So I scream a lot and piss myself, which is breaking character a little. Cut me some slack. Artaxes at least doesn't *bite.* In between screams, I amuse myself planning how I'm going to kill her next time we meet. Rusty, jagged metal will be involved. There may be, like, a little corkscrew bit on the end, possibly some kind of barbed flanges. I'll use my imagination.

Eventually I pass out, thank God. When I wake up, there's a teenage girl in the uniform of the palace healers, the glow of green thaumite leaking between the clenched fingers of her shaking hand. A small pool of vomit by the door marks where

---

3 This isn't really true. I'm just trying to piss her off. No offense to my flat-chested sisters!

382

extras

she lost her lunch at the sight of me. I wonder what the wilders have threatened her with.

She grows back most of my missing bits, but leaves me with a few open wounds just for shits and giggles. Dark Lord's orders, presumably. Fucker likes to twist the knife, figuratively and distressingly literally. At least when he killed Johann, my poor beautiful himbo boyfriend, he didn't have time for any of this sadistic bullshit.

Now that I can think without being *completely* submerged in white-hot agony, I'm getting pissed off. I know you're thinking, Davi, *just now* you're getting pissed off? And it's true, this anger has been building for a while. It's taken some time to bubble to the surface, but it's been stewing down there in the acid swamps of my subconscious.

To put it bluntly: I am about done with this shit. The whole being-tortured-to-death thing, *obviously*, but also the rest. Finished. Kaput. No more. Fuck every last little bit of it. I have a new plan and it's time to get started.

Fun fact: Did you know that snakes lose their teeth and constantly grow more, like sharks? Actually I have no idea if snakes do that, what the fuck do I know about snakes, but snake-wilders do. I know this, as of today, because I have one of Sibarae's fangs embedded in my palm.

The healer has grown the skin back over it, but it's merely the work of an excruciatingly painful eternity to dig it out with my fingernails. The fang has a nice curved shape and a vicious point, and I grip it between two fingers and press it against my wrist, right on the artery. I don't have much leverage, so the best I can do is work the point back and forth, sawing through the skin. Hurts like a motherfucker, but sometimes a girl's just gotta die, you know?

When the artery finally pops, the spatter of blood hitting the floor is like music to my ears. I keep tearing at the cut, opening

extras

it wider, willing my stupid heart to pump harder and get my whole blood supply out before someone notices. The fang slips through my fingers about the time my vision starts to go gray, but by then I can taste victory. Also blood.

I slip into the sweet embrace of death with a contented sigh. So long, #237. Go fuck a porcupine.

Life #238

"Well now." The voice is frustratingly familiar. "That won't do at all."

CHAPTER ONE

I sit up out of the cold water of the pool, gasping for breath. Again.

Twelve seconds.

Done done *done* with this shit, for real. No more.

Still naked, of course. Death, birth, nudity, very mythic. Frankly if it has to be that way, I'd rather die in bed during an epic fuck[1] than bleeding out after weeks of torture in my own fucking dungeon, but beggars, choosers, you know.

Ten seconds.

Anyway. Naked in a rancid pool of chilly water at the top of a hill. Edge of the Kingdom, right up against a wilder-haunted

---

1 Managed it once!

extras

forest. I'm healthy and hale of limb once again, and also about three years younger, with a lot less muscle tone and a ghastly sort of pixie cut. Same as always. I figure it's what I looked like when all of this kicked off, when whatever happened happened and I got here from Earth some-fucking-how.

Six seconds.

I focus on breathing. Calm and centered, that's me.

Four seconds. Sound of someone scrambling up the rocks.

Take a deep breath. Hold it. Let it out.

Two. One.

"My lady!" Tserigern says. I mouth the lines with him. My timing is perfect. "So it's true, then. Gods preserve us. We have a chance."

I look over at him with my best expression of doe-eyed innocence. He climbs the last few feet, dusts off his motley robe, and approaches reverently.

Tserigern is a wizard, a very old and famous one. Everyone says he's the most powerful wizard in the Kingdom, but *frankly* I've never seen him do magic for shit. Light the way in caves and get cryptic messages, that's about it. You could replace him with a flashlight and a walkie-talkie. But he at least looks the part: He's a bony old motherfucker with a beard you could lose a sheep in, like Santa Claus after a debilitating illness. He has kind, crinkly eyes and a sly grin, a weathered, avuncular voice perfect for laying out the mysteries of the universe for an awestruck young naïf. Just the guy you want on your side when you wake up all nudie in a weird fantasy universe with no idea what the fuck is going on.

He bends to one knee and offers me his gnarled hand.

"My lady," he says as I wrap my fingers around his, "I—"

He doesn't get to finish, because I grab the back of his head with my other hand and slam his face into the fucking

extras

rocks. I hear his nose break with a *crunch*, and my heart sings, it's so goddamn cathartic. He lies out flat and I swing astride his back, both hands in his hair, and start pounding his stupid fucking face into mush against the stone edge of the pool.

Seeing as how he's a little occupied, I say his lines for him.

"I know you must be frightened"—*crunch*—"but I swear to you, I mean you no harm"—*crunch*, you fucking liar—"I have hoped against hope for your coming, and I thank the gods my reading of the texts was true"—*crunch*, they didn't predict this, did they, motherfucker?—"you must come with me, the fate of the Kingdom is balanced on the blade of a knife"—*ca-crunch*.

Holy fuck, it's better than sex. I don't stop until long after his legs have quit kicking and bits of blood and brains are floating in the water.

"I'm done," I tell the body, leaning back and breathing hard. "Hear me? Done. I'm not some holy savior here to protect your fucking kingdom." I've been doing that for, hold on, let me check my watch, *fucking ten centuries*, and where the fuck has it gotten me? A fucking snake-woman eating my goddamn fingers, that's where.

I strip off his nasty-ass robe and wrap myself in it. He's wearing trousers, too, but I'm not touching them without a hazmat suit.

"What am I going to do instead?" I say in response to an inaudible question. "I will tell you what I am going to fucking do. We have an expression back home concerning what course of action to take if you find yourself under no circumstances able to beat 'em. I intend to follow its advice."

I tie the corners of the robe under my chin, plant my hands on my hips, and let it flap behind me like the cape of an extremely inappropriate superhero.

386

extras

"I," I announce to the world, "am going to become the *fucking Dark Lord.*"

* * *

Okay. I've been going full speed ahead in the interest of keeping my *res* fucking *in medias*, but it's possible you have some questions, such as:

1. How could you beat a friendly old man to death like that? and
2. Didn't you die, like, two pages ago? What's the deal?

To which I answer:

1. The key is getting a good grip on the wispy bits of hair on the back of his bald-ass head. Once your fingers are really dug in there, then it's pretty simple.
2. It's a long fucking story.

To keep confusion to a minimum, though, here's the airline safety video version: Hi! I'm Davi. I'm in my early twenties, dark hair, light brown skin, freckles like someone flicked a paintbrush at my nose, body you'd probably swipe right on but maybe not brag to your friends about afterward.

For the last thousand years,[2] I've been trapped in a time loop, like in that movie or that other movie. When I die—and I always die, for reasons I'm about to explain—I wake up here, now, naked in the pool. Tserigern turns up to give me his spiel. What he would have told me, had I not enmushified his

---

2 Give or take a few hundred. I try to count but it's not like I can keep a fucking diary.

extras

head, is that the Kingdom is in dire peril from the impending rise of the Dark Lord, and *only I* can save humanity from the monstrous armies of the Wilds. Chosen by the fucking gods, promised by prophecy, generally just absolutely lousy with momentous portent. Get your ass in gear, Davi, there's heroing to do.

There was a time when I bought this horseshit. I mean, it's not like he's completely off base here. Try to maintain appropriate humility all you want, it's hard to believe the world doesn't revolve around you when it rewinds the tape every time you fall on your head. And whatever prophet wrote the one about the Dark Lord destroying the Kingdom makes Nostradamus look like a stock-picking hamster, because that shit happens *Every. Fucking. Time.*

It's not always the *same* Dark Lord, and sometimes it takes a little longer, but they always turn up. And as of a few minutes ago, I have fed 237 quarters into this fucking game and I *cannot* get past the last boss. I have tried *everything*, and it always ends with me getting sliced into sashimi. I am becoming *a little peeved* about this, hence my admittedly emotional outburst slash face-smashing.

So! Yeah. Davi. Freckles. Time loop. That's me.[3]

---

3 Where was I before the time loop? Honestly, I don't fucking remember. Somewhere on Earth, obviously. I speak English. I think I was an American because I'm kind of an aggressive asshole. I know stuff: Superman is Clark Kent, Darth Vader is Luke's father.* That really fucking awful guy is president. Not that one, the other one. At this point, I've been here in the Kingdom five hundred times longer; how much do *you* remember from the first month of your life?

* Is Superman Darth Vader's father? This shit all kind of blurs together.

Follow us:

f /orbitbooksUS

𝕏 /orbitbooks

▶ /orbitbooks

Join our mailing list to receive alerts on our latest releases and deals.

orbitbooks.net

Enter our monthly giveaway for the chance to win some epic prizes.

orbitloot.com